STOLEN KISS

Before she realized what he was about, he threw one arm around her shoulders and dragged her ruthlessly against his chest. His lips descended on hers, claiming them in a kiss that tore her breath away. To her shock, she found herself returning this unfamiliar caress, acting upon a previously unknown passion that flooded through her with alarming intensity.

He released her slowly, and in the dim light of the interior of the hackney, she could see his dark eyes glinting. "I was going to apologize, but I think maybe I won't, after all."

She stiffened, furious, pulling free of the arm that lingered about her. "I see. And to what do I owe the—the dubious honor of being mauled by you?"

He laughed, low and soft, and her bosom heaved with indignation. "I cry pardon, my lady. But Kennington walked by. It was the—the impulse of the moment, I fear, an attempt to keep our identities hidden."

A deep flush of mortification tinged her cheeks. "You can have no notion how glad I am to have been of some use," she informed him with heavy sarcasm.

Deverell chuckled, a soft deep sound. . . .

Midnight Masque

BY JANICE BENNETT

ZEBRA BOOKS
KENSINGTON PUBLISHING CORP.

For Wynne—For all of them.

ZEBRA BOOKS

are published by

Kensington Publishing Corp.
475 Park Avenue South
New York, NY 10016

First printing: November, 1988

Printed in the United States of America

Chapter 1

The storm, which had hovered with threatening intent over London for the past three days, broke at last with a crash of thunder and a veritable fusillade of pelting rain. Lady Leanora Ashton peered out the window in the Home Office complex in Whitehall, looking down on the chaos created in the street below. Stately gentlemen ran to and fro, pulling greatcoats more firmly about themselves or clutching at tall curly beavers that threatened to be blown from their heads as they darted for shelter in doorways or waiting carriages. Black clouds hung low, creating an unreal night. And through it all, the melancholy strains of Mozart's *Requiem* played through her mind.

Lady Leanora shivered in spite of the warmth of her merino pelisse and hugged closer the pug puppy that squirmed to curl more tightly into her arm. The impending storm, combined with those haunting chords, had filled her with the most ridiculous sense of foreboding ever since she attended that concert at the Opera House the night before. She was being missish, foolish beyond permission, to allow herself to fall into a fit of the blue megrims just because of the weather!

The pug, as if sensing her distress, twisted within the crook of her arm and licked anxiously at her face. Her lips twitched upward, and she rubbed the little dog's preposterous head, reducing it to a state of panting idiocy.

Turning away from the storm, she looked back into the earl of Sherborne's elegantly appointed office. In contrast to the darkness outside, the room was brilliantly lit by several branches of candelabra. The pug squirmed again, and she set him down to dance delightedly about her feet and make short darts in his excitement about the comfortable desk chair.

"Yes, you may walk downstairs," she informed the ecstatic puppy. "But mind you walk, Puglet! I will not have you tripping me."

The pug came to a near-sitting position before her, his whole body trembling in his glee. Leanora shook her head, a sudden smile lighting her clouded blue eyes.

"What ever possessed Aunt Charlotte to give you such a name? But never mind, Aunt Amabelle will give you another—*if* you can turn her up sweet," she admonished the animal in terms that would have shocked either of her aunts.

Slipping the puppy's lead over her wrist, she transferred her attention to the stack of papers that lay on her father's desk and quickly glanced through them. For the most part, they concerned Lord Grenville, the new prime minister, though several still referred to Mr. Pitt, who had died a bare three months before. And there, near the bottom, was the single sheet that had brought her to the Home Office that afternoon, the guest list for the earl's upcoming dinner party.

It was just like her father to consign sensitive documents into her keeping whenever it was not convenient for him to transport them himself. Smiling at the eccentricities of her parent, she tucked the bulky pile of papers under her arm and went out through the antechamber to the corridor.

After taking the first three of the wide oaken steps, she realized her mistake in setting down the little dog. It leaped merrily from one stair to the next, intent, it seemed, on entangling her feet in its lead. Somehow, they reached the bottom of the staircase without mishap and started across the marble mosaic floor toward the door.

Abruptly, this flew wide, and freezing wind and rain gusted into the entry hall, swirling Leanora's skirts about her ankles and tearing the ermine-trimmed hood of her pelisse from her golden curls. She caught at it, the unstable stack of papers shifted, and before she could save either, a man, head still lowered against the storm that raged outside, slammed against

6

her, almost knocking her from her feet. The papers went flying across the floor, and Puglet burst into a frenzy of high-pitched puppy fury.

"I beg your pardon!" The gentleman grasped her elbow, steadying her. He blinked as his gaze took in her dismayed features. The puppy made a savage foray against his mud-splattered Hessians, but he fended it off. "Lady Leanora," he murmured, barely to be heard over Puglet's frantic yips. The cynical smile that twisted the lips on his swarthy face did not reach his eyes. "Allow me to assist you."

"Thank you, Lord Kennington. It is quite unnecessary. Oh, do be quiet, Pug," she added, and the puppy retreated to the safety of her long skirts. Her smile, charming as always, concealed her discomfiture. It was not only that Lord Kennington was a powerful member of the Opposition party who irritated her father regularly that caused her to shrink from accepting his aid. The man's manners, indeed, his unbearable haughtiness, left her with a sense of uneasiness and a marked distaste for his company.

She knelt down and hastily began to collect the papers that lay scattered amidst the mud and rain that had been tracked across the normally spotless floor. Puglet eyed them with true puppy fervor and crept forward to try out his new teeth. Lord Kennington, eyeing the pug askance, dropped down on one knee at Leanora's side and snatched up sheets at random. Several, she noted in shocked amazement, he looked at closely, then tucked under his arm.

A glance at her outraged countenance caused his cold smile to widen. "Mine, I fear. You were not the only one carrying papers." He held out the closely written pages that he had retained. "Just notes for a speech, but as it is vehemently opposed to something Lord Sherborne is actively supporting, you must agree that it would be most indiscreet in you to read it."

An angry flush lent delicate color to her cheeks. "Indeed, he has no need of—" She broke off, forced to swallow her scathing retort as the sound of booted feet, hurrying unevenly down the staircase behind her, recalled her to a sense of her surroundings.

7

The footsteps paused, then crossed over to where Leanora and Lord Kennington still knelt with papers scattered about them. Leanora glanced up into the rugged, deeply tanned face of a gentleman who was a complete stranger to her, and her breath caught in her throat. The man's thickly curling dark locks ran riot beneath his high crowned beaver, defying any attempt to comb them into a fashionable style. Vaguely, she took in his towering figure with a driving coat that boasted only two capes hanging over broad shoulders. From beneath this, she was permitted a glimpse of the neat military cut of a coat of blue Bath cloth that could only have come from the hands of the great Scott himself. An unobtrusive waistcoat bespoke a quiet elegance, and muscular legs covered in buff pantaloons disappeared into Hessians gleaming with a mirrorlike sheen.

Her gaze rose slowly back to his face and encountered a penetrating intelligence in the depths of dark, sparkling eyes that coolly assessed her softly flushed countenance. Hot color rose to her cheeks, and instantly she looked away, back to the papers that Lord Kennington still tried to sort, which she had forgotten completely at the sight of this powerful, disturbing gentleman.

The pug advanced on him, quivering all over with interest as one who senses a friend. The man bent to offer his hand, which the shortened nose sniffed thoroughly. Pleased with his new acquaintance, the puppy licked the fingers with enthusiasm as the man attempted to scratch him behind his short, flopped-over ears. This ritual accomplished to the apparent satisfaction of both parties, the man stepped forward.

"May I help?"

His deep, commanding voice sent an unnerving shiver through Leanora. Without waiting for her response, he dropped carefully down to one knee and began to pick up the damp and dirtied documents. Puglet leaped joyfully into the middle, only to be set aside by the man. The puppy submitted meekly, which did not surprise Leanora—she would not herself choose to defy the aura of authority that hung about this gentleman.

In a few moments, their task was completed, and the stranger stood stiffly, then offered his hand to help Leanora.

8

She hesitated, then placed her small hand into his large one. The warm firmness of his clasp sent a giddy, nervous sensation dancing through her, and her gaze flew to the impenetrable mask of his rugged face. She could read nothing there and was glad when she was safely on her feet and he relinquished his hold.

Lord Kennington stood also, ran a quick glance over the papers he held and made a leg to her that held just a hint of mockery. "My apologies, my lady," he murmured. With a curt nod to the gentleman who had assisted them, he continued on his way up the stairs.

Leanora also turned to the gentleman, who retained the heavy stack of documents. He was of undoubtedly good ton, she decided, with an air of reserve and breeding that she liked. Yet there was something dashing, almost dangerous, about the set of those broad shoulders and the firmness of the jutting chin. The cumulative effect was both attractive and rather frightening.

It required a struggle, but she mastered her fascination and, with a semblance of calm, extended her hands for the papers. "I must thank you for coming to my aid," she said, vexed that her soft, musical voice sounded oddly breathless. She dropped her gaze, startled to find herself as gauche and flustered as a schoolroom miss.

"My pleasure." A note of amusement lurked in his deep voice, as if he guessed the unsettling effect he had on her.

She raised searching eyes to his but could not fathom their mysterious depths. She felt both confused and intrigued, an unusual condition for a young lady who had always considered herself to be well up to snuff. But even though she had been on the town any time these past seven years, never had she encountered the like of this gentleman. To her dismay, she found she was not as immune as she would have liked to his alarming, yet compelling, appeal.

"Do you have a carriage awaiting you?" His polite question broke across her tangled thoughts. When she nodded, he continued, "Then will you permit me to escort you? The weather outside does not appear to be of the best."

The stack of papers did not seem so very great or heavy when

9

tucked neatly beneath his arm and sheltered by his driving coat, and Leanora found herself unable to protest their remaining in his possession. She scooped up the wriggling puppy, accepted the man's free arm and allowed her disturbing giant to lead her from the building. He limped slightly, moving his right leg stiffly from the knee, but it did not seem to trouble him overly much.

As soon as the door opened again, the full force of the raging storm swept over them. Stinging rain and icy wind slashed into their faces. Leanora cradled Puglet closer and unconsciously tightened her grip on the arm she held as if to keep from being blown from her feet.

In a moment, a liveried groom came running up the steps to help her to the covered barouche that waited only a few feet away. Leanora hurried down to this, set the pug safely onto the carriage boards and climbed into the shelter herself before turning back to her escort. He handed over the papers, and impulsively she held out her hand.

"Could I take you somewhere? Or—or do you have your own coach?"

He took the proffered hand and raised her fingers to his lips. "It's very kind of you, but I have my curricle. I hope we shall meet again." With that he stepped back, allowed the groom to put up the step and remained where he was, watching as her barouche drove off.

Leanora peeped out the window for one last look at him. He still stood in the street, as if oblivious to the pelting rain and wind that set his driving coat flapping. A tiny thrill shot through her, disturbing by its very existence and undeniable in its strength.

Who was he? She had been a frequent *habitué* of the Home Office building since long before she let her skirts down, and no one was unknown to her, at least by sight. He must have been new, perhaps invalided home from the war that raged on the Continent. But did he serve the party or the Opposition? She would have to ask her father—or better, Sir William Holborne, assistant to Lord Petersham, the Home secretary. Sir William always seemed to know everything about everybody.

By the time the barouche pulled up before stately Sherborne House in Berkeley Square, the worst of the storm had blown itself out. The rain continued to beat down with a steady determination, but the icy gusts of wind no longer penetrated the carriage. Leanora picked up Puglet, sprang down lightly and hurried up the steps to where Tremly, that most efficient of butlers, held the door open for her.

"Terrible storm, Miss Leanora," Tremly commented. Not by so much as a blink did he betray his surprise at seeing the little dog that nestled damply in her arms. He relieved her of the wet animal, then the armload of papers and her drenched pelisse. Casting a searching and paternal eye over her, he seemed to reach the conclusion that his young mistress had not sustained any lasting harmful effects from venturing out in such inclement weather. Satisfied, he consigned the dripping garment into the hands of a waiting footman to be conveyed to the laundry maid's care.

"Thank you, Tremly. And you, too, James," she added as the young second footman entered the hall from outside, bearing several purchases she had made and left in the barouche. "This—" She broke off, regarding the pug with disfavor as he shook the dampness from his short coat. "This is Puglet. I greatly fear he will be living with us."

The footman, wooden-faced, passed her and made his way up the staircase with her packages.

Leanora picked up the stack of papers from where the butler had laid them on a small occasional table. "My father will not be back until late tonight. Is Mr. Edmonton in his study?"

"No, Miss Leanora. He went out shortly after you did. To the City, I believe, on business for his lordship." Not by so much as a glance did Tremly, that ever correct retainer, betray any interest in the pile of documents.

"Leanora, is that you, my love?" A small lady of comfortable proportions, well advanced into her middle years, appeared on the landing in a cloud of lavender gauze. Fluffy gray curls surrounded a face that had once inspired a young gallant of romantic turn of mind to compose sonnets in her honor. Her features still retained much of their former prettiness, and a naturally sweet disposition had softened the ravages of time.

11

"Thank heaven you are home and safe, my dear," she continued in her fluttery way. "I never can feel quite easy when you are out in such terrible weather, even though you did have our good coachman to drive you, and I am sure he took the greatest care. Do come up and put off your gown, for it must be quite wet."

"In a moment, Aunt Amabelle," Leanora called up to her. "I must first put these somewhere."

The widowed Mrs. Amabelle Ashton clucked her tongue disapprovingly. "I suppose your father will be dining out this evening, not that I know any reason why he should not, of course, for I could not face Almack's tonight, not with all this dreadful rain; and we are not actually pledged to anyone this once, though to be sure, if your father remembered that before making his plans, it is more than one could expect of him when he is so busy. Still, it would be so very pleasant to be able to dine *en famille* with him, though you may be sure that if he had not gone out, he would have brought someone dreadfully important home to dine with us, without sending us a word of warning, so that Cook might prepare something suitable, and—" She broke off, eyeing her niece in mild surprise. "Have I said something to make you laugh, my love?"

"No, indeed not, dear aunt. I will be up in a moment, and only wait until you see the ravishing lace cap I found in Brook Street this afternoon. You will like it excessively, I make no doubt, and it will be just the thing for you to wear with your new dressing gown."

Between her aunt's exclamations that her dearest niece should not have put herself to the trouble of purchasing this trifle for her, and her demands to be allowed to view it on the instant, Leanora started down the hall. The puppy, which had nestled contentedly against the back of her ankles, now sprang up and ran in a circle about her.

"What is that?" cried Mrs. Ashton, who still leaned over the banister.

"This is Puglet," Leanora explained, hoping to win the favor of her aunt for her protégé. "He is quite alone in the world, I fear. Aunt Charlotte purchased him, but she goes into the most violent fits of sneezing whenever he comes near. So she

12

thought that perhaps you might like him."

"A pug?" Mrs. Ashton exclaimed in dismay. "Oh, no! Leanora, you must know that I have the greatest dislike of animals in the house! If you wished to keep him I would not raise the least objection, to be sure, but to be expecting me—"

"Then I shall keep him," Leanora said shortly, cutting off her aunt's protests. "He is really quite a dear." Calling the pug to heel, she continued along the hall to her study, which lay at the front of the house, overlooking the square.

It was a cluttered apartment at the moment, for here she kept the household records and planned the numerous and exacting state dinner parties in which her father reveled. Lord Sherborne entertained his official cohorts regularly and lavishly, and Leanora had served as both his planner and hostess since shortly after her sixteenth birthday when the death of her mother had precipitated her emergence from the schoolroom. Mrs. Amabelle Ashton, although a suitable chaperone for her unmarried niece and a notable society hostess, found herself to be wholly at sea when confronted with the intellectual and political guests among whom Leanora moved with ease.

Shoving various menu plans aside with ruthless abandon, Leanora set the papers on the center of the cluttered cherrywood writing desk. Somewhere, in the midst of all those sheets, lay the finalized guest list she needed for the state dinner her father would give in three days' time. But she would extract it later. First, she must see Puglet suitably established and then dress for dinner.

A glance at the mantel clock warned her that it lacked only five minutes until six. With a muttered exclamation, she hurried back into the hall, almost colliding with Tremly, who appeared as if at her summons.

He bowed and took charge of the puppy's lead. "I have already conveyed to the cook that his lordship will be away from home this evening, Miss Leanora," he informed her. "And dinner has been set back to six-thirty."

"Thank you, Tremly," she sighed in relief. She hated the thought of scrambling into a dry gown. Her aunt's insistence upon keeping country hours when they ate alone frequently

13

proved inconvenient.

Tremly looked down at the pug, which wound the lead about his legs, and sapiently picked the little animal up. "I shall myself convey him to the kitchen and see that a suitable dinner is procured, Miss." He bowed again, tucked the pug under his arm and retreated with amazing dignity.

Secure in the knowledge that all would be taken care of, Leanora made her way up the several flights of curving stairs to her bedchamber on the second floor. Here, she rang for her abigail, then set about removing her half-boots of green kid that bore stains from the puddles and mud. The package with the lace cap, she noted with a smile, was nowhere to be seen. Her aunt must have claimed it at once.

When she was warm, dry and suitably gowned, she descended to the lower floor. Mrs. Ashton awaited her in the Gold Saloon, seated in a comfortably padded chair and sipping a glass of warm negus. She waved for her niece to join her, and greeted her with the news that Mr. Edmonton had been delayed by the storm but had sent a message that he would be dining with Lord Sherborne's man of business.

"So we are indeed alone, dear Aunt. I am almost afraid to tell you that I shall have to work tonight. Pappa gave me the guest list for Saturday's dinner."

Mrs. Ashton gave an eloquent shudder. "How I do hate such affairs." She sighed, as she always did when faced with a state occasion. "I cannot like those people, forever arguing and talking about things I cannot understand, try as I may. And it is no use asking me to help you, my dear, for you know I can never remember who must not sit next to whom. How you can bear such parties, I vow I have no idea!"

"But then, I was brought up with them constantly going on in the house," Leanora explained apologetically. Affectionate amusement danced in her bright blue eyes. She loved her aunt dearly, but on occasion had wondered how her father's younger brother had ever come to marry such a bird-witted creature, lovely and sweet though she undoubtedly was.

When dinner came to an end, Amabelle Ashton withdrew to the drawing room where a new fire screen awaited her exquisite embroidery. Knowing that her aunt would be happily

14

occupied with this pursuit for some time to come, Leanora, with the dried and fed puppy scurrying in her wake, retired to her study and resolutely bent her mind to the placement around the long dining table of a number of persons who cordially detested one another.

A brace of candles had been lit for her, and their warm glow bathed the closely written lists that lay spread out across her desk. The pug, curling at her feet, let out a contented sigh, scratched an intrusive flea and settled down to sleep. Thoughtfully, Leanora bit at the tip of one long, delicate finger and considered the tentative arrangement she had previously created. She abstracted the final guest list from the stack of papers, groaned as the documents slipped and scattered over the already cluttered surface of her desk, but made no move to gather them together.

She consulted the list, then crossed two names off her seating chart. These, she tried placing at opposite ends of the long dining table sketch, then studied the plan again. That simple alteration meant three more people would have to have their places changed. She reinserted the names back in their original positions and turned her attention to their troublesome partners instead.

The ticklish problem was made no easier by the continual obtrusion into her thoughts of a certain tall, broad-shouldered gentleman whose rugged features showed a disturbing tendency to rise up before her mind's eye. Those eyes, so dark and mysterious . . . but here her memory faltered. All she remembered for certain was that they had glowed, and there had been both humor and secrets hidden in their depths; and she would very much like to gaze into them again.

With difficulty, she dragged her mind back to the seating arrangement. Daydreams were a foolish pastime and one in which she had not indulged for many years, not since she was a silly damsel fresh from the schoolroom and her dashing cousin Vincent had donned his first pair of scarlet regimentals. . . .

She brushed away a sudden errant tear. It was all a long time ago! He was dead now, killed—though she alone of the family had any suspicion of the truth—because of the intervention of his best friend, who had sent him on one of their mysterious missions behind French lines. She had little time now to spare for nonsensical notions. And her difficult guests refused to be happy, wherever she tried to seat them.

She moved another name, considered the consequences and replaced it. Before long, the tricky problem once more held her full attention. So involved was she, that she never heard the soft knock that fell on the door. Not until a breath of air sent the flames from the candles dancing did she realize that it had opened.

"What is it, Tremly?" she asked with a sigh, still staring at the chart in her hands. Absently, she twisted her fingers through a long yellow-gold ringlet that lay against her shoulder.

"Dash it, Leanora!" The earl of Sherborne, his dapper figure framed on the threshold, cast a considering eye over the smooth-fitting cut of the elegant long-tailed coat that he had received only that morning from the masterful hands of Weston. From the intricate folds of his starched neckcloth to the high gloss on his Hessian top boots, he could detect no fault in his appearance. In spite of a few extra pounds that had somehow attached themselves to his middle, he remained a fine figure of a man, a fact that afforded him considerable pride. "I may not be a Tulip," he expostulated, "but to have the infernal impudence to be taking me for a butler . . . ! I must say, it's the outside of enough!"

"Pappa!" Leanora looked up at her father's quizzing countenance, and sudden laughter replaced the strain that had drawn down the corners of her eyes. "I didn't hear you come home. How was your meeting?"

Lord Sherborne pulled up a Hepplewhite chair and seated himself across the desk from her. Dropping the handful of papers he carried onto the already cluttered surface before him, he settled comfortably back against padded cushions. "Petersham grows more tiresome by the hour. How that prosy old bore ever came to be secretary of the Home Office in Grenville's cabinet, I shall never know."

"He undoubtedly knows a dreadful secret about the prime minister, and his position is the price for holding his tongue," Leanora responded promptly. "What was the reason for

16

tonight's urgent dinner?"

"State secrets, my dear. I am sworn to silence." He smiled across at his daughter, sharing the joke. "Since Pitt's death, everything must needs fall under that heading for our dear Lord Petersham. He would do better to concentrate on those missing funds."

"You still have no idea who could have taken them?"

The earl shook his head. "Nor *how* they were taken—or even how long it has been going on. And at the rate Petersham is moving, we never will discover the answers."

"And Sir William?"

"Petersham's ways exasperate him, as ever, but he shows remarkable restraint." Lord Sherborne raised the quizzing glass that hung about his neck by a black satin riband and examined a minuscule speck of dust that rested on his sleeve of mulberry superfine. He brushed it away with care, then allowed his glass to fall. "Sir William asked after you, my dear."

"Did he?" she asked, her smile one of coy innocence.

Her father gave a deep bark of laughter. "No, child. That won't fadge. Our dandified Sir William Horborne is no match for you."

Leanora gave an exaggerated sigh. "No man is, Pappa."

At that, her loving pappa frowned. "Not still wearing the willow for Vincent are you?" he asked with surprising gentleness.

She managed an almost creditable laugh. "Don't be absurd, Pappa." Her gaze dropped to her desk, and she shuffled papers unnecessarily, fighting back memories of loss. She had not missed her cousin with that bleak, dull ache for some time now, not until the concert last night when the music, so very solemn, its subject death, brought it all back to her as fresh and painful as the day she first heard the news.

She swallowed hard and forced a laugh. "How—how Vincent would have stared at such a suggestion! I was always quite fond of him, of course, but—" She broke off, shaking her head. "I doubt I am cut out for marriage," she added with an attempt at her usual funning humor. "I have been on the shelf for years, and by choice, mind you, not for lack of offers. I am a positive ape-leader, or so I have heard said."

Her father's eyes flashed at that. "Who would have the confounded impertinence to come out with such a farradiddle of nonsense? You may be four-and-twenty, but to be spouting such ridiculous fustian—" He broke off as his reprehensibly mischievous daughter dissolved into a fit of the giggles.

"It was Aunt Charlotte," Leanora confessed, her eyes still brimful of determined merriment. "Poor dear. She has tried so very hard to see me suitably established, you know, and constantly blames poor Aunt Amabelle for not producing any eligible suitors. I greatly fear I have not made it an easy task for either of them." Her tone was one of mock contrition. "Aunt Charlotte told me I was in grave danger of dwindling into an old maid when I refused to encourage that silly moonling Cassady."

"Cassady!" Lord Sherborne's head came up, and he almost dropped the enameled snuff box he drew from his pocket. "I should certainly hope you'd have the sense not to let that nodcock dangle after you! Is that the sort of match Charlotte has in mind? Never had any sense, any of your mother's family!"

"Well," Leanora said fairly, "at least Cassady isn't a gazetted fortune hunter like John Kelson."

"Has he been making up to you?" her father demanded. "Good God, girl. Is that the best you can find, with all of London to choose from?"

"You don't think just *any* man would do for me, not after the standards you have set?" Leanora shook her head with mock sadness. "Serving as your hostess these past eight years have left their mark on me."

"Saucy minx," her doting Pappa told her, apparently satisfied. "Did you not go out this evening? I thought there was some rout party or other."

"Almack's, dearest. It's Wednesday. But Aunt Amabelle did not want to go out in this terrible storm, and I am sure it would have been quite dreadfully thin of company. Besides, I still have not solved this problem."

"What is it?" He leaned across to better examine the plans she held out to him.

"That 'little dinner party' of yours. Why you ever invited so many people with so many different political views is beyond me. You realize, of course, Lord Broughly would never come if he knew you had also invited Glasden?"

Her father chuckled. "Can't stand a dull evening. What's this?" he demanded suddenly. "You can't possibly put Petersham next to Countess Lieven. Do you want to have your vouchers to Almack's withdrawn?"

"It was either that or put her next to Broughly, and you know what *that* would come to." Their eyes met across the desk, and both burst out laughing as the last of Leanora's lingering depression vanished. "The only way we can achieve a reasonable seating arrangement," she gasped, "is to place Broughly and Lady Glasden in a separate room. And even then, they cannot be put in the same one."

Lord Sherborne rose, still chuckling. "You have three days ahead of you, my dear. I am sure you will have contrived something by then. Lord, I'm tired! And I still have a few notes to make on tonight's meeting. Do you go up to bed, now?"

"In a few minutes. I want to finish this." She swept some of the papers on the desk together and handed them to her father. "You can take these with you; they're the ones I brought home today."

Her movements disturbed the sleeping puppy. He stretched, sneezed and came to his feet. Seeing the earl for the first time, the little dog danced up to him and snuffled at his gleaming boots.

"Good God!" the earl exclaimed, eyeing the pug with something akin to revulsion. "What is that?"

The puppy, ignoring the words, shivered all over in delight and emitted a series of short, demanding yips. Sherborne set down the papers and picked the animal up, holding it in one arm as he raised his quizzing glass to subject it to a minute scrutiny.

"Puglet." Leanora introduced it. "Aunt Charlotte has given him to Aunt Amabelle, but I fear she does not want him."

"*Puglet?*" the earl exploded in tones of loathing. "Charlotte always was a foolish woman. *Puglet*, of all things." He allowed his glass to drop and raised the puppy's ludicrous black face

19

with his hand. The quick, darting tongue went to instant work on his fingers, and the whole little body trembled with its intense pleasure. "So Amabelle won't have it, will she? No wonder, with a name like that. It should be something solemn, don't you think?"

Leanora observed the instant rapport between the two and with difficulty kept from laughing. "To be sure. Something noble, to befit his stature."

"Exactly," agreed her father, ignoring her sarcasm. He considered the pug. "Artaxerxes," he decreed suddenly, and the pug wriggled with delight. "Any idea how old he is?"

"About six months, I believe. And he is really quite well trained, though somewhat rambunctious."

"Artaxerxes," the earl repeated. He stooped down and set the puppy on the floor. Instantly it sat before him, trying to wag the tail that curled up over its back. Sherborne gathered up the papers once more and left the room with the newly christened Artaxerxes scurrying at his feet.

Still smiling, Leanora returned to her work. But the names on the pages ceased to make sense. She yawned and knew it was time to give up for the night. Ruthlessly, she shoved the remaining sheets into a drawer, slammed it closed and went in search of her father.

She found him in his study at the back of the house, seated at his great desk with the puppy curled up at his feet. The earl looked up as she entered, nodded absently and scribbled the last of his notes onto the paper before him. Collecting several sheets together, he locked them into a drawer and stuffed the key in his pocket.

"Finished?" he asked.

"Not even close," she admitted. "Though when I shall get back to it, I have no idea. I have a full day tomorrow."

"Do you good to get away from it for a while," Sherborne encouraged her. "You'd be surprised what inspiration can come to you in the night."

She picked up the chased, silver snuffer and began to extinguish his candles. "It would take a visitation of nothing less than a muse to seat this dinner amicably. Have you—" She broke off, alert, staring hard in the direction of the window that looked out over the mews. "Did you hear something?"

Artaxerxes rose, growling softly, the hackles rising on the back of his neck. The earl of Sherborne silenced the puppy, then cocked his head, considering. "No," he said at last. "Must have been the rain. With those branches scratching against the window, it's no wonder you're jumpy."

Leanora crossed to the window and looked out, scanning the darkness that was all she could see. It had not been a twig brushing the windowpane that she heard. It had been a heavier sound, of something—or someone—falling or dropping to the ground. But there was no sign of anything now.

"What a taking you're in!" the earl exclaimed, laughing. "No, really my girl, you're not one to be afraid of a storm! Seen you tramping happily all over the estate in worse weather than this!" He grinned suddenly and put a comforting arm about her to lead her from the room. "That Requiem music still bothering you, is it? Never seen you so moved by a concert before. Tell you what, I'll take you to that *soiree* tomorrow night, and we'll listen to some livelier tunes. That will cheer you up!"

She managed to smile, for she recognized the truth in his words. It was not like her to let her imagination run wild, but between Mozart's solemn score, the storm and that intriguing gentleman, she had certainly been indulging in fantasy this day!

Together, they returned to the main hall where candles had been left for them on the small table at the foot of the staircase. Lighting these, they started up to the second floor where their bedchambers lay with Artaxerxes scrambling along with them. When they reached her room, Leanora stood on tiptoe to kiss her father's cheek.

"If you can think of where to seat Lord Petersham where he cannot bore anyone, do please tell me," she urged her father. "That will do the trick and cheer me up."

"To bed with you, my girl," he told her with a half-laugh. He continued down the hall to his own room, still smiling to himself, and to Leanora's amusement, the puppy followed blithely at his heels.

She entered her apartment, found her abigail waiting for her and felt insensibly better. It really was nothing but her imagination upsetting her so. But in spite of this, she would not have objected to little Artaxerxes spending the night curled on her bed, and she cast an uneasy glance at her curtained window as she finally slid between sheets.

Chapter 2

The storm continued throughout the night, but by morning a pale, watery sun peeped out from between gray clouds. A flock of birds took possession of the trees in the square across the street and melodically announced the arrival of a late spring. Leanora, roused from an uneasy sleep at an early hour by their determined singing, settled back against her pillows and considered the day ahead.

In the light of morning, she found it easy to banish her foolish, nervous flights of the night before. She had other matters, of a more practical nature, with which to deal. And the first was to pay a morning visit in Mount Street, where her brother, the Honorable Mr. Gregory Ashton, and his wife Lady Julia had set up their residence.

To Leanora's surprise, she descended the stairs to the breakfast parlor and found her Aunt Amabelle there before her. Mrs. Ashton, who rarely left her bedchamber before ten o'clock, sat in the cozy apartment, sipping tea and eating delicate fingers of toast. She smiled wanly at her niece, who promptly went to drop a kiss on her cheek.

"Are you quite well, dear Aunt?" Leanora asked solicitously.

"This dreadful weather!" Mrs. Ashton murmured in failing accents.

Leanora made a sympathetic response and turned her attention to the sideboard, where a variety of dishes were laid out. Lifting the lid of one, she inspected its contents, then

23

selected a thin slice of ham and a roll. She poured herself a cup of chocolate and returned to the table.

Mrs. Ashton sighed deeply, shaking her head. "I vow and declare, my love, I did not close my eyes once all night. You must know how I hate storms, and the wind did blow so, I feared at any moment my window would be broken; and then I should have all that rain, not to mention leaves and twigs, for I am sure they were blowing about all over. And what with all that dreadful clatter in the streets, which I made certain you must have heard, for it was enough to awaken anyone from the soundest sleep, which I must say, I do envy you very much, for I have the most terrible time dropping off; and if ever I am awakened I can never get back to sleep, but—" She broke off, momentarily perplexed, having lost the thread of her narrative.

"Just so, ma'am," Leanora agreed, her eyes twinkling. "But it is over now, I assure you. Only look out and you may see."

Her aunt complied, leaning back in order to look out the long, mullioned window that provided a view of the garden in the center of Berkeley Square. The pale sunlight, glinting off rain drops that still clung to the black, iron fence, did not overly impress her. She shook her head sadly. "It will be days, still, before it will at last be warm and dry."

Leanora smiled. "You will see how delightful it is outside. Remember, we are pledged to call on Julia this morning."

"This morning? Oh, no, my love!" Mrs. Ashton cried, dismayed. "It is far too damp! I should catch a chill!"

Leanora considered. "Well, I do not think you would, but there is no need for you to accompany me, if you do not feel quite the thing. Julia will understand."

Indeed, her sister-in-law would understand, and all too well, Leanora reflected. Mrs. Amabelle Ashton, a gentle creature, had never gotten along well with her nephew Gregory, whose restless energy and propensity for playing pranks left her somewhat bewildered. Nor did she feel comfortable with the dashing Lady Julia, who had been the reigning Beauty for two seasons before accepting Gregory's hand, much to the delight of her father, the impoverished marquis of Windemere.

"For, my love, I cannot hide from you that I believe her

24

to be *fast*," Mrs. Ashton had sighed tragically upon the announcement of the engagement. "I should be sorry to see any daughter or niece of mine behave in so forward a manner." These strictures were not quite just but rose from the fact that Mrs. Ashton's own son, her beloved Reginald, had once shown a tendency to dangle after the undoubted Incomparable. Rather than being relieved when Reggie's interest had waned, she held the Beauty to be at fault for treating him with an unwarranted callousness and cruelty.

"You will call out the carriage, will you not, my dear?" Mrs. Ashton asked now as Leanora rose from the breakfast table.

"For a journey around the corner?" Leanora's ready mirth bubbled just beneath the surface. "I shall come to no harm walking such a short distance. The weather is quite mild, I assure you."

"But—but the proprieties! At least take a footman with you!" her aunt begged.

At that, Leanora laughed. "Dearest Aunt! Mount Street is not at the end of the earth! I shall walk less than two blocks! And I am not a green girl, you know. It will be quite proper for me to go such a short distance alone. Or no! I shall take that pug puppy with me. Unless my father has taken him to Whitehall?"

Mrs. Ashton shook her head. "Your pappa is still in his study. Such a fancy as they have taken to each other! Why, when he took that little dog to the kitchens for its breakfast, it whimpered so to be parted from him, it quite wrung my heart!"

"No, did it?" Leanora demanded, amused. It seemed the bond between the two had only been strengthened over night. "Of a certainty I shall take it with me then, to keep it from pining when Pappa leaves. Now, do not worry yourself, dear Aunt. You shall lie down in your sitting room; and if you feel more the thing later, I shall take you to that milliner's shop I visited yesterday, and you may see for yourself their delightful hats."

Leaving her aunt, Leanora went in search of the puppy Artaxerxes. She found him in a corner of the pantry, exercising his teeth on a formidable ham bone. This he could not be induced to abandon, and Leanora gained the impression

25

that having been handed over into the care of the staff, there the puppy intended to remain until claimed by his chosen master. Leanora was not one to waste time on hopeless causes and soon gave up her plans for the pug's entertainment.

A very few minutes later, she left the house, warmly garbed in a pelisse of golden-brown merino and with her hands safely tucked into an ermine muff. A ragged urchin, lounging against the iron-work fence, darted across the street and planted himself firmly in front of her. Leanora looked down, her eyes registering both surprise and dismay at the boy's disheveled appearance.

"There's a dentical fine cove as is keeping 'is peepers glued t' that ken o' yours," the lad hissed at her in an urgent undervoice.

Leanora blinked. Close association with her father and brother had done much to extend her vocabulary in directions that shocked such high sticklers as Mrs. Ashton, but these mysterious words proved beyond her comprehension. The urchin, noting this, frowned at her slowness.

"A nib cove!" he explained. "Flash cull, too."

"A gentleman!" Leanora exclaimed, pleased to have one part of the peculiar utterance explained to her, though she had a sinking suspicion that "flash cull" meant that the person in question was not quite honest. "And what was this gentleman doing?"

"I tol' yer. Watchin'."

"Watching? The house?" she asked, incredulous. Involuntarily, she glanced about the street as if she expected some menacing stranger to accost her at any moment.

"Lor' love ya, miss, 'e ain't wheres you'd see 'im!" the boy exclaimed. "Been 'ere all morning, 'e 'as. Piked on the bean when you come out."

"Piked on the. . . ." Leanora, once again wholly at sea, transferred her bemused gaze back to the dirty face before her.

"Loped off," the boy explained patiently.

"I see," she said slowly. Had someone been watching the house, then disappeared as soon as she came out? The idea was ludicrous, but a shiver ran through her. The storm, that strange thud outside her father's study window—it was all

26

nerves, nothing more. And this boy undoubtedly had made up the whole story in the hope of extracting largesse from her. She turned a stern eye on the lad, and her resolve to send him packing melted. He was quite thin and dressed in the shabbiest fashion. He must be cold in those rags, she mused. Impulsively, she drew her reticule from within the warm confines of her muff and handed him a shilling.

The boy's eyes rounded with delight. "Thank 'e, miss!" With a touch to the disreputable cap that perched on his head, he bounded off.

Leanora watched his retreating figure, wondering whether she had made a mistake. If money was all that he had been after, she might never be rid of him! But he had seemed surprised at the coin she had given him. Either he had not expected so much for his tale, or . . . or his story was true, and his telling her had been an honest warning. She tucked her hand back into her muff and walked on more swiftly, her mind in a whirl.

She was not granted much time for reflection. Only a few steps farther took her to the corner, and she turned onto Mount Street. The house her brother had rented was halfway down the block, and she reached it quickly. The door was opened to her at once by Retlaw, senior footman in her father's household until he had been called upon to fill the important role of butler for his young master's new home.

Retlaw bowed low to her, permitting himself the prim smile of welcome that Tremly had taught him could be allowed when greeting members of the Family. "Good morning, my lady." Deftly, he relieved her of her muff and pelisse, laying these tenderly aside. "Her ladyship is in the morning room, if you would care to go up."

"Thank you, Retlaw." Firmly putting aside her uneasiness, Leanora hurried up the wide staircase to the first floor and entered the second room to the right of the landing without bothering to knock. The sight that met her eyes brought her up short.

Lady Julia Ashton sat perched on the edge of a gilt chair, her lovely head lowered in her hands and her dark curls disarrayed as her shoulders shook with sobs. Over her, his face flushed with anger, stood the Honorable Mr. Gregory Ashton. He looked up, an angry scowl crossing his features at the intrusion. This faded, to be replaced by a tight-lipped frown as he recognized his sister.

"Lord, what are you doing here, Nora?" he demanded with true brotherly affection.

"I came to visit Julia, but it is nothing important. If—if this is a bad time. . . ." She broke off, unsure of her ground. Julia had always struck her as a very self-possessed young lady. Her present tearful state seemed unaccountable.

"No! Oh please, Leanora, do stay!" Julia sobbed. She raised her large, reddened eyes beseechingly to her sister-in-law. "Gregory is being so unkind, but you will reason with him for me!"

Leanora crossed the room, sank down before the distraught young lady and possessed herself of her hands. "What is this all about?" she asked gently. "Surely it is only a misunderstanding! Gregory, do ring for some refreshment. I am quite cold, and I am sure Julia will be better for something."

Gregory, his scowl returning to mar his classically handsome countenance, tugged at the bell pull with enough force to bring Retlaw bounding up the stairs to discover what had occurred. While they waited for chocolate and biscuits, Leanora drew up a chair beside Julia and sat quietly until that lady composed herself enough to be able to speak.

"He is being very cruel to me!" Julia wailed when the butler had once more removed from the room.

Gregory let out an exasperated exclamation, and Leanora directed a quelling glance at him while she poured out cups of chocolate. "Do be quiet, Gregory, or you will upset her all over again. I cannot understand you, distressing her so."

"Nora, if you knew the half of it," Gregory began, but she held up a silencing hand. He let out a frustrated "Phaugh!" and strode over to stare out the window, rocking impatiently on his heels.

Julia gave a delicate sniff. "He—he has ripped out at me in the most horrid way for spending! But I only bought a new ball gown, and you must know the ones I have would not do at all for—" She broke off, quailing under the furious glare directed at her by her husband.

"But where is the problem? I know he makes you a generous allowance. Surely you could not have spent the half of it, for we are only just past the quarter day!" Leanora looked from Julia's chagrined expression to Gregory's glowering one, startled.

"Spent before she ever received it!" he said shortly. "Gaming debts! Good God, I would have thought she'd know better, with her father practically rolled up. Must be in the blood!"

"They—they were only the most discreet card parties, I promise you!" Julia protested. "I went with Dalmouth."

Gregory swore softly. "Damn it, Julia, just because he's your brother don't mean you should go jauntering off with him to those hells he frequents!"

"It was not a hell! It—it was a quite respectable house, and I did not like it above half; so you may be sure gaming is *not* in my blood!" She ended on a sob, once again hiding her face which, to Leanora's unending envy, was lovely in spite of the tears.

"Am I to understand that *you* do not visit hells in the company of Viscount Dalmouth?" Leanora asked her brother with a false sweetness. If gaming was the issue sending the young couple's finances into desperate straits, then she knew where the real blame should be placed. She and her father had watched with increasing concern Gregory's growing addiction to any form of gambling.

Gregory flushed an unbecoming scarlet beneath his carefully combed golden locks. "Lord, Nora, how you do take a fellow up! Nothing wrong with a man's gaming. Expected of him!" He hunched an angry shoulder as she raised dubious eyebrows. "Damme, if I weren't held to such a beggarly allowance, no one would think twice about it!"

Leanora stared at him. By no stretch of the imagination could the allowance the earl of Sherborne made to his heir be considered beggarly. Gregory must have been dipping very deep of late, and that knowledge could not make her easy. She regarded her brother searchingly through lowered lids. His appearance indicated a Top-of-the-Trees Corinthian, a buck of the first head, and she knew it was his greatest ambition to be declared a Blood, a Go amongst the Goers. It had been an easy step for Gregory to go from emulating his heroes' sporting abilities to following their lead in betting heavily on the outcome of cock fights, races and boxing matches and frequenting such haunts of the Out-and-Outers as the Daffy Club and Watiers.

From there, a young gentleman who was not quite as up to snuff as he would like to think, nor had yet learned to tell a flat from a leg, could easily fall into the hands of a Captain Sharp, whose business it was to lure young pigeons, ripe for the plucking, into discreet but not necessarily honest gaming hells. Although Leanora found it hard to believe that Viscount Dalmouth, son and heir to the marquis of Windemere, could be a professional gamester, she had no doubt that it was Gregory's ramshackle brother-in-law who had first introduced him to a certain house in Pall Mall.

She could not like the situation. How badly was Gregory scorched? He must have had very deep doings of late to object to Julia's buying a gown. But asking him directly would not serve, she guessed shrewdly. A year younger than his sister, he accepted her advice when he chose and jealously guarded his dignity the rest of the time. Perhaps she could find out from Sir William Holborne. As well as being an associate of Lord Sherborne's at the Home Office, he always seemed to know the latest gossip and *on dits*, and could be counted on to drop a hint in her ear if Gregory were indeed in trouble.

She glanced at her sister-in-law's tear-streaked face, then up into Gregory's deeply lined one. He was worried, but the experience would do him more good than harm, she decided. She stood abruptly and said in a rallying tone: "Well, then, you are both making a great deal of fuss over the merest trifle, I am persuaded. Julia has learned her lesson and will conduct herself from now on with the utmost propriety and economy."

"Economy!" Gregory ejaculated. "She doesn't know the meaning of the word. You should see our household accounts. The amounts she squanders on candles alone! She—"

Leanora, casting a rapid glance at Julia's quivering chin, hastily broke into her brother's diatribe. "Houses are always

30

shockingly costly to maintain. I am sure you never so much as glanced at the expenses for Sherborne House. But now that you have explained the situation to Julia, I am sure that you will both contrive to live more circumspectly. I must take my leave of you now, but will you see me out, Gregory?" She turned her fine, compelling eyes on her brother, meeting and holding his gaze.

He shrugged and strode to the door, which he held open for her. She moved out onto the upper landing, then grasped his wrist and drew him into the breakfast parlor next door.

"Dash it all, Nora, what are you up to?" he demanded, not pleased.

"Gregory, tell me the truth," she instructed. She looked up into his handsome face and studied the tiny lines about his eyes. He had been racketing about too much of late. If she could persuade him to retire to the country for a repairing lease, he would be the better for it. And so would Julia. "Are you keeping company with Dalmouth?" she demanded.

"What if I am? Good God, he's my wife's brother, you know, not some social-climbing mushroom!"

"No, but the company he keeps is not of the best *ton*, and well you know it. If half the things I've heard are true, they're a dangerous lot. Anything from boxing the watch to—to I do not know what!"

"No, how should you?" His lip curled in a sneer, which faded almost at once. "A regular set of hellions, they were. But no need to worry about them. Dalmouth gave up that lot. Whole new set of interests. Quite a reformed character, you'd scarcely believe it!"

"You are quite right there, at any event. What are these new interests? Gaming?"

Gregory flushed. "Lord, Nora, you were never one to preach so! You'd think a fellow never had a flutter before!"

She placed one hand on his shoulder and stood on tiptoe to plant a light kiss on his cheek. "Just don't go throwing good money after bad," she told him. A reprehensible amusement suddenly lit her eyes. "That's the way to come home by Weeping Cross."

A reluctant smile twisted his lips into a singularly charming

31

expression. "Look who's lecturing whom on propriety! You mind your tongue, my girl, or you'll be thought fast! Where do you pick up your cant phrases?"

"From you, my dear. And Pappa. If you find yourself in a bind, let me know. Do you go to Lady Castlereigh's *soiree* tonight?"

He hesitated. "I believe we do."

"Then we shall see you there."

She took her leave of him, reclaimed her pelisse and muff from the waiting Retlaw and soon emerged onto the street. The sun was stronger now, taking the chill out of the air. If the morrow proved to be fine as well, the puddles of water that made the walkway treacherous would quickly dry up.

Had her father noticed Gregory's troubles? Leanora could not be sure. The earl had been so preoccupied of late with Lord Grenville, the new prime minister. And surely, the last time Gregory and Julia had come to dinner—was it already three weeks ago?—there had been nothing amiss! She could only hope that her father would be able to attend the party with her that night so that he would see for himself how things stood with his son and heir.

Her thoughts remained concentrated on her reckless brother, but as she paused on the corner before crossing to Berkeley Square, she looked up and chanced to see a gentleman walking some distance ahead of her. His limp, as well as his size and the quiet elegance of his dress, instantly identified him for her as the stranger who had helped her retrieve those papers the day before.

A fluttering of nerves took uncomfortable possession of her stomach. Why would the mere sight of the man throw her into such chaos? She wanted to run away and hide, yet the desire to speak to him, to stare into his marvelous eyes, almost overwhelmed her. She bit her lip, torn by unfamiliar, conflicting desires.

As she resolutely turned to walk away, another figure strode purposefully toward the unknown gentleman. With a touch of surprise, Leanora recognized Lord Kennington. He seemed about to pass the other man, then paused, looked hard at him and spoke. The other gentleman nodded, Kennington turned

32

his steps to accompany him, and the two walked off together, still in conversation.

Her heart sank. Why should that association dismay her so? There was something mysterious—even dangerous!—about that man. But still, he had not seemed to be of Kennington's ilk. The knowledge that she might have been wrong distressed her more than it should.

Suddenly, the sun did not seem to shine as brightly. Irritated with herself for reacting like some foolish chit, she quickened her pace and within a few minutes reached the house. As she started up the steps, a grubby little hand tugged at the long skirt of her pelisse, and she turned about in surprise.

"Oh, it's you again, is it?" She regarded the ragged street urchin with a touch of suspicion.

"That flash cull come back, miss, soon as you was gone. 'Ung about, 'e did, 'til a swell cove come out o' the ken. Loped off after 'im, keepin' back, like, so as the swell cove don't see 'im." The huge eyes regarded Leanora not without hope.

"What did he look like, this—this 'flash cull,'" she asked. A sudden, unsettling idea took possession of her mind.

The boy hesitated, obviously thinking. "Well," he began slowly, "'e weren't nothin' special, wore fancy mish an' carried a fancy tattler. . . ." He broke off, frowning.

"What color hair did he have?" Leanora prompted. "And was he short or—or tall? Very tall?"

"Dark," the boy finally decided. "Couldn' see 'is 'air rightly unner 'is 'at," he added apologetically. "An' 'e weren't tall, neither, nor short."

"In effect, quite ordinary." So it wasn't that man! Her relief startled her. She did not like the idea that he might have some sinister purpose.

"That's it, miss! 'E were jus' ordin'ry." The boy seemed pleased to find her of so ready an understanding.

"Well, thank you," Leanora sighed. "If you see him again, let me know." She drew another shilling from her purse and handed it to the boy, who accepted it gleefully. She would probably never see the end of him, now, but if there really was someone watching the house and following her father. . . . Trying to banish the incident from her mind, she went inside.

33

She found her Aunt Amabelle laying down on a couch in her pretty sitting room with a cashmere shawl cast over her feet and a scented handkerchief held in one hand. A fire burned merrily in the hearth. As Leanora entered, Mrs. Ashton's eyes fluttered open.

"Is that you at last, my love? I swear, you have been gone this age!"

"Are you feeling more the thing, now?" Leanora asked as she sank down into a delicate chair near the fireplace and warmed her hands.

"Indeed I am. Did you find your sister-in-law well?" she added civilly, though with no real interest.

"Yes, and Gregory was there, too. I have seen very little of him of late, you must know. They will both be present at the *soiree* tonight."

"Oh, do we go out?" Her aunt brightened perceptibly, then cast an anxious glance toward the curtained window. "Do you think the weather will hold?"

"I am quite sure of it. Now, you will have to hurry if you wish to accompany me to Bond Street. And after we come back from shopping, would you care to drive in the Park? I should be delighted to take you up in my phaeton."

Her aunt embarked upon a tangled speech in which she maintained that while a gentle airing would be just the thing, provided that the weather were indeed mild, she was not at all sure that she wished to be conveyed in her niece's dashing and precarious high-perch carriage. As Leanora had been accustomed to driving herself about Hyde Park in this vehicle for several years, and was accounted an excellent whip, this only made her laugh and pledge herself not to overturn her beloved aunt, whom she saucily apostrophized as a "dear goose."

Subsequently, after the ladies partook of a light nuncheon, they sent for the barouche and prepared to set forth on the projected visit to the newly opened milliner's shop in Brook Street that Leanora had discovered the day before. As Leanora stepped out the front door, a dashing racing curricle bearing two occupants pulled up in the street opposite their waiting carriage. The budding Pink of the Ton who sat beside the driver waved to her.

"Nora," her cousin Mr. Reginald Ashton called. "Are you and my mamma still planning on being at the Castlereigh's tonight? Got a little surprise for you. See you then!"

Leanora blinked. "But Reggie—"

He laughed. "Not a word. By, Nora!"

The driver, who had been mostly obscured from view behind her cousin, leaned forward, and almost in disbelief Leanora recognized the nameless gentleman who had been disturbing her thoughts. It was almost as if he haunted her! And what on earth did he have to do with her cousin Reggie?

The man turned to glance at her, and his dark eyes widened in recognition. Reggie, oblivious of his companion's sudden intentness, urged him on. The gentleman hesitated, then gave his matched bays the office. His gaze, though, remained on Leanora's face until he had driven past.

Mrs. Ashton emerged from the house in time to see the curricle depart. "Was that not Reggie?" she demanded. "Why did he not stay?"

"He—he said he would see us tonight," Leanora managed. Bemused, she watched as the vehicle turned the corner and disappeared from sight.

Mrs. Ashton sighed. "It has been an age since he has paid us a visit, so unnatural a son as he is, not to be calling on his poor widowed Mamma more often. We do not see him nearly often enough. But then, I suppose all young men must have lodgings of their own, though why they should prefer to live in mere rooms, when I am sure your dear pappa would give him a suite of his own in this great house, I cannot imagine; for dear Reggie cannot be looked after as well as one would like, and if they air the sheets properly it is more than I can hope for!" She ended on a challenging note, as if defying her niece to claim that her only surviving son could receive better care at the hands of a pack of strangers than with his devoted mamma.

Leanora, who would not for a moment consider anything so foolhardy as to engage in an argument with her garrulous relative, firmly repressed a smile. "Just so, dear Aunt."

The combination of Gregory's problems, someone watching the house and Reggie's acquaintance with that unsettling gentleman kept her mind in a whirl the rest of the day. She could not be easy, yet never could she remember looking forward to a party with such eagerness. It was in this unsettled state that she descended the stairs that evening, ready to depart for the Castlereigh's *soiree*. She was joined almost at once by her aunt, and together they sat down to wait for Lord Sherborne who, not unexpectedly, had been held up in a late meeting with Lord Petersham.

When the earl joined them at last, he was, as always, precise to a pin, a tall, elegant figure in his long-tailed coat of blue superfine. Leanora experienced a feeling of pleasurable pride, for it was not often he had the time to accompany her to a non-political function. She enjoyed his escort, for he had the rare ability to set his fellow guests at their ease. His manners were easy, and he could never be accused of being the least bit high in the instep, despite the importance of his position.

The carriage arrived at the door, and the earl ushered the ladies outside. As she waited for her aunt to precede her into the barouche, a slight movement in the darkness across the street caught her attention. A tree, blowing in the wind? But it had almost looked like a man, disappearing into the shadows of the garden.

It was nothing but her overactive imagination again! She tried to laugh it off, but the words of the disreputable street urchin had taken root in the back of her mind. It had to be all nonsense! A pack of moonshine—as Reggie would say. Still, she cast an uneasy glance back over her shoulder as their carriage moved off.

Chapter 3

By the time the barouche pulled up before the Castlereigh's town house, Leanora had almost banished the worst of her uneasiness from her mind. Firmly, she placed the blame for her nerves on the storm and the effects of the melancholy chords of the *Requiem*, which still haunted her. Tonight she would hear other, more lively music, that would once and for all drive away the moody memories.

As she expected, the drawing rooms, which were thrown open so that one led into the next, were sadly crowded, filled with members of the *haut ton*. She looked about, recognizing a great many of the guests. One face, though, she did not see, and the realization that she even looked for him startled her. And why did the absence of that mysterious man disturb her? The thought was unsettling.

"You are looking uncommonly solemn this evening," a familiar voice spoke behind her.

Leanora turned and smiled as she saw the Exquisite who had joined her. "Sir William, I am surprised to see that Lord Petersham has given you the night off. Until the last moment, I feared he would keep even my father at one of his meetings."

Sir William Holborne took her offered hand and raised her fingers to his lips with an elegant grace. Nothing could exceed the precision of his manners or the perfection of his dress. Had he not entered the complex world of politics, Sir William would have been hailed as a Tulip, a veritable Pink of the Ton. As it was, his dandified airs were kept to a minimum out of

37

deference to the position he held. His collar points might reach above his cheek bones, but they did not prevent him from turning his head. His coat, as he had once assured Leanora, had come from the hands of no less a personage than the great Schultz, as had his flower brocade waistcoat. His pantaloons were of the palest buff, and his gleaming white-topped Hessians were decorated with golden tassels. His brown locks, cut and curled *a la Titus,* were carefully anointed with Russian oil, and only a genius would have attempted the intricate, visionary folds of his pristine neckcloth.

"But Petersham is himself here this night," Sir William told her with mock astonishment as he released her hand. "I believe I saw him in one of the other rooms, boring some poor acquaintance."

Leanora tried to frown at him but found it difficult. His waspish tongue might be the one thing she deplored about him, but on occasion she was forced to admit the truth, if not the kindness, of his words. "I believe he means well," she countered.

"And worse you can say of no one" came Sir William's prompt retort.

Leanora threw a considering glance at her companion. If she wanted to know the extent of her brother's difficulties, Sir William Holborne was certainly the person to ask. The words were on the tip of her tongue, but she checked herself. Sir William might be justly famed for knowing everything about everyone, but he was also quite ready to impart this information to anyone who asked. She did not want her brother's affairs whispered about town as the latest *on dit.* Instead, with studied casualness, she asked: "Is Viscount Dalmouth here, do you know?"

"Now, why would you be interested in that gentleman?" Sir William watched her narrowly. "Or is it his connection with a certain Mr. Gregory Ashton?"

Sir William's reputation for quick-mindedness was well earned, Leanora reflected. With reluctance, she admitted that this was her concern, then added, trying not to sound too worried: "What do you know of Dalmouth's set?"

Sir William turned from her to bow to a turbaned dowager

who was bent on attracting his attention. Smiling and nodding to another acquaintance, he addressed Leanora without actually looking at her. "Gregory is showing less than his usual good judgment in this case, I fear—as you seem to suspect, or you would not be asking, would you, my dear? Dalmouth plays deep, and it is usually at certain elitest hells that are designed to pluck young and wealthy pigeons."

"Dalmouth is hardly wealthy," Leanora murmured, half to herself, as she turned to acknowledge a greeting from an ardent young buck. "Where does he get the money?"

"Now, that would be most indiscreet in me to hazard a guess, would it not? Mind, I am not claiming that he is a Captain Sharp or an ivory turner himself, of course, but that is the sort of company he has been keeping of late."

Leanora took a deep breath and turned back to Sir William. "I have known you for a very long time and hope I can rely on your discretion. Tell me honestly, and without roundaboutation, is my brother much in Dalmouth's company?"

Sir William hesitated, then nodded. "He is. But it has only been of recent date, so there may not have been much damage done as yet. If only they were not related by marriage, I would say it should be no difficult thing to wean your headstrong brother from this undesirable friendship. I have considered dropping a word of warning in Lord Sherborne's ear, but I fear he might think I was interfering in what is none of my concern."

"My father has enough worries of his own at the moment, with all the dust up over changing prime ministers," Leanora sighed. Her gaze scanned the room, rested a moment on the corpulent figure of Lord Petersham who had just come through a doorway, and moved on. She would try hinting to Gregory that the knowledgeable considered Dalmouth to be dangerous. In his current, unhappy state, that information might be enough to give him pause.

She separated from Sir William and moved to join her Aunt Amabelle. So far, there was no sign of Gregory and Julia. Nor of her cousin Reggie, she noted, though without much surprise. He had promised to attend for his mother's sake, but music was not his idea of entertainment.

Lady Castlereigh appeared and began ushering her guests into the largest drawing room, where rows of chairs had been set facing a small area that contained a pianoforte and a harp. Leanora found her father, tucked her hand into his arm and led him, over his murmured protests, to a seat.

When the first set of performances at last ended, Lord Sherborne muttered something about insipidity and made good his escape to the card room. Mrs. Ashton, though, lingered in her chair, commenting at length on the delightful young lady who had played the harp, and that romantic gentleman with the most wonderful baritone voice who had sung such a lovely ballad. In this opinion, Mrs. Ashton was seconded by the dowager Lady Ingersoll who sat nearby, and the two ladies seemed content to remain where they were throughout the interval, reviewing every performance in detail.

Seeing her aunt so comfortably established, Leanora slipped away to find refreshment. As she entered the room in which several long tables had been lavishly arrayed with food and punch bowls, she almost collided with the bulky figure of Lord Petersham. He blinked, then smiled as he recognized his associate's daughter.

"Well, my dear, quite a pleasant evening, is it not?" he asked, beaming on her. A muscle twitched nervously at the corner of one eye, and he rushed into speech. "Can always count on the Castlereighs for a spot of excellent entertainment. I remember one night, *soiree* much like this, you know, but she managed to get an Italian Opera singer of all things. Exquisite! Had some wonderful music that night. And then there was the time, just a rout party you understand, unless it was that Venetian breakfast. Capital, though, I assure you."

Leanora let him drone on for several minutes, an artificial smile firmly held to her lips. Was she mistaken, or did he seem ill at ease? She considered for a moment, and the feeling grew. Definitely, something was amiss.

She regarded him with concern while trying to pretend an interest in the lengthy story he related. He was an amiable man, but he did tend to bore on indefinitely, making his company about as exciting as his moldering collection of

Classical antiquities. His plump, vacuous countenance exactly mirrored his meager intelligence, and what nature had neglected in height it more than made up for in girth. He looked a jovial country squire, which he might have been had not the importance of his office taken precedence over everything else in his mind, giving him a consequential air and a conviction that his opinion must naturally be desired by all of his numerous acquaintances.

As quickly as she could without giving offense, Leanora escaped from him. Arming herself with a glass of lemonade, she mingled through the crowd, greeting friends, but her thoughts drifted back to the gentleman she had just left. The last time she had seen him so distressed was when another collector had purchased the Roman bust he had ardently desired.

Halfway across the room, she was stopped by Sir William, who desired, with a wave of his quizzing glass, that she observe a dowager in a purple turban resplendent with ostrich plumes. Leanora cast a quick glance in the direction he indicated and agreed that the woman looked a frightful quiz.

"And there," Sir William added in mocking tones, "is a sartorial vision to delight any eye. Leanora, my dear, I believe your cousin Reggie has arrived."

Leanora turned to see the young dandy approaching with delicate, if not mincing, steps. His appearance would inspire awe in any aspirant to fashion, for every line of his bearing proclaimed the *dernier cri*. His long-tailed coat was of the palest powder blue, nipped in tightly at the waist and padded at the shoulder to provide a modish silhouette. Silver thread shot through the floral brocade waistcoat, and his pantaloons, rather than being a delicate yellow, were of the most pristine white. A sapphire pin pierced the marvelous folds of his neckcloth.

But Leanora spared no more than the briefest glance for her cousin's splendor. For at his side, limping slightly, came the dark-haired, elegant giant with deep, turbulent eyes.

Leanora's full lips parted slightly as her gaze met and held that gentleman's. A strange, exciting sensation fluttered within her, and she started to take a step forward before she recollected herself and dropped her gaze, holding her ground.

41

There was something compelling about him, something she had never before experienced, something that made her feel all giddy like the silly heroine in an improbable romance!

Mr. Reginald Ashton cast a measuring glance at Sir William's cynical smile and seemed uncertain whether envy or derision lay behind the other man's patent disapproval. He nodded briefly to him, then turned his attention to his cousin.

"Here's my surprise, Nora. Like you to meet a friend of mine. Actually of Vincent's, you know," he corrected himself conscientiously. "Up at Eton and Oxford together, then in the army. Captain Lord Deverell, my cousin Lady Leanora Ashton."

A shocked, icy chill engulfed her, followed by a wave of heat as the blood rushed to her cheeks. She had sensed he was dangerous, from the first moment she saw him, but never would she have guessed. . . . How dare Captain Lord Deverell show his face to Vincent's family, after what he had done! How he could pretend friendship for Vincent at one moment, then lure him into undertaking the secret missions that cost him his life. . . .

Her hand was taken in a warm, firm clasp. She stared at it in revulsion, then raised her eyes to look up into the deceitful face whose dynamic features had crept about the fringes of her mind since she first saw him in Whitehall the day before. Hatred welled within her, vying with the lingering shreds of her fascination.

"And this is Sir William Holborne," Reggie went on, having not the least suspicion of the cannonball he had exploded in his cousin's face. "Associate of my uncle's."

The two men exchanged bows, but before Sir William could speak, his attention was claimed by Lord Petersham, who strode up to them. Petersham halted abruptly, his eyes started, and his expression took on a distinct resemblance to a stuffed trout as he beheld Reggie and his companion. Sir William, a wicked gleam lighting his sharp eyes, took in this situation. With great presence of mind, he excused himself to the company by expressing the hope of expanding his acquaintance with Captain Lord Deverell at the earliest opportunity, and neatly removed with his superior.

42

"What was the matter with him?" Reggie asked, watching the departing figure with distrust.

"Don't ask," Deverell recommended unmercifully. "I told you that coat was too outlandish."

"It is not! It's the highest kick of fashion! Isn't it, Nora?" he beseeched.

"I—I have never seen one to equal it at any evening party," she managed, responding with both truth and diplomacy.

Her answer seemed to satisfy her cousin, for he beamed at her. "Glad we found you in this crush, Nora. Dev seemed devilish anxious to meet you."

"Indeed?" she asked, her tone frigid.

Deverell, who had been watching Petersham and Sir William walk off, directed a quelling glance at his young friend. "Your cousin is a deplorable rattle, Lady Leanora." His heavy brow lowered thoughtfully as his quick gaze took in the flashing of her magnificent eyes and the stiffly regal bearing that made her seem taller than her meager inches. "Do not let him embarrass you."

"That is something he could never do. My cousin is a gentleman who can be trusted to hold the line." She subjected the man before her to a slow, sweeping gaze that took in every detail from the top of his tightly curled black hair to the toes of his gleaming Hessians. Danger—and excitement—lurked in every line of his bearing.

Deverell reached for the quizzing glass that hung from a black satin riband about his neck. For a moment, Leanora thought he would return her insulting scrutiny, but he merely pulled it off and offered it to her with a mock bow. "It is a pity ladies do not as a rule carry these," he told her politely. "They greatly facilitate setdowns."

Had he been anyone else, she would have burst into laughter at this masterly turning of the tables on her. As if sensing her reaction, his dark eyes glinted as if he invited her to share his amusement. But not even her ready sense of the ridiculous could overcome the utter contempt she felt for Captain Lord Deverell. She ignored his offering, saying instead: "Thank you, I have not the need for artificial aides to make my sentiments known."

Reggie stared, open mouthed, as Leanora's hostility finally penetrated his preoccupation with the uncertain reception of his new coat, with which he had hoped to lead fashion. He gave her a pointed nudge with his elbow. "Thought you'd like to meet him. Great friend of Vincent's, you know."

"He spoke of you often, Lady Leanora." Deverell regarded her through half-lidded eyes. "I feel as though I have known you any time these past ten years."

His brooding expression sent an enticing thrill through her that infuriated her. "Vincent told me a great deal about you, also," she replied, her voice cold.

"You call me a rattle!" Reggie tried with a forced laugh, dismayed by his cousin's lack of cordiality. Never had he known Leanora to be less than polite, and this untoward situation left him nonplussed.

"Yes, when it came to wagging tongues, there never was anything to choose between you and Vincent," she said tartly. "Whenever we kicked up a lark, one or the other of you could be counted upon to blurt it all out, and at the most inopportune moment."

To her dismay, Captain Lord Deverell chuckled, a deep, enticing sound that tugged at the loneliness she had closed away deep within herself. "It was the same at Eton and Oxford," he said. "Whenever we went on a spree, it was Carlton House to a Charley's shelter that Vincent would—er—'blow the gaff.'" He threw her a look brimful of challenge, as if daring her to call him to book for using cant phrases.

Did he think her missish? Little chance she had ever had of that, being raised by a father like Lord Sherborne and with a brother and two male cousins sharing the house with her since they were all in leading strings. She ran a far greater risk of being considered a shocking hoyden by the high sticklers, though she had taken the greatest care to avoid that disparaging epithet. She wondered, suddenly, what sort of female this disturbing captain preferred, then reminded herself instantly—and sternly—that it mattered not a whit.

"Vincent's record in the army was quite distinguished," Deverell said with deliberation.

The deep, compelling tones of his voice left her trembling,

44

and she braced herself against the inexplicable appeal he held. "It is a pity his career could not have been longer," she shot back.

Something flashed in the depths of his dark eyes. "It is difficult to control one's destiny in battle. It is a choice every officer is forced to make when he purchases his commission."

She raised her eyes to his, meeting his gaze squarely. "At least in battle one may die with one's comrades. But there are other ways to be killed during war, are there not?"

"Lord, Nora," Reggie broke in, uncomfortable. "No one likes the war. Let's change the subject. Poor Dev here has only just been invalided home. Assigned to the Austrian forces, you know. Can't want to keep prattling on about it all night. Let's go find m'mother. She'll be delighted to see you again, Dev. Been a few years since you stayed with us."

Her aunt's greeting for her eldest son's friend would make up for her own coldness, Leanora reflected. But then Mrs. Ashton had no idea that it was this very friend who was responsible for Vincent's death. She averted her face, willing down the stinging tears that pressed against her eyes. Her beloved cousin had been so full of laughter and vitality that the thought of his life being extinguished was still unbearable for her.

"Coming, Nora?" Reggie prompted. "Where is she?" He looked about the room and became aware that three gentlemen were regarding him in a manner that was far from admiring. One even went so far as to chuckle before turning away. Reggie, bearing a marked resemblance to a disgruntled puppy, turned his back on the trio. "Devilish flat party, ain't it, Dev? Want to make our excuses?"

"We were about to find your mamma, I believe," Deverell reminded him. "Ah, I believe our hostess is trying to attract our attention."

Lady Castlereigh, with all the air of a mother hen gathering her brood, was once again ushering her guests back toward the drawing room from which the sounds of a violin warming up could now be heard. Captain Lord Deverell made a mocking bow and offered Leanora his arm. She hesitated but was loathe to make a scene. She placed her fingers lightly on the soft, wine velvet sleeve of his coat and, to her utter fury, a tingling sensation ran up her arm at the contact. As if she were a silly miss in her first Season, instead of a mature lady who had been on the town for a good many years! She was being foolish beyond permission, and over a man as despicable as Deverell!

They entered the larger drawing room and within minutes joined Mrs. Ashton. That lady greeted them with delight, and nothing would do but that she must exclaim over her son's daring appearance, admiring wholeheartedly what other, more prudent, dressers eyed askance. Under her effusive compliments, Reggie was quickly restored to his normal good humor. He bent to kiss her hand and cheek, then brought forward his companion.

"Lord Deverell!" Mrs. Ashton exclaimed, clasping his hands between her own and shedding a motherly tear. "So very long!" She sighed with gusto. "Do sit beside me, dear boy, and tell me how you go on. So wonderful as it is to see you again. But injured! Though to be sure we can only be glad that you have been, for now you are home where you can be safe, which you could not be, of course, as long as you were in foreign parts. Such a terrible thing to be at war, for it seems that no one can truly be safe as long as that monster Napoleon is at large."

Deverell, his eyes twinkling but his expression somber, agreed with every word she uttered, causing her to beam even more warmly upon him.

"You must tell me everything you can remember of the last time you saw my dear Vincent," Mrs. Ashton urged him.

"I will do my best," he said, and Leanora was surprised at the catch in his voice. Did he have the grace to feel ashamed for what he had done? But in all honesty, she recognized that it was more than that. Her own sense of loss made her acutely aware of a similar sentiment in someone else. For the briefest of moments, she experienced an unwanted, compassionate tie with Deverell.

"A—a *soiree* is hardly the place," she declared abruptly.

"You are quite right," Deverell said, almost disguising the note of sadness that still lurked in his voice.

Fighting down an urge to warm toward him, she asked the first question that came to her mind. "Reggie said you were with the Austrian forces. Were you at Austerlitz, then?"

He raised an assessing eyebrow. "You have been following the war closely, it seems. Yes, I was there, and got a ball lodged in my leg for my efforts."

"It still bothers you?" Mrs. Ashton asked at once with deep sympathy.

"The Austrian field surgeons are not noted for their skill," he said evenly.

"Surely the ball has been taken out?" she exclaimed, her motherly instincts engaged.

At that he laughed. "After I got back to England."

"Good thing you are invalided home," stuck in Reggie, who had been quiet throughout most of this exchange as he kept a surreptitious eye on Sir William, who sat with Beau Brevin, the current arbiter of the dandy set. "You wouldn't believe what those damn blood-letters have done to him!"

"Oh, I came off easy, compared to many," Deverell said lightly. "And now, as you see, I have the pleasure of visiting London at the height of a Season and am spared the necessity of standing up for every country dance."

"You've no notion how lucky you are!" Reggie said with feeling.

"Are you enjoying London?" Mrs. Ashton asked. "You must come and dine with us some night soon. Must he not, Leanora?"

"Certainly," she responded repressively, and to her indignation she noted that sparkling glints of amusement began to dance in his disturbing eyes.

"I should be delighted," he assured Mrs. Ashton promptly. "It has been several years since I have been in London. It seems odd to have the leisure to renew old acquaintances—and make charming new ones."

Before Leanora could prevent herself, her wrathful gaze flew to his and held for a very long, charged moment. He acknowledged her animosity, but unless she was very much mistaken, he had just thrown down the gauntlet to her! Shaken and angry, she dropped her gaze. "You are an ardent flirt, sir," she declared with an attempt at a sneer in her voice.

"Dev?" Reggie asked, surprised, momentarily emerging

47

from his uneasy contemplation of the gentlemen only a few rows before him. "He ain't in the petticoat line, Nora."

"As you say, bantling," Deverell responded, but an unsettling smile played about the corners of his mouth.

A string quartet now struck up the opening notes of a Bach concerto, and the assembled company lapsed into silence. Concentration on their excellent performance, though, proved impossible. Every moment Leanora was vividly aware of the imposing—and unwelcome—presence of Lord Deverell at her side. Her preoccupation with him was impossible! If only she had known who he was before she saw him and fell prey to the overwhelming magnetism that beckoned inexorably to something deep within her!

Considering him objectively, which for Leanora was not possible, he was everything she would have expected in such a close friend of Vincent's. His manners and address were all that they should be, and lurking just beneath the surface, she detected a reprehensible sense of the ridiculous, a dashing, carefree, devil-may-care attitude that intrigued her, whispering to similar yearnings within herself. Only in Vincent had she ever before experienced such a sensation of meeting a kindred spirit.

And it was this same spirit that had induced Vincent to yield to his friend's entreaties and follow him into a very dangerous and secret branch of the army. Like Deverell before him, Vincent had become a spy. And unlike Deverell, he had failed to return from his last mission.

At the beginning of the next interval, Deverell offered to obtain refreshments. Reggie stood at once.

"Come with you," he announced. "No point just sitting about. M'mother will expect you to go into raptures over the music," he explained in an undervoice as he made good his escape.

Lord Deverell glanced down at Leanora. "Would you care to stroll?"

Leanora hesitated, wondering what it would take to make him understand that she could never like or forgive him—indeed, that she could never look at him without reopening the still-painful wound of Vincent's death. She shook her head, lowering eyes that showed an alarming tendency to blur. She could not think clearly in his overpowering presence. He was so disconcertingly masculine, setting off unfamiliar and wildly erratic sensations within her. He was so very much alive. . . .

The matter was taken out of her hands. "Oh, yes, do go, my love," Aunt Amabelle exclaimed. "I am persuaded you would not care to remain, so restless as you are. I promise you, my lord, she is never still, but must always be doing something. So unsettling, when one wants to have a nice, quiet cose, as you must know I quite enjoy. Do go off, my dear, and do not give me a thought. I shall be quite comfortable, for here comes Lady Ingersoll."

With resignation, Leanora accepted her dismissal and accompanied Reggie and Deverell out of the room. She would be civil to him, for propriety demanded nothing less in the middle of a *ton* party. But she would firmly resist the disturbing wave of attraction that swept over her whenever their eyes chanced to meet.

"That sent us to the rightabouts, did it not?" Deverell asked with great affability as soon as they were out of earshot of Mrs. Ashton.

Leanora stiffened, remembering that the same deceitful, compelling voice had lured Vincent from the comparative safety of his regiment to almost certain death. "I fear I am too restless for her tastes," she snapped. "And I cannot rapturize for hours over ballads, no matter how hard I try."

"I should think not!" Reggie exclaimed, shocked at the idea. "Devilish dull things. Never understood what she sees in them."

"Does that mean you do not enjoy concerts?" Deverell addressed Leanora, ignoring Reggie's interpolation.

"Indeed I do." She kept her gaze firmly away from him, dreading a repetition of that strange, fluttery sensation that he created in her. "I am also quite partial to the Opera. It is just that I do not enjoy discussing every performance in minute detail."

His low, disturbing chuckle sounded once more, but he returned no answer. She risked a glance up at him and caught him watching her with an odd glow in his dark eyes. Dangerous

49

was the only word for him.

"And you?" she asked. She was merely being polite, she told herself. She did not care a fig for his answers.

"Like you, I would rather be doing something than just sitting around talking about it."

That was something she could readily believe. An air of energy hung about him, even here, and she sensed the adventurous spirit that lay barely hidden beneath the propriety of his manners. She felt drawn to him again and fought against it.

"Do you play an instrument, then, or sing?" she asked with thinly veiled sarcasm.

"Of course," he responded promptly. "But no one in their right mind would sit through my performance."

"Have to be dicked in the nob to come to an evening like this at all," Reggie stuck in. "Mind, I don't say they don't know one note from another, but to be listening to a lot of rubbishing ballads all night! Well, I ask you!"

Leanora made the mistake of glancing at Deverell's face to see how Reggie's comment struck him, and it was nearly her undoing. His expression was so completely bland as to be unbelievable, and she choked back a reprehensible giggle. He raised his brows in mild surprise, but amused lights danced merrily in the gaze that held hers.

The next instant, all desire to laugh deserted her. Just inside the doorway, making their apologies to Lady Castlereigh for their late arrival, stood Mr. Gregory Ashton, his wife Julia and her brother Viscount Dalmouth. Gregory, to Leanora's despair, looked to be about half-sprung already, to borrow a term of her father's, and Dalmouth was no better. Julia looked up, and Leanora saw that her eyes sparkled with anger. At least Gregory was not gaming, Leanora reflected, thankful for that meager crumb.

As soon as they left their hostess, Julia dropped her husband's arm. Without so much as another glance at him or her brother, she headed straight toward a lively group of young people. Two of her former suitors greeted her arrival with delight and, apparently ignoring the fact that she was now married, proceeded to shower every flattering attention upon her.

Gregory threw a fulminating glance at his wife, then pointedly turned his back, linked his arm through Dalmouth's, and the two made their unsteady way toward the card room with unerring accuracy. At least her father was there, Leonora reflected. Gregory could hardly get himself into a scrape under the watchful eye of his sire. As Gregory himself would say, Lord Sherborne was a right downy one, up to every rig and row in town.

Deverell, noticing the sudden worry in her large blue eyes, touched her arm gently. "Is something amiss?" he asked softly.

Leanora glanced up, then away. "No!" she declared with force. He had been responsible for enough chaos in her private life. She did not welcome his unwarranted interference with her brother as well as her cousin!

"Just Leanora's brother and his wife, arriving late," Reggie stuck in, attempting to cover the unusual gap in her normally perfect manners. "If I know anything of Julia, she'll be sorry to have missed so much of the program."

Deverell turned to regard the beautiful Lady Julia Ashton. She held a pierced ivory fan in one hand, which she fluttered restlessly before her face. A trill of delighted laughter escaped her at a sally from one of her *cicisbei*, and a bright flush added becoming color to her otherwise pale countenance.

Reggie raised his quizzing glass to better view the lovely picture she made. "Julia's in looks tonight, ain't she, coz? What's Gregory thinking of, to be running off like that?"

"We promised to obtain refreshment for your mamma," Leanora replied, avoiding his comments. If it was not obvious to him that something was terribly amiss between Gregory and Julia, she was certainly not going to bring it to his attention. Suddenly, she wondered whether her father was aware of the strain between the couple. Lord Sherborne had been very preoccupied of late. He might not know that his son and heir was steering a shaky course amid muddy shoals.

Lord Sherborne did not emerge from the card room until

51

well after the music had ended and Leanora had begun to despair of him. He came at last, and she was glad to see that Gregory walked at his side. She studied their faces carefully but could gain no clue as to what had been the topic of their conversation. Her father was no slow-top, though, and only a few minutes in his son's company should have been enough to alert him that all was not well. He would feel his way with care, spring subtle questions and soon know the whole.

As they made their thanks and farewells to their host and hostess, Leanora glanced one last time about the room. Deverell still stood where she had parted from him, his eyes resting on her in a manner that left her nervous. Delicate color rose to her cheeks, and uncomfortable, she turned to the door.

Mrs. Ashton, following her out, gave a deep sigh of contentment. "Such a wonderful evening, was it not, my love? I vow, I could listen to music for hours on end and never notice the time passing, though to be sure it is always nice to be able to talk about it, too; and so fortunate as it was that dear Lady Ingersoll chanced to be sitting so near, for you must know, we were able to enjoy the most comfortable cose, which is what I enjoy of all things. And such a delight to see Captain Lord Deverell again, for I have not seen him this age, and then only briefly, of course; but you would not remember it, I suppose, dear Leanora, for you were not at home at the time. Such an amiable gentleman as he is, and his manners and address such as must always please. I cannot tell you what a relief it is for me to know that my dear Reginald is going about in his company."

Leanora could not feel the same. Although it was most unlikely that Deverell could lure Reggie into any dangerous pursuit, his intimacy with her cousin must naturally lead to his being often in her company, as well. She had no desire to further the acquaintance.

"Might do Gregory a bit of good, too, if this fellow is such a model of all the virtues," Lord Sherborne stuck in. "Sounds a dull dog."

"Dear sir," his sister-in-law Amabelle laughed. "Why, he is nothing of the sort! I believe him to be what the young people call a—a 'dashing blade.' Have I that right, Leanora?"

Leanora bit her lip, and her eyes glinted with a reluctant amusement. "I believe so, dear ma'am," she managed with a creditably straight face.

They had entered the barouche by this time, and the coachman gave his horses the office to begin the short trip back to Berkeley Square. While Mrs. Ashton rattled on happily about the evening and the company, Lord Sherborne sat staring out into the street, an abstracted expression on his solemn face.

"Do you know, Leanora," he said suddenly, breaking in on Mrs. Ashton's recital of Lady Ingersoll's sufferings with rheumatism, "I don't think we've been seeing enough of Gregory of late. Work's been keeping me too busy. Haven't given it much thought before, but do you think the boy's getting bored? Doesn't seem to have any purpose. Been thinking of letting him go down to Sherborne Abbey, to take charge of the property. Don't get down there often enough myself, these days. Place needs someone there to keep an eye on it. About time he learned estate management, while we still have old Grimsby to teach him. Time Gregory started thinking of his inheritance."

"That's an excellent idea!" Leanora exclaimed, relieved. It would be the perfect solution to the problem, if her out-and-outer brother could be induced to leave the entertainments of the Metropolis. If it were only the fall, he would go gladly, for there would be the promise of partridge and pheasants, and the all-consuming task of bringing his hunters into condition. But the countryside of Kent in the middle of spring would seem dreadfully flat to an ardent sportsman.

"I'll talk to the boy about it tomorrow," Lord Sherborne decided. There was a note of satisfaction in his voice at having found an answer to a difficult problem. He settled back in the carriage, relaxing. No mention of their worries for Gregory passed between them, for there was no need.

Amabelle Ashton had lapsed into silence during their discussion and for once showed no tendency to resume speaking. Leanora watched her beloved aunt through half-closed eyes as the barouche jostled along the cobbled streets.

53

She was glad that she had enjoyed the evening. And her father would take Gregory in hand. On the whole, if it had not been for the unwelcome discovery that her intriguing stranger was in fact someone she could never regard with pleasure, she would have been quite satisfied with the *soirée*.

The barouche swayed as the horses came to a stop. Lord Sherborne sprang down lightly and turned to assist first Mrs. Ashton and then Leanora from the carriage. The two ladies started toward the stairs as the front door opened.

Tremly hurried out. "Your Lordship!" he called. He held out a salver, on which rested a sheet sealed with a Home Office wafer. "An urgent message has just been delivered, my lord."

Sherborne took it and tore the sheet open. He scanned the single page by the light from the doorway, then crumpled it, his brow lowering in concern.

"You do not have to go back there tonight, do you, Pappa?" Leanora exclaimed.

"No." He shook his head slowly. "There's nothing I can do." He looked at the message again. "It's Holloway, my clerk. His body has just been pulled out of the river, near the Serpentine."

Mrs. Ashton gasped, and Leanora regarded her father in dismay. "His. . . . He is dead?" Leanora managed.

The earl nodded. "Poor fellow. Decent young man."

"What—what happened?"

"Apparently, he killed himself. I suppose this has to do with the missing funds at the Home Office, but I had no idea he was under suspicion."

Leanora closed her eyes. It was too terrible! She had known Holloway for years. Never would she have thought him capable of theft—or of suicide. He had a family. . . .

The earl slipped an arm about her waist and gave her a quick hug. "Come on inside, my dear. We—" He broke off as a low voice hailed him. He turned to see the dark figure of a man detach itself from the shadows of the garden on the other side of the street and come a step toward them. He raised a hand and called Sherborne's name again.

The earl frowned. "Now what?" he muttered. "You go on in, Leanora. I'd best see what the fellow wants." He started across toward the garden.

The wild pounding of shod hooves on cobbled stones was their only warning. A large traveling chariot drawn by four runaway horses veered around the corner, rocked at a crazy angle and bore down on the hapless Lord Sherborne, slamming into him before he could get clear of its path.

Chapter 4

Leanora screamed, horrified, as her father was thrown to the side of the cobblestone road. He lay there, a crumpled heap, frighteningly still as the carriage, unheeding, raced on.

"Pappa!" The name tore from Leanora's throat, and she ran, oblivious of everything else, desperate to reach her father. She fell on her knees at his side, her anxious hands reaching for his head.

"Don't touch him!" The butler's sharp command came from behind her.

She raised large, terrified eyes to the ashen face of Tremly. "No, you—you are quite right," she gasped.

Still breathing hard from the unaccustomed exertion of running, the butler knelt down and carefully felt for a pulse at the earl's neck.

"Is—is he . . . ?" Leanora's voice broke on a sob.

"He is badly hurt. Best send for a doctor at once, Miss Leanora. Don't try to move him." He looked over his shoulder to where Mrs. Ashton stood paralyzed with shock on the walkway. The coachman still held the heads of his excited horses, trying to quiet them. "Go for the doctor!" Tremly ordered. The coachman hesitated, then mounted back onto his box and drove off.

"We—we cannot leave him here, in the street," Leanora cried. "We must at least—"

A wail from the walkway announced that Mrs. Ashton had recovered from her stupefaction and was now succumbing to a fit of hysteria.

"If you could take madam inside, Miss Leanora, and send the footmen to me?" Tremly suggested.

Leanora nodded. She rose, finding to her dismay that her legs trembled alarmingly. With shaky steps, she went to her aunt who stood on the sidewalk sobbing loudly, and folded that lady's ample form into her arms. Turning her gently, she led her up the steps to the house.

The commotion had brought the footmen and Mrs. Tremly, the housekeeper, onto the scene. Leanora sent the former to assist the butler and the housekeeper after her aunt's abigail. With Mrs. Ashton leaning heavily upon her, Leanora helped her into the front saloon and settled her on the couch.

Mrs. Tremly returned quickly, accompanied by Sutton, Mrs. Ashton's abigail. The two women set to work at once on Leanora's prostrate aunt, chafing her wrists, waving burnt feathers before her and holding a silver vinaigrette bottle to her nose. Beyond the closed door, Leanora could hear the sounds of the men carrying the inert form of Lord Sherborne into the house.

The next twenty minutes passed in a nightmarish daze for Leanora, torn between Mrs. Ashton's uncontrolled wails and her fear for her father. She had just induced her aunt to take a draught of laudanum when an imperious knock sounded on the front door, followed moments later by the doctor's calm voice.

Leanora stood at once, but her aunt grasped her hand. "Don't leave me!" the woman cried, clinging to her.

"I must. The doctor has come." Gently, she tried to disengage the fingers that gripped her tightly.

"Begging your pardon, Miss Leanora, but the doctor won't be needing you just yet," Mrs. Tremly said. "I'll just go and see if there is anything he'll be wanting, though Tremly can easily order things just as he wishes." With that, the housekeeper hurried out of the saloon.

Leanora sank back down beside her aunt, seeking comfort by returning the firm pressure of her clasping hands. Slowly, these relaxed as the laudanum took effect. She had given Mrs. Ashton enough to allow the distraught woman to slip safely into sleep, and for a brief moment she envied her aunt this escape from the distressing reality.

It was some time before Mrs. Ashton's breathing slowed to the steady, regular rhythm of sleep. Leanora looked down at her, dismayed, for she should have first seen her to her chamber, into her night things and between sheets. But it couldn't be helped. Disturbing her would only have set off her violent sobs once more. For this one night, she would be all right where she lay.

"I'll stay with her, Miss Leanora," said Sutton. "But first I'll fetch her a quilt."

"Thank you." Leanora looked down at the cloak that now inadequately covered her aunt. Sutton returned in a very short time, bearing not only the needed quilt but several soft pillows and her mistress's nightcap. Leanora assisted the abigail in rendering her aunt as comfortable as possible, then hurried out of the room.

She paused in the hall, looking about, unsure. The door to the other saloon stood open, but a quick glance through this assured her that the room was empty. They must have taken her father to his room. She ran up the several flights of stairs and down the hall. As she neared his door, it opened and his lordship's valet came out.

"Pagget!" She almost ran up to him. "How is he?"

The old valet turned a haggard face toward her. "We have him resting as comfortably as we can, Miss Leanora. I am just going to get him a nice hot brick for his bed." With his shoulders drooping under the strain, he moved off.

Leanora slipped through the door into the antechamber and peered into the great bedroom. Her father lay in the massive four-poster, a still figure beneath the sheets. The silken hangings were drawn back, and a large candelabrum rested on the bedside table, casting its light over the scene. Beside it rested a basin of reddish water and several blood-stained cloths.

The doctor, a youngish man of medium build and competent manner, half-sat on the bed as he examined the earl's head. A number of bandages and plasters were already applied. Leanora ventured a few slow steps farther into the room, watching intently.

59

Sensing her entrance, the doctor glanced up. "That was a nasty accident," he said, then ignored her to return to his examination.

"Will—will he be all right?" She found she had come up against a chair and gripped its back for support.

The doctor was silent for a moment. "What?" he asked, abstracted. "Oh." He shook his head. "Too early to tell yet. It's always difficult with head injuries. His arm is broken, and I've strapped up three of his ribs; but that will all mend." He sat back, directing a steady look at Leanora. "He's unconscious, and I've no idea how long it will last. He may come out of it tomorrow."

"Or he may not at all?" She forced herself to ask the question.

To her dismay, the doctor nodded. "I'm sorry." He looked back down at the disconcertingly still figure of the earl. "I've done all I can for him tonight. His man has promised to sit up with him and send a message to me immediately if there's any change. I'll call again first thing in the morning. I should be able to tell more then."

While he talked, he repacked his things into his large bag and in a very few minutes took his leave. Leanora remained by her father's bedside, feeling very much alone and frightened. Pagget returned, carrying a hot brick wrapped in towels as if it were breakable, and together they placed it under the quilt at the earl's feet. Leanora sank down into the chair that until recently had been occupied by the doctor's bag and stared at her father's gray face.

"You might as well go to bed, Miss Leanora. I'll stay with him." Pagget's eyes, which seemed to have sunk deeply into their sockets, held a stricken expression.

"I would like to sit here for a bit," she said. She pulled the bellrope which hung near the bed and, when Tremly presently answered the summons, requested a pot of chocolate and two cups. When he returned with this, he was not alone. A very subdued Artaxerxes followed at his heels, for once not dancing.

The animal slunk into the room and came to stand on his hind legs by the bed, his front feet pawing at the top that he could not quite reach, his ridiculous short nose snuffling. Leanora scooped him up and held the little dog tightly in her lap, not sure which of them derived the most comfort from this contact.

Tremly poured her some chocolate, and she insisted that the shattered valet join her in this much needed refreshment. They sat for a very long time in a silence unbroken except by Artaxerxes's soft, sad whimpers.

Leanora must have dozed off, for when she moved her aching neck and opened her eyes, a pale ray of sunlight seeped in through a crack in the drapes. She stood, stretched to ease her stiff muscles and crossed to the window, throwing the hangings wide.

"It's morning," she said unnecessarily.

"Yes, Miss Leanora." The valet stood also and moved closer to the bedside to study his master's face.

Leanora turned to look at her father. Artaxerxes lay on the bed, curled into his master's side, his nose resting on his paws. The earl did not seem to have moved at all during the night, and Leanora shivered with a sudden cold fear. When she spoke, her voice sounded tense and unnatural even to herself. "How—how is he?"

The same fear seemed to have gripped Pagget. The man reached out a shaking hand to touch the earl's, which lay atop the silken coverlet. He let out a deep sigh of relief. "He's still with us, Miss Leanora."

She released a breath she had not realized she held. "He has made it through the night. That *must* be a good sign, Pagget. He *will* get better."

"Yes, miss." The valet turned his head to wipe a surreptitious tear from his eye.

"I am going to my room now. Please have me called when the doctor arrives."

But when this individual finally put in an appearance over two hours later, he was unable to give a more encouraging report than he had the night before. Yes, he agreed, it was a good sign that the earl had lived through the night. More than that he would not venture to guess. He was inclined to take a hopeful view of the case, saying that the earl, a robust man in

61

excellent health, might come out of it at any time. But honesty forced him to admit that there was also a chance that he would slip deeper into this coma from which he might never awaken. His views on animals in sick rooms he mercifully kept to himself, in spite of the fact that Artaxerxes set up a low growl upon his arrival and maintained a *sotto voce* disapproval throughout the visit.

After his departure, Leanora donned a simple morning gown and refreshed herself somewhat by vigorously washing her face and hands. She then made her way down to the breakfast parlor, where she discovered that she had no appetite. Instead, she stared moodily at a cup of tea that she was disinclined to sip. She remained there for some time, lost in worried thought, before the door opened and Sutton, her aunt's maid, entered and sketched a curtsy.

"If you please, Miss Leanora, Mrs. Ashton is wishful to see you as soon as you are ready."

Leanora started guiltily. So preoccupied had she been with her father's dreadful state that she had not spared a single thought that morning to her aunt's delicate sensibilities. Resisting a craven impulse to go for a long walk instead, she stood and followed the abigail out of the room. In the hall, she stopped Tremly and asked him to request Mr. Edmonton to come to her in her father's study in half an hour's time.

"Did my aunt pass a comfortable night?" she asked Sutton as she began to climb the stairs.

"As well as could be expected, Miss Leanora. She is in a dreadful state this morning, though, for nothing will convince her that his lordship has not suffered a Fatal Injury."

Firmly rejecting from her mind that she, too, shared this fear, she entered her aunt's bedchamber with a determined smile on her lips. Mrs. Ashton must have awakened and sought her bed at some time during the night for the bedclothes were sadly crumpled and her evening garments lay strewn about the room where Sutton had not yet had the time to collect them. This the tired abigail set about doing while Leanora faced the more difficult task of soothing her distraught aunt.

It took considerable effort and tact, but Leanora convinced Mrs. Ashton not to rush to her brother-in-law's sickbed but to lie upon her own couch for the rest of the day. A passing reference to the chaos into which the servants had been thrown was enough to warn her aunt that grave discomforts might await anyone unwise enough to venture downstairs, and that the best course would be to permit the staff to recover and resume their normal duties.

This feat accomplished, Leanora next sought out her father's secretary. Mr. Edmonton, as she quickly discovered, had not been idle. Messages had already been dispatched to Whitehall, and he was even now engaged in preparing a complete report on his activities of the last few days on his employer's behalf. Leanora, as she glanced through these, could only hope that her father would soon be in a position to appreciate this efficiency.

The next task, she decided, would be to send for Gregory. This Mr. Edmonton offered to do personally, saying that the news would best be broken gently rather than entrusted to a letter. Thankful to be able to leave the matter in the secretary's capable hands, she returned upstairs to sit, staring helplessly at her father, clasping the squirming pug in her lap.

A short while later, Tremly knocked softly on the door and announced that Mr. Gregory had arrived and had gone straight to his lordship's study with Mr. Edmonton. Leanora was surprised, for she had expected her brother to come at once to their father's side, though she realized there was nothing he could do. It seemed strangely unlike Gregory to take any interest in practical concerns, and she could only admire the tactics that must have been employed by Mr. Edmonton to bring this about.

The next news carried to her did not please her as much. Tremly, hesitating once more on the threshold of Lord Sherborne's chamber, apologized for the intrusion and begged Leanora to spare him a few moments. Leaving her father under the watchful eyes of Pagget and Artaxerxes, Leanora stepped out into the antechamber.

"What is the matter? Is it not something that Mr. Gregory can take care of?"

"Begging your pardon, Miss Leanora, but that's the crux of the matter, as you might say. Mr. Gregory has requested that

Mrs. Tremly turn over all the housekeeping papers to him."

"But that's not her province!" Leanora exclaimed, surprised. "Just tell him that I handle all the household matters."

"I did relay such information to him, but he is insistent," replied the harassed butler. "And not wanting to take it upon myself to go through your papers, I thought it best to lay the matter before you."

Leanora let out an exasperated sigh. "Thank you, Tremly. I will come at once."

With a last glance at the recumbent figure in the massive four-poster, Leanora made her way down the flights of stairs and to the back regions of the great town house. Here, in her father's study, she found her brother Gregory seated behind the large mahogany writing desk. Five piles of papers were neatly stacked on the surface of this, and Mr. Edmonton bent his tall, lean figure over a sixth, carefully arranging the loose pages.

"Leanora!" Gregory exclaimed, frowning.

Her eyes narrowed. He did not seem overly pleased to see her. Well, in a moment he would be even less so.

"You did not come up to see Pappa." Her tone was mildly accusing as she came to stand beside the desk.

Gregory looked down, unable to meet her penetrating eye. "Well, Tremly told me there was nothing I could do." He glanced up and had the grace to look sheepish. "Dash it, Nora, you know I can't abide a sickbed! Never know what to say!"

"In this case, nothing would be necessary. You must know that he has not yet regained consciousness."

"I do know," he said. His fingers clenched on a pen he held, and his knuckles whitened. He cared deeply, his sister realized, though he would never admit it.

"I came to settle a misunderstanding," she said, more gently than she had begun. "You need not concern yourself with any of the household matters. Those are my province, not Pappa's."

"Oh, I understand that," Gregory said with an attempt at unconcern that merely sounded defensive. "But if I'm to take command for a while, I'll need to know how the land lies. Surely you understand that, my girl? Now, you just bring all the accounts in here to me and let me look them over."

Leanora hesitated, watching the odd sparkle in her brother's normally pale blue eyes. He was up to something, or she was sadly mistaken—which she took leave to doubt. But what? To learn how to keep proper household records and see how much certain things should cost? Remembering his tirade of the day before over Julia's lack of ability, this might be the explanation. Gregory was too proud to ask her directly for advice, but he would not be beyond pretending to help her while in reality helping himself. If that were so, she would let him have his way. Without another word, she headed for her own study and began to gather together the account books.

A soft cough came from the doorway, and she turned to see Mr. Edmonton.

"Allow me to carry those for you, Miss Leanora." He came forward, holding out his hands, and she let him take the heavy books.

"If you would not mind, Mr. Edmonton," she began, then paused as she realized the impropriety of what she was about to ask.

A slight twinkle lit the man's eyes behind his heavy spectacles. "With your permission, Miss Leanora, I would like to stay with Mr. Gregory to—to offer him any assistance he might need."

"Thank you," she declared with profound relief. She knew him of old, and there were few men more capable of keeping a quiet but protective eye on her brother. He would not let Gregory pry where he should not, nor dabble too deeply in her father's concerns.

She hurried back upstairs to where Artaxerxes once again lay on the bed. Pagget sat hunched over, his tired eyes never leaving his master's face. There had been no change, the aged valet was sorry to report, his expression morose in the extreme. Leanora sank down in the chair on the other side of the bed, trying very hard not to fall prey to her fears.

Barely half an hour passed before Tremly again knocked on the door, this time announcing that Sir William Holborne had called and desired speech with her. Taking a protesting Artaxerxes with her, she made her reluctant way downstairs.

She handed the indignant pug over to James, the second footman, with the request that the puppy be given a walk. Then bracing herself, she entered the Gold Saloon where she found her guest pacing restlessly before the hearth.

"Sir William," she said by way of greeting. "It was good of you to come."

"Unless I am intruding." He took her hand and gave her fingers a reassuring squeeze. "Dare I hope there has been any improvement?"

"Not yet." Her voice remained steady, a fact upon which she congratulated herself.

"Then you must be wishing me at the devil for taking you from your father's side. I assure you, though, only the utmost urgency has caused me to disturb you. Lord Petersham has ordered me to retrieve all the documents your father took away with him from our meeting two days ago. It seems that he needs to check some information, and as it is a matter of the greatest importance we dare not let it wait until your father can return them himself."

A tired smile lightened Leanora's strained countenance. It was very good to hear someone talking of "when" her father would recover instead of "if." "I'll have Mr. Edmonton find them at once," she told him. She rang for the butler, then invited Sir William to take a glass of wine while he waited. This he declined, though he did accept a seat. When Tremly arrived, she relayed her instructions, and in a very few minutes Mr. Edmonton himself appeared, carrying a small handful of documents.

Sir William received them eagerly and leafed quickly through the pile. Suddenly he frowned, then started going through them more slowly. He looked up at Mr. Edmonton. "And where are the rest?" he asked.

Mr. Edmonton and Leanora exchanged perplexed glances. "These are all he left locked in his top drawer, Sir William," the secretary avowed.

"But there were more," Sir William declared. His brow furrowed with an effort of memory. "I remember distinctly that he carried quite a pile when he left my office. Are you sure these are all that he brought home?"

66

"He might have left some of them in Whitehall," Leanora suggested. "He would not have brought them all home, I am sure, especially if there were so many. He could not possibly have gone over them all in one night. Have you asked—" She broke off in consternation, remembering that Holloway, her father's clerk, was dead.

"Just so. This has been a terrible day for the Home Office."

Leanora nodded. "Have you—has anyone seen his family? My father would have wanted to help."

"Rest assured, we are taking care of the matter. I have myself ordered an investigation into the circumstances."

"I cannot believe he would have embezzled funds! My father trusted him implicitly."

"I am looking into it," Sir William repeated. "But at the moment, it is those papers we must find." His tight smile clearly betrayed his concern. "I checked your father's office myself before disturbing you. Might he not have put them somewhere else, other than his desk?"

Mr. Edmonton regarded Sir William with a frown. "You must understand, sir, that the household is in considerable upheaval following the terrible accident. At the earliest opportunity, I will myself go through his study."

"Could we not do it now?"

"Mr. Gregory Ashton is in there at the moment, sir."

"Gregory?" Sir William's brow snapped down. "What is he doing there?"

Mr. Edmonton raised his eyebrows a fraction. "As Lord Sherborne's son and heir, it is only right that he should assume control of household matters during his lordship's indisposition."

Sir William waved this aside as being of complete unimportance. "There are any number of confidential documents in that study! It is in the highest degree improvident to have someone not closely connected with the Home Office to have access to such matters."

"My brother is completely to be trusted," Leanora said in what she hoped were reassuring accents, then added, somewhat spoiling the effect of her loyal statement: "He has no head whatever for government affairs. I doubt he will so

67

much as glance at anything of a sensitive nature."

Sir William considered this statement and, from the circumstances of having been acquainted with Gregory for close on six years, was inclined to agree. "Forgive me," he apologized. "This is an upsetting time for us all. I meant no slur on your brother. If you will send for me as soon as it is possible to search your father's study, I will be grateful."

Mr. Edmonton gave a deprecatory cough. "If you will let me know what these documents concern, I will myself conduct a thorough search."

"I will not put you to so much trouble. I can quite easily look for them myself." Sir William looked down at his impeccably manicured hands, then directed a piercing glance at Mr. Edmonton. "It would be best, in fact. As you may have guessed, the matter is of some delicacy, and I am not permitted to divulge the details to anyone, even yourself."

"Then you will understand, I am sure, that I am not at liberty to permit anyone to search his lordship's study—without his permission. It would be most—indiscreet of me."

The two men's eyes met, and Leanora experienced the oddest sensation that they were sparring, testing the strength of each other's wills. The idea had no sooner flickered across her mind than it was banished, for Sir William laughed.

"One can understand why Sherborne values you so highly, Edmonton. No, were I in your position, I should not allow anyone in there, either. Very well, if you will permit, we shall look together, and you may make sure I do not read anything that does not meet with your approval. I warn you, though, if we do not find those damned documents soon, you will have Petersham calling on you, next."

Leanora accompanied Sir William to the door, where he again expressed his sorrow for the accident that had befallen her father and for the necessity of disturbing her at such a time. She watched him depart, then requested Tremly, in tones that betrayed her stress and exasperation, not to call her from her father's side again for anything less than a catastrophic emergency. The butler, managing a prim smile, assured her that no further callers would be permitted to cross the threshold.

She returned upstairs to discover that Pagget, despite his good intentions, had fallen asleep in his chair. She doubted he had closed his eyes at all the night before, and could only be glad to see him get some rest. Entering the room silently, she draped a shawl over the elderly man and returned to her own seat to keep a lonely vigil.

Several hours passed before the door again opened. Leanora raised her eyes from her father's pallid face to see her brother Gregory standing uncertainly in the doorway. She rose and went to him, drawing him into the antechamber more for the sake of the sleeping valet than for Lord Sherborne, who at the moment was beyond being disturbed by mere voices.

"Hasn't he awakened at all?" Gregory asked, peering past Leanora for a glimpse of the figure in the bed.

Leanora shook her head, suddenly not trusting herself to speak. He *would* recover. He had to. He could not remain like this, slipping slowly but inexorably away from her.

"Don't worry, old girl," Gregory said in a rallying tone, accompanying his words with a sound buffet to her shoulder that nearly knocked her sideways. "He'll pull out of it, you'll see. He's a tough old egg."

Leanora smiled her thanks but switched to an emotionally safer topic. "Did you find what you needed?"

A strange smile lit his eyes, and they seemed almost to dance in the half-light of the room. "Oh, yes," he said with studied casualness. "Well, I must be off. I'll stop in again soon and see how he goes on. Don't wear yourself to a thread, Nora."

With that he was gone, but he left his sister with an uneasy feeling that she could not quite place. There had been something disturbing about his manner, as if he had been pleased with himself over something. Had he learned what he wanted to know, or—or had he gotten something that he needed?

Suspicion became certainty, and after a quick glance back into the room to assure herself that both master and valet rested comfortably, she hurried down to her father's study. She looked about, but there was nothing outwardly amiss. Papers remained neatly stacked; the drawers to the desk were all locked, the keys nowhere in sight.

69

Leanora almost ran to her own study, where her set of keys to her father's desk were kept. She brought these back and opened the bottom drawer, where only two days before she and Mr. Edmonton had placed the housekeeping money that he had withdrawn from the bank while in the City. This amounted to a considerable sum, for the wages of the household staff were included. She jerked the drawer open, lifted out the money box and raised the lid.

It was empty. Not so much as a single shilling of the nearly three hundred pounds remained.

Chapter 5

Leanora swore softly, drawing on a vocabulary culled from her father and brother that would have shocked her Aunt Amabelle had that lady been privileged to hear. She should have known what her brother would be up to, Leanora told herself savagely. And instead of taking the simple measure of removing temptation, she had never even considered the possibility that he might steal the housekeeping money. She would have this out with Gregory the very next time she saw him. But at the moment, even this shocking piece of behavior could not overshadow her concern for her father's continued unconsciousness.

Pagget, who awakened late in the evening, assured Leanora of his readiness to resume his watch, with the faithful pug as his companion. At his continued insistence, Leanora was at last persuaded to seek her own bed. She did not enjoy a restful night's sleep, however, and rose early to once again return to her father's room.

The morning brought no change in Lord Sherborne's condition. He remained still and pale; but his pulse was slow and steady, as the doctor assured Leanora during the course of an early visit, and his breathing, although shallow, was not unduly ragged.

Mrs. Ashton, stopping at her brother-in-law's room a little while later, cajoled Leanora to come downstairs with her and keep her company at the breakfast table. Although Leanora had eaten very little the day before and had not touched her chocolate that morning, she declined the invitation, preferring to stay by her father's side. But in this she was firmly overruled by both Pagget and Mrs. Ashton, and the latter carried her off to seek nourishment.

"For what good would it do your poor, dear father to have you collapsing from weakness, which I am persuaded you will do soon if you make no attempt to keep up your strength, my love?" her aunt demanded as she bustled Leanora into the sunny room that had been laid out for breakfast.

More from a desire to be done with the meal and return to her father than from any wish to eat, Leanora consumed a few morsels of the ham that Mrs. Ashton piled on her plate. The rest she placed into a napkin, feeling that the pining pug must stand in need of a snack.

Her aunt droned endlessly the entire time, wondering how they would manage to go on. "For you must know, dearest Leanora, that we were pledged to attend a dinner party last night, but that terrible accident drove it completely out of my mind. I must write on the instant to beg dear Mrs. Cheval-Hampton's pardon, though I am sure when it has been explained to her she will understand perfectly why we did not come. Yes, and that puts me in mind of it; are we not promised to Lady Barnsbury for a rout party this evening?"

Leanora looked up at this. "Oh, no! Aunt Amabelle, we cannot go!"

"No, of course not, my love, for it would be quite shocking in us to go jauntering about town seeking amusement when your poor dear father is so ill. I shall write to her, also, with our excuses."

"You will be quite busy then, this morning, crying off from all of our engagements." Leanora stood and set her cup down beside her almost untouched plate. "I shall leave you to it and go back to my father." Before her aunt could object, she made good her escape from the parlor.

Armed with some long-neglected embroidery, she entered Lord Sherborne's bedchamber to find Pagget tenderly raising the earl's bandaged head while an upper housemaid adjusted the pillows. Laying him gently back down, the valet lovingly smoothed the coverlet back into place. The maid, bobbing a curtsy, carried a basin of water from the room, leaving Leanora, Pagget and the puppy to watch over the master of the house.

Settling the pug on the floor at her side, Leanora handed him the scraps of ham one by one. For some reason, it comforted her that these were not disdained. Pleasantly full, the puppy curled up at her feet and soon began to snore peacefully.

Artaxerxes settled, Leanora turned her attention to the embroidery, but this pastime could not long occupy her worried mind. After setting a number of stitches in the wrong place, she threw the handkerchief she was decorating aside with an exclamation of frustration. Pagget looked up, an expression of such compassion in his tired eyes that she instantly felt ashamed of herself.

"You might take the little dog for a walk, Miss Leanora," the valet suggested. "The fresh air will make you both feel better, and you will be ready to sit with his lordship while I try to sleep this afternoon."

Irresolute, she looked down at her father's face. There was nothing she could do but wait for a change, to wait for whatever damage his head had suffered to begin to heal. She did no good here at the moment—the reverse, in fact, for her fidgeting only served to distress the good valet.

With Artaxerxes padding along behind her, she went to her room, collected a bonnet and spencer to ward off the cool breeze that blew in gusts outdoors and made her way back downstairs and outside. She let herself into the private garden with her key and strolled aimlessly, trying very hard to convince herself that this was pleasant. Artaxerxes gamboled about her, pouncing on insects and flowers that waved in the breeze. Leanora sank down on a bench to watch him but only stared at her hands with unseeing eyes.

She was roused from her troubled reverie by the sound of a light carriage pulling up before the house. Lord Petersham climbed laboriously down from the vehicle and made his stately way up the steps to the front door. Tremly opened this for him as he reached it, and Petersham stepped inside.

Well, Leanora reflected as she stood and shook out her narrow skirt, Sir William Holborne had warned her the day before. They had never sent for him after Gregory left the study, so she really had no one to blame for this invasion but herself. Yielding to a craven impulse, she remained where she was. If she were needed, Mr. Edmonton would send for her.

Over half an hour passed before Petersham emerged from the house. As the door closed behind him, he stopped on the porch, trembling, his countenance ashen. Drawing a handkerchief from his pocket, he mopped at his brow. His rotund face bore such an expression of acute anxiety that Leanora came to her feet, startled. Before she could go to his aid, his groom hurried forward. Petersham stumbled down the steps and leaned heavily on his servitor, who assisted him into his carriage.

As the vehicle drove off, Leanora collected the protesting puppy and hurried across the street. Leaving Artaxerxes in the care of James, she went at once to her father's study, where Mr. Edmonton sat behind the huge desk.

"Whatever happened to Petersham?" she demanded. "He looked as if he had seen a specter!"

"It seems the details of your father's accident upset him somewhat," her father's secretary said. "Though I admit, his reaction seemed somewhat excessive."

"Did he come for those papers Sir William could not find?"

Mr. Edmonton nodded, but the creases in his brow deepened. "We couldn't find them, of course, even though we turned out every drawer and cupboard. I'll take my oath they are not in this study!" He raised frowning eyes to Leanora. "His concern at not finding them seemed out of all proportion, I must say. I have never seen him in such a taking. Kept hinting at something secret, and dire consequences if the documents fell into the wrong hands."

Leanora sank into a chair opposite him. "Do you know what this project is all about?"

"That it concerns Lord Grenville, and the complexities of his assuming control of the government after the untimely death of Mr. Pitt, is all I could gather from him." He shook his head. "I had thought that I enjoyed Lord Sherborne's complete confidence, but it seems that I was mistaken. I am not aware of any project that requires such carefully guarded

74

secrecy. But I do wonder what became of those papers."

Leanora sighed.."Well, I hope we find them soon, if only to keep Sir William and Lord Petersham from haunting our doorstep."

The sound of the knocker, vigorously applied to the front door, drifted back to them. Leanora threw a dismayed look at Mr. Edmonton.

"He cannot have come back already!" she exclaimed.

Mr. Edmonton grinned unexpectedly at her expression. "If he has, I will not let him disturb you. You can escape up the servants' stair if you hurry," he added invitingly.

She had just started to carry out this plan when Tremly opened the massive front door. She paused, for it was not Lord Petersham's anxious voice, nor even Sir William's dulcet tones, that reached her. Her cousin Reggie wished the butler a brisk good morning and asked after his uncle.

Leanora retraced her steps and hurried up the hall to greet him, then stopped short. Behind him, his large figure framed in the doorway, stood Captain Lord Deverell. A welter of indefinable sensations surged within her, with dismay and an unreasonable pleasure jostling for the upper hand. She went forward slowly, confused by the chaos the mere sight of him created.

"Hallo, Nora." Reggie slipped an arm about her slender waist and kissed her cheek. "Came as soon as I got my mamma's message. Holding up all right?"

"Yes, thank you. Captain Lord Deverell?" After a brief hesitation, she offered her hand. To her consternation, he raised her fingers to his lips.

"We won't take up much of your time," he said. "We just called to see how Lord Sherborne goes on, and to ask if there is anything we can do to help."

He seemed more capable to her of doing harm than good, but she kept that reflection to herself. An aura of mystery hung about him, intensified by the alert intelligence in his keen eye and the restless vitality that seemed impossible in a man so large. Why did he cultivate the vacuous Reggie as a friend? The combination of these two seemed so improbable as to make her instantly suspect an ulterior motive on Deverell's part.

75

Gathering her shaky courage, she invited her visitors to step into the Gold Saloon. Tremly appeared at her elbow, and she requested him to inform her aunt of the gentlemen's arrival and then bring refreshments to the saloon. With a disturbing inward trembling that would not be quelled, she turned to follow her guests.

Lord Deverell's presence filled the large apartment, making her acutely aware of him. He possessed an energy that vibrated through the room, reaching out, filling her with a dancing sensation of nervous impulses. He turned and smiled in a manner that caused sheer havoc to her normally orderly mind.

"Came to see if we could do anything," Reggie repeated. He lounged down into a comfortable chair and crossed a booted foot over his other knee. "I must say, Nora, you're looking fagged to death."

Leanora colored, not from her cousin's frank comment but from the searching gaze directed at her by Lord Deverell. He stood leaning negligently against the mantelpiece, his thickly curling black locks glinting in a beam of sunlight that came through the window.

"You need to get outdoors for a bit," he said bluntly. "If you would care for it, I should be delighted to take you for a drive in the Park this afternoon."

"I will not put you to the trouble," she responded coolly. Escaping from the tense atmosphere in the house could not but tempt her, as did the prospect of riding through the comparative peace of Hyde Park behind those splendid bays she had seen harnessed to his curricle. But she could not tolerate the company. "I dare not go far from the house just at present," she ended on a note of finality, glad to be able to fall back on the truth.

He smiled, displaying even, white teeth that flashed against the deep tan of his skin. "I am completely at your disposal Lady Leanora, if at any time you should change your mind."

A most unladylike sensation rippled through her as their eyes met. Why did he persist in challenging her undisguised dislike of him? Of course, he would have no idea that Vincent had told her of his secret work, and of the friend who had lured him into taking it on.

76

The door to the saloon opened behind her at that moment, and Mrs. Amabelle Ashton advanced unsteadily into the room, a handkerchief clutched dramatically in one hand.

"Reggie, my son!" she cried in faltering accents.

Reggie sprang instantly to his feet and went to support his afflicted parent. Tenderly, he led her to the sofa, then seated himself at her side as he continued to hold her hand.

"Dear Aunt!" Leanora sank into a chair near her. "Has anything more happened?"

Mrs. Ashton gave an expressive shudder. "Oh, my love, I have just been reading over the notes of condolence that we have received! There is nothing more lowering, I assure you, than being the object of sympathy from all of one's friends. And so many from people with whom we are barely acquainted! I know they mean well, but when they speak of our 'tragedy,' it quite sinks my spirits, for it makes me fear the worst! And dear Sherborne will get better, will he not, dearest?"

"Of course he will, Mamma," Reggie stuck in, disgusted. "Lord, if it ain't just like people, to be writing you such fustian! Much better to be sending cards to my uncle, wishing him a speedy recovery!"

"Let me answer the letters, Aunt Amabelle," Leanora suggested, a martial light in her eyes. "You may be sure they are mostly from a set of vulgar, prying busybodies who hope to goad you into disclosing all the details of the accident. You may be sure I shall know how to deal with them." A slight noise from Lord Deverell made her glance suspiciously at him, but he met her gaze with one of complete blandness.

"Just so," he murmured, and she could not help but notice the amusement that lurked in his dark eyes. "Lord Sherborne is a public man, you must remember," he pointed out. "Anything that befalls him is naturally of interest to society. Particularly at such a time, with Lord Grenville so newly in office."

Leanora sighed. "It is too true."

"Is his illness causing trouble in Whitehall?" he asked.

"The situation is even worse than you know. My father's clerk was killed on the same night as the accident."

Deverell straightened up, and his eyes narrowed. "Was

77

he, now?"

"A terrible thing. And that reminds me, dear Aunt, we must have Mr. Edmonton visit Mr. Holloway's family and give them whatever help they need."

"I should imagine your father's colleagues are beside themselves," Deverell commented.

To Leanora's relief, he did not pursue the subject of the clerk's death. She tried to smile. "They have been here, you must know, both Lord Petersham and Sir William Holborne."

"Why?" Reggie demanded. "I mean, can't talk with your father or anything like that."

"Apparently he took some papers away from a meeting with them, and they are quite anxious to lay their hands on them. If you could only have seen how upset Petersham became when we could not find the documents he needed. . . ." She broke off, dismayed. Her chaotic reactions to Deverell were leading her into an indiscretion unworthy of the earl of Sherborne's daughter! It was most unlike her, for she knew how to guard her tongue. She had been raised from her cradle to respect political secrets! And just what was Deverell's interest in her father's affairs, anyway? The concerns of the Home Office were hardly a fit subject for polite inquiries! Her reserve—and suspicions—closed about her like a cloak.

Deverell's gaze rested on her heightened color, and he moved away from the mantelpiece. "We shall not trespass on your time any more at the present. But if there is any way in which I might be of assistance, please do not hesitate to call on me. Reggie, do you come?"

Reggie stood slowly, giving his mamma's hand a final pat. With a speaking glance at Leanora that she had no trouble in interpreting as a desire to have a word with her, he started for the door.

"Nora," he began as soon as she joined him, "look after m'mother, will you? Hate to see her so distressed."

"Don't worry. We are taking the greatest care of her. Perhaps tomorrow I can start taking her about a little to try and distract her mind. And if you can stop in to visit, that will do more good than anything. She is always so happy to see you."

Deverell, having taken his leave of Mrs. Ashton, emerged

into the hall behind them and possessed himself of Leanora's reluctant hand. "I repeat, if you have need, do not hesitate to call on me," he directed. The significant look that accompanied these words startled her, robbing her of breath, and she could only stare up helplessly into the rugged face so far above her own.

With an effort, she commanded her voice to remain calm as she thanked him. It was almost as if he sought to warn her of something—or perhaps to frighten her! Recovering her hand, she led the way to the door. Deverell reached over her shoulder to open it, and the smooth cloth of his mulberry riding coat brushed her bare arm, sending a disturbing shiver through her.

The two gentlemen departed, but Deverell's unnerving presence lingered, leaving Leanora with the growing conviction that some menace underlay his words. Uneasy, she returned upstairs. Here she found Mrs. Tremly, engaged in mending a table cloth, sitting beside Lord Sherborne's bed. Pagget, that good woman explained, was laid down on a truckle bed in his lordship's dressing room, having left instructions to call him if his master so much as moved a muscle. Artaxerxes once more lay on the coverlet beside the earl.

Leanora returned to the chair she had occupied earlier and idly picked up her embroidery. The next few hours were spent in alternately trying to set stitches neatly in a row and watching her father's still face. She was roused at last by the puppy, which stood near the door, whining softly.

"Do you need a run, Artaxerxes?" she asked. Suddenly, the idea of getting out for a few minutes proved irresistible. What she needed more than anything was a breath of fresh air and some exercise. Scooping up the puppy, she sent for her pelisse and a leash, and together they set off for a brisk walk.

This afternoon, the garden in the center of Berkeley Square seemed too confining. Instead, she turned her steps down the street. Artaxerxes frisked happily at her heels. A chill breeze ruffled her curls and whipped color into her pale cheeks, and suddenly she wanted to keep walking forever.

But she couldn't let herself stray too far from the house, in case . . . just in case. At the corner she turned, then made her way along the narrow alley behind the stately row of mansions.

Artaxerxes dashed to and fro, sniffing frantically at the unfamiliar smells, pulling her along with him until she almost ran to keep up.

Suddenly the puppy stopped dead, his hackles rising. A low growl started in his throat and crescendoed into frantic, yelping barks. He surged forward, dragging Leanora.

A man in a dark greatcoat, hidden before from her view, broke away from the sheltering wall of one of the houses and began to run. Without thinking, Leanora started after him. Artaxerxes darted between her feet, tripping her, and she stumbled, barely catching her balance short of a puddle left by the rain. The man disappeared around the corner.

Leanora slowed to a stop and abandoned the chase. She had no real idea why she had pursued him in the first place, except that his behavior had been suspicious in the extreme. Curious, she turned to see what he had been doing.

She walked along the row of houses until numerous footprints in the mud showed her where he had lurked. They were concentrated primarily beneath one window, as if he had been trying to gain entrance. She examined the back façade and realized with a sense of shock that this was her own home. And the window, which sat just above the level of her head, would be that of her father's study.

Disturbed, she retraced her steps back the way she had come, lost in thought. As she approached the front stairs, running footsteps came up behind her. She whirled about, but it was only the street urchin who had accosted her before. Artaxerxes growled but apparently sensed no menace, for he began to wag his reprehensible little tail.

"'E come back, miss." The boy regarded her hopefully. "That flash cove I tol' yer of."

Leanora swallowed hard. "Just now?"

He nodded. "Come aroun' from th' back o' the ken, 'e did. Lopin' off like some'at scared 'im right proper."

Leanora felt in the reticule that dangled at her wrist and found a shilling. "If you see him again, come tell me at once. Come right up to the house and knock on the door." She added a second coin to the first, and the boy's eyes widened.

"Thank 'e, miss," he breathed. He touched his cap and ran

across the street, as if bent on beginning a vigil over the house at once.

Leanora mounted the steps and went inside. Someone watched the house. And someone had followed her father. What was going on? If only she could think clearly! But with her father so dreadfully hurt, nothing made sense to her.

Through the door into the parlor, she glimpsed Tremly refilling the wine decanter. She went in and told him what had just occurred. "If you see anyone—anyone!—loitering about, please tell me at once," she ended.

Tremly blinked. "Yes, Miss Leanora."

In spite of his training, his tone betrayed his skepticism of her story. Leanora sighed. He must have thought she had run mad under the strain of her father's accident. If she had not seen that man herself, she would be inclined to believe the whole thing a farradiddle of nonsense. But she had seen him and thought she had glimpsed someone before.

With the puppy scampering between her feet on the carpeted stair, she made her way back up to the earl's bedchamber to resume her vigil. Here she found her Aunt Amabelle, who quietly knotted the fringe for a shawl. Her aunt looked up and smiled.

"So you have been out, my dear? I am so glad, for you must know I cannot like you sitting up here for hours on end. Not that I would have you desert your poor dear father, of course; but I know how you prefer activity, and to be ever sitting at a sickbed is not good for you. But I see that your walk has brought your color back, so I may be comfortable again. Though how odd it is to be talking of comfort, with poor Sherborne like this. You must know, my dear, that—"

But Leanora was spared from hearing what she must know. Tremly tapped lightly on the door, interrupting the rambling speech.

"Excuse me, Miss Leanora, but Lord Kennington has called and is anxious to see you."

"Kennington! But—" She broke off, recollecting herself. But why should Kennington, of all people, pay her a visit? Of condolence? Her scant acquaintance with that gentleman made this explanation seem in the highest degree unlikely.

Filled with curiosity, Leanora made her way down to the drawing room. She entered to find the budding light of the Opposition party standing before the hearth, his manner relaxed. He smiled as he saw her and came forward, his hand extended to take hers. The supercilious manner that normally characterized him was absent on this occasion, a fact that made Leanora instantly suspicious rather than setting her at ease.

"You must forgive me for intruding on you," he said, retaining her hand in a firm clasp. "This is a trying time for you, I fear."

She drew back, obliging him to release his hold. Gesturing toward a sofa, she invited him to be seated.

He waited for her to take a wing-back chair, then himself perched on the edge of another, leaning slightly forward in a confiding manner. "I will come straight to the point, Lady Leanora, for I am sure you will be anxious to return to your father's side. Do you remember the unfortunate collision we sustained just three afternoons back?"

She stared at him in surprise. If he were coming to apologize, he would better have done so immediately, not delay it so long!

He must have caught the slight tensing of her expression, for his own smile became instantly contrite. "So very clumsy of me. But I fear I have come by my deserts. I have lost some of the papers that I carried and wondered if perhaps they had become confused with yours. You must understand, of course, the delicate situation? Imagine my embarrassment if it became known that I permitted Opposition papers to fall into the hands of so notable a party member as Lord Sherborne!"

A sudden smile lit Leanora's eyes, for she was well able to appreciate the difficulty of his position. The gleam in their blue depths suddenly became arrested as a new thought occurred to her.

"Those papers!" she exclaimed. Her father's accident had completely driven them from her mind! She, not Lord Sherborne, had transported a very large stack of sensitive papers to the house! And Mr. Edmonton had found only a small pile for Sir William. She cast her mind back, trying to remember. She had given them to her father, she was sure, and he had carried them to his study. But what had he done with them then? She simply could not remember! They should all have been there, not just a few. Why had they not been found?

She looked back at Kennington to find that he watched her intently. "I am sorry, my lord. My father's accident drove the incident completely from my mind. And the worst of it is that we cannot seem to find all those papers I brought home."

His brow snapped down. "You cannot, my lady?" he asked smoothly.

"No, and there are documents that Lord Petersham is anxious to lay his hands on, as well. Oh, what a muddle this is!" she exclaimed. "I assure you, Lord Kennington, we will do everything in our power to locate your papers, if they are indeed here. And no one, I give you my word, will look at them! I feel quite dreadful, having caused so much trouble with my wretched memory."

Promising to send for him the instant the papers should turn up, Leanora saw him to the door. Turning back down the hall, she wracked her memory. Sir William, Petersham, Kennington. . . . Oh, what a muddle she had created! She had best see to the recovery of those wretched documents at once.

Mr. Edmonton was not in the house, and she was forced to wait a considerable time before he was due to return from the City, where he had gone to replenish the missing housekeeping funds. Leanora passed this time in her father's room, sitting quietly while the doctor subjected the unconscious earl to a thorough examination. There were no changes yet, the doctor confirmed with a shake of his head, and he refused to hazard any guesses.

As soon as Mr. Edmonton entered the house, Tremly informed him that Leanora was anxious to speak to him. He went immediately to Lord Sherborne's chamber, where Leanora sat with the puppy stretched out in her lap and her embroidery untouched. Together, they went down to her father's study, where she sank down into the desk chair and told him about her bringing home the papers entrusted to her by her father, and of Kennington's belief that some of his own had become mixed with these.

Mr. Edmonton leaned back in his chair and pursed his lips.

"And you have no idea what happened to them?" he asked.

"None." She shook her head. "I gave them to Pappa in my study, and I am sure he carried them directly here. But we have searched this room thoroughly! And no one has been in here except us and Lord Petersham."

"And Mr. Gregory, of course," added Mr. Edmonton conscientiously.

"Yes, and my brother." Slowly she raised her head, her eyes meeting those of her father's secretary. "My brother?" she repeated, her tone incredulous as the horrible thought forced its way into her mind.

Chapter 6

Leonora and Mr. Edmonton stared at each other in disbelief. "It—it cannot be!" Leonora finally managed to say.

"Of course not, Miss Leonora. He would have no reason to take them. But it might be possible that he moved them, if they were in his way."

"I will ask him at once." She had wanted to talk to him, anyway, for the little matter of her housekeeping money still lay between them. A quick search of the desk provided her with pen and paper, and she scribbled out an urgent summons for her brother to come to her on the instant. This missive she entrusted to the footman James, then sat back to await the response.

James returned in less than twenty minutes with the unwelcome tidings that Mr. Gregory was away from home. It were believed in his household that he was visiting his club, and he was not expected to return until the early hours of the morning.

Leonora sank her head into her cupped hands. If Gregory was at his club—or anywhere else, for that matter—the chances were very good that he was gaming. In her mind's eye, she envisioned her housekeeping money floating away.

Gregory did not, in fact, present himself before his sister until late the following afternoon. Although dressed with impeccable taste, his eyes were bleary, and he showed all the signs of a young Blood who had spent a convivial evening with like-minded cronies.

He lounged back against the cushions of the most comfortable chair in Leanora's sitting room and winced as his tousled blond head collided with the carved wooden trim along the top. "Fact is," he explained apologetically to his indignant sister, "not in plump currant today."

"No, it looks like you made a pretty batch of it last night," she agreed with acid sweetness. "Or is your misery due to the ivories?"

He tried to grin, then winced once again at the pain this effort caused him. "Devilish against me," he admitted. "Cards, too. Never known such an evening of ill luck. What was so important that it could not wait until tomorrow?"

"You know perfectly well!" she exclaimed, exasperated. "What on earth do you mean by taking my housekeeping money?"

"Oh, was that what it was?" he asked with studied nonchalance. "Thought it was there for an emergency. And I can tell you, Nora, it was certainly that! Damned if I'll know what to do if my luck don't change."

"Gregory, you stole almost three hundred pounds!"

He straightened up, attempted to look down his aristocratic nose at her, found himself unequal to it and flopped back in the chair. "Lord, you make such a fuss over nothing! Merely borrowed the flimsies. No need to set up a screech over it! Pay you back on Settling Day."

"Oh, Gregory! You did not bet some of the money on a horse, did you?" she demanded, dismayed.

"Well, of course I did. Fellow who twigged me at Tat's swore the filly couldn't lose! Got handsome odds, too. You just wait for Settling Day, and everything will be all right and tight."

"It will more likely be a Black Monday," she retorted. "If you ever take money from this house again without asking me, I'll—"

"You'll what?" he broke in with a true brotherly challenge.

"I may not be able to land you a—a facer, but you may be sure I shall have you thrown out of here!" she exclaimed.

At that, Gregory collapsed into helpless laughter, clutching at his throbbing head. "No, Nora, please! I—I'm not up to this! Lord, how I'd like to see you try! Game as a pebble, that's what you are. Now, don't put yourself in a pet. I'll pay that blasted money back."

She stood up and took an agitated turn about the room. He was a shocking scapegrace, a disgraceful reprobate, but he was not wholly ramshackle. She doubted that he viewed taking money from her father's desk as stealing. He would not intentionally do something dishonest—would he? She turned back to face him. "Did you take any papers away with you as well as the money?"

"Papers? What the devil would I want with anything like that?" he demanded. "Lord, Nora, just because I borrowed a few rubbishing rolls of soft don't mean you have to accuse me of taking things! What interest could papers possibly have for me?"

She was inclined to agree with him, but the defiant note in his voice gave her pause. How desperately did he need money? Would he do something as despicable as stealing their father's papers to sell? As quickly as the thought occurred to her she dismissed it, thrusting it to the back of her mind. This was her brother! She could not suspect him of anything so vile! But still, the possibility took root and began to haunt her.

She stood, staring down at his unrepentant countenance, a frown creasing her brow. If only her father would regain consciousness! If only. . . . But that was just wishful thinking. Until Lord Sherborne was once again himself, she would have to deal with her problems—and his—on her own.

"Gregory," she began slowly, then broke off with a vexed exclamation as a gentle tap sounded on the door.

Tremly entered in response to her call, bowing slightly as he held out a silver salver on which rested a neatly engraved card. She took it, and her brow snapped down in displeasure as she read the imprinted name of Captain Lord Deverell.

"Is he waiting?" she asked curtly.

"In the Gold Saloon, Miss Leanora."

Gregory peered over the edge of her arm and read the name on the card. "A suitor, my girl?" he asked with a sublime disregard for the presence of the butler. "I must say, it's about time. You run along and flirt with him before he gets away."

"Oh do be quiet, Gregory!" she snapped. She folded the card

87

with suddenly nervous fingers. If he was alone, as his sending up a card indicated, this might be a very good time to establish an understanding of the revulsion that engulfed her whenever she thought of Vincent's tragic—and unnecessary—death. It would not do to be forever meeting Deverell in company and never be able to tell him what she really thought of him. She glanced at Gregory, who regarded her with the utmost interest.

"I shall leave you to your swain," he offered magnanimously. He straightened his lanky form and grimaced as he came to his feet. "Let me know what the doctor says, will you?"

The doctor! Leanora's gaze flew to the clock that stood on the mantel, but was relieved to see that the time wanted only twenty minutes before four. The doctor was not due to arrive until at least six, and she had only left her father's bedside a bare half hour ago, when Gregory arrived. She could quite easily allow a few minutes to put Captain Lord Deverell in the possession of a few home truths.

She found him in the saloon, his restless energy driving him to pace its length with his long, uneven stride. Just the sight of him sent an errant thrill coursing through her, as if she were a schoolroom miss in the clutches of her first *tendre!* she reflected in disgust.

His dark eyes lit with something that might have been pleasure as they rested on her, and he came forward at once with his halting gait. Taking her hand in his, he raised her fingers briefly to his lips.

"I am glad you could spare me a moment," he said. "But tell me, have I come at a bad time? You look vexed."

She fought down the responsive chord that the timbre of his deep voice struck within her. "I doubt I have looked anything else since I had the dubious honor of at last making your acquaintance," she informed him coldly, taking the proverbial bull directly by the horns. He released her hand, and she experienced a wave of satisfaction at having penetrated the imperturbable calm with which he surrounded himself.

"This is plain speaking indeed," he said. "Perhaps you will be so kind as to tell me what I have done to incur your censure?"

"There is no mystery about that. It is Vincent." She swallowed hard to prevent an uncomfortable lump from rising in her throat. Her eyes, though, remained clear and icily disdainful as they rested on him.

Deverell's brow snapped down. "Vincent was as a brother to me," he informed her. "And from things he said . . . forgive me if I speak out of turn, but I understood that he did not regard you in the light of a sister."

"He did me the honor of asking me to be his wife the last time I saw him." To her relief, her voice only quavered slightly.

"Then I am at a loss to understand. . . ."

"I know that he was not with any regiment when he died," she said more steadily. "He told me of the secret work that you—*you*, who were supposedly his friend—had coerced him into undertaking."

Deverell took a deep breath and exhaled slowly. "So you hold me responsible. I am sorry, Lady Leanora. If you believe that Vincent did not know full well the dangers of the job, or that he did not take it on willingly, then I think you must not have known him as well as you thought."

Leanora walked past him to stare blindly out the window. "He was not hen-hearted," she said softly. "Of course he went into it, and gladly, I should think. He was always hey-go-mad, looking for adventure." She spun about, tears slipping unheeded down her cheeks. "But if you had not suggested it to him—" She broke off, unable to control her voice.

"Since you know so much already, I will not scruple to tell you that it was I who was first recruited for the work by a senior officer. He asked me to recommend other officers of sufficient intelligence and daring to work in the effort. Vincent was a logical choice." He paused, but she returned no answer. "Vincent would want no man to take the responsibility for his death. The choice was his, and his alone. He knew what he was doing."

She turned away, wishing desperately that she had a handkerchief upon her. Booted footsteps crossed the Aubusson carpet behind her, and his hand appeared over her shoulder, offering the needed article. She took it, dabbing at

89

her eyes and resolutely blowing her nose.

"Why do you persist in blaming me? The rest of his family does not."

"They do not know the truth," she answered bleakly. He stood so close that his breath stirred the hairs on the top of her head. If she leaned back even slightly, she would brush against the crisp, olive-green cloth of his riding coat. "They believe he was attached to the Austrian forces."

"And so we were." His voice was strangely gentle. He moved away abruptly, taking a quick turn about the room. He stopped behind her once again. "Will you never forgive me?" he asked.

She bit her lip, fighting back tears. How could she? She had hated him for so long, partially for recruiting Vincent to that dangerous way of life, but mostly for being alive while her cousin had died. And beneath the strength of this overpowering emotion, she had buried a guilt of her own. It had been easy to blame the unknown Deverell while trying to forget that she had not loved Vincent enough to promise to become his wife. Her cousin had returned to the war without her answer, and she had never seen him again.

"I believe the best thing for us will be to call a semblance of a truce," Deverell said, breaking the long silence that stretched between them.

"What—what do you mean?" She did not turn to face him but made use of his handkerchief which she still held.

"Unless you wish to tell his mother and brother how he really died, you will need a good explanation for why you cannot stand the sight of me," he said in a tone of perfect reasonableness.

"I—" She broke off. "What do you suggest?"

"We understand one another," he said deliberately. "There is no reason why we should not put animosity aside and be commonly polite."

"We." She almost managed a smile at that. "You mean me."

"You need not like me," he pointed out affably, "but it will be less awkward if you do not give me the cut direct whenever we chance to meet. Let us say no more of what is past."

"Begin again as if this conversation had never taken place?" She turned to look up at him over her shoulder, experiencing a slight surprise as to how very far above her he towered. "Very well." She offered him her hand. "How do you do, Captain? It is very kind of you to call."

Unexpected lights twinkled in the depths of his dark eyes as he raised her fingers to his lips. "I have come to see how your father goes on."

Her eyes clouded on the instant, and she found her hand clasped in a sustaining manner.

"No improvement? But then it has not been very long, yet." The pressure of his fingers increased. "It is often so with head injuries, I believe. He may stay like this for a week or more, then suddenly awaken as if nothing at all has been amiss."

She managed an odd, grateful smile. "It is kind of you to offer words of encouragement."

A boyish grin broke across his rugged face, and to her surprise, her heart lifted at the sight. "Actually, I came to ask you to drive in the Park with me."

She shook her head. "I dare not. If I were to be from here at a moment when he might need me. . . . I must stay here."

"That is precisely what you ought not to do," he replied promptly, that devastating smile still playing about his lips. "Forgive me for being blunt, but you are looking strained. Some fresh air will do you a world of good."

She hesitated, sorely tempted. As odd as it would have seemed to her only fifteen minutes before, she found comfort in his company. Was it because no pretenses now lay between them? They had been honest with one another. Vincent had called him friend, and though she could not go that far, she did Deverell the credit of believing that he had not perceived the harm he did her cousin in introducing him to the world of espionage.

It would be such a relief to forget her problems for just a little while, to enliven the afternoon with his rich laughter and energetic spirits. Crossing verbal swords with him might even sharpen her dulled wits. But her father lay so still, his face so very pale and lifeless. . . .

Her conflicting desires reflected themselves clearly in her expressive countenance. Lord Deverell watched her, the gleam in his eyes brightening as her distress became clear to him.

"Your father would not like to think of you tying yourself up indoors," he persuaded. "And he would most definitely not want you to worry yourself into a decline."

"I am not such a poor creature as that," she responded, smiling slightly at the wilting picture of her his words conjured up. Her resolve wavered, and the strain of her father's illness and the worry for the missing papers decided the issue. "Just allow me to fetch my bonnet," she begged, and hurried from the room.

Less than five minutes later, he handed her up into a sleek curricle that could only have been designed for racing. A cool breeze ruffled the golden ringlets that curled from beneath her chip straw hat, and she shivered slightly though welcoming the refreshing crispness of the air. Deverell climbed up beside her and from beneath the seat drew a lap robe which he arranged across her knees.

"You were right," she declared as his groom swung up behind and the matched bays stepped out at a brisk trot. "I have not been getting out often enough."

"Do you just sit in his room?" He slowed his team as they approached the corner and turned the horses neatly off the Square, maneuvering around a cart heavily laden with boxes.

"That, and search for those missing papers."

"You have not found them yet?" He cast a quick glance at her face, then returned his attention to his pair as he negotiated another turn.

She let out a deep sigh. "I wish I had never heard of them!" The heat of her response surprised even herself. "No, we have not found them, and I cannot think where they can be. And now it seems that I have also lost some pages of a speech that Lord Kennington wrote. Oh, if ever there was such a tangle! People are positively haunting the house, asking after those wretched documents! How I wish my father would recover!" To her consternation, her eyes misted with tears again so that she was obliged to avert her face.

"He is getting no worse," Deverell pointed out in heartening accents, "and that is a good sign. Now," he continued, his tone rallying, "I wish you will give me some advice, for your cousin Reggie assures me you are up to every rig and row in town."

That drew a shaky smile from her. "Of course I shall do what I can, though from what little I have seen of you, you do not seem to stand in need of any help."

"But I do. I find manners here in London very odd and have begun to live in constant dread of offending someone."

"Do you, indeed?" Resolutely, Leanora bit her lip to keep her chin from quivering in amusement. The idea of anyone as confident and self-assured as Captain Lord Deverell quaking in his boots appealed to her sense of the ridiculous. "Has some turbaned dowager stared you out of countenance?" she asked wistfully.

"Worse than that. Reggie introduced me to Lady Carmody and her daughter Eliza at a party last night that turned into an impromptu hop. And when I solicited Miss Carmody's hand to sit out a waltz with me, I thought she would burst into tears!"

"Poor Eliza!" Leanora laughed in spite of herself. "She has only just been presented, you must know, and last week finally received approval to waltz by the patronesses of Almack's. She must have been dying to dance it in public, and then here you come, requesting that she sit it out as she has been forced to do ever since she came to London!"

Deverell's deep, rich chuckle rolled over her, enveloping her in his merriment. "I shall never offend another lady by asking her *not* to waltz!" he vowed.

An unfamiliar sensation tugged at Leanora's heart. Just because she could not like him did not mean that she was unaware of his attractiveness. The prospect of being held in those strong arms, of swirling about the floor guided only by the pressure of his hands, appealed reprehensibly to her. Poor Eliza, indeed, to discover that this mountain of masculine appeal could not yet dance because of his injury.

"*Do* you waltz?" she asked before she could stop herself.

He looked down at her, a smile still lurking in his dark eyes. "I did a great deal, in Vienna. I imagine I could still drag myself around the floor, but I doubt if any lady would be pleased to stand up with me."

He was wrong there, and that realization only served to confuse her further. To cover this, she cast a roguish eye at him. "I fear you underrate the appeal of a war hero. You must

93

know your injury makes you above anything romantic." She fluttered her long lashes at him in feigned worshipful innocence.

He laughed. "Minx," he said with appreciation. "I must remember to thank Cousin Reggie."

"Why?" she demanded, instantly suspicious.

"For recommending a companion who would not bore me," he responded promptly.

They had entered Hyde Park by this time, and she had barely time to inform him, in no uncertain terms, that that was something she had no ambition to be, when they were hailed by an acquaintance of Lord Deverell's. They pulled up, exchanged greetings, and by the time they started forward again she had regained her composure. Determined to keep to a safer topic, she asked him about society in Austria.

"Napoleon was not making himself popular," he replied lightly. "There seems to be a young lady on the path, just over there, anxious to attract your attention."

Leanora turned, then recognized the daughter of one of her Aunt Charlotte's friends; and Deverell obligingly pulled up to allow them to exchange greetings. It soon became obvious that Miss Sophia Wentworth's intent was not to speak to Leanora but to discover the identity of her intriguing escort and to make certain that she attracted his notice. This she attempted to accomplish by adopting an arch manner and relating an *on dit* that Leanora considered too warm by half.

They were interrupted before this had gone too far by a gentleman in scarlet regimentals astride a neatish chestnut hack, who hailed Deverell as a long lost friend. This, it transpired, was exactly the truth, for the two gentlemen had last met on the battlefield at Austerlitz, from which both had been removed on stretchers.

After this, they were able to proceed for some distance before being stopped once again. It was pleasant to get out, Leanora decided, in spite of her companion, and she made a silent vow to herself to try and ride or drive every day throughout her father's illness. She was relaxing somewhat, which she needed badly.

On their third turn about the Park, Leanora caught sight of

her sister-in-law, Lady Julia. She sat alone in her commodious landau, leaning over the side to converse with a tall gentleman. To her astonishment, Leanora recognized Lord Kennington. Julia looked about quickly, then leaned closer and whispered something in Kennington's ear. He responded, his manner casual, and she went off in a merry peal of laughter.

Leanora frowned, finding the exchange strangely unsettling. She should be only too glad to find her brother's wife in better spirits than when she had last seen her, but she could not be pleased that she appeared to be on such friendly terms with a notorious rake.

Julia spoke to her coachman, and the landau drove on. Kennington stood by the carriageway for a moment, his eyes on the departing vehicle, then he turned and strode quickly off to the foot path.

The meeting bothered Leanora. She glanced at Deverell, who had fallen silent while easing his pair around a curricle with an obstreperous pair of colts harnessed to the shafts. This feat did not appear to tax his ability to any great extent, but it did occupy his attention. She could only be relieved that he had not noticed her concern.

"Reggie tells me that you drive yourself," Deverell said as they resumed their forward progress. "Perhaps you will take me up one afternoon. He assures me you will not overturn the carriage."

Leanora managed a laugh that almost sounded natural to her ears. "No, that I will not do. But my Aunt Amabelle vows that I am in the gravest danger of being labeled fast for choosing such a dashing carriage. And not even the passage of several years has convinced her that my high perch phaeton is considered quite a normal sight. You are an excellent whip," she admitted judiciously. "Are you being put up for membership in the Four-In-Hand Club?"

"I don't believe I am acquainted with any of the members, yet," he told her, and his eyes, when he turned them on her, twinkled in a most disconcerting manner. "I fear that any recommendation on the part of Reggie would not be greeted with much enthusiasm."

"It would not, indeed!" she agreed, an unexpected

merriment welling up within her. Grudgingly, she granted that he seemed to possess the knack of making her feel that her troubles were not so very bad, after all. "Have you been privileged to ride with Reggie yet?"

"Once, when I first came to town. I purchased my curricle and pair the next day," he added on a reflective note.

The conversation slipped comfortably into the rival merits of driving two, three or four horses, with Deverell stoutly and not very seriously advocating the unparalleled joys of the almost suicidal pastime of driving unicorn through traffic. Leanora was still smiling at his absurdities when they drew up before Sherborne House in Berkeley Square.

The amusement died from her expressive eyes as her problems, for the most part forgotten for the past hour, once again descended upon her. She had been gone longer than she intended, leaving Pagget and her Aunt Amabelle to sit by her father's bedside. The sooner she relieved them, taking her lonely turn, the better she would feel.

She turned to thank Deverell, surprised that her sentiment was genuine, and once more encountered dancing lights in the mysterious depths of his eyes. His warm smile was infectious, and she found herself returning it as his strong hand clasped hers. His touch created disturbingly pleasurable sensations.

He sprang lightly down from the curricle, came around to her side and offered his hand to assist her to the street. Leaving his pair in the charge of his groom, he escorted her up the stairs, only leaving when Tremly opened the door and she had gone inside.

She stripped off her gloves and dropped them on the hall table, lost in the aura of Deverell's masterful personality that lingered even after his departure. He made her feel that he was more than capable of dealing with any problem that might arise. How very odd to feel that way about him. But he was no longer there, and she had been too long from her father's side.

"Excuse me, Miss Leanora." Tremly coughed slightly.

Reluctantly, she set aside her abstraction, aware that the butler stood before her, politely waiting to speak.

96

"Mr. Edmonton would like to see you at your earliest convenience."

Yes, she had returned to her problems, indeed. Firmly repressing an urge to sigh, she thanked Tremly. "I just want to check on my father. Is Mr. Edmonton in his study? Then I shall join him in ten minutes."

She hurried upstairs to her father's bedchamber. Pagget sat at his side, hands folded in his lap, his eyes fixed anxiously on his master's empty face. Mrs. Ashton sat opposite, her needle plying in and out of the picture that was beginning to take form on the firescreen. Artaxerxes raised his head from the coverlet and tried to wag his curling tail in greeting.

"Ah, my love," Mrs. Ashton, who faced the door, looked up as she entered. "Did you have an enjoyable time? Though to be sure, with a gentleman as considerate as Lord Deverell, I am sure you must, for there is nothing more pleasant than to be able to leave everything in the hands of a capable man, though so very few of them really are. Capable, that is. Not that I mean to say anything against Lord Deverell or your father, my dear, for I am sure that they are both able to deal with any problem, and dear Reggie, of course, can always be counted on to make sure that one is quite comfortable and everything is arranged just as one would like."

Leanora ignored this speech as she moved over to the bedside and laid her hand over her father's. His skin was tightly drawn, almost transparent. He had always been such a hearty man, so strong and vibrant and fun-loving. It was as if only the shell remained, empty of his soul, of the life-force that made him what he was.

Hot tears stung her eyes. He would recover! He had to! She would not let him slip away like this! But what could she do? A painful constriction gripped her throat, and half-blinded, she turned from the room.

In the hall she paused, trying to master her despair. She would do what she had to. She would carry on with the conviction that her father would get better, make sure that everything ran smoothly so there would be nothing to trouble him when he at last resumed control of his own affairs. On that

97

note of resolution, she made her way down to Mr. Edmonton's study.

She found him seated behind his writing desk, his tall, lank frame bent almost double as he studied the sheets of paper that lay spread out before him. He glanced up as she entered, then stood at once.

"I am sorry to bother you, but—" He broke off, lifted the pair of spectacles that rested on the bridge of his nose and rubbed thoughtfully at a reddened spot made by the frame.

Leanora took the chair nearest his. "Has something happened?"

"Not exactly." He seated himself again. "It is just something that seemed a bit strange. I thought you should know about it. Lord Petersham came to call."

"That is vexatious, certainly, but hardly strange," she pointed out.

He awarded this sally a perfunctory smile. "It was his manner that did not seem to be quite normal."

"Do you mean he did not bore on?" she asked, prompting her father's secretary as he again fell silent.

"Oh, yes, he most certainly did. He talked endlessly about those missing papers, going on and on about how they must be found, but he was talking in circles, repeating himself over and over, using the same phrases."

At that, Leanora frowned. "You are right. That is not quite like him. Normally he finds endless new ways to say precisely the same thing."

"That is it!" Mr. Edmonton agreed, glad to have made her understand his own perplexity. "It was almost as if he had rehearsed a short speech and did not know how to vary it. He kept hinting at a reward if the papers could be found quickly."

"A reward?" Leanora demanded, amazed. "Are you quite sure? It is so easy to get confused, you know, with his involved periods and endless flow of words."

"He most definitely used that term, and at least a score of times if he used it once! It sounded to me," he added with more than a touch of indignation, "rather like he offered a bribe."

But this Leanora could not allow. "A bribe?" she repeated skeptically. "There would be no reason! It is not as if you were

98

a member of the Opposition party, or even new to my father's service! If we knew where the papers were, we would naturally hand them over on the instant!"

Mr. Edmonton nodded. "So I informed him, Miss Leanora. He then had the goodness to say that he never doubted our loyalty and implied that we merely did not realize the importance of those documents and were not really trying to find them."

"Petersham!" she sighed. "I doubt if *he* has any real idea how important they are! It has always seemed to me that it is Sir William or my father who manages everything for him."

"He must be frantic without Lord Sherborne's help," Mr. Edmonton agreed, and not without a certain satisfaction. "He has never appeared to me to be a gentleman quite suited for his high office."

Leanora was silent for a moment, considering. "I shall ask Sir William what this is all about," she decided. "But I cannot like Petersham's coming here and offering you money to do no more than your job." She shook her head. "I shall be very glad when those papers finally turn up."

With this, Mr. Edmonton was in full agreement. When he suggested that they make one more search, Leanora agreed. For the remainder of the afternoon, and then again after dinner, they turned out every drawer and cupboard in Lord Sherborne's study, but not so much as a single sheet could they find mentioning the new prime minister.

At last, Leanora sank back on her heels from where she had been kneeling at the bottom shelf of a bookcase. About her were strewn the chaotic results of their labors. It would take the better part of the morrow to restore the room to any semblance of order, but on one point at least she was satisfied. The missing documents could not be in this room.

Only one person had been alone in this study. As much as she did not like to consider the possibility, only her brother Gregory would have had the opportunity to take those papers. But why? They would only be of importance to the Opposition party, but surely Gregory would not betray their father, not even for money!

A sudden, unwelcome picture rose up before her mind's eye.

Julia, Gregory's wife, whispering something into the ear of Lord Kennington, a rising power in the Opposition. She had assumed it was Julia's beauty and Kennington's rakish reputation that formed the tie between them. Could it in reality be something more, something even less savory? And if so, was Gregory involved?

Chapter 7

The unanswered questions about the missing papers and the connection between Julia and Kennington continued to haunt Leanora throughout the following day. It was almost with a sense of relief that she received her Aunt Amabelle's reminder that this was the night of Lady Carmody's dinner party, and that this was one event from which they simply could not cry off.

"I made certain you must see that we cannot, my love," Mrs. Ashton told her anxiously. "For as much as I enjoy a comfortable cose with her whenever we meet, which has not been as often as I should wish of late, though to be sure with your dear father so ill I could hardly expect to enjoy *anything*, could I, dear? But there can be no denying that she is the most shocking gossip, and you may be sure if we do not attend her wretched party she will spread it about that it is because Sherborne has taken a turn for the worse; and then we will have every vulgar busybody paying us visits, though to be sure it seems that the knocker on the door is never silent now." She ended on such a note of appeal that it would have taken a very firm resolve to have turned her down.

If Leanora were honest with herself, the prospect of going out could not but appeal to her. Contrary to her determination of the previous afternoon, she had not been able to set foot out of doors since. She had spent the entire day between sitting with her father and helping Mr. Edmonton restore Lord Sherborne's study to some semblance of order. This latter

101

was not an easy task, for her father's secretary, ever efficient, took the opportunity to reorganize a great many of the papers. He might have been satisfied that everything was now far more orderly than it had been in years, but Leanora considered this to be of less importance than discovering why they had been forced to make such a thorough search in the first place.

She did not again think about Lady Carmody's dinner until she left her father's room to go and dress for the party. It should be an adequate diversion, she reflected, for she would be sure to meet a great number of acquaintances. Lady Carmody did not consider any entertainment to be complete without a liberal sprinkling of *ton* notables, and her husband preened himself on being able to draw members of the government circles. There should be no one there unacquainted with her father's accident; so there should be little awkwardness on that score, and their hostess would not object when they took an early leave.

Only one question remained in her mind as she approved the half-robe of peach crepe that would be worn over a white satin underslip. Would Lord Deverell be there? He had not mentioned the engagement when she had seen him the day before, but then he had only just met Lady Carmody. Considering the fact that Eliza was only the first of a long line of Carmody girls, Leanora felt sure that her matchmaking mamma would find a way to include such an eligible gentleman.

She knew she had been right as soon as they were ushered up the wide staircase and into the drawing rooms of the Carmody house in Curzon Street. Lord Deverell's presence filled the room, making her vitally aware that he was there even before she saw him. It was more than just his physical size which dominated everyone in his vicinity; vitality emanated from him in a tangible wave.

He stood at the far end of the room, in conversation with Reggie and Miss Eliza Carmody. Leanora found herself drawn toward him, against her will. He looked up as if he also were aware of the magnetic force that palpitated between them. A sudden gleam lit his mysterious eyes, and they began to sparkle with his barely repressed energy.

102

With a word, he excused himself to his two companions and strolled over to her side, taking her hand and raising her fingers to his lips. A challenging smile lit his face, as if daring her to snub him before so many important people.

"I had not expected to see you here this evening, Lady Leanora," he said, and the deep, resonating tones of his voice vibrated through her.

She found the experience disturbing. Had her sentiments undergone so drastic a change since their talk? She no longer hated him. She had come prepared to regard him with tolerance, but she had not expected to be captivated by the sheer power of his presence! Forcing herself into a semblance of her usual calm, she managed to reply: "We—that is, my aunt—felt it would do us good to go out."

At that moment, Lady Carmody bore down upon them to welcome Leanora and Mrs. Ashton. She remained talking with them for several minutes, though her eyes frequently strayed from the tall, distinguished figure of Lord Deverell to her daughter Eliza. That she wished to maneuver the two together was obvious, as was the fact that she did not know how to bring it about.

Leanora firmly repressed a mischievous smile. She was very fond of Lady Carmody, and Eliza was a sweet creature though somewhat lacking in conversation, a fault of her youth. She would show her hostess how the trick could be done neatly.

"Dear Aunt," she cried impulsively. "There is Reggie, talking to Eliza. Let us go join them."

Her hostess blinked, then bestowed a beaming smile on Leanora. "Yes, do so at once, dear Mrs. Ashton, for I am sure you are quite anxious to speak to your son. And Lord Deverell, I know I can leave them safely in your hands." Her problem solved to a nicety, Lady Carmody hurried off to welcome more newcomers.

A muscle at the corner of Deverell's firm mouth quivered in amusement. "Whatever possessed you to play so perfectly into her hands?" he murmured as they started across the crowded room.

"Poor Lady Carmody. She has four daughters, you must know, and not the least notion how to manage," she whispered

103

back over her shoulder. "It was such a simple maneuver, and one she desperately needed to learn."

His deep chuckle rumbled forth, and an answering ripple of appreciation swept through her. Firmly, she squelched it. She could not allow her errant senses to control her reason! Just because she no longer hated Deverell did not necessarily mean that she had to like him.

"She will need considerably more practice if she hopes to get off so many girls," he said dryly as they neared their quarry.

They never made it. Just as Mrs. Ashton reached her son's side, Leanora felt a touch on her arm and turned to see Sir William.

He took her hand and bowed low over it, his laughing eyes meeting hers. "My beautiful life!" he greeted her effusively. "How delightful to see you once more in company."

"Have you been bored?" she asked promptly with mock sympathy. "Poor Sir William, is there no one to listen to that stinging tongue of yours?"

"Fair fatality, you wrong me! There are any number of ladies only too willing to listen to the latest *on dits*. But none, I assure you, as able as you to appreciate my retelling of them."

"Be glad, or you should find yourself challenged to a duel in a trice," she told him tartly. To her surprise, she experienced no inclination to remain and talk or listen to his never-ending supply of gossip. Why did she find no amusement in his cheerful rattling this evening? Was it because for the first time she had serious troubles to face? Sir William would be only too ready to divert her with lighthearted bantering, but she had never detected a compassionate or sensitive side to his nature.

Another unnerving thought struck her. Those eminently desirable qualities were to be found, in perfect measure, in her other companion. This put her in mind of her duty, and she turned to Lord Deverell. "Are you acquainted with Sir William Holborne?"

"I believe we met a few nights ago," Deverell said. "At the Castlereighs' *soiree*."

"Quite so," Sir William drawled.

The two men eyed each other measuringly as they shook hands, and Leanora experienced the uncanny sensation that they were considerably more acquainted than they let on.

Deverell spoke again, dispelling the illusion. "I believe I have seen you about Whitehall, as well."

Sir William raised the quizzing glass that hung from a black riband about his neck and surveyed the larger man with apparent interest. "Ah, that would explain why you seem so familiar," he agreed. He allowed the glass to drop, then turned back to Leanora. "A veritable mountain," he murmured. "My love, it devastates me, but I must leave you to him. I see the fair Sophia Wentworth in the corner over there, with Lord Kennington bearing down upon her. I must, really must, make a push to protect her fortune from so vile a seeker." With an elegant bow, he took his leave of them and in a very few moments neatly removed Miss Wentworth from Lord Kennington's vicinity.

"He would seem to have the knack of making enemies," Deverell commented in a soft voice.

"Enemies? Sir William?" Leanora considered. "He was rather rude, but then you must realize that his shoulders are not naturally as broad as yours, which makes it difficult to display his coats to perfection."

Deverell smiled. "He shows considerable restraint for an aspiring dandy. He should study our Reggie. His neckcloth is certainly a masterpiece, but those collar points are quite moderate."

"Out of deference to his position as Lord Petersham's assistant. I fear he is quite envious of Beau Brevin—even of Reggie! Nothing, I assure you, would please him more than to devote his genius to becoming the chief Pink of the Ton."

"Then why doesn't he?"

"Ah, he is intelligent enough to know that that would require considerable funds." She shook her head, her eyes dancing. "It takes a great deal, you must realize, to induce Weston or Schultz to risk their reputation with such dashing articles of clothing as Reggie—indeed, all the dandies—designs. And each one must manage to outdo the others, you see."

"A never-ending circle, it seems. I can only be thankful I chose to go into the army."

105

Leanora laughed. "No, I fear you could never be mistaken for a Tulip."

Lord Deverell cast a considering glance at his smooth-fitting coat of blue superfine and the elegant brocade waistcoat beneath. "I suppose I should need a Cumberland corset to nip me in at the waist," he agreed. "And that I could not stomach."

Her eyes brimmed with amusement at the picture his words conjured up. "And you would be obliged to have white tops added to your Hessians."

"Good God," he said, revolted. "They'd be black with mud before I cleared the third fence in the hunting field!"

"You are quite right; you would never make a dandy." She shook her head with mock sadness. "You know nothing about the matter. You must retire from the field long before that, so as not to fatigue yourself or damage your appearance. But do not fear, I am sure Reggie could be induced to take you in hand. Or would you prefer Sir William?"

"I doubt he could be induced to be more than civil to me," Deverell murmured.

"You mustn't mind him," Leanora urged. "He has a dangerous tongue, but I doubt that anyone takes him seriously, except in Whitehall. Poor Sir William, I fear he is quite unhappy, with his greatest ambition blighted. But he is excellent at his position. My father says Petersham could not manage without him."

"That is a compliment, indeed," Deverell agreed, though with a certain measure of reserve.

"Yes, it is." It pleased her to be able to compliment another man. Deverell was dominating her thoughts a little too much just at the moment. "Sir William can be amusing when he chooses," she went on quickly, "which fortunately is a great deal of the time."

Deverell returned no answer, instead offering his escort to join her cousin Reggie. This gentleman regarded them both morosely, then returned to his contemplation of Beau Brevin's wondrous neckcloth.

"Can't see how he does it?" Deverell asked lightly.

Reggie shook his head. "Never seen the like of it! Do you think his cloth is wider than two feet?" he asked hopefully.

"Might explain some of those folds."

Deverell turned to subject the neckcloth in question to a brief scrutiny, but fortunately, since such things did not hold out much interest for him, an interruption occurred with the influx of more guests. Leanora turned to see her sister-in-law Lady Julia sweep into the room on the arm of her brother, Viscount Dalmouth. Leanora's lips tightened, for Gregory did not accompany them.

Apparently these late arrivals were the last of the guests, for in a very few minutes the butler entered and announced dinner. Lord Deverell offered her his arm, and after hesitating a moment, Leanora placed her fingers on the smoothly fitting blue cloth. It would be shockingly rude in her to refuse, she told herself, and tried without success to ignore the surge of fluttery nerves that swept through her at the contact between them. She would avoid his company later, during the musical portion of the evening, thus letting him know that she had no desire to encourage any degree of intimacy between them.

Her resolution nearly crumbled when the gentlemen rejoined the ladies after the protracted meal. She sat in a far corner of the drawing room, feigning interest in the lengthy description of Miss Carmody's visit to a fashionable modiste that morning. Throughout this rambling tale, Leanora kept an eye on Julia, who loudly bewailed her husband's indisposition that had made it necessary for her to accept the escort of her brother.

In the midst of this tirade, the door to the drawing room opened and Lord Carmody ushered in his male guests. Leanora looked up, met Deverell's searching gaze, and an inexplicable desire for his company swept over her like a wave crashing on the shore.

He started toward her, and she looked quickly away, back to Eliza Carmody. With every ounce of her resolution, she fought to overcome the urge to meet his eyes. It was too tempting, and potentially too dangerous. She could easily lose herself in their dark depths, and she found the prospect unnerving. Never before had she felt such a strong desire to just gaze at a man. Not even Vincent.

Deverell had barely joined her when the double doors at the

107

opposite end of the room were thrown wide by liveried footmen and Lady Carmody rose and announced that the entertainment would now begin.

"For I hope to persuade many of you to honor us with your musical talents this evening. And to start us off, my own dear Eliza shall perform upon the harp."

A number of her guests gave at least the appearance of looking forward to this rare treat, and the rest had little choice but to follow along politely. Leanora found herself seated between her aunt and Reggie, with Deverell on his other side. She was glad of this and took the opportunity of ringing a silent peal over her own head for the shocking behavior of her wayward senses. She could not like Deverell, she reminded herself firmly. To be attracted to the man who had virtually caused Vincent's death was ludicrous!

After Eliza's quite creditable performance, another young lady was led forward and induced to sing a lovely old ballad while accompanied by her sister on the pianoforte. Leanora forced herself to concentrate on the sweet, lilting voice, and tried not to wonder whether or not Deverell enjoyed it. After all, that was a matter of complete indifference to her.

When at last an interlude was called, Deverell took Reggie with him to carry punch to the ladies. Resolutely, Leanora turned her back on them so that she could not watch his powerful figure making its purposeful way through the milling guests. Suddenly restless, she rose and wandered about the room until she found herself standing next to Julia.

"A delightful evening, is it not?" her sister-in-law remarked with a noticeable lack of enthusiasm.

Leanora could not help but smile. "It is. Though it feels strange to go out in company when my father is still not himself."

Impulsively, Julia clasped her hand. "Poor Leanora. It is too dreadful. And though Gregory tries so very hard to hide it, I know he worries terribly. Please, do not be vexed that he does not come more often to Berkeley Square."

"He was always one to avoid any emotional display," Leanora commented dryly.

Julia flushed. "He dislikes it of all things," she agreed in hollow voice. "I fear it—it makes him acutely uncomfortable."

Leonora bit her lip, vexed to have distressed the lovely Julia. If Gregory was ignoring her, she would comb his hair with a joint stool, to use his own parlance, and at the earliest opportunity. If he was indeed experiencing monetary problems, he would do better to talk it over with his wife than to throw up a wall between them. Julia, despite her undeniable beauty, was no pea-goose. More than once she had proved herself to be quick-witted and practical. Gregory should treat her as an ally rather than keep her in ignorance.

"I suppose he will—" Leonora broke off, for Lord Kennington bore down in their direction. Would he speak to Julia? she wondered. To her surprise, he accorded them the barest nod and walked past.

"How odd!" she declared without thinking.

"What is?" Julia looked at her enquiringly.

Did her voice sound too casual? Leonora shot her a piercing glance but found that her sister-in-law had already turned away. "Lord Kennington," she said. "He did not stop to speak to us."

Julia shrugged. "I would have thought it odder if he had! Or have you taken to consorting with the Opposition?"

"No, though I have . . ." she broke off, a slight smile curving her lips, "run into him several times of late."

"He seems most uncivil," Julia retorted with a total lack of interest. "Gregory and I are barely on speaking terms with him."

She moved off then, leaving Leonora staring after her in surprise. That had not been the impression she had gained in the Park the other day. She found this unsettling and strolled off on her own to consider the matter. The chatter in the drawing room distracted her, so she crossed the hall into the Conservatory, a large room almost buried in plants, overlooking the back of the house.

The door stood open a crack, and as she pushed it, the sound of carefully modulated voices reached her. She would have withdrawn, for it was obvious that an argument took place, but she stopped as she recognized Lord Petersham's angry tones.

"Let me remind you that my position is unassailable!"

"No man's is" came Kennington's amused response.

"This is little more than polite blackmail!" Petersham went on.

"No, would you use such a term? It is hardly that. I merely make suggestions." Leanora could almost hear the smile in his voice.

Petersham gave an uneasy laugh. "You are talking nonsense. May I remind you that if you try anything so—so foolhardy, I can—and will!—create such a scandal that it will ruin your career!"

"Will you, my dear Petersham? Now, why do I not believe you?" Kennington's laugh was far from pleasant. "If we are to talk of scandals. . . ."

"There is no need," Petersham broke in hastily, almost blustering.

Leanora, forgetting the proprieties, leaned closer to the door. She could not hear the exchange that followed, but it was punctuated by a spluttering protest from Petersham. This he followed with a rush of words, from which she only caught "funds" and something about "selling out."

Footsteps approached the door, and Leanora, deeply aware of the impropriety of her eavesdropping, hurried away. Disturbed, she returned to the drawing rooms where a sudden silence indicated that the music was about to begin again. What lay between Petersham and Kennington? Here was an ill-matched pair indeed, and it had sounded like threats on both sides. She could not like it, considering the opposing political importance of these two gentlemen. There were already too many problems at the Home Office, what with the missing funds and papers, Holloway's death and her father's accident.

"Can you not face the prospect of more ballads?" Deverell, a glass of punch in his hand, leaned negligently against the doorjamb, just inside the room where a young lady was taking up her position at the pianoforte. "You look positively ferocious."

Leanora looked up, startled, and encountered a considering glint in his dark eyes. "Do I?" she asked as lightly as she could manage. "How unkind of you to point it out."

110

That drew a deep chuckle from him. "Here," he said, handing her the glass. "I believe I went to fetch this for you a little while ago."

"Oh!" she exclaimed, stricken. "I am so sorry. I—I started wandering, to think. . . ."

"To worry, you mean." He placed her free hand on his arm and led her to one of the few remaining seats as the young lady struck the opening chords of her piece. "We shall have to do a better job of diverting your mind. You cannot spend all of your time distressed."

"Oh, can't I?" she murmured to herself, then realized that he had heard. His hand came up to cover hers with the briefest of touches, then dropped away. Still, she felt immeasurably better, comforted in some intangible way, and realized it was because he was offering her his support. Not, of course, that she would allow herself to take advantage of this, but oh! for a moment it was tempting.

It took only another moment for her to realize she was doing precisely what she had vowed not to do: spending the evening in Deverell's pocket. A soft flush of mortification left her cheeks burning. It would seem to him as if she had emerged from her self-imposed seclusion for the sole purpose of casting out lures to him!

As soon as a brief lull occurred in the performances, she excused herself to her companion and went to join her aunt. In an undervoice, she suggested it was time for them to take their leave.

"For I cannot be comfortable so far from home, dearest Aunt. There is Lady Carmody now. Please, say we may go."

Mrs. Ashton gave vent to a deep sigh, but agreed. Their hostess exclaimed in dismay, and in the same sentence assured them that she understood perfectly how it was and added her sincere hope that they would find Lord Sherborne much improved upon their return. In record time, their barouche drew up before the door.

"You are leaving so soon?" Deverell's deep voice sounded beside Leanora. She looked up into his dark eyes and for the briefest of moments gained the impression that he was not quite pleased. It must have been a trick of the light, for at once

111

a smile twisted his lips upward. "Will you allow me to escort you home?"

"It is not in the least necessary," she told him curtly. "Your carriage. . . ."

"I walked. I have taken lodgings not far from here." He must have sensed her hesitation, for he turned to her aunt and repeated his offer.

Mrs. Ashton cast a measuring glance at Leanora and accepted with an enthusiasm that could only have been gratifying to the gentleman. "For if you are leaving anyway, then it is not as if we are taking you away from the party, which is a thing I could not want to do. I cannot deny that I always feel so much safer with the escort of a gentleman, for you must know I have the greatest dread of footpads and Mohocks. Not, of course, that we see very many of those in London these days, but in my youth they were rampant!" Somehow, as they entered the vehicle, she managed to take the facing seat, leaving Deverell to sit beside her niece.

Resolutely, Leanora turned to stare out the window. After several moments of silence, Mrs. Ashton admirably filled the gap by chatting to Deverell about the dinner and the ability—or lack thereof—of the various performers. Leanora sank back in her corner and tried very hard not to look at, or even think about, Captain Lord Deverell. She was behaving like an infatuated fool, falling victim to the aura of energy and mystery that hung about him. She was not normally one to make such a cake of herself. What had Reggie called her? Up to snuff, a right knowing one? Well, as of now, she would stop allowing her errant senses to rule her normally intelligent mind!

Unfortunately for this decision, they were still several blocks from Berkeley Square, which provided her ample time to fall back under the powerful spell of his presence. Against her explicit orders, her thoughts errantly wandered about their forbidden, enticing subject who sat so close beside her.

At last the carriage pulled up before Sherborne House. The front door, to Leanora's surprise, remained firmly closed. No Tremly to greet them, no footman to run down the steps and assist them to alight from the coach.

Deverell sprang out, then turned to perform this office for Mrs. Ashton and saw her safely to the paving. Leanora stepped down quickly before he could assist her as well.

A slight frown creased her brow as she regarded the dark front of the house. Had something happened within, something that claimed the servants' attention? Had her father at last taken a turn for the better—or worse? Panic gripped her, and she ran up the steps.

The door, fortunately, had been left on the latch. A candle burned low on the hall table, not yet replaced. And Tremly was not in sight. She rushed for the stairs, heard a noise from above and dashed headlong as far as the first landing. Ahead of her, just coming down, she saw the tall, angular figure of Mr. Edmonton.

"Is my father all right?" she cried.

He stopped, surprised. "Yes. I have just come from his room." Her distress dawned on him, and he came quickly to her side, taking her hands in his. "Has something happened?"

She shook her head, almost laughing in her sudden relief. "No. But—but Tremly did not come to the door, and we saw no servants, and I feared. . . ." She broke off, unable to voice the horror that had engulfed her.

He patted her hand gently and led her back down to where Mrs. Ashton stood in the hall, bewildered, clutching Deverell's supporting arm.

"Where is everyone?" that lady demanded. "Leanora, where is Tremly? It is most odd in him not to have been at the door, though to be sure, he had no way of knowing when we would return. But he always seems to know, which is one of the things that makes him such a particularly good butler, though of course there are other things equally important; and I have no idea why. . . ." She broke off as Deverell neatly disengaged himself and strode over to where Leanora and Mr. Edmonton extracted tapers from a drawer in the hall table.

"Whatever are you doing, my love?" Mrs. Ashton wailed.

"They are about to look for your butler, I believe." It was Deverell who responded.

"I saw him less than half an hour ago in the dining room," Mr. Edmonton put in, "polishing silver while he awaited

113

your return."

"Did you leave a candle burning in my father's study?" Leanora asked suddenly. "There is a light back there."

Mr. Edmonton frowned. "I did not go in there this evening. I worked in my own room, but I extinguished the candles when I left."

Deverell had already started down the hall toward the back of the house, and Leanora and Edmonton hurried after him. The door to Lord Sherborne's study stood slightly ajar, allowing a thin stream of pale light to seep out into the hall. Deverell pushed it back, then froze on the threshold.

Leanora, standing on tiptoe to see over his massive shoulders, gasped at the total chaos that met her gaze. Books and papers were scattered about, thrown at random. Several chairs had been flung on the floor, their backs and seats slashed and their padding torn loose. And sprawled in the center of the room, with blood seeping sluggishly from a gash in the back of his balding head, lay Tremly.

Chapter 8

Leanora stared, immobilized by shock, then shoved the massive figure of Deverell out of her way and rushed forward. She fell to her knees beside the still form of the butler, only to find herself neatly set aside. Deverell took her place, his careful fingers seeking the feeble pulse. Reassured that the man was alive, he felt around the back of his head. A large swelling rose about a puckered gash, and blood dripped slowly into a brownish pool on the dark green carpet. He turned him over gently, pulling a fallen pillow from one of the chairs to cushion his head.

"I—I will send for the doctor." Mr. Edmonton, his face unnaturally pale, turned from the room and hurried back up the hall.

Leanora rose slowly. "We—we need a cold wet towel to hold against that wound," she said shakily. And she would have to tell Mrs. Tremly. . . .

A shocked exclamation from the doorway warned Leanora that this task was no longer necessary. Her gaze flew to the housekeeper, who clutched at the jamb for support, her eyes wide with horror as she stared at her husband's fallen form. Leanora went to her, took her hands and led her to a chair that Deverell righted for them. The woman dropped into it and raised frightened eyes to her mistress.

"When—when Mr. Edmonton came to the servant's hall and sent a footman for the doctor, never did I believe it was for my poor Tremly. Oh, Miss Leanora, they do say that tragedies

115

happen in threes, and what with his lordship first, and now Tremly. . . ." She swallowed hard. "I dare not think what may happen next," she wailed.

Leanora stared at her. "But they are not connected! Surely, you cannot believe. . . ." She broke off, and her frightened gaze met Deverell's grim expression. The housekeeper referred to an old superstition, but the thought her words had conjured up for Leanora was too terrible to be believed. It had to be utter nonsense!

A low moan from the floor interrupted her wildly leaping imagination, and both she and the housekeeper went to Tremly's side. His eyes opened but remained blurred, unfocussed. Slowly, he shook his head as if to clear a fuddled mind. He winced and lay still once more.

These signs of returning life buoyed his wife. With a recollection of what was necessary, she bustled off to the kitchens to obtain a compress to hold to Tremly's head. Leanora sank down into the chair the housekeeper had vacated and stared about the room. Deverell stood amid the litter, his expression a thoughtful mask.

When Mr. Edmonton returned, carrying a basin of water for Mrs. Tremly, Leanora went to find her aunt and explain what had occurred. This so shocked the woman, who had retreated to her dressing room, that she collapsed upon the day bed there and Leanora was obliged to locate her vinaigrette and hold it for her while her abigail went in search of feathers to burn.

It was some time later before Leanora was once again able to return downstairs to find out how Tremly went on. She found him sitting in one of the righted chairs with the doctor at his side. Deverell and Edmonton wandered about the room, examining the damage.

The doctor glanced up as she entered, then returned his attention to his patient. He shook his head as he examined the swelling. "You'll have a bad head for a while," he declared with irritating cheerfulness, and began to smear an evil-smelling salve over the gash. "Could be worse, though. Consider yourself lucky and take it easy for a few days. No lasting harm done."

The butler raised his eyes, caught sight of Leanora and at

once tried to rise to his feet. He was prevented from this both by his own weakness and the doctor's firm hand on his shoulder, and he sank back down, defeated.

"I am sorry, Miss Leanora. I have made a dreadful mull of the business."

"Nonsense!" she declared. "All that matters is that you will be all right. When you are feeling better, you will tell us what happened."

"I am deeply ashamed, Miss Leanora. I never suspected what was toward." He put his hands to his aching head. "Never did I think to fail you so completely."

"You have done no such thing," Leanora assured him, touched by the butler's devotion to what he felt to be his duty.

"How did this come about?" Deverell asked sharply.

The butler raised his head to look at him but did not question his undeniable air of command. "It was while I was locking up, sir. I noticed a light flickering back here and assumed it must be Mr. Edmonton. I came to see if there was anything he might be needing, but the room was empty. I went in to snuff out the candle, and that is all I remember. Someone must have hit me from behind."

"And rather hard, too," the doctor commented. He fastened a piece of sticking plaster over the wound, then secured another. "I recommend you spend the next couple of days in bed."

"But I cannot!" Tremly exclaimed, horrified. He turned too quickly to face the doctor and was obliged to hold his head in his hands once more until the throbbing settled.

"Of course you will," Leanora said at once. "Mrs. Tremly will oversee the setting of everything to rights, and you may relay your instructions to the footmen through her. Now, Mr. Edmonton, if you will assist the doctor, I believe we should get him to his room."

Edmonton, returning to the study a bare half hour later, discovered Leanora and Deverell kneeling on the floor as they sifted through the scattered papers. "I thought you'd be here," he commented.

She almost jumped. "I—I did not hear you. You might have been anyone, coming up behind us." She sat back on her heels

117

but could not repress the shiver that ran through her.

"No one is likely to try again on the same night," Deverell pointed out dryly. He came stiffly to his feet, then assisted her to rise as well.

"It is a simple break-in," Mr. Edmonton enunciated carefully. "Come, let us look in the other rooms to see what has been taken."

Leanora threw an uncertain look at Deverell. "Yes," she agreed shakily. "And—and send for the Runners."

To her relief, Deverell offered to accompany them on their search of the house. It was ridiculous of her to still feel nervous, as if housebreakers lurked behind every door, waiting only for some unwary soul to enter before bashing them over the head with whatever was handy. There was something so very reassuring about the captain's size. She doubted that anyone would tackle him without due deliberation.

They began the tour in the front saloons, but found these to be undisturbed. The dining room, however, showed signs of a hasty going over—too hasty, it seemed to Leanora. The lock on the drawer that contained the silver had been forced, and its contents scattered haphazardly about, but it did not appear as if much were missing. Several of the salt dishes that had been displayed across the back of the buffet were no longer there—but some remained.

The only other room that appeared to have been touched was Mr. Edmonton's study. Here, also, signs of a thorough search could be seen, for books and papers had been scattered almost as freely as in Lord Sherborne's room.

"We—we had better not touch anything until the Runners arrive, Miss Leanora," Mr. Edmonton said.

She stood in the center of his study but turned to face him thoughtfully. "This is no ordinary robbery," she said to herself, then could have bitten her tongue as she realized she had spoken the indiscreet words aloud.

Mr. Edmonton hesitated, then removed his spectacles with deliberation and began to polish them with a handkerchief he drew from his pocket.

Deverell filled the uncomfortable gap. "You are suggesting that someone broke in here with the express purpose of

118

stealing Lord Sherborne's papers."

"No! That is—" She broke off, distressed, for that was exactly what she meant.

Mr. Edmonton returned his spectacles to his nose and regarded the black-haired giant who stood near the door. "We need hardly tell you that this might prove to be a sensitive matter. You must forgive us; you find us somewhat shaken this evening."

A slight smile played about Deverell's lips, as if at some secret joke. "I know how to keep my tongue," he assured the ruffled secretary. "If you would prefer it, I shall take my leave. But you agree with me, do you not?"

Edmonton hesitated, then nodded. "I wish I did not, though," he admitted.

"Oh, it is absurd!" Leanora declared, forgetting for the moment that it was she who had made the initial suggestion.

"A normal thief would not have ransacked these two studies," Deverell told her. "He might have gone for the locked drawers in Sherborne's desk, looking for household money, but he would never have torn the rooms apart like that."

Restless, Leanora took several strides about the room, righting a chair in her way as she did so. "Tremly must have surprised the man after he had already searched in here," she said slowly.

"He must have gone to Sherborne's study next." Deverell took up where she left off. "He hit the butler, finished in there, then took a few things from the dining room to make it look like a normal robbery."

Leanora eyed him, dismayed, for this tallied with her own suspicions. She looked at Mr. Edmonton and found that he was frowning. "You do not agree?"

"I do," he said slowly. "But why? What could someone have wanted so badly?"

She shook her head. "Someone must believe that Pappa has something of vital importance. Those horrid papers we have been unable to find, most likely. Oh!" she exclaimed suddenly, vexed. "None of this makes any sense! What could someone want so desperately? Why is everyone interested in papers all at once? Between Petersham, Sir William and Kennington, we've had a never-ending stream of people parading through here demanding to . . ." she broke off, then continued in an odd voice, "demanding to search Pappa's study."

Mr. Edmonton nodded. "Yes."

"Everyone else seems to want them; why not our housebreaker?" she asked flippantly, trying to disguise from herself the fear that began to take root in her heart. Tremly, struck down viciously to keep him from interrupting the search. And her father. . . . What if someone believed Lord Sherborne to be a danger to them, because of his possessing some mysterious paper? Could it have been cause enough to try to silence the earl? Permanently? She closed her eyes, again seeing the maddened horses bearing down on her father, the heavy coach they drew rocking and pitching at a wild angle.

It was impossible! Only a madman—or a very desperate one—would have attempted anything so dangerous and uncertain. How could anyone know that Lord Sherborne would be in the center of the street at the precise moment. . . .

She shivered, her skin cold and clammy as the blood drained away. Someone had called to her father, someone who remained hidden in the shadows across the street, luring the earl into the path of the carriage. What had become of that man? She had thought of nothing but her father, not reflected back over this strange circumstance of the "accident."

And then there was Mr. Holloway's death. . . . What if that had nothing to do with those missing funds? As her father's clerk, he could have seen any of those papers that she had picked up that day in Whitehall. Or someone might have believed that he had—

"Lady Leanora?" Deverell's deep, gentle voice sounded above her.

She looked up, surprised to discover that she had sat down on a hard-backed Chippendale chair. Deverell held out a glass to her, and she took it, taking a cautious sip as she recognized the pungent odor of brandy. She choked on the amber liquid, took another swallow quickly and felt the burning sensation race down her throat, warming her and steadying her nerves.

"It is all nonsense!" she declared hotly. "I am being foolish

120

beyond permission to even consider it!"

Deverell righted another of the chairs and settled down at her side. He took a long swallow from his own brandy glass, then turned to regard her worried face. "Consider what?"

She opened her mouth to tell him, but a soft cough from Mr. Edmonton caused her to break off. Color flamed hotly in her cheeks, and a strange iciness slid down her throat into the pit of her stomach, dispersing the warmth of the brandy. Her wretched tongue, running away with her so! She must be shattered, indeed, by the events of the last few days to so far forget herself!

"It would seem that I am being indiscreet," Deverell murmured, his eyes dancing as they took in her discomfiture. "My lady, forgive me for asking questions you do not feel yourself capable of answering. If all is now under control here . . . ?" He raised a questioning eyebrow at Edmonton.

Lord Sherborne's secretary eyed Deverell consideringly. "I believe it is," he said slowly. "I am grateful for your support."

"As am I," Leanora said stiffly, annoyed by her gaucheness. She had as good as informed him that she did not trust him. And much to her dismay, she discovered that she had a very strong desire to take him fully into her confidence and seek his guidance. He looked such a capable man. But Vincent had trusted him, and only see where that had led!

Deverell smiled, and somehow it seemed as if he understood her dilemma. "I shall take my leave of you. I am sure there are matters that will best be discussed between just the two of you. If I may, I shall call tomorrow to see how you go on."

"Yes, thank you." For some reason, she was relieved that he had not taken offense.

Mr. Edmonton escorted him back to the hall and saw him out, then returned to where Leanora still sat in his study. Closing the door behind himself, he turned to face her. "What occurred to you?" he asked directly.

She threw him a shaky smile. "Thank you for stopping me from blurting it out."

"I must say, it is difficult *not* to trust Captain Lord Deverell," he said musingly. "He appears to be a truly admirable gentleman in every respect."

121

She considered telling Mr. Edmonton the truth but realized it was not her right to disclose Deverell's secret work to anyone. Instead, she said: "We really do not know much about him, except that he is a friend of Reggie's—and Vincent's."

Mr. Edmonton emitted a strangled sound. She looked up and encountered the amused cynicism of his expression. Edmonton was right. Association with Reggie could hardly be considered a recommendation in this case. Or with Vincent, for that matter, for throughout his life he had been almost as erratic as his young brother.

Edmonton picked up the decanter and poured a liberal dose of brandy into the glass Leanora held. Still shaking, she managed to swallow a sip and almost at once felt steadier. Another swallow did the trick, and she leaned back against the cushions, exhausted.

She gestured toward the chair that Deverell had drawn up to hers, and Edmonton seated himself. Weighing her words with care, she told him of her suspicions concerning Mr. Holloway and her father's accident. "Now please," she begged as she finished, "tell me I am being absurd. No one would murder Pappa's clerk for such a reason, and that runaway carriage cannot have been a deliberate attempt on his life!"

He rubbed his chin thoughtfully. "I wish I could be sure," he admitted at last. "I don't like any of this."

She let out a deep breath. "But who would do such a thing? There must have been an overwhelming reason! Lord Petersham? The idea is ridiculous! Lord Kennington is a better candidate! Or perhaps we should suspect Sir William, or better yet, Gregory!"

Mr. Edmonton allowed himself a tight-lipped smile. "I would be more inclined to agree that it is all nonsense if Lord Sherborne's accident had been less serious. The doctor did not say so in your presence, but it is nothing short of a miracle that your father is still alive."

Leanora took a gulp of the amber fluid in the cut-crystal glass. "I—I had guessed as much."

Mr. Edmonton reached across, covering her hand for a moment. "Go upstairs," he directed. "I will deal with the Runners. You must be fagged to death."

"I—I would like to see my father," she admitted. "Mr. Edmonton, if this was no ordinary robbery, but involves some sensitive government matter. . . ." She allowed her sentence to trail off as they regarded each other.

He nodded. "We had best mention nothing of papers to the Runners."

"Thank you," she said, relieved. "If we are right, the less publicity the matter receives, the better. I wish we had not said so much before Lord Deverell. We must turn it over to the proper authorities as soon as possible."

At that, a slight smile crossed his lips again. "Not Bow Street. I strongly suspect they lack the finesse needed in such a case as this."

Secure in the knowledge that Mr. Edmonton would prove more than capable of dealing with the Runners, Leanora made her way up to her father's bedchamber. Pagget looked up as she entered, eager to hear news of what had occurred below stairs. Artaxerxes sprang to his feet and ran to her, the whole little dog shivering in his welcoming fervor. She scooped him up, holding him close as she told Pagget what had occurred. She made no mention of her fears, but her eyes remained on the immobile serenity of her father's countenance.

To whom should she turn with her suspicions? Feeling suddenly very much alone, she tried to consider with care. Lord Petersham? He would be the proper person, of course, but she hesitated from following such a course. A close acquaintance with him over the past few years had done nothing to encourage her to have much faith in his abilities. He was the perfect figurehead, if one delved no deeper. Her father had the disconcerting habit of referring to him as "that old bumbler." And now, there was that strange association with Kennington that left her uneasy.

Then what of Sir William Holborne, Lord Petersham's assistant? He might be at heart a dandy, but that said nothing against his intelligence. To the Polite World he appeared little more than an amusing rattle, but Leanora had been acquainted with him any time these last six years and knew well that his foppish exterior hid an alert mind and quick wit. He could probably advise her.

Strain and the lateness of the hour finally took their toll. Dropping a kiss on her father's pale forehead, she restored the puppy to his side and left to seek her bed. But in spite of her exhaustion, sleep did not come easily nor stay for long. She tossed restlessly throughout much of the night and rose, not much rested, when the first meager rays of the sun seeped into her chamber.

If she had hoped that the more rational light of morning might make her fears of the night before seem ludicrous, she was wrong. Tremly's absence from the breakfast parlor, where normally he would have been arranging pots of coffee and chocolate, brought it all back to her with terrible reality. She could only be glad that her aunt would not yet be astir, for she doubted her ability to follow the thread of that garrulous lady's rambling chatter this morning.

A short while later, she was made to feel very guilty for this sentiment. Mrs. Ashton sent a message to her, by way of her abigail Sutton, saying that she was far too distressed by the events of the last few days and would remain in her room.

Leanora rose at once to go to her but paused just inside the entrance to the breakfast parlor as a loud knocking from below indicated the arrival of a visitor. She had no desire to speak to anyone, so she stayed where she was, dismissing Sutton to return to her mistress. In only a few minutes, Leanora heard measured footsteps crossing the hall, then a slight creak as the massive front door opened.

A moment of silence followed, then Gregory's strained tones reached her. "Good morning, Charles," he greeted the senior footman who now stood in for the invalided butler. "Where's Tremly?"

"There—there have been certain goings on here, Master Gregory," Charles informed him in what he obviously hoped was a properly impressive tone.

"Have there?" Gregory came into the hall, divesting himself of his hat and cane. "Where's my sister?"

"Up here, Gregory," Leanora called, stepping out onto the landing. "Do come up and have some coffee."

Gregory turned to look up at her where she leaned over the

railing. "Good God, Nora! You look a fright!" Her loving brother bounded up the stairs two at a time and grasped her hands as he reached her side. "Not another accident, is it?"

"Worse! No, I do not mean that, of course. Poor Pappa! But someone broke into the house last night and hit poor Tremly over the head."

Gregory let out a long whistle. "Did they, by Jove! No wonder the place is at sixes and sevens. Where's that coffee you promised? Come on, I want to hear the whole!" He dragged her back with him into the sunny parlor.

She poured each of them cups of the steaming brew, then reviewed, as briefly as possible, the events of the night before. Only her suspicions did she omit. Gregory sat quietly throughout the whole, listening with an unusual interest, then shook his head as she came to the end.

"Can't say I like that above half! Lucky thing that fellow Deverell was here to give you a hand." He fell silent a moment, frowning. "*Why* was he here?" he demanded suddenly. "Dash it all, Nora, don't seem to be quite the thing, the man escorting you home and coming in like that."

That idea had already occurred to her, but it did not please her to discover that it seemed peculiar to someone else. "I am sure there was nothing the least bit odd about it. He was bored and wished to leave, and we offered a convenient excuse. And as for his coming in, I believe my aunt dragged him inside when she realized something was amiss."

Gregory shook his head. "Too smokey by half, Nora. Not like you to take up with strange men like that."

Delicate color warmed her cheeks. "I did not 'take up' with him at all! You make it sound improper! He was a friend of Vincent's, you know."

At that, Gregory let out a tight bark of laughter. "Lord, Nora, what a goose you are! Bunch of care-for-nobodies, Vincent's lot. Ramshackle, that's what they were. You take my advice, my girl, and have nothing further to do with this fellow."

"You speak from experience?" she shot back, angered by his words.

He stiffened, then his features relaxed. "Well," he admitted, "I'm no saint, but I'm no vulgar make-bait, either."

"And Captain Lord Deverell is?" she asked with deceptive sweetness.

Gregory crossed to the sideboard, found a decanter of brandy and poured a shot into his coffee. He returned to the table, apparently still considering her question. "Can't say that I really know him," he said at last.

"This is getting us nowhere," she exclaimed. She set down her cup with unnecessary force. Why was Gregory so ready to discredit a man he hardly knew? That her own feelings about Deverell were uncertain in the extreme she now ignored.

She cast a shrewd glance at her scapegrace brother. He looked terribly strained and unwell this morning. What had he been up to last night? The thought that flickered across her mind was too terrible to contemplate, but still it intruded, nudging at her, demanding her attention. She lowered her eyes, concentrating on the swirling liquid in her cup. Would— *could*—Gregory have staged a fake robbery to cover his own thefts from the house? More money, or those papers. . . . Instantly she was ashamed of herself for letting such a disloyal thought so much as enter her mind.

She looked back up at Gregory and found him watching her with a strange, closed expression on his face. Abruptly she stood and crossed with agitated steps to the sideboard. Picking up a roll, she looked at it and then set it back.

"We—we have turned the matter over to Bow Street, so they may handle it now. You did not go to Lady Carmody's last night." This last was said with an attempt at casualness, and she had the satisfaction—and relief—of seeing her brother relax somewhat.

"No. Don't care for that sort of thing. Had some private matters that I needed to take care of."

"You did not miss much," Leanora conceded. "I believe poor Julia regretted going."

At that, Gregory sat up. "Julia was there?" he demanded. His brow snapped down in displeasure.

Leanora blinked at him. "But of course. Did you not know— or did you forget?"

"That's it," Gregory declared, seeming relieved to have this excuse for his ignorance provided. "Did—she didn't go alone, did she?"

"No, of course not. Dalmouth was with her."

If she had hoped that this would relieve her brother's mind of the fear that his wife had sought the escort of one of her *cicisbei*, she was mistaken. His color darkened alarmingly to an almost purple hue, and for a moment she thought his tightly clenching fingers must snap the delicate china handle of the cup he clutched.

"Dalmouth, eh?" he breathed coldly.

"For heaven's sake, Gregory, he's her brother! Who else should escort her when you must be away?"

"Damned loose screw!" Gregory snapped. "He may be her brother and a viscount, but that don't make him acceptable! She should have called on you!"

"We had no idea until the last moment that we would attend," Leanora told him soothingly. Here was a new comeout! She had believed that perfect harmony marked her brother's relationship with Dalmouth. If this were no longer the case, she could only be glad.

"Did he stay with her, or wander off?"

Leanora considered. "I don't really remember. There was a musical portion to the evening—"

"I suppose she was the center of attention," he broke in.

"Julia has always had a great many admirers," she replied tentatively, not wanting to cause trouble.

"*Male* admirers," he said shortly. He lapsed into silence, brooding.

"Naturally. Very few young ladies dare risk comparison with her," Leanora assured him breezily. "She takes the shine out of the lot of them."

His lips twitched slightly. On the whole, Leanora was not displeased by his reaction. If he were beginning to worry that his wife was developing a roving eye, it might make him more attentive to her. Or was there a particular basis for his annoyance? The thought was unpleasant, but she could believe it of a man as ramshackle as Dalmouth to help his sister cover up an amatory indiscretion. With someone like Kennington, perhaps?

Leanora took a deep breath as the thought took hold. Unless she was very much mistaken, she greatly feared that an irreparable rift might be forming between her brother and his wife.

Chapter 9

As soon as Gregory took his leave, Leanora retired to her father's room where she relieved the tired valet from his vigil at the earl's side. The puppy, after barreling up to her and snuffling noisily as she rubbed his head, retired to a corner to finish an extremely thorough job of shredding a stocking.

Leanora sank into her chair and picked up her neglected needlework. For some time she sat with her needle suspended in midair, considering her various problems. And at the moment, Gregory came at the head of this list.

It had been Lord Sherborne's idea to send his heir into the country to manage the Abbey, where he could not get into serious trouble. On the whole, this plan still seemed the best. But how could she broach it to him, make the idea acceptable? Gregory would never leave London as long as their father remained so ill.

Of Deverell she tried steadfastly not to think, but it proved a losing battle. Now that she had talked to him about Vincent, she felt a strange bond with him. And that, to her dismay, made it easier for his undeniable masculine appeal to wreak havoc on her normally well-behaved senses. In truth, she found that she liked him far too well.

But she could not escape the fact that there were certain mysteries surrounding him. He was present at the Home Office in Whitehall, yet neither Petersham nor Sir William seemed to know anything about him. She had seen him talking to Lord Kennington, but not since that time had either gentleman openly acknowledged the other. Deverell was one subject on which she had trouble thinking clearly, and at the moment she was not even up to making the attempt.

Nor had she yet told anyone her fears and suspicions about the housebreaking, or about Mr. Holloway and her father's accident. She must see Sir William, but she did not look forward to his inevitable laughter if he refused to take her seriously.

She felt a touch on her leg and looked down to see the pug sitting before her with a hopeful expression on his comical face. She scooped him up, scrubbed him behind the ears, and he panted happily. Her lips curved in a slight smile. "Well, Artaxerxes? Heavens, what a mouthful your name is. Shall we shorten it? Arty?" She considered. "No, Xerk. You are definitely a Xerk."

The puppy shivered all over with enthusiasm at this abbreviation of his name, and she hugged him tightly, finding comfort from his company.

Toward the early afternoon, Mrs. Ashton entered the chamber on tiptoe. She sank into the empty chair on the opposite side of the great bed and stared down at her brother-in-law with misty eyes. "If only our presence *could* disturb him," she sighed.

"It will," Leanora responded firmly. She hugged the little puppy, which dozed peacefully in her lap. "And then we will be in constant terror of making any noise in here. But, oh! how glad I will be when that happens."

They lapsed into silence, each engaged in her embroidery. This was an occupation that could not hold Leanora's interest, and her mind returned to her suspicions. *Should* she tell Sir William, or was it all nothing more than her overactive imagination and nerves? Irresolute, she threw the delicate handkerchief down in disgust.

"When Paggets returns, would you care to drive in the Park?" she asked.

Mrs. Ashton blanched visibly. Despite Leanora's reputation as an excellent whip, her doting aunt could never contemplate her dangerous high-perch phaeton with any degree of equanimity. She set another stitch carefully, avoiding her niece's sparkling eye. "If it is all the same, my love, I believe I will stay here. But why not send a message to Reggie? I am sure he would be only too happy to bear you company."

The prospect of a turn about the Park with Reggie, who would take the opportunity to scrutinize and discuss in detail the attire of every gentleman they passed, was more than Leanora could bear. She did not press her aunt further, and as soon as the valet took her place, she retired to her room to change her gown. What she really wanted, of course, was a long gallop. The image of riding *ventre a terre* through the Park, and the subsequent scandal such behavior would cause, brought a fleeting smile to her lips. In her present mood it was too tempting. She had better confine herself to her carriage.

As she was about to send a message to the stables requesting her groom to bring the phaeton around, Charles, the upper footman, announced that Sir William had arrived and awaited her in the Gold Saloon. She jumped to her feet, glad to have her indecision settled for her. She would speak to him at once. Snatching up her driving gloves, she hurried down to her visitor.

She strode into the saloon, tossed the kid leather gloves onto a table and went up to him, her hand extended. "Sir William, how fortunate that you called. There is a matter I would like to discuss with you."

He turned from his contemplation of his reflection in the gilded mirror and raised her fingers to his lips. "How delightfully refreshing! Leanora, my love, I am all admiration. A lady who is not afraid to say what she feels!"

She would not let his snide humor divert her. "Do be seated. I assure you, I quite meant what I said. I have been on the verge of sending for you several times this day."

"Then do me the honor of driving with me."

Leanora agreed at once, and they went out to the street where Sir William's groom stood, holding the heads of a pair of long-legged chestnuts harnessed to his curricle. She mounted into this vehicle, and Sir William joined her and took the reins.

"How may I be of service to you?" he asked as soon as his horses were set in motion.

"Tell me how things go on at the Home Office," she said by

way of an opening. After all, one did not start screaming espionage and murder without some preamble.

To her surprise, Sir William laughed. "Are you still worried about those papers that have gone missing? My dear Leanora, you may dismiss them from your mind."

"But—" She turned to stare at him, wide-eyed. "But Lord Petersham—"

"You are suffering from a visit by him, I can tell!" His voice still quivered with his amusement. "I assure you, only in his eyes are those documents important."

"But there has been such a fuss! And you were anxious to recover them, as well!"

"Only on Petersham's orders. When I questioned him more particularly, I discovered that there was nothing in the least bit urgent about the matter. I am sorry if he has distressed you, but you may be easy now."

She blinked, considerably taken aback. Could she dismiss the business from her mind? *Had* it all been imagination and worry over her father? What a precious pack of fools they must have looked, sifting through those ridiculous papers time and again as if the fate of England itself rested on their discovery!

She managed a laugh that sounded artificial to her ears, glad now that she hadn't blurted out any nonsense about murder. "How thankful Mr. Edmonton will be to learn this has all been a hum. And how typical of Petersham to terrify us for nothing!"

Sir William shook his head with mock gravity. "My dearest Leanora, never, but *never* question his dedication to state secrets."

She returned a light answer, asked him about a play that he had attended several nights previously and sat back against the cushioned seat to think while he described this event. She still could scarcely believe it had all been a mere tempest in a teacup. Her father's accident must have been nothing more than an unfortunate occurrence, with no sinister or murderous overtones. Mr. Holloway must have been involved with those missing funds, after all, and the vicious attack on Tremly. . . .

No, that was not altogether innocent. She cast a curious

glance at Sir William, who was now well into a description of the dress and appearance of several notables who had been present at the theatre. She may have been on the wrong track as far as Petersham's documents were concerned, but something had drawn an illicit and dangerous visitor to Sherborne House.

And if not the Home Office papers, then what? Lord Kennington's speech? Or had he carried other papers, of a more sensitive nature, that had become mixed with those that she carried? The only way to learn what was behind all this would be to find the missing sheets, and at the moment she had not a single clue as to their whereabouts. Unless Gregory. . . . No! She shied from that idea, refusing to accept it.

Sir William slowed his horses, and Leanora emerged from her abstraction as she realized they were passing through the gate into the Park. In a matter of minutes, they joined the fashionable throng.

Her companion threw her a sideways glance. "Would you care to avoid the busybodies, or shall we let them stop us and ask impertinent questions?"

She wrinkled her nose. "Let us be no more than commonly polite," she decided. "I do not think I could bear vulgar inquisitiveness today."

They accomplished their purpose with little trouble for two full circles of the Park, and Leanora was beginning to relax, when she saw two gentlemen astride horses bearing down on them. Reggie, atop a neatish black hack, waved to her, but her attention riveted on his companion. Captain Lord Deverell, resplendent in a riding coat of olive-green drab, swayed easily on the back of a playful roan stallion. He brought the animal firmly into line and drew up smoothly at the side of the curricle.

They exchanged greetings, and Sir William gave his chestnuts the office to move on. Neither Reggie nor Deverell seemed the least bit disconcerted, merely turning their horses to ride along with them. Sir William gave vent to a deep sigh, which brought a fleeting smile once more to Leanora's lips.

"That was a dashed unpleasant business last night, Nora," Reggie said. "Dev here has just been telling me about it."

133

"What business?" Sir William demanded, instantly agog with curiosity. "Leanora, my love, have you been keeping secrets from me?"

"No," she assured him, suddenly reluctant to talk about the incident. "Our butler merely surprised a housebreaker and was hit over the head for his efforts."

"Dear me," Sir William murmured, his eyebrows flying upward in comical dismay. "I hope no lasting injury?"

Leanora shook her head, not wanting to discuss it. If she closed her eyes, she could still see Tremly's fallen figure with the blood seeping from the swelling on his head. It left her shaken, feeling ill once more.

"Just an unpleasantness they could easily have done without at the moment," Deverell said smoothly. "I am glad I was able to be of help."

Sir William reined his horses to a stop, turned to Deverell and raised his quizzing glass to better observe the other man. Deverell watched this process with an expression of amused interest, and Sir William allowed the glass to drop. "Just so," he murmured as he started up his pair once more.

Leanora glanced from one to the other, surprised at the thinly veiled animosity displayed on the part of Sir William. Did he object to the aura of amusement that hung about Deverell? His own wit ran more to the derogatory, an appreciation of the failings of society. While Sir William laughed *at* it, she sensed that Deverell would laugh *with* it. This was a very strange distinction, but one of which she had never before been so vividly aware.

"I—how fortunate it is that your injury does not prevent your riding." She rushed into speech, saying the first words that sprang to her mind. Almost immediately she wished them unsaid, for Deverell's humorous eye, alight with enjoyment, came to rest on her. He was fully aware she had spoken to cover Sir William's rudeness!

"Yes," he agreed, and his restrained laughter vibrated from him as tangibly as if it had been released in the deep sound that she should not enjoy so much. "It is a most convenient wound, for I find it only prevents me from doing the things I have no desire to do."

134

"Such as standing up with young ladies at balls?" she asked.

"It is very sad," he agreed, shaking his head in dismay. "I am quite unable to dance a step."

"How fortunate for your partners," Sir William murmured. "Or perhaps how wise of you, to know where you will not appear to good advantage."

Leanora stared at him, shocked by his want of manners. As far as she knew, Deverell had done nothing to earn his censure, yet here he was, ripping out at him as if some unpleasantness lay between them. She shot a quick glance at Deverell, but he remained unperturbed, as if unaware of the dislike directed at him.

"You're out there," Reggie stuck in. "Quite a neat dancer, in the old days. Remember Vincent saying so. Took the shine out of 'em all. Must be all those years nipping about among Boney's troops making you rusty, Dev. Nothing like secret missions to put a fellow off his company manners."

Leanora glanced swiftly up at Deverell and surprised an irritated expression in his normally amused eyes. So Reggie knew of his secret work! She was sure, though, that he never suspected that Vincent had also been involved. But it was not a matter that Deverell wanted discussed, of that she was certain.

"He certainly did help us out last night, and for that I am grateful," Leanora declared warmly, ruthlessly sacrificing herself to take Sir William's suddenly piercing eyes away from Deverell. "I do not know what we would have done without him."

"A man of many talents, it would seem." Sir William directed a long, steady gaze at the other man.

Deverell laughed. "I merely soothed Mrs. Ashton."

"Yes, there is something so very comforting about such a large man," Leanora agreed promptly.

She was rewarded by a swift chuckle on Deverell's part and a reluctant smile from Sir William. The situation, which a moment before had felt uncomfortably charged, now returned to normal.

"You have told me nothing about it, yet," Sir William complained. "Was anything taken?"

"Only some silver. Our butler must have disturbed the men

135

before they could take more. And they ransacked my father's study, but only imagine, they did not have time to find the housekeeping money!"

"You were most fortunate, it would seem. But how distressing, to have such an unpleasantness follow so closely upon your father's terrible accident."

"It was that which made my aunt so particularly grateful for Lord Deverell's presence," she agreed. She cast a sideways glance up at this gentleman and found, to her consternation, that he watched her closely through half-closed lids.

Reggie had fallen silent through most of the last exchange and now leaned over Deverell to address her. "Think I'll come back to the house with you, Nora. Want to see my mother. Must be pretty badly cut up over all this."

"Yes, please do, Reggie." He would monopolize his mother, giving her a respite from that lady's sweet but vacuous and never-ending conversation.

As they neared the gate, Sir William turned his pair toward it. Deverell and Reggie rode with them, but as soon as they reached the street, Deverell took his leave and turned his powerful roan in the opposite direction. Sir William watched him ride off with a brooding look that did not make Leanora feel easy.

"You do not like the captain," she said softly when Reggie was forced to drop behind because of traffic.

"Do I not?" Sir William asked with an air of one considering a momentous problem. "I believe you are right. I most definitely *do* not."

"Why?" She could not contain her curiosity.

Sir William smiled suddenly. "My training is leading me into bad manners. I am suspicious, that is all. I have seen him several times at Whitehall, but I cannot discover, try as I might, who it is he has been visiting. And now to find him upon such easy terms with both you and dear Reginald, with your father so very ill, I began to wonder if he might have . . . an ulterior motive, shall we say?"

"He was a very old friend of Reggie's brother Vincent," Leanora told him. "They were at Eton together, and in the army."

136

Sir William's brow cleared. "So simple an explanation. You must forgive me, my dear. I have been too much in Petersham's company. I am beginning to see state secrets everywhere. Was he really a spy, do you know?"

She hesitated, then nodded. "Vincent told me so," she explained.

Her companion let out a sigh of relief. "Then that settles my worries. If he has been engaged in espionage, then it is only natural he should be poking about Whitehall and no one willing to admit to it." He frowned suddenly in exaggerated and comical dismay. "I suppose I must now beg his pardon for my rudeness."

Leanora laughed, glad to have the reasons for Sir William's dislike of Deverell explained—and resolved. She could not like to have the men enemies, for she very much counted Sir William her friend, and as for Deverell. . . . A soft flush crept into her cheeks, and she spoke hurriedly. "Do not, I beg of you, apologize! I doubt I could bear up under the shock of such an unprecedented spectacle!"

He laughed and, as Reggie drew abreast of them, directed a lighthearted comment toward him. They reached Sherborne House shortly, and after handing Leanora down from his curricle, Sir William drove off to return to the Home Office.

They found Mrs. Ashton reclining upon the day bed in her dressing room. Seeing her son, she emitted a low moan, extended a shaky hand and begged him not to leave her side. Leanora assessed the situation at a glance and slipped away to warn Cook that there would be another cover to set at dinner.

As she emerged from the great kitchens in the basement beneath the house, she saw her housekeeper coming toward her with a purposeful stride. For one moment she nourished a craven impulse to fob her off. She had been through a great deal of late, but then so had the servants, especially Mrs. Tremly. She had ignored normal household matters completely for the last few days, she realized to her dismay.

"Miss Leanora," that determined woman hailed her. "If you have a moment, I was wishful of having a word with you."

"Of course, Mrs. Tremly. Would you care to come up to my study?"

137

"There's no need for that, Miss Leanora, not when you must be anxious to go upstairs to see how his lordship goes on. But when you have some time, Cook will be needing the menus for next week, though to be sure if you don't want to be bothered with such things we'll manage."

"Of course." Suddenly, the mundane, normally boring procedure of planning meals appealed strongly to Leanora. It would occupy her mind, give her something orderly to think about. For the first time in many years, she found herself looking forward to this routine occupation. "I will see to it first thing in the morning."

"Thank you, Miss Leanora. It will do the servants good to get things somewhat back to normal around here." With a warm smile, the housekeeper bustled on past, bent on making her own inspection tour of the kitchens.

Get things somewhat back to normal. The phrase ran through Leanora's mind as she sat by her father's bedside that evening. How she longed for that normality, but it would be a long time in coming. As soon as Lord Sherborne was well enough to travel, she would take him into Kent, perhaps spend the whole summer at the Abbey. She would invite Gregory, Julia and Reggie to bear them company. And the Abbey, which was situated near Canterbury, was not so far removed from London as to make it ineligible for a certain robust and energetic gentleman to come down for visits—if he wished to see Reggie, of course.

These thoughts still lingered in her mind the following morning when, after a light breakfast, she retired to her study to work on the menu plans. The surface of her cherrywood writing desk was still cluttered, and she realized, with an odd sense of shock, that she had not worked in there since the day before her father's accident.

She seated herself in the large, comfortable desk chair and started drawing the scattered pages together into a neat pile. In her top drawer lay the troublesome seating chart that would not now be used for a very long time. She set this aside and began to leaf through the pages beneath it. Here was the menu plan she had balanced so carefully to match a variety of finicky appetites. She picked up the remainder of the stack, glancing each page before setting it down.

She froze, for the next sheet had nothing to do with the dinner party whatsoever. It was a page of notes, in Lord Petersham's spidery fist. She scanned it quickly, noting references to Lord Grenville and a meeting with a French agent. Her eyes widened as the import sank home. These must be the missing papers! No one had stolen them, they had merely become separated from the rest on her chaotic desk. She started to giggle, a release of worry and suspicion. She, and she alone, was responsible for the fuss. How Sir William would roast her for this!

The next page was one of her own, notes on the culinary preferences of several of the more important guests to the dinner that had never been held. She set this aside, found a sheet in Sir William's neater hand concerning safety precautions for the prime minister, and placed this with Petersham's sheets.

Following these, she came across several pages that were closely written in a clumsy hand she did not immediately recognize. She started deciphering the words, then realized it must make up a portion of a speech. Lord Kennington, she supposed. She glanced down the page, reprehensibly aware that she should not be looking over the contents. It certainly could not hold her interest. Only Lord Petersham, in his finest form, could sound forth in so boring and pompous a style!

She laid the page aside, then stared in surprise at the next. It was complete gibberish! She looked over the random collection of letters, bewildered.

```
YEMLAFWWM   HFWW   QOOMLI
EMVGFMS   SQNVGM   QN
DWQLLMI   /   QNNQNNFLQOFXL
OX   OQCM   DWQPM   QO
SFILFYBO   IX   LXO   SQCM
PXLOQPO   /   HQOPB   I
```

Bored scribblings? A puzzle game? She regarded the sheet with curiosity. Yes, now that she studied it, the letters did seem to be grouped, as if to form nonsensical words. And there were two slashes, as if to break up a line—or sentence.

A puzzle was far more to her taste than Kennington's speech. She studied the sheet, turning it about to examine it from different angles, and became more certain that it was not just idle scribblings. But what was the solution? Or better yet, what was its purpose, for that would surely provide a clue to the answer. A quote? Several lines from a poem? Who had written it, and for whom was it meant?

How odd that it turned up in the middle of the missing papers. To which of the gentlemen whose pages she had did it belong? It must be the one item she had lost that no one was demanding.

An icy chill washed over her like a wave. The one paper no one asked for. Could it actually be the one that everyone—or at least one very desperate person—wanted? Her eyes widened, and her flesh tingled in an eerie combination of horror and excitement. Her father's accident, the burglary, the attack on Tremly—could this single sheet of paper be the cause of so much trouble? And if it was, what terrible secrets might it reveal?

Chapter 10

Leanora's fingers tightened on the paper. She had better turn this over to someone who would know what to do about it, and as quickly as possible! Lord Petersham and Sir William must be in their offices this morning. She would take it immediately to them and tell her entire story.

She jumped to her feet, then slowly sank down as a partially buried voice of reason took over. This was all supposition! What a fool she would look if she went running to them with a crazy story of danger and murder, only to discover it was nothing more than a word game—or worse, a child's puzzle!—designed to pass the time during a boring meeting!

If she held a mere nursery rhyme, she would rather be the one to discover that fact for herself, without causing a derogatory stir in Whitehall that would leave the government officials snickering. Determined to find out one way or the other, she made a neat copy of the letters, checked it against the original, and sat down to figure it out. In a very short time the problem held her completely absorbed.

Something over an hour passed, and she was forced to make a clean copy, for she had scribbled so many wrong possibilities on hers as to render it almost illegible. With a clean sheet in hand, she set once more about the task of decipherment.

She had only just begun to grow frustrated, when a gentle tap sounded on her door and Tremly, a bandage still wound about his head, entered to announce that Lord Kennington had called. Leanora sprang to her feet, glad to be able to return the missing portion of his speech to him. But as she reached for the papers she hesitated, biting her lip. What if this puzzle were his? He would realize at once that she had not returned it and must be keeping it. And what if her guess was correct, that it was a dangerous code? Until she was sure, she had best deny any knowledge of any of the papers having been found. She thrust the cipher into her desk, locked the drawer and went next door to the Gold Saloon.

Lord Kennington stood by the window with his hands clasped behind his back, staring out across the square. The rigidity of his stance betrayed his displeasure even before he turned and allowed her a glimpse of his scowling face. His expression smoothed at once, and he came forward with his hand extended.

"I hope I have not come at a bad time?"

"No, but I fear I have nothing further to tell you. As you may have heard, the house was broken into the other night, and all has been in chaos since then."

Kennington's brow snapped down hard. "Broken into, you say? Was anything stolen?"

Closely, she studied his reaction as she repeated her well-rehearsed story. He seemed honestly surprised. Did that mean that he had nothing to do with it, that the paper was not his? Or did it mean that he had had plenty of time to practice his artless manner of listening, and his sincere interest stemmed from a desire to know how much they guessed of the real purpose of the robbery?

Kennington let out a slow, measured breath as she finished her tale. "I am glad there are no serious repercussions from the event," he said, but a shivery sensation flickered along Leanora's spine, leaving her uneasy. He looked down at his gleaming Hessians, then thoughtfully glanced back up at her face. "Do you still have no idea where those papers might be?" he asked gently. "Have none of them at all turned up?"

She shook her head resolutely. "I am very sorry. Only that one stack." It was her turn to drop her eyes, for she found his piercing gaze unnerving. "Could—could your missing pages not be somewhere else?" she asked, almost desperately.

"Are you quite sure they became entangled with mine?"

The moment she spoke, she realized it had been a mistake. His eyes narrowed, and the look to which he subjected her made her feel as if he could see right through her and know her words for lies.

"What makes you think they did not?" he asked softly.

"Why, nothing!" She tried a laugh, then decided it was too shaky. "It was a forlorn hope, I admit. I just wish that you did not have to suffer because I had been so careless."

To her relief, he seemed to relax. "There is no great harm done," he admitted. "It is only that I should like to recover that speech before it is discovered that I ever lost part of it."

"I promise you, Lord Kennington, I shall spend the entire day searching."

"Then we shall hope for a happy outcome." He took her hand, made her a half-mocking bow and left the room.

Leanora sank down into the nearest chair. Had he believed her that the papers had not been found? He must have, or he would not have left. She sensed a ruthlessness about him that both chilled and frightened her. If he had doubted her word, she felt sure that nothing would have prevented him from locating and taking what he wanted.

The sooner she deciphered the paper, the better! If it was truly dangerous, she did not want it in the house a moment longer than was necessary. Intent on this purpose, she returned to her study.

She had just reached the disturbing conclusion that the key to the cipher did not lie in a simple letter progression when she was interrupted again by Tremly. Master Gregory, he informed her, had called and was at that moment upstairs with Lord Sherborne. Leanora nodded absently and nibbled on the end of her quill. Unless her brother specifically needed to see her, she would do better to remain where she was and keep working. The fact that the solution was neither simple nor obvious indicated that it had not been designed for a child's amusement. That did not necessarily make the message sinister, but it did not set her at her ease, either.

The defeating combination of hunger and headache finally

caused her to shove the papers back in her drawer and give up. She glanced at her clock and was surprised to discover that it was already past two. No wonder she was so tired! She would order a light luncheon, stroll in the garden and then take the cipher upstairs with her to work on while she sat by her father's bedside. It would prove more diverting—though no less frustrating—than her embroidery.

Fortified by a roll and wedge of cheese, she hurried up the stairs to peep into Lord Sherborne's room. There she found her aunt quietly sewing while Xerk chewed noisily on a bone in the corner. Gregory must have departed long ago.

Mrs. Ashton looked up at her niece and managed a wan smile. "There you are at last, my love. Such a morning as it has been, with Gregory coming in when I did not expect him in the least, though why he should not come and sit with his poor dear Pappa I do not know; only it seems so strange having him here so much, though of course he has not been living away for so very many years. And that puts me in mind of it, Leanora, my love. Do you think we should ask Reggie to dine with us more often? To be sure, he is forever out with parties of his friends, and I am sure I am one to be glad he is so popular; but do you not think he might join us and perhaps bring that very nice Lord Deverell? I should so enjoy talking over old times," she sighed.

Leanora dropped a light kiss on her aunt's wrinkled brow. "Of course we must invite Reggie, and whenever and however often you desire. But I believe we should wait to ask Lord Deverell until we are formally entertaining once again. We cannot offer him anything in the way of amusement just at present, you know."

Amabelle Ashton looked somewhat dismayed. "Such a nice gentleman," she tried. "And he seems to be quite partial to your company, my love. I could not but notice how he admired you. And I am certain he and your Pappa would deal famously together." A deep sigh escaped her as her sad gaze came to rest on the earl's unmoving figure.

Leanora stiffened and could only hope that the dim light in the room hid the soft flush that burned in her cheeks. "It is a great pity you had no daughters, Aunt. You would make a splendid matchmaking mamma. But in this case you are fair and far out. Captain Lord Deverell and I should not suit."

"Well, my love, it is early days yet, is it not? You are barely acquainted with him. He reminds me so of my Vincent, so dashing and full of life. And though it hurts me as a mother to admit it, I cannot but feel that Deverell is steadier and more dependable than Vincent." She dabbed at the corners of her misty eyes. "You must have been aware, my love, that it was the dearest wish of my heart to see you wed to Vincent."

"If you are thinking that Deverell would do as well, you are quite wrong," Leanora informed her with a touch of asperity. "I will thank you to put any such ideas aside. And only think how singular it would make us look, to be inviting him here when we entertain no one else!"

Mrs. Ashton, although struck by the force of this argument, was not daunted. She spent several minutes trying to hit upon a scheme where they might invite a small number of very close friends for an enjoyable evening without actually holding a party. "And cards are always popular," she exclaimed suddenly. "Gregory is quite partial to a rubber of whist, as I remember. Perhaps we could invite him, and Julia as well! I cannot think dear Sherborne would have the least objection. Not to a quiet family gathering, at any rate. And the doctor said only this morning that your father goes on very well."

Leanora nodded. If only she could see visible signs of this supposed improvement! "I am sure it would distress Pappa if he knew what recluses we have become for his sake," she told her aunt, forcing a smile to her lips. "I should love to stay and help you make plans, but I am going to step outside for some fresh air."

"What a delightful idea! It will be just the thing for me. And dear little Artaxerxes, too." Mrs. Ashton discarded her needlework at once and stood. "Let me just send for Pagget to sit with your father, and we can go into the garden for a comfortable cose, which is what I have been wanting of all things. Do you go and put on your bonnet, my love, while I arrange everything here."

145

Recognizing defeat, Leanora stooped to kiss her father's pale forehead and went away to don a chip straw bonnet and fetch a shawl. Xerk trotted at her heels. She had no desire to discuss parties, for her mind was too fully occupied with mysterious puzzles and papers. But nothing, she knew from experience, would turn her aunt from her purpose.

Mrs. Ashton joined her in a very few minutes, and Leanora was forced to put her troubles aside once more. Together they strolled about the tiny park in the center of the square while the puppy frolicked in glee, dashing after every bird or butterfly that chanced in his way. Seating themselves on a bench in the shade of a huge laurel tree, they watched the pug while Mrs. Ashton rattled on about the proposed family dinner.

"And no one will think it the least odd if we invite Lord Deverell as well, for he is so often in Reggie's company," that lady finished on a determined note.

Leanora regarded her aunt with dismay. Was the whole project merely an attempt to throw Deverell in her way? Under normal circumstances, Amabelle Ashton would shrink at the prospect of sitting down at table with her nephew and his wife. It was possible, though, that she did her aunt an injustice. She was a gregarious woman who loved nothing more than society parties and visits. Once the shock of her brother-in-law's accident had worn off, and the immediate sense of tragedy faded, the subsequent tedium of the waiting for him to regain consciousness must naturally wear at her.

As they started back to the house, a dashing pair of bays harnessed to a sleek curricle rounded the corner in style and pulled up before the house. Mrs. Ashton, spotting her son seated beside Lord Deverell, hurried forward, calling out to them in delight. Xerk darted ahead, yipping his enthusiastic welcome, amazingly not frightening the high-bred horses. Leanora followed more slowly, trying hard to control the wave of pleasure that rippled through her at sight of the tall, dark gentleman who held the ribbons. She could not be so vulgar as to give in to sheer masculine appeal!

He sprang lightly down, entrusted the bays to a young groom

146

whom she did not recognize and came to meet them. Leanora held back, allowing her aunt to greet both her son and his friend before strolling up.

"What an unexpected surprise," she declared as she joined them. To her intense satisfaction, her voice sounded perfectly composed, with just the right degree of casual friendliness. No trace of the erratic quavering that jolted through her as Deverell clasped her hand reached her calm surface. "My aunt was just saying how much she wished for company."

"Do not you?" Deverell murmured as he raised her fingers to his lips. His dark eyes, glinting with challenge and a suppressed amusement, met hers.

"An occasional diversion is always welcome," she assured him, with difficulty controlling her leaping response to the force of his presence. He was flirting with her! Very well, then. She could indulge him in a bantering argument. It might prove amusing to match wits with a gentleman of his caliber.

Mrs. Ashton and Reggie had already started up the front steps, and Leanora and Deverell followed. She felt his eyes resting on her and glanced up at him sideways in a manner that might have been mistaken for coquetry. As she accompanied this with a mischievous smile, he was in no danger of assuming that she cast out lures. He chuckled, a deep, rich sound that filled her very being, and she prepared herself for an enjoyable battle.

Reggie, unaware of the subtle nuances passing between his friend and his cousin, paused at the door to the Gold Saloon. "Just been telling my mamma, Nora. We've been to the Peerless Pool!"

"Oh, no, Reggie! You cannot be serious! Have you really?" Her eyes danced with sudden laughter at such an outrageous expedition to this far from genteel resort. "Did you swim, or perhaps bowl on the green, or . . . heavens, what else can one do there?"

"Admire the fish pond," Deverell informed her. "Reggie assured me no gentleman of fashion could survive in London without making such a visit."

"What a—a whisker!" she exclaimed. "If that is not just like

147

you, Reggie, to so hoax poor Lord Deverell. You must know," she added, turning to the dark giant who stood disconcertingly near, "it has been an ambition with him to visit the Pool for as long as I can remember. Until now, we have been able to dissuade him, for I assure you it is not at all the thing."

"Only for a female," Reggie protested. "Dev and I had a capital time."

While Leanora rang for refreshments, Mrs. Ashton settled down on the sofa with Reggie at her side. Deverell remained standing, obviously waiting for Leanora, so she deliberately took a chair at some distance from him. Appreciation lit his dark eyes, and he strolled over to lean in a negligent manner against the mantelpiece.

"Are you already bored with the more usual entertainments to be found in London?" she asked.

"A little," he admitted, watching her closely. "One tends to see the same people at every party, night after night."

"But so comfortable," Mrs. Ashton assured him. "One may always be assured of meeting friends." Her gaze strayed to Leanora. "Or furthering an enjoyable acquaintance."

"Have you been introduced to Watiers or Whites?" Leanora asked quickly, hoping to cover her aunt's obvious intention.

"I have been put up for membership," Deverell admitted.

"Not a gamester," Reggie explained. "Thought I should take him around to Jackson's Saloon and the Daffy Club, but not really my sort of places."

"Oh, but I am sure he would like it of all things!" Leanora exclaimed. "Why, to—er—'pop in a hit over Jackson's guard' is a prime ambition of my brother's. Gregory would be only too delighted to introduce you to him, or take you to drink Blue Ruin at the Daffy Club. And he always knows where a mill is to be held. Or would you perhaps prefer a visit to the Cockpit Royal?"

"I would not," he declared decisively, his eyes twinkling. "Although I should be interested in visiting Gentleman Jackson. I find I do not get sufficient exercise 'on the toddle' about town. Nor do my horses," he added thoughtfully. "They—and I—stand in dire need of a good gallop, which is something everyone tells me I must not indulge in."

"Very true," Leanora agreed with feeling. "Though if you go to the Park early enough in the morning, there would be no one to see you."

"I will remember that." His words held both an understanding and an invitation.

She threw a quick, considering glance at him and met his clear eyes. There was intelligence revealed in their dark depths, a hint of a quick mind in search of challenging diversion. He would welcome the mental exercise of a problem like her cipher.

"Reggie," Mrs. Ashton broke in upon her thoughts. "Leanora and I were just discussing holding a small family dinner party. What do you think?"

"Family party?" he asked, revolted at the prospect of meeting his relatives. "Good God, ma'am. Whatever for?"

While his doting mamma entered into a tangled web of reasons, Leanora lapsed into silence. At all times, she kept a surreptitious eye on Deverell. It would be best if that letter puzzle were to be solved as quickly as possible, she knew. If it proved to be harmless, then she could return everyone's papers and the matter would be settled. But if it were a dangerous document. . . . The sooner they learned the truth, the better.

But could she trust Deverell? With his undeniable intelligence and his experience with espionage, he might be able to solve the code. And she had to trust someone! What better choice than an outsider, who was not involved in the Home Office, who came in recently to the political circle that she had known for most of her life? As such, he would be bound to see things more clearly and without the prejudices that marred her own objectivity. And now that Sir William had provided an explanation for Deverell's mysterious presence at Whitehall, she could—must!—banish her suspicions about him.

"Have you visited the Royal Menagerie at the Tower?" Mrs. Ashton inquired, apparently having exhausted the topic of her dinner and turned her attention to other schemes for

Deverell's entertainment.

"We have," that gentleman responded, his eyes taking on a reprehensible twinkle.

"Rather liked the wild beasts," Reggie admitted. "And they let us watch them making coins in the Mint. But the rest of that devilish gloomy place!" His expression took on a martial gleam of remembered wrongs. "Well, I ask you! Who wants to stare at a bunch of rubbishing old prisons? Must have looked a rare couple of flats, wandering all over the place with that curst guide book."

"I fear he has refused to accompany me to the British Museum this afternoon," Deverell admitted, his eyes dancing.

"I should dashed well think I did!" Reggie exclaimed.

Deverell looked toward Leonora to share the joke but encountered her unusually strained face. He frowned, trying to interpret her expression. "Would it be possible to persuade you, Lady Leonora, to take your cousin's place?"

Her brow cleared. "Of course!" she breathed. "Yes, I would enjoy it of all things."

Deverell's eyes narrowed, for he was no fool. He dropped his gaze, studied his coat sleeve for a moment and removed an infinitesimal speck of fluff. "I had meant to go this afternoon. Would now be convenient for you, or would you rather go another day?"

"What a splendid idea, Leonora," Mrs. Ashton chimed in. "You must know, my lord, that she does nothing but sit in this house and worry about her poor father. And such a relief that I shall not be obliged to accompany you, for I am persuaded that she will come to no harm in your care. And as unexceptional a place as the museum is, I—"

"Now would be a perfect time." Leonora broke ruthlessly in on her aunt's wandering sentences. "If you will just give me a few minutes?" She hurried out of the room.

It took her something under ten minutes to collect her bonnet and reticule, look in on her father's immobile figure and restore the eager Xerk to his side. The doctor gave only encouraging reports—so why did he not recover? It distressed her, seeing him lying so very still, but it also increased her determination to get to the bottom of the mystery. Before returning to the Gold Saloon, she slipped into her study and made one more clean copy of the cipher. The rest she locked safely away.

Reggie, not to anyone's surprise, loudly disclaimed any desire to accompany them. "Think I'll stay here for a bit," he murmured in an aside to Deverell. "Make sure m'mother takes a drive in the Park."

With her mind relieved of that worry, Leanora accompanied Deverell out to the curricle that his groom had been walking around the square. When the vehicle pulled up before them, Deverell assisted her to climb in, then came around and took the ribbons from the groom who sprang lightly down.

Deverell beguiled the drive with the most commonplace and unexceptional small talk, confining himself to the splendid weather and the many advantages attached to visiting the metropolis at the height of the Season. As Leanora knew very well that he found these to be an utter bore, she was hard pressed not to dissolve into a fit of the giggles at his mouthing of complete inanities. It was her nerves, she realized, and for the first time she wondered whether or not he would take her puzzle seriously. If he did not, she would have wasted the afternoon.

The British Museum was housed in the former Montagu House, a fine old seventeenth century mansion. This was presently reached and the bays once more handed over to the custody of Deverell's lad. As soon as the vehicle drove away, Deverell turned to Leanora.

"An excellent groom, in his way, but I shall be glad when my own returns," he confessed. "Now, there is an individual of many hidden talents." He chuckled softly to himself as he took her arm and started up the walk to the massive building. "He has been taking care of a little matter for me. And now, if you please, you may tell me to what I owe the pleasure of your company."

"Was I that obvious?" she asked with a sigh, ashamed of how clumsy she must have been.

He smiled down at her in a very disconcerting manner. "You

151

have shown no great desire for my company on other occasions."

"I am sorry if I have appeared rude," she told him stiffly.

By this time they had reached the museum, and he escorted her inside. "What would you care to see?" he asked. He consulted the listings. "Printed Books? Manuscripts and Medals? Or would you prefer Natural and Artificial Products?"

"Let it be the Egyptian Antiquities," she decided. "Though heaven knows, I should have had my fill of those from listening to Petersham. He is a collector, you must know. Are you interested in such things?"

"Indeed I am. This way, then." He led her through a large doorway and along a hall. "You have not answered my question, yet," he added.

"No. I. . . ." She glanced up at him, then looked down.

He regarded her through half-lidded eyes. "Does this concern the searching of your father's study and the missing papers?" he asked shrewdly.

"It does. You see, I found them."

It was impossible for him to respond, for at that moment they were joined by a group of people. Together they entered the hall devoted to the Egyptian artifacts captured from the French less than four years before. For a very long while they were silent as they strolled among the ancient objects that never failed to fill Leanora with a sense of awe. At last they came up before a large broken stone, part of a basalt stele, found near the Rosetta mouth of the Nile River. On it were three sets of carvings, one in Greek and two in strange, unintelligible symbols.

Leanora stared at it, lost in thought. "I have often wondered what it says," she said at last.

"My Greek is rather rusty, but I could try to translate that part of it if you are serious." He sounded amused.

She cast a sideways glance at him. "Do you enjoy deciphering puzzles, then?"

His dark eyes began to sparkle, and the corners of his mouth twitched upward into a decidedly charming smile. "My lady, I am entirely at your disposal. But is such a service needed?"

He took her elbow and led her on. "From my experience, government papers take a certain amount of wading through, but I have never yet had to resort to a translator."

"I believe I have been indiscreet enough so that you realize I misplaced a number of documents. Do you remember that afternoon we first—encountered—each other in Whitehall? I was carrying some of my father's papers from a meeting he had had with Lord Petersham and Sir William. Lord Kennington knocked them out of my hands. He also dropped some of his own papers. We gathered them together at random, and when I got home I lost some of them."

They paused before a display of ancient pottery, then moved on. Deverell kept them toward the center of the room, where the chances were very slim that their low voiced conversation would be overheard.

"I found the papers this morning," she continued when an elderly couple, who had paused for a moment beside them, moved on. "There is one sheet of particular interest, and I have no idea to whom it belongs."

"I am to understand that you do not wish to ask any of the possible owners?"

She nodded, pleased at his quickness. It seemed that she had chosen her assistant well. "It is a sheet of absolute gibberish. My first thought was that someone had created a word puzzle to while away a boring meeting. It is probably perfectly harmless, but it has not proved easy to solve."

"You suspect a code?"

"You will probably think me foolish beyond permission." She turned to look earnestly up into his ruggedly handsome face. "Indeed, I hope you may be able to tell me that I am."

"But you think not."

It was a simple statement, and she was glad that his expression betrayed none of the amusement that seemed so characteristic of him. She needed to have this taken seriously, she realized.

"Where is it?" he asked.

She drew the copy from her reticule and handed it to him without a word. He unfolded it and studied it in silence for several minutes. "This is a copy?" He did not so much as glance at her.

"Yes. I have made several. My—my first attempts at deciphering it were not very successful. I only hope you will be able to tell me that it is nothing more than a child's rhyme."

At that he smiled, and his entire face seemed to brighten. "I hope so, too. I can probably solve your little puzzle, for I am not entirely without experience in such matters." He fell silent, thinking. "Do you go to Almack's tomorrow night?" he asked suddenly.

"I had not planned on it, but I can." She looked up, surprised.

"Get Reggie to escort you. That should be easy, for he has a new waistcoat he wishes to spring on Society. Have you told anyone that you found the papers?"

"No, not even Mr. Edmonton."

"Good. Do not do so until we know exactly what we have here." He refolded the paper and slipped it into a pocket of his coat. Taking her arm once again, he led her into the next room. He looked down upon her with that singularly devastating smile on his lips and the merry lights of amusement dancing once more in his eyes. "I must thank you," he said. "I find myself deeply in your debt."

She glanced suspiciously up into his face, and for a moment forgot to breathe. With difficulty, she mastered her unruly senses. "Why?" she asked, as lightly as possible.

"For offering me something that will relieve my boredom. I can never resist an intriguing mystery—or someone who is capable of sharing it with me."

Leanora was of both an imaginative and humorous turn of mind, but the suspicion that the earth shook beneath her feet as their gazes held did not seem the least absurd to her. "It—it is I who am glad, to be able to turn this over to someone who will know what to do. If you knew how afraid I have been, you would not joke so."

"You have shown the greatest presence of mind," he said simply. He drew the paper once more from his pocket and ran an appraising eye over it. "In a way, it will really be too bad if this turns out to be nothing more than a word game."

There was a decided twinkle in his eye, and Leanora realized

154

he would welcome danger every bit as readily as he did the challenge. To her surprise, this did not worry her further but actually gave her the oddest sense of security. Here, indeed, was a man capable of dealing with anything. And he did not alarm her with unfounded theories or try to jolly her by making light of her fears. He respected her opinion, and that knowledge filled her with a warm glow.

Chapter 11

Waiting throughout the next day proved almost unbearable to Leanora. Not willing to rely on Deverell alone, she took the cipher with her to her father's room and spent the entire day in fruitless attempts. By evening, she was exhausted and no nearer a resolution than she had been at the beginning.

She actually welcomed the interruption of her abigail, who came looking for her with the information that it was well past the hour when she should be dressing for dinner. And if she were to go on to Almack's, her woman chided her, she could not just scramble into any gown in a haphazard fashion.

For some reason, it took her longer than usual to select just the right dress for the evening. Not that it mattered, she kept telling herself, but somehow the round dress of green muslin did not seem sophisticated enough and the gold satin was too fussy. At last she settled for a half robe of peach crepe worn over a white satin slip with a single flounce at the hem.

Her long, golden hair the abigail dressed simply, smoothing it back and then up into a knot at the crown of her head. From there, it was brushed into long ringlets that fell about her shoulders. The remaining short wisps were teased into feather curls that framed her oval face.

Next, her maid drew out her jewelry box from the locked drawer and rummaged within for the diamond drop earrings and pendant. As Leanora watched, the woman frowned, then began to search again.

A strange chill of suspicion gripped Leanora. "Can you not

find them?" she asked, her voice strangely hoarse.

"No, my lady." Her maid frowned. "I am sure I put them back last time you wore them."

"You did." This was something that her father had always insisted she watch with care. Leanora looked about the room, her slow gaze taking in every detail. Nothing else appeared to have been disturbed. Someone must have taken the diamonds —someone who knew where they were kept and where to find the key. That narrowed the suspects considerably. With difficulty, she cast back in her mind. When was the last time she had seen the diamonds? Not for several days, she was sure. She had not been going out much of late.

"It is all right, Ripton," she said at last. After the business with the housekeeping money, she really had no doubts. Part of her hoped she was wrong, that Gregory would not have stooped so low as to steal her jewelry, but it seemed the only possible explanation. She would confront him tonight—if he went to Almack's. If not, he was bound to come to the house on the morrow. Since their father's incapacitation, Gregory was showing a remarkable interest in all of the household affairs. She turned back to the distressed maid. "Do not look so worried. I believe I know where they might be. Never mind, I shall wear the pearls instead."

When she finally descended the stairs, she found Reggie bearing his mother company. At first glance, he was quite conservatively attired in a long-tailed blue coat, black satin knee-breeches and striped stockings. And then she beheld his waistcoat. It was not so much the cut, though that was certainly unique, that lent this garment its distinction. Embroidery in gold and silver thread covered almost every inch of the black satin fabric so that it shimmered in the candlelight.

Leanora thrust the incident of the diamonds from her mind and went to admire her cousin. After taking his hand, she stood back as he obviously wished her to do, to better take in the full glories of his latest sartorial achievement.

"I must say, Reggie, it's—it's bound to set them all on their ears!" she exclaimed dutifully. "You will cast Beau Brevin himself in the shade!"

Her cousin preened himself with justifiable pride. "Took me all of a week to convince my snyder to make it up. No vision, that man. He'll listen to me next time, though," he added with a smug smile.

The cook, a tyrant of French extraction who ruled his domain with an iron hand, had done justice to the occasion. Having had a full twenty-four hours notice that there would be a guest for the meal, he had set about his preparations for so small a party with a lavish hand. The result was that they sat down to a first course that consisted of a roast sirloin of beef, a rack of lamb with an array of sauce boats, white collops, a baked fish, clear soup, two different vegetables and a variety of removes. This was followed by a second course, consisting of a roast chicken, several pigeons stuffed and baked in the Flemish way, an assortment of lobster patties, apple tartlets, a Renish cream, a raspberry souffle and an array of pastries.

The dinner, which went a long way to stiffening Reggie's nerve to spring his waistcoat on his fellow dandies, only served as a disturbing reminder to Leanora of how much her aunt loved to entertain. Frivolous parties, beloved by the members of the *haut ton*, were exactly suited to her temperament, unlike the weighty State affairs she begged her niece to hostess in her stead. The idea of having to welcome anyone to the house could not appeal to Leanora, but she knew they would have to hold the quiet family party that Mrs. Ashton had already begun to plan.

As the meal drew to a close, Tremly entered the dining room to inform Leanora that the doctor had arrived for a belated visit. Excusing herself hurriedly, she went up the stairs to find that individual already with her father.

He looked up as she entered the room, nodded briefly and returned to his examination of his patient. Leanora remained by the door, watching, almost not daring to breathe in her anxiety. Would there never be any improvement?

"Of course there will," the doctor replied testily, and she realized she had spoken that last thought aloud. "Has been, already. Just you leave him alone, let him recover in his own time. That was a nasty accident."

Leanora nodded but derived little comfort from his words. Her father still lay there in the bed, pale and almost lifeless. She brushed aside an errant tear, waited while the doctor repacked his instruments and accompanied him down the stairs.

Her aunt and cousin had retired to the drawing room on the first floor, where she found Reggie attempting to instruct his mother in the intricacies of piquet. As neither player was a gamester at heart, and Mrs. Ashton became hopelessly fuddled when trying to understand the complex scoring, they both welcomed her arrival with relief. Mrs. Ashton retired from the lists, saying that she would be content to watch and see how the game *ought* to be played.

"No turn for cards, that's your problem," her loving son pointed out affably. Leanora took her place at the card table, but as her mind was elsewhere, she several times provoked her cousin into complaint at her random play.

All were relieved when it was finally time to set forth for Almack's. They arrived quite early at the select club in King Street, dubbed the *holiest of holies* by the irreverent, and Leanora looked anxiously about the spacious rooms. Deverell had not yet arrived.

Another, and quite unwelcome, sight met her searching gaze. Lady Julia, more beautiful than ever in a seductive gown of the thinnest crepe that clung enticingly to her full curves, was just being led by a very dashing young officer into a set that formed for a country dance. They made a striking couple, Leanora reflected. What on earth was Gregory thinking about to leave his lovely and very young wife to seek amusement with others?

She had the opportunity to ask him, had she so desired, barely a moment later. As she turned to follow her aunt to a group of empty chairs, she found herself face to face with her brother. Her first reaction was not for Julia, though. She had other business to settle with Gregory, and the thought of her diamonds sprang uppermost in her mind.

"I want to have a word with you," she informed him tartly. His chin jutted out in a belligerent manner. "Well?"

"Not here. In private. Come and see me first thing in

the morning."

For a fleeting moment, something that might have been uneasiness flickered across his handsome face. It was replaced at once by a supercilious smile. "Sorry, Nora. Got other fish to fry tomorrow. I'll come see you when I can."

"You *can*, and first thing in the morning."

"Really, my girl, just what do you think you're doing, giving me orders like that?" He refused to meet her compelling eye, a circumstance that confirmed her suspicions.

"You know perfectly well, Gregory. Or would you care to discuss the matter here?"

He glowered at her. "Don't know what maggot you've taken into your head," he grumbled unconvincingly. "All right, I'll stop by tomorrow."

"In the morning," she repeated, and moved off.

She had not gone many steps when a gentleman of her acquaintance presented himself before her and solicited her hand to join the next set. Forcing her irritation to the back of her mind, she allowed him to lead her onto the floor. Her partner soon had her smiling at his lighthearted banter.

She glanced about the room as the dance ended, wondering about her cousin and the reception of his remarkable waistcoat. Poor Reggie, if no one was smitten with envy, his evening would be ruined.

The musicians struck up a quadrille, and as if summoned by her thoughts, Reggie appeared at her elbow.

"Dance with me, Nora," he begged.

"What, reduced to asking your own cousin?" She took his offered arm and allowed him to lead her into a set. He was an excellent dancer, knew the intricate moves to perfection and could have had his pick of a host of young ladies anxious for such a dependable and elegant partner.

"Don't feel like doing the pretty." The movements of the dance separated them, and when he rejoined her he was glowering. "Lord, what a disagreeable lot have come tonight!"

The reason for his ill humor was not hard to discern. Since the quadrille had begun, Leonora had seen more than one amused glance cast at her cousin. Apparently the child of his genius was not winning the admiration he felt to be its due.

A moment later, a shadow fell over her own evening. As the dance ended, she looked up and saw Lord Kennington standing in the doorway. His gaze scanned the room, then came to rest on her. The expression in his cold eyes left her shivering. Had he not believed her, after all? Did he know that she had found those papers—and that scribbled code?

She kept a nervous eye on Kennington. He drifted with apparent aimlessness about the room, but in a very short time he stood near Lord Petersham and Sir William Holborne. He bowed stiffly to Sir William, then bent down to murmur something in Petersham's ear. Petersham stiffened, cast an agitated glance in Leanora's direction, and the two gentlemen stepped out through a nearby doorway together.

Leanora shivered as if with a presentiment of danger and tried to swallow. She found her mouth uncomfortably dry. What lay between those two? And did it concern her—or at least those papers?

Sir William strolled up and bowed before her. "I believe there is to be a waltz next."

She forced a smile to her lips. "And no young female has yet solicited your hand for it? Poor Sir William! What a terrible blow!"

He led her onto the floor. "Have you enjoyed the rare privilege of trying to hold a conversation with some of these chits? Fresh from the schoolroom, without an ounce of conversation between the lot of them! How their mammas hope to pop them off, when they have done nothing to prepare them for the Marriage Mart, is beyond me!"

"Poor things," Leanora said with feeling. "They should be allowed to try their wings at country balls before being pitchforked into London society."

Sir William shuddered. "Imagine the manners and conversation they would pick up from a pack of dowdy country squires! No, thank you."

"I see. You prefer to find your amusement with a jaded spinster?"

He laughed at this, but to Leanora's surprise she realized that a touch of irritation lay beneath her bantering words.

162

Looking about the room, it seemed to her to be packed with young ladies of barely seventeen years. Ladies over twenty were either already married or accepted the fact that they never would be.

For the first time in a very long while, it struck Leonora that she really had consigned herself to the ranks of the ape-leaders. A female of four-and-twenty, who had turned down every offer ever made to her, was certainly beyond her last prayers. For what did she hope? A knight on a gleaming charger to sweep her off her feet? Such gentlemen rarely sought out capable maidens beyond their first blush of youth. A helpless damsel in distress was far more to their liking.

Effortlessly, she followed Sir William's able lead, and they swirled about the floor. Reggie, she was relieved to see, danced with Julia. At least that kept her sister-in-law safe for the moment. Now if only Gregory would show such proper spirit, she could be relieved on that head. And where was Deverell? If he did not arrive soon, the doors to the exclusive club would be closed to him, for no one, under any circumstance, could enter the sacred portals after the hour of eleven.

Sir William emitted a deep sigh. "I must be losing my touch," he complained. "Am I boring you?"

She looked up, surprised. "Of course not!"

"Now, what could have made me wonder?" he asked of the room at large. "You appear quite distracted this evening. Has something happened to distress you? Or has my long association with Petersham begun to bear distasteful fruit? Have I been prosing on unbearably?"

"I have yet to be bored by your company," Leanora informed him, quite truthfully.

He laughed softly, his eyes glinting, and they slipped easily back into a comfortable repartee. There was a great deal to be said for an old acquaintance, Leanora reflected. She knew what was expected of her, could respond without straining her mind—which unfortunately left her free to think of other matters.

As the music ended, they stopped quite near Lord Petersham. He sat against the wall, ostensibly in conversation with Lady Carmody, but his small eyes remained focused on

163

Kennington. Leanora took a deep breath.

"What is between Petersham and Kennington?" she asked.

Sir William shrugged. "A man with political ambitions uses what tools he may."

"But Kennington? Consorting with the Opposition would hardly advance him within his own party!" Leanora objected.

"Perhaps he wishes to hedge his bets, in case the Opposition comes into power," he said softly. "And now, my dear, I fear I must leave you. I see your next partner bearing down upon us."

Before she could object, he slipped away, leaving her to face Viscount Dalmouth. She turned her large, blue eyes on him in a measuring gaze that failed to discompose him. He was a handsome, rakish young man, a year older than she, but with lines of dissipation already etched on his countenance. His dress gave the impression of the dandy, for along with a neckcloth that would have won Reggie's approval, he sported several fobs, chains and rings. The shoulders of his exquisitely cut coat were padded, adding unnecessary breadth to an already wide frame. His bearing was more that of a Corinthian, and she knew that his preference lay in playing at single sticks at Jackson's Saloon rather than going on the toddle down Bond Street.

He bowed low before her, his manner for once bearing no trace of the mockery that normally characterized him. "May I have the honor of this next dance?" he asked. "Unless you are already promised?"

"I should be delighted," she lied, and accepted his arm.

"Perhaps some lemonade, first?" he asked as if anxious to see to her every comfort and enjoyment. "I see that the musicians are taking a break. If we hurry, I am sure we can get something to drink before the next sets begin to form."

Curious, Leanora allowed him to escort her into a room where tables of refreshments were laid out. Leaving her safely away from the crush, he worked his way through and in a surprisingly short time reemerged bearing filled cups.

He handed one of these to her, took a sip of his own and made a face. "I am sorry I could not bring you better."

"Almack's is not known for their refreshments," she replied

lightly. What was he up to? Never in the long course of their acquaintance, even in the past year since his sister had married her brother, had he been more than passingly polite. He had certainly never set himself out to charm her before. She would play along, she decided, see to what end he was leading. But on what topic could they converse? As far as she could tell, gaming was Dalmouth's only interest at the moment.

"Has your father shown any improvement, yet?" There was only honest concern in his voice, nothing at which she could take offense.

"The doctor says so. He holds out a very hopeful view," she replied, keeping her voice steady.

"Then I am sure you must, also. Medical men do not lightly give one hope, I have discovered."

There was an odd note in his voice, and she cast a quick look up at him. His hazel eyes remained devoid of any clue as to his meaning, but Leanora sensed that something disturbed him. For what did he have little hope? Certainly not his health, which appeared to be excellent in spite of his dissipation. His finances, then? Did his associates in the gaming hells press him to pay debts he could not meet?

She finished her lemonade, and he took the glass from her and set it on a table. As he offered her his arm once again, he said, with an almost forced casualness: "I am thinking of going into the country for a few days. Repairing lease, you know. Been trotting too hard these last few weeks. Do you think Gregory would care to go with me? He is always such a pleasant companion."

Pleasant and compliant, she guessed. Did he hope to make up a party devoted to gaming? Considering the great show of friendship Dalmouth made toward Gregory, she could only wonder at the trouble into which he led him. She bit back hasty words.

"You will have to ask him," she said coolly.

"Have I offended you?" He appeared all concern. "I assure you, I quite value your brother's friendship."

That proved too much for her. Her missing diamonds rankled. "Yes," she replied with feigned sweetness. "It has been very valuable to you, has it not? You have introduced him

165

to any number of hells."

Dalmouth stiffened, then suddenly gave a laugh that did not sound quite genuine in her ears. "Now, there you are quite out, Lady Leanora. What I have done is to steer him away from the worst, the ones whose honesty is not above suspicion. I have taken him only to ones that are safe—just to satisfy his curiosity and desires." He looked down at her, his eyes narrowing slightly. "I do not think I flatter myself when I say that I am a bit older and more worldly wise than your brother. Young gentlemen—not quite at home to a peg, shall we say?—find these hells fascinating. I have done my poor best to keep him from falling into the hands of gull catchers."

"Then it is very kind of you," she replied, not satisfied. If Sir William had spoken the truth, then Dalmouth himself fell into that last category of unsavory gentlemen. Showing open animosity would not help matters, though—a tame Dalmouth was infinitely preferable to an angry one out to do her a mischief. What might he be capable of doing in revenge? She felt uneasy, suddenly aware that she was almost afraid to cross him. She was being goosish, shockingly poor spirited, but for once she did nothing about it. With Dalmouth, she feared, she had better move carefully.

The dance with him seemed interminable. She could not keep her eyes from the doorway, for the minutes ticked inexorably by, every moment drawing closer to eleven. If Deverell had not arrived by then, she would have accomplished nothing by coming out this night. Dalmouth, aware of her abstraction, took the opportunity of quizzing her about it the next time the movement of the dance brought them together. She laughed it off, saying that in truth she was eager to return home to her father, and could only hope Dalmouth was satisfied.

He appeared to be, for as the dance ended he took her back to her Aunt Amabelle, stayed chatting for a couple of minutes in the most amiable fashion, then strolled off to seek his next partner. Leanora watched him narrowly, convinced that he had sought her out with an ulterior motive. Had he accomplished his purpose? Had it only been to make himself pleasant to her—for a change—or had there been more?

The question was driven from her mind almost at once. There, filling the doorway with his overpowering presence, stood Lord Deverell. He greeted Lady Jersey, who happened to be nearby, and came slowly into the room, his eyes scanning the crowd. His gaze flickered over her, barely acknowledging her presence, and moved on. Limping more than usual, he crossed to an empty chair and sat down.

A wave of disappointment swept over Leanora. He did not seem the least interested in speaking to her! Did that mean he had been unable to decipher the code? Then why did he not come to tell her so? That she wished very much that he would come to her side, she tried hard not to acknowledge. And not only because of the letter puzzle, she admitted at last, as she watched him rise and join a group of gentlemen. He was the most striking, attractive and irritating man of her acquaintance!

She danced the boulanger with an inarticulate young buck many years her junior. Probably too shy to solicit the hand of a damsel nearer his own age, Leanora reflected ruefully. All at once she became bored with the evening, wanting nothing more than to go home. If Deverell had nothing to report to her, she could see no point in remaining.

She left her partner as soon as the dance ended and started across the room to where the chaperones sat. Her aunt, she noted, had been joined by Lord Petersham, and only he appeared to enjoy the situation. Mrs. Ashton directed a pleading gaze at Leanora. No, she would have no trouble in that quarter about leaving.

She was caught by Sir William before she could reach her aunt, and had no choice but to go down a country dance with him. Before she could escape, she heard halting footsteps coming up behind her. This gave her a moment to prepare herself, and when she turned it was with a distantly polite smile on her lips. No trace of her sudden and unaccountable inner trembling betrayed itself.

"Evening, Deverell," Sir William greeted the newcomer. He made no move to leave Leanora's side.

"Good evening, Sir William." Deverell gave the man a slight bow, then took Leanora's hand and raised it fleetingly to his lips. "Lady Leanora, I find myself in a dilemma. There is to be a waltz next, and you are the only lady I can be certain will not be insulted if I ask you to sit it out with me."

"How unkind of you," she responded lightly. "You should say rather that you desire my company."

"As you have given many indications that you have no desire for mine, I thought I should do better to appeal to your kind heart." This was accompanied by such a twinkling in his dark eyes that she was forced to laugh.

"Shameless," she informed him. "Do let us be seated, then. If you will excuse me, Sir William?" She glanced at her last partner and detected a slight frown creasing his brow. There was something so very free and easy in Deverell's manner, it was no wonder that the fastidious Sir William could not be pleased. Deverell, his limp still exaggerated, led her to a couple of empty seats placed between potted plants.

"I had begun to despair of your approaching me this evening," she murmured as he handed her to her chair.

"I fear this is not the place for the discussion you have in mind." His quiet tone matched hers.

She looked up into his rugged face, then hurriedly dropped her gaze. He could be shatteringly attractive. He certainly appeared to advantage in his impeccable evening dress. How could a man look so natural in buckskins and riding coat, astride a dancing stallion, and yet appear so sophisticated, so completely at home in a long-tailed cutaway coat in the middle of a ballroom? She discovered in herself a reprehensible desire to delve deeper into the matter, and with difficulty dragged her mind back to the subject at hand.

"Does—does that mean you have solved our little puzzle?" she asked, distressingly breathless.

"I have." His voice took on a grim undertone, though his smile remained fixed. Anyone watching them would think they indulged in a mild flirtation.

"It—it was not a nursery rhyme, then?" She gazed out over the dancers, knowing his answer even before he spoke. Still, his confirmation of her fears sent an uncomfortable sensation creeping through her.

"It was not. I will call upon you tomorrow morning, if I may.

Would you care to ride in the Park? I understand it is not overly crowded at that time and we may indulge ourselves in a gallop." She agreed, and they fell silent for a moment as his gaze swept the room. "Tell me," he said abruptly. "What do you know of Lord Petersham?"

"Petersham?" she asked surprised. Surely he could not be responsible for that mysterious code! But then Deverell was not acquainted with him and would have no idea how ineffectual that gentleman was. She gave him a quick summary of what she knew, based primarily on her father's observations.

Deverell nodded as if she confirmed his own opinion. "And Sir William?" he asked when she finished. Here she was able to be more complimentary, and Deverell listened with interest. Next he wished to know a little about Kennington, but she was considerably surprised when he also asked about Lord Dalmouth.

"What has he to do with this?" she demanded.

"I have no idea. How could I, when I do not know him? But he appeared bent on making himself agreeable to you this evening."

That surprised her. Had he been there longer than she realized? Dalmouth's attentiveness had made her curious as well. Could it have something to do with the mysterious paper? But try as she might, she was unable to connect him with it.

There was time for no more that evening. The waltz had ended long before, and Mrs. Ashton, unable to bear another moment of Petersham's interminable conversation, came in search of her niece. Deverell offered politely to bespeak their carriage for them, with the result that when they detached Reggie from a friend of his, the vehicle had already pulled up at the door.

"Which only goes to show, my love," Mrs. Ashton told Leanora as they drove home, "how useful a gentleman can be. For I never would have thought to send a message for it before finding dear Reggie, and then we would have been obliged to stand in the vestibule for who knows how long!"

"Yes, Lord Deverell is quite adept at obtaining carriages,"

her infuriating niece replied calmly.

Mrs. Ashton threw her a darkling look. "*Such* a gentleman! I cannot but be struck by it whenever I see him. Such an air, and so romantic, with his war injury."

"Dear ma'am," Leanora replied, a spark of mischief in her eyes. "I fear you are on the verge of losing your heart to him! What a hardened flirt he must be!"

While Mrs. Ashton did her best to disabuse her of this notion, Leanora sank back in the seat. The one adjective that her aunt failed to apply to Deverell, which suited him to perfection, was "aggravating." In all the time they had sat together, he had given her no hint as to the actual contents of the mysterious message. But he would come in the morning, and she would lose no time in demanding a complete disclosure from him.

Chapter 12

With this intention, Leanora rose early the next morning and dressed in her riding habit. Going directly to her father's room, she took up her accustomed place at the bedside. For a very long time she sat quietly, gazing down at the earl's still face and stroking the puppy which settled in her lap.

"Do not worry, Pappa," she whispered. "We are very close to getting to the bottom of this." She blinked back misty tears, then suddenly stared. Was it her imagination, or was there a little more color in his face this morning? Was it only the way the light struck the bed? She studied every line and plane of his countenance and at last came to the unhappy conclusion that there was no real change.

The door opened behind her, and she jumped. To her surprise, not Tremly but Gregory entered the room. It took her a moment to interpret his antagonistic expression, then memory of her diamonds flooded back to her. Handing the protesting Xerk to Pagget, who emerged from the dressing room, she left them to watch over her father once more while she led her brother down to her sitting room.

Gregory followed her into the apartment with an air of studied casualness. Lounging down in a chair, he crossed his booted feet on a low table before him. "Going out this morning, Nora?"

She ignored him. "Did you take my diamond earrings?" she demanded without preamble.

He sat up straight in the chair. "Damme, if that's any way to

171

greet your own brother! What would I be wanting with your trumpery jewelry, anyway? Diamond earrings, of all things! Why, I daresay they would not bring as much as four hundred pounds!"

"Cut line, Gregory. That is exactly what they would bring, as you well know. Tell me the truth, for once!"

"Dash it, Nora." He looked down at his hands. "You make it sound worse than it is. I only borrowed them for a bit."

"And what do you consider to be 'a bit'?" She stood before him, hands on hips, her eyes flashing.

"Just until the quarter day. I only put them up the spout, anyway. I wouldn't sell your earrings!"

She let out a deep sigh and sank down into a chair opposite him. "You had best tell me, Gregory. How badly are you scorched?"

He gave her a wan smile. "Not the sort of thing a female should be involved in, Nora."

"Gregory!" Her tone was menacing. "When you take my diamonds, you have already involved me. Now, let us have this with no more roundaboutation. Just how much money do you owe?"

He seemed uneasy, and for a moment she received the strong impression that there was something he desperately did not want her to know. Just what sort of trouble was he in? Was it only that he had gotten himself into the clutches of unscrupulous moneylenders, known among the knowledgeable as cent-per-centers? Or was it more?

She regarded him uncertainly, not knowing which question to ask. Nothing could more surely make Gregory belligerent than the interference of an elder sister. She stood again and took a few paces about the room.

"Gregory," she began, then broke off in vexation as a soft knock sounded on the door. It opened, and Tremly stood on the threshold.

"Excuse me, Miss Leanora. Captain Lord Deverell has called. Would you wish your horse brought around from the stable?"

Gregory was on his feet in a moment. "I'll take myself off now, Nora. Want to talk to Edmonton, if he's in the house

172

Don't you keep the horses waiting."

Before she could protest, he was out the door like a fox with the hounds hot on its heels. Once again, he had escaped before she learned what she needed to know. With difficulty, she controlled her rising temper. Lord Deverell waited, and the information he brought her might well prove of far greater importance.

She hurried down the stairs to greet him. While they waited in the hall, they exchanged the merest commonplaces until her groom rode up to the house, leading her gray mare. She had not had leisure to ride of late, and the mare was frisky and anxious to play off her tricks. For some time they did not speak while the horse wore off some of its freshness.

At last, as they entered the Park, Leanora was able to rein in quietly beside Lord Deverell. Her groom kept a discreet distance to the rear, out of earshot if they kept their voices low.

"Are you going to tell me now?" she demanded. "Or are you waiting to see how far my patience can stretch?"

He gave a deep, rich chuckle that sent the blood pounding through her veins in a very disconcerting fashion. "Can you spare a hand to read this?" He drew a folded paper from his pocket and handed it over.

She transferred her reins to one hand and tore open the sheet. It was a copy of the original code, only with the solution printed neatly beneath each letter. Her hands shaking with excitement, she read aloud:

"GRENVILLE WILL ATTEND REQUIEM MASQUE AS PLANNED. ASSASSINATION TO TAKE PLACE AT MIDNIGHT. DO NOT MAKE CONTACT. WATCH D."

She stared at it, then read it again as if unable to take it in the first time. At last she looked up at Deverelll, her eyes very wide.

"Are you playing a practical joke on me?" she demanded.
He shook his head. "And I do you the honor of believing the message you gave me was genuine and not a joke on your part."
"What have we stumbled upon?" she whispered as shock

173

began to take effect.

"Offhand, I would say a plot to murder the prime minister."

Leanora turned and stared at him. "But whose plot?"

They regarded each other for a very long moment. The gray mare shook its head, restless, and Leanora was forced to pass the page back to Deverell and take the reins in both hands once again as her mount began to dance.

"I—I don't believe it," she said at last as the mare settled down.

"Then why are you so upset?" His amusement, which was never buried very deeply, resurfaced.

She threw him a fulminating glance. "The whole thing is absurd. It must be! Why should the prime minister attend a masquerade in the first place, and why one with such a peculiar name? Have you ever heard of a 'Requiem Masque'?"

"I have not," he admitted. "Do you have any idea what it might mean?"

She shook her head. "And who is behind it?" she threw at him, getting back to what she felt to be the most important question. "There are no names mentioned, only one initial 'D'! It might be anyone! Why, it might even be you!"

Deverell laughed. "I agree. At the moment, it seems pretty hopeless, but let us consider. You found the sheet among your father's papers. That narrows down who it might have belonged to."

"Petersham, Sir William, Kennington. . . ." She broke off, reflecting on the possibilities. "Not a 'D' among them. It might not even be a real initial, but a code name. Like calling him Number Four."

"Could anyone else have touched those documents?"

She shook her head. "No one except my father." Her fingers clenched on the reins, sending her mare skittering sideways. Her father could not be involved! The idea was ridiculous! Somehow, the paper *must* have become mixed up with his by accident! He could never have had anything to do with this treasonable plot.

She urged her mare into a canter, more from the need to be doing something than anything else. Deverell caught her up easily, and the horses, both eager, extended their gaits until

174

they raced neck and neck. Behind, the groom kept determinedly up with them.

The Requiem Masque. The phrase ran over and over through her mind. The Requiem Masque. So much like Requiem Mass, the music for the dead. *Requiem*. . . . Mozart's *Requiem* that she had heard only a week before . . . that she had heard the night before she came into possession of that stack of papers. Could it be connected? Had that message been written by someone who had also attended the performance of Mozart's *Requiem*? Someone besides her father!

It had been at the Opera House. Anyone could have been there. Suddenly her thoughts focused, like a hound picking up a scent. She drew up her horse and turned excitedly to Deverell, who followed suit.

"The Opera House!" she exclaimed. Quickly, she explained about the performance of Mozart's *Requiem*. "And public masquerades are held there from time to time. What if, for some unfathomable reason, the prime minister plans to attend a public masquerade at the Opera House?"

"It doesn't seem likely, does it?" Deverell mused, but she had his attention. "I wonder when? How often are they held?"

"I have no idea." A mischievous smile suddenly replaced her frown of concentration. "Prime ministers are not the only ones who do not attend public masked balls."

Deverell shot her a quick grin. "This may be one to break all the rules." At once, a grave expression replaced his humor. "But we will do our best to make sure that one, at least, is not broken. I take a somewhat dim view of murder."

"When you say that, it—it scares me." She shuddered and urged the mare into a trot.

"I very much wish I did not have to. In fact," he added with considerable feeling, "I wish you were not involved in this at all."

"Well, I am," she said tartly. "I'm the one everyone is coming to about this wretched paper!"

"Not everyone. Only one person wants this. The others are after quite legitimate documents."

"How nice! Only one person haunting my house is a murderer! You have no idea how relieved that makes me feel!"

175

He laughed, and it was a pleasant sound in spite of the seriousness of the matter. "I don't believe you stand in any danger."

"And what of my father and Holloway?" she shot back.

"Someone panicked, I should think, when the paper went missing. Their first thought was to silence your father and his clerk. And since that damned code has not yet turned up— as far as they know—they must feel that your father did indeed have it and that they accomplished their purpose in keeping him from talking."

Leanora digested this. "And what do we do now? Turn it over to Bow Street?"

Deverell shook his head. "This is too delicate a matter for them, I fear. No, I think the Horse Guards are a better possibility—but not until we know what is involved. A fine mull we would make of it if we laid our story before one of the conspirators in this pretty plot."

"Do you think someone in the Horse Guards might be behind this?"

He frowned. "Could you positively state that no one there knows anything about this?"

"No," she admitted. "I suppose anybody could be involved. But what should we do?"

She knew his answer even before the broad grin spread across his dynamic face. Suppressed energy emanated from him in tangible waves, filling her with his eager excitement.

"I think I will look into it myself a bit," he said with a casualness that did not fool her for a minute.

"*We* will," she corrected without thinking. "I'm in this, too."

Whatever possessed her to say anything of the sort? she wondered a moment later. No sane woman would actually try to involve herself in an assassination plot! But she was already involved, and when she saw those devils of anticipation dancing in Deverell's eyes, she suspected that he was not entirely sane, either.

"Lord, how bored I've been!" he breathed, ignoring her last words. He was vibrantly alive, and his energy filled her as well. "I wonder if this is the only copy."

176

"They will have sent one to each conspirator, however many there are," she said, her quick mind keeping pace with his.

"It's been a week," he agreed. "It will have been replaced." He drew the page back out of his pocket and read it again. "I wonder who 'D' is," he mused. An amused expression hovered about his lips.

"It says to watch him closely, does it not? Do you think he is to give the signal for the assassination?"

"Or warn everyone if the plot is discovered," he suggested, obviously enjoying himself.

"Well, it has been. And the sooner they know, the better. *That* should stop them."

A strange smile quirked up the corners of his mouth. "Do you know, I don't think we should tell them."

"What? Are you mad?" She pulled her mare to a halt and stared at him. "We cannot let them murder Lord Grenville!"

He laughed again and urged his horse back to a trot. The gray followed. "No, but if this plan fails, they will only try again. Do but consider!"

Leonora did. "What do you propose, then?"

"I believe we should pretend we know nothing about this, then set a trap to capture the conspirators. That will be the only sure way of preventing the assassination, either now or in the future."

"But how? Unless I continue to say that all those papers are still missing. . . ."

Again, Deverell ignored her. "This copy's only value lies in the proof that the plot has not been discovered. Somehow, we must preserve that illusion." He fell silent, his eyes resting on her in a manner that she found strangely disconcerting. His gaze held not the least hint that he saw her as an attractive young lady. Her sole interest for him lay in whether or not she would make a capable assistant in whatever plan his fertile brain devised. She was not at all sure that she liked this scrutiny but could not help wondering if she measured up to his standards.

"I think," he said at last, "if you do not mind, it is time we returned to your house."

Did he not think her capable of helping? The possibility stung. "You mean there is an aspect of this you have not yet

177

worked out?" she demanded in mock astonishment to hide her chagrin.

He awarded her sally a quick grin. "Several aspects," he admitted.

They were silent for most of the return journey. At the door of Sherborne House, Deverell jumped lightly down to the pavement and turned to Leanora. She hesitated, then allowed him to grasp her slender waist and lift her from her saddle. She tried very hard not to enjoy the sensation of being held so capably in his strong hands, but it proved to be a losing battle. All too quickly he released her.

To her surprise and dismay, he swung back up onto his great roan stallion. "Are you not coming in?" she asked.

"Not at the moment. If you will excuse me, I have a number of plans to make. May I call upon you later?"

She gave her assent, glad she was not to be completely excluded, and watched him ride off. She turned the mare over to her groom to take back to the stable and climbed the stairs to the front door, lost in thought.

Donning a simple morning gown, she went to her father's room and found her Aunt Amabelle had joined Pagget and Xerk in their steadfast vigil. She took the valet's place, releasing him to seek some much needed rest, and settled down with the pug snuggled in her lap. If Lord Deverell intruded upon her troubled thoughts as often as did the plot to assassinate the prime minister at this Requiem Masque, she tried to convince herself that it was only because the two were at the moment inextricably entangled for her.

As the day wore on, her irritation with Deverell grew. How dare he leave her without any definite course of action to follow? She could only continue as she had, pretending ignorance of the papers' whereabouts, hoping she did not betray her knowledge to the wrong person.

Toward late afternoon, as she sat alone with her father, her aunt sent up the message that Reggie had called. Leaving Mrs. Tremly at the earl's side, she hurried downstairs, glad of the interruption to her uneasy thoughts. She could use an amusing half hour.

As she entered the saloon, Reggie looked up. "Nora, just the

178

person I need!" He held up a small embroidered box for her inspection. "What do you think?"

She took it and examined the intricate floral pattern. "Quite pretty," she pronounced. "What is it for? The era of patches is long passed."

He took it back, affronted. "Snuff," he uttered succinctly, his gaze challenging her to object.

"Oh." There was little more she could say. The delicate fabric box might indeed be unusual, but it would wear from handling and become stained from the finely ground tobacco. If Reggie was hoping to hit upon a new quirk of fashion, he was sadly out, here.

Reggie frowned. "You don't think it will catch on?" he asked, trying not to sound concerned.

Her reply, fortunately, was cut off by Tremly, who appeared in the doorway to announce the arrival of Captain Lord Deverell. All thoughts of snuff and fashion fled from Leanora's mind. Her gaze flew to the doorway, where his tall figure stood just behind the butler.

"Dev, huh?" Reggie looked up, momentarily emerging from his own preoccupation. "Lord, Nora, is he dancing attendance on you? Seems he's forever in your company."

Deverell grinned, his eyes brimful of amusement at these overheard words. Leanora froze in embarrassment, then her own sense of the ridiculous won out. She stood and moved forward easily, and as she took Deverell's offered hand, only a soft flush colored her cheeks.

"My dear Deverell!" Mrs. Ashton beamed on her visitor. "How delightful to see you." She threw a speculative glance at him, noted that he remained at her niece's side and smiled in a very satisfied manner. "Leanora, my love, do you keep Deverell company for a while. I have something of a most particular nature I wish to discuss with my son, so if you will excuse us?" Grasping Reggie's arm, Mrs. Ashton bustled him from the room.

"No, I say! Really, Mamma," could be heard before the door closed firmly behind them.

Leanora made the mistake of meeting Deverell's humorous glance and burst into a fit of the giggles. "I—I am sorry, my

179

lord," she apologized.

"On the contrary, I am quite flattered. You cannot fool me into believing she regards every gentleman with such complacency."

"That she does not!" she agreed with feeling. "But to be blatantly throwing me at your head . . . ! It is beyond anything!"

An odd smile twisted his lips into a decidedly charming expression. Leanora, vividly aware of this, thought it prudent to say no more. Instead, she looked away and busied herself with taking a seat. "Have you come to any conclusions about—about the matter we discussed this morning?"

"Yes. I think we had better return the original copy of that message as quickly as possible."

"Just give it back?" she demanded, dismayed. "But—to whom? Petersham and Kennington have both been asking for papers, and so has Sir William. Do you think it is Kennington?"

"At this point, I would not dare to hazard a guess," he admitted.

"Then what would you have me do? Would it not be potentially dangerous if we gave it to the wrong person? I can hardly show it to each of them and ask if they know anything about it!"

That drew a deep chuckle from him, and the compelling sound created the most unsettling sensations within her. "Most unwise, I should think," he agreed. "No, I believe we should give it to Petersham."

She searched his face but could read no clue as to his thoughts. "Do you think it is he, then, who is responsible?"

"Let us say rather that he will be the most harmless. If the paper is not his, he is more likely to return it than to decipher it." He met her worried gaze. "Kennington, unless I am much mistaken, would use it to create a nasty scandal—if he is innocent."

"Yes," she said slowly. "But if it *is* Kennington's, he will miss it at once!"

"If we handle this carefully, I believe we may be able to pull this off with success. I want you to contact Lord Petersham and tell him you have found the papers. Then give him a handful, and assure him you have not looked at them. You said you found them with your dinner plans? Then tell him that, and include a menu or two at the bottom of the stack so that he will believe you did not examine them. Do you think you can do it so that he will believe you?"

Leanora cast him a scornful glance. "Of course. He has the poorest opinion of women, you must know. I doubt he would suspect for a moment that state documents could interest me." The only objection she had to the plan was that she found herself willing to trust Deverell unquestioningly. That fact disturbed her, but for the moment she set it aside. "And what about Lord Kennington?"

"You will tell him exactly the same, only you will not, of course, give him the code. If he says anything that makes you think he is asking about it, you may tell him you found a sheet of idle scribblings and threw it out."

With this, she had to be satisfied. Deverell departed a few minutes later, taking Reggie with him. This left Leanora to face a eulogy from her aunt on Deverell's many estimable qualities, which she was only able to stem with difficulty. She then excused herself and went in search of Mr. Edmonton.

She found her father's secretary in his study, taking copious notes from a copy of the *London Times*. He set this aside and invited her to be seated.

"Just keeping up," he explained. "Lord Sherborne, if I know anything about him, will demand a summary of all major news events as soon as he awakens."

"Thank you, Mr. Edmonton," she said warmly, and knew he understood. It made all the difference in the world to her spirits when people behaved as if they expected her father to recover—and soon. She met his gaze and tried very hard to look her mischievous self. "You will never guess what I have just found," she said.

"What, those papers?" he asked dryly. Suddenly he sat up straight. "Are you serious? You have found them?"

She nodded. "Among my dinner plans. They must have gotten mixed up on my desk, and I shoved them all into a drawer without looking." How many more times would she

181

have to repeat that story? she wondered. "Do you think we should send a message to Petersham at once?"

He agreed, and she left him to take care of this while she went to prepare the papers that she would give him. The less neat they were, the better, she decided. First she collected all of the sheets she had decided belonged to him. Then she took the original copy of the code and several pages of notes on the dinner party that had not been held, and mixed these last together, putting them on the bottom of the stack. She then went upstairs to her father's room to await events.

Not for the world would she have admitted it to Deverell, but with every passing minute she grew more nervous. What if she seemed too eager as Petersham took the papers? What if he guessed that her artless reorganization of their order was intentional? What if she betrayed any knowledge that she should not possess?

When Tremly arrived less than an hour later with the information that Lord Petersham awaited her below, she was actually trembling. She stood hastily, knocked over her chair and almost ran from the room. She went first to her study, picked up the papers, then made her way to the back of the house. She paused outside the door to Mr. Edmonton's study to compose herself, then entered.

Petersham rose at once. "Lady Leanora!" He went to meet her, clasping her free hand between his own damp ones. His eager eyes fixed themselves upon the documents she carried. Was he as nervous as she? That prospect went a great way to calming her, for in his present state of agitation he would not be thinking clearly.

"Thank you for coming." She seated herself, then held out the papers. "I cannot tell you how ashamed I am of myself. I have had them all this time, locked in my desk, and never knew it. I can only offer my father's accident as my excuse."

Petersham took hold of the documents eagerly, as if afraid they might vanish. With hands that shook, he leafed through the stack, then heaved a great sigh of relief. "I—I cannot tell you how much work this has saved me, my dear," he said at last. Calmer, he glanced through the documents once more, this time smiling. "You have not even looked them over, I

182

see," he said, sounding immensely satisfied.

"No, I did not," she lied, trying to sound puzzled. "Should I have?"

"No, indeed not. Boring things for a lady. You merely did not notice these." With a broad grin on his pudgy features, he held out her dinner notes.

With a pretty show of embarrassment, she received them back. "I am so sorry!" she exclaimed. "I fear you see how it all happened. Just carelessness. But I have had a great deal on my mind. . . . Please forgive me."

He gave a hearty laugh that sounded to Leanora like the release of tension. "Nothing to forgive, my dear. Just glad to have these back, all right and tight. Now, you just forget all about this botheration. Won't keep you any longer; know you'll be wanting to go back to your father. Don't trouble to see me out."

This Leanora allowed Mr. Edmonton to do, while she sank back in her chair, shivering and chilled. He had noticed her menus but had not mentioned the sheet with the code. Lord Petersham, a respected member of the government, could very well be involved in the plot. But to what extent—if at all? She still recognized the possibility of his innocence. But if he was involved, who else joined in this treason? Kennington? Sir William? Or, as long as she was being ludicrous, what about her own father? And she could not forget Mr. Edmonton while she was at it! She knew she was being sarcastic, yet suddenly, terribly, she felt there was no one she could trust, except for Deverell and her cousin Reggie.

What a perfectly dreadful afternoon she was having! At least with Petersham it had gone more easily than she had feared, but then she had never really expected much trouble from him. And she had no clue as to whether his relief sprang from seeing the code or the documents.

She forced the questions from her mind. She still had Lord Kennington to face. As soon as Mr. Edmonton returned, she requested that he send a message to this gentleman, as well. Mr. Edmonton set about this at once, and Leanora, armed with her useful dinner notes, went to prepare a second stack of papers.

Kennington, to Leanora's surprise, arrived within the half hour. He had been on the verge of going out, he explained as he greeted her, and came at once. He took the papers she held out to him, waved aside her apologies and scrutinized each sheet with care. As he reached the bottom of the stack he smiled, then handed her the dinner notes.

"Is this all you found?" he asked gently.

Was that a touch of anxiety she detected in his voice? What else did he expect? The code? She stiffened, then forced herself to relax. "There were several documents belonging to Lord Petersham, which I have already given to him," she said slowly. "Oh, and a sheet of odd scribblings. I thought it might be his, but he just crumpled it up and threw it away. Was it yours?" She ended on a note of concern. "I could search again right now if you think anything is missing."

"That will not be necessary. I fear my clumsiness has already put you to a great deal of trouble." With repeated thanks for sending for him, he took his leave.

Leanora retired to her housekeeping room, desiring only to be alone for a few minutes. Which of the men was really responsible for this Requiem Masque plot? She could not force the question from her mind. Which of them wanted the prime minister dead? Or was it either of them? Did that dreadful paper in fact belong to someone else? But not her father! She repeated that, over and over, hanging onto it as if to her one tie to sanity.

Chapter 13

It was not until dinner had ended and Leanora had returned to her father's room that it occurred to her that she had no idea what to do next. So far, all she had thought about was the coded message. Now that it was no longer in her hands, she experienced the strangest sensation of loss and lack of direction.

She ought, of course, to send a message to Deverell, assuring him that she had complied with his instructions and telling him of the reactions she had observed. She could think of no way of doing this, though, for to send a footman with a missive to a gentleman's lodgings would not be in the least proper. Deverell should have thought of that, she fumed, and arranged to call upon her.

As the evening progressed and he did not put in an appearance, she grew steadily more irate. She fully recognized that her distressed mood was a direct result of having completed her current role, but that did not soothe her growing temper. Why did Deverell not come to see how she had fared? Did he not consider her help to be of sufficient importance? And what plans did he make for confounding the conspirators that he did not bother to mention to her? By the time she retired to her bed, she practically seethed with indignation.

Nor did the night watches bring calming relief. Sleep proved elusive, and she rose in the morning, looking every bit as haggard as she felt. A period of quiet reflection over breakfast served to convince her that Deverell must have had previous plans the evening before which had prevented him from hurrying to her side. This mollified her somewhat, and she was able to go to her father's chamber with the happy conviction that Deverell would arrive upon their doorstep at the earliest possible moment.

She was disturbed only a short while later, but by Edmonton, not Deverell. The morning's mail had brought a letter from old Grimsby, the bailiff at the Abbey, who had suffered an accident.

"A broken leg," Edmonton explained. "He wishes me to come down and oversee the last of the planting, if I can be spared."

"Of course you must go!" she exclaimed. "Oh, poor Grimsby. Go at once, he will be fretting so! I will write to you if—if anything should happen."

Mr. Edmonton departed within the hour, leaving Leanora to wonder what else could befall her. She felt very alone, bereft of any support, and found herself longing for Deverell to come.

He did not, but Reggie put in an appearance shortly after noon. His purpose, he quickly disclosed, was to invite his mother and cousin to join a small party of Deverell's arranging at Vauxhall Gardens that evening. Leanora, on the verge of declining because of her father, suddenly hesitated. Might this be a part of Deverell's plans? Not one to leave anything to chance, she instantly suggested that Reggie and Deverell dine with them before departing for the evening's entertainment. This Reggie agreed to gladly, though he could not at that time speak for his host.

If Leanora had hoped that Deverell would respond to the invitation in person, she was disappointed, for shortly after two, a wiry little man whom she recognized as his groom brought a brief letter to the house, thanking them for the kind suggestion and promising that he would present himself not a moment later than seven o'clock.

With this, Leanora was forced to be satisfied. The day seemed unconscionably long to her, and even Mrs. Ashton remarked that her beloved niece seemed sadly out of sorts. No

186

even riding in the Park served to divert her mind; for Deverell was not there, and at this point only a long talk with him would soothe her jaded nerves.

Even a conference with her father's doctor, who arrived in the late afternoon, did little to comfort her. The earl's pulse remained strong, the man informed her, but she could place little faith in his assurances that it was only a matter of time. Her father remained so still and pale, giving no sign of life except for his shallow breathing and steady heartbeat.

Restless, she went to her room and tried to interest herself in dressing for the evening. This did not take as long as she had hoped, and she made her way down to wait in the drawing room a full half hour before Reggie and Deverell were due to arrive. Mrs. Ashton, entering this apartment nearly twenty minutes later, beamed on her in approval.

"How lovely you look, my dear," she sighed. "The gentlemen are sure to admire you, for you must know that shade of rose becomes you so very well. Why, that is the very one I helped you pick out, is it not? I knew it would make up to admiration." She nodded, preening herself on the happy circumstance that had led her to urge her wayward niece to purchase that particular pale rose crepe. On a darker female the delicate color would have been lost, but on Leanora it only served to enhance her fair loveliness.

Leanora had not much longer to wait. The two gentlemen arrived punctually at seven, which led her to believe that Deverell and not Reggie was responsible for getting them there. She stood as they were announced, and Deverell's dark eyes, full of laughter, met her outraged gaze. He knew perfectly well how anxious she was to speak to him! That knowledge only served to further infuriate her.

He came forward, his eyes twinkling with suppressed amusement, and raised the hand she held out to him to his lips. 'Lady Leanora. Mrs. Ashton." He released her and turned to include her aunt in his devastating smile. "I must apologize for sending my invitation for Vauxhall through Reggie."

"And we must apologize for sending ours for dinner through him as well," Mrs. Ashton tittered.

"Poor Reggie, we have been treating him like a footman," Leanora said dryly.

"Quite disgraceful of us," Deverell agreed, "but then I had a number of . . . plans . . . to arrange."

Leanora's gaze flew to his, but could read no hint of his meaning in the dark, humorous depths of his eyes. She could only suppose that the evening had been arranged for a purpose, but what that might be escaped her.

Before she could frame a suitable question, Tremly entered to announce dinner. This was a simple affair, for there would be a lavish supper later at Vauxhall Gardens. As soon as they had eaten, the barouche was bespoken, and they set forth.

It was shortly discovered that Deverell had spared no pains to assure the ladies' enjoyment of the evening. They drove to Westminster, where they found sculls waiting to ferry them across the river. Opposite, Leanora could make out the countless glowing globes that lit the pleasure gardens.

They alighted at the water gate, then proceeded along the beautifully lit paths toward the center of the grounds where an orchestra could be heard playing. Here, amid the groves and colonnades, stood the magnificent rotunda where a concert was already in progress. Small supper boxes were laid out in two sweeping semi-circles that opened onto the colonnades. At every angle, gaily festooned paths led off through the groves offering the enticement of romantic strolls.

They joined the throng in the rotunda to listen to the orchestra. Deverell guided them to seats near one side, assured himself that his party was quite comfortable, then leaned back to look about the softly illuminated crowd.

Leanora, although always enjoying a concert, found herself more interested in Deverell and whatever plan he was carrying out. This was not the place for private speech, but later, after supper, she would try to entice him down one of the paths, perhaps to one of the tiny summer houses that were scattered about the gardens, and demand an explanation from him.

Sitting so close at his side, his presence could not but affect her. He was so very large, so very powerful and so elusive and enticing. . . . Unable to prevent herself, she peeped up at him

188

only to discover that his gaze had become fixed, that he watched someone intently.

She looked over at the side of the rotunda. A small party had just entered but did not appear the least bit interested in finding seats. Lord Kennington stood at their lead, his head bent down to catch the words of the dark, ethereal lady slightly behind him. He laughed softly, moved a step forward, and Leanora recognized her sister-in-law Julia. That beauty fluttered her fan, peeked up at Kennington in the most shockingly coquettish manner and moved back outside with an obvious invitation for her admirer to follow.

It was then that Leanora became aware of her brother. Gregory leaned negligently against the wall, watching his wife and Kennington with a fixed sneer on his lips. As the two moved away into the darkness outside, he attempted to straighten up, wavered alarmingly and sank back against the wall. Three parts disguised, Leanora realized with disgust. If he were not in his cups, surely he would have made some move to break up his wife's flirtation! It was not in the least like Gregory's hot temper to make no objection to her outrageous behavior.

She glanced back up at Deverell and noted that his narrowed gaze remained fixed on Gregory. Cold uncertainty engulfed her, tearing her apart. *Why* did Gregory do nothing? What power did Julia hold over him to make him turn a blind eye to her behavior? Or was it Kennington who held Gregory in check? The thought took root in her worried mind. She was being ridiculous! She was seeing conspirators everywhere! Oh, if only she had never heard of that hateful Requiem Masque! It made her doubt everyone, even her own brother!

The first portion of the concert ended, and Deverell shepherded his party outside to find the box that bore his name. Although Leanora would much rather have strolled about the grounds, she dutifully remained with her aunt, who exclaimed delightedly over everything. At Mrs. Ashton's request, Deverell had chairs placed at the front of the box and seemed content to sit and watch the passersby.

Leanora studied his profile covertly as she tried to decide

how best to separate him from her aunt and cousin long enough to demand a few answers that she shrewdly guessed would not be readily forthcoming. A never-ending parade passed before their box, watched closely by Deverell's amused eyes. As Leanora transferred her gaze to this crowd, she became aware of a gentleman in a nearby box staring fixedly across at them. In surprise, she recognized Sir William Holborne. She waved to him, and he at once excused himself from his own party and went to greet her.

He bowed low. "How delightful to see you, my fair wit. Never has it been my misfortune to be with such a boring party. I had begun to despair until I saw you."

She could not help but smile. She glanced across at his box again and recognized several prominent members of the government and their staid wives. "Good heavens!" she exclaimed before she could prevent herself. "Whatever has brought them to Vauxhall? Surely, they will not enjoy themselves here!"

"It was my Lord Petersham's suggestion that I bring them," he informed her, his manner inviting her to share the joke. "He, you will note, had the excellent good sense not to join us as of yet."

She cast a quick glance at Deverell to see if he noted Petersham's absence, but he appeared to pay no attention. Irritated with him for this lack of proper interest, she turned back to Sir William.

"May I be so rude as to steal you from your party for a few minutes?" he asked her. "I have a great desire to stroll through the grounds, but there is no one in my party capable of such exertion."

That he wished to speak to her, and preferably alone, she had no doubts. Would he have anything of use to tell her? She glanced at Deverell, hoping that he would give her some clue as to what she should do, but met his bland expression. What did he want? Out of pique, she decided to take matters into her own hands. She excused herself politely and went to the door at the back of the box to take Sir William's arm.

She waited until they had wandered a little ways along a

190

discreetly lit path, then turned to look up at her companion. "Well?" she asked, a mischievous smile playing about her lips. "To what do I owe the pleasure of this invitation?"

He laughed softly. "You would not believe me, I suppose, if I told you that your company was all that I desired?"

"No," she said frankly after a moment's consideration.

"I thought not," he admitted, his amusement clear to be heard. "I wished to tell you that you have made Petersham a very happy man."

She smiled. "He made that extremely clear."

"To think you had those papers all along," he mused, shaking his head. "How ever did they become mixed up with your menu plans, of all things?"

She told him, and he laughed. "What a pity you never found out if your seating plan would have worked," he said at last. "My dear Leanora, you must always be a political hostess. Never, but never, marry a man who will not force you to use your talents to the fullest!"

"I promise you I shall not," she assured him. They reached a crossing of paths, and Leanora turned down one that would eventually take them back to her box. "I am glad the papers are all safely back where they belong."

With this, Sir William agreed. "And to think of all that fuss made over something that was not even all that important," he added, shaking his head. "But that is Petersham, all over. By the by, there was an odd page of gibberish mixed up with the papers. Petersham threw it away. I do hope it was nothing of importance?" He ended on a note of query.

"Gibberish?" she asked, stalling. Did that mean the code was not Petersham's, after all? "It—it must have been one of Kennington's pages, then. It is odd; I do not remember seeing anything like that. I must have missed it when I sorted the pages out. I fear I did not examine any of them very closely."

"Kennington?" Sir William stopped, turning to look down at her. "What has Kennington to say to anything?"

"Why, only that I had some of his papers, as well. Did I not tell you? It was the stupidest thing!"

Sir William listened to her story, his eyes narrowed but a

smile playing about his lips. He laughed softly as she described that gentleman's discomfiture. "My dearest Leanora, did you not learn a single thing from his speech that we could use? It might not be exactly . . . *comme il faut,* shall we say? But would it not be delightful if you had discovered something to put that dashed disagreeable fellow at a disadvantage?"

Leanora could only agree and shook her head in mock contrition. "It is too true. I see that I am quite unworthy of being my father's daughter, for I did not read so much as a single page."

He laughed again and in a very short time returned her to her box. As she approached, Deverell looked up and directed a very penetrating gaze at them. To her dismay, a thrill raced through her as those dark eyes sought hers. In a moment the effect vanished, for she drew close enough to detect the amusement that lay just beneath the surface.

As soon as Sir William had returned to his own party, Reggie stood. "My mamma wants to see the fountains. Will you bear us company, Nora? Dev?"

Deverell came to his feet. "Unless Lady Leanora is tired of walking," he said dryly.

This sally she awarded no more than a perfunctory smile. She led the way, with Deverell at her side, along the colonnade to the first of the magnificent fountains, which glowed brightly with an array of colored lanterns. While Mrs. Ashton admired this loudly, Leanora prepared herself to answer Deverell's expected catechism. To her further irritation with him, this was not forthcoming. Instead, he, too, evinced a considerable enjoyment in the dancing water before them.

She was on the verge of telling him, in no uncertain terms, what she thought of his provoking conduct, when her name was spoken in apparent delight by a gentleman. Turning, she beheld Lord Dalmouth.

"I dared not hope to see you this evening," Dalmouth declared as he took her hand in his. To her surprise, he raised her fingers to his lips, then pressed them in an intimate manner before releasing her.

"Did you come with Gregory and Julia?" she asked,

ZEBRA HOME SUBSCRIPTION SERVICES, INC.

P.O. BOX 5214

120 BRIGHTON ROAD

CLIFTON, NEW JERSEY 07015-5214

Get a Free
Zebra
Historical
Romance

*a $3.95
value*

FREE

BOOK CERTIFICATE

ZEBRA HOME SUBSCRIPTION SERVICE, INC.

YES! Please start my subscription to Zebra Historical Romances and send me my free Zebra Novel along with my first month's Romances. I understand that I may preview these four new Zebra Historical Romances Free for 10 days. If I'm not satisfied with them I may return the four books within 10 days and owe nothing. Otherwise I will pay just $3.50 each; a total of $14.00 (a $15.80 value—I save $1.80). Then each month I will receive the 4 newest titles as soon as they come off the press for the same 10 day Free preview and low price. I may return any shipment and I may cancel this arrangement at any time. There is no minimum number of books to buy and there are no shipping, handling or postage charges. Regardless of what I do, the FREE book is mine to keep.

Name _____
                     (Please Print)

Address _____ Apt. # _____

City _____ State _____ Zip _____

Telephone ( ) _____

Signature _____
        (if under 18, parent or guardian must sign)

Terms and offer subject to change without notice.   11-88

ACCEPT YOUR **FREE GIFT** AND EXPERIENCE MORE OF THE PASSION AND ADVENTURE YOU LIKE IN A HISTORICAL ROMANCE

Zebra Romances are the finest novels of their kind and are written with the adult woman in mind. All of our books are written by authors who really know how to weave tales of romantic adventure in the historical settings you love.

Because our readers tell us these books sell out very fast in the stores, Zebra has made arrangements for you to receive at home the four newest titles published each month. You'll never miss a title and home delivery is so convenient. With your first shipment we'll even send you a **FREE** Zebra Historical Romance as our gift just for trying our home subscription service. No obligation.

BIG SAVINGS AND **FREE** HOME DELIVERY

Each month, the Zebra Home Subscription Service will send you the four newest titles as soon as they are published. (We ship these books to our subscribers even before we send them to the stores.) You may preview them *Free* for 10 days. If you like them as much as we think you will, you'll pay just $3.50 each and *save $1.80 each month* off the cover price. *AND you'll also get FREE HOME DELIVERY.* There is never a charge for shipping, handling or postage and there is no minimum you must buy. If you decide not to keep any shipment, simply return it within 10 days, no questions asked, and owe nothing.

Zebra Historical Romances Make This Special Offer...

IF YOU ENJOYED READING THIS BOOK, WE'LL SEND YOU ANOTHER ONE

FREE

a $3.95 value

No Obligation!

—Zebra Historical Romances Burn With The Fire Of History—

unnerved by the warmth of his demeanor.

"I did," he admitted. "But I seem to have lost them. There was no one in our box when I went there just now."

"I am certain they will return in time for the supper." She tried to move away from him, but he accompanied her. Why was he going out of his way to be so abnormally charming? The situation confused her, leaving her ill at ease.

"I hope that your presence here means that there has been an improvement in Lord Sherborne's condition?" he asked.

"The doctor is taking an optimistic view." Firmly, she fought the rude impulse to tell him that it was none of his concern. Why was he interested? Was it part of the attentive role he played? Or did he have another reason, a secret one, for being curious?

Dalmouth spotted a friend nearby, bowed low over her hand and took his leave—but not before promising himself the pleasure of stopping by their box before the evening was over.

Perturbed, Leanora watched him walk away. There was a certain grace to his movements she had not noted before, an elegance to his dress and bearing. Had she allowed her initial dislike of the company he kept to cloud her judgment of him? Was he, as Gregory had averred, a reformed character?

So lost in these tangled thoughts was she that she started when a hand touched her arm. She looked up into Deverell's rugged face and met his dark, mocking eyes. His lips quirked into a disturbing half-smile.

"Would you care to stroll about the gardens?" he asked.

At last! Dalmouth fled from her mind as she accepted Deverell's arm. As soon as they were alone, far down one of the innumerable paths, she could ask him the questions that tumbled about in her mind.

"It is a beautiful evening," he commented as they strolled along a path lit by colored globes.

She agreed. A warm breeze ruffled through her hair, but she had no need of the cashmere shawl that hung about her elbows. Just ahead of them, another fountain spurted and danced, sending flashes of colored light shooting high in the air. If only such a serious topic did not lie between them, she could easily relax in this idyllic atmosphere.

They left the vicinity of the fountain, and he guided her along another softly lit path, through one of the groves. His hand was warm where it lightly grasped her arm, and for once she enjoyed the knowledge that there was a very capable gentleman in control of her troubles.

Ahead of them stood a tiny summerhouse, decorated about the outside with numerous lanterns. Would this be private enough? she wondered, looking about at other strolling couples. Reprehensibly, she knew she would not mind if it took them a very long while to find a safe place on this beautiful night.

To her surprise, but not her displeasure, he did not lead her inside the kiosk. Instead, he directed her steps along a side path, then paused in a patch of shadows. Somehow, she stood very close to him, the crisp cloth of his mulberry sleeve brushing along the bare skin of her arm, sending enticing thrills through her. The heady scent of the gardens filled her, and something more, something strictly masculine and overpowering and very urgent, stirred strange sensations within her. Succumbing to the spell, she raised her face, hesitant, nervous, yet longing for the kiss she felt sure would come.

He was not looking at her. He stared back the way they had come, at the kiosk. Leanora stiffened, furious with herself for allowing Deverell's undeniable appeal to run riot over her. Her mind should have been on the Requiem Masque, not him!

As she subjected herself to a mental rake-down for her foolish—and badly misplaced!—romantic fantasies, a woman slipped from the kiosk, paused to look about, then fled down one of the other paths. Leanora straightened, casting a quick glance at Deverell's dynamic profile. Was he waiting for something to happen? Had they followed someone here?

A minute passed, and a gentleman appeared in the kiosk's doorway. He, too, looked about, then sauntered off in another direction. Something about him seemed vaguely familiar, but in the dim light it was hard to be sure.

To her surprise, Deverell made no move to follow the man.

Instead he continued to wait. Leanora looked about, puzzled. Was there someone else nearby? Was it not the kiosk that he watched, after all?

"What are you waiting for?" she demanded at last, exasperated beyond endurance.

"Waiting?" He turned innocent dark eyes on her.

"Don't try that game with me, it won't fadge!" she informed him roundly if improperly. Then, in a near-whisper, she added: "I thought you brought me down here to tell me what has been going on and what I am to do next!"

He raised humorous eyebrows. "My dear Lady Leanora, as far as I am aware, there is nothing for you to do next."

She almost stamped her foot in impatience. "Do not be so provoking!" she ordered in an angry undervoice. "You know very well what I mean. I have returned the papers to Petersham and Kennington. Do you not want to know what they said?"

"Very little, I would suspect," he said dryly. "Are you trying to tell me that one of them gave himself away?"

"No," she admitted, and fumed as his soft chuckle shook his massive frame. "Oh, you are the most odious creature alive!"

"Because I do not want to thrust you into the middle of danger?" he asked.

"I would seem already to be there," she shot back.

Abruptly, he grasped her arm and propelled her down the path. She started to protest, thought better of it, and instead peered ahead into the near darkness, trying to see who it was that they followed. There seemed to be no one about at the moment, which perplexed her further.

As suddenly as they had started up, they stopped again. To her irritation, Deverell peered off through the trees and shrubs at an angle that was beyond her inches to achieve.

"I do not suppose you would care to tell me what we are doing?" she whispered in exasperation.

"Watching, at the moment." His voice held a suppressed excitement not untinged by enjoyment.

"Who?"

His only response was a soft, provoking laugh. He started

slowly forward, but she grasped his arm and stood her ground.

"I will not go one more step until you explain!" she threatened.

"Then you had best let go of me, unless you wish to be dragged." With infuriating ease, he removed her hand from his coat sleeve and continued without her.

She remained where she was for something less than ten seconds. Her refusal to go on would hurt no one but herself, for being with Deverell was the only likely method of getting information out of him. She caught up with him quickly, met his laughing eyes with a stare of steely hauteur and stalked on beside him with what dignity she could muster.

"Was my returning the papers to Petersham and Kennington of no importance at all?" she asked, curiosity at last getting the better of her.

"Of course it was. Why do you ask?" He did not so much as glance at her.

"Because you were not the least bit interested in it!"

"Unlike you, my dear Lady Leanora, I have faith. I believed you were more than capable of carrying out so simple a task. Had anything untoward happened, you would have let me know at once, would you not?"

"How could I? You must know it would be quite improper of me!"

He looked at her, a quizzical expression on his face. "Would that have stopped you in an emergency?"

She glared at him. "It is odiously disagreeable of you to be right," she sighed. They continued in silence for some distance. Absently, she took his arm when he offered it. "What am I to do next?" she asked at last.

"Nothing" came the prompt reply.

"*Nothing?* But—no! I cannot and will not do nothing! You know what the plot is! How can I just forget about it?"

"I said nothing about forgetting it, did I?" he asked with his calm imperturbability. "It is just that I want you to *do* nothing."

"Why? Or do I mean 'why not'?" She considered.

That drew his deep, compelling chuckle from him once more. "Because any change in your normal routine might occasion interest from our guilty party. I am not sure it was wise to let you admit you ever had those papers in your possession. You may be watched."

That sent a shiver of fear through her, but not for the world would she admit it to Deverell. Involuntarily, her grip tightened about his arm. With his free hand, he covered her cold fingers. For a long moment he left it there, then released her with what almost amounted to a soft caress.

"If we stay here any longer," he said softly, "we will be late for supper."

Her head jerked up to stare into his laughing eyes. "Where is our—our quarry?"

"Heading back to the boxes. Come, let us do the same."

They emerged from the path into a gaily lit colonnade. In a very few minutes they were back in their box, and while her aunt rapturized over the beauty of the pleasure gardens, Leanora cast a surreptitious glance about. Lord Petersham, she noted, had joined Sir William's party. She could not see Dalmouth and must suppose her brother's box to be out of her sight.

Supper was served almost at once, and Leanora emerged from her abstraction to find her plate being filled with exquisitely thin slices of ham. Deverell himself was engaged in carving a pheasant, and the air about them filled with delicious aromas from a wide variety of side dishes.

As the remnants of the meal were finally cleared away, Deverell refilled everyone's glasses with the excellent rack punch. "I believe the fireworks will soon begin. Shall we find places?"

Still carrying their glasses, they left the box and joined the throng heading toward the clearing where the fireworks would shortly be ignited. To her surprise, Leanora heard her name called. She turned to find Gregory, Dalmouth and Julia bearing down on her. Gregory, although his eyes still glittered alarmingly from drink, appeared to have overcome the worst of his earlier mood. He seemed abnormally delighted to find his sister, complimented her effusively and fell into step beside her. Dalmouth, beginning to succumb to the amount of wine he had obviously imbibed at supper, somehow moved in on her other side. With difficulty, Leanora prevented her punch from being spilt as the two gentlemen each tried to take her arm.

She was never quite sure how he managed it, but suddenly it was Deverell who walked protectively at her side. Neatly, he guided her through the growing crowd, leading her and her aunt to a place where they could be sure of a clear view of the fireworks. Grateful for this masterly bit of maneuvering, Leanora smiled her thanks up at her companion.

The look in his dark eyes warmed her with security. As provoking as he might be at times, she could be glad of his presence at others.

At that moment, her arm was jostled. Steadying her punch once more, she looked up, startled to recognize Lord Kennington. He apologized, smiling at her in a manner that made her acutely uneasy. Did he seek to draw near to Julia? If so, he might find that Gregory was approaching a belligerent stage of inebriation and might very well object.

She moved away, a step closer to Deverell, only to find that he had fallen back to make way for several elderly ladies: members of Sir William's party, Leanora realized, as she saw Lord Petersham approaching with his assistant following in his wake. Both Petersham and Sir William stopped to greet her, then moved on.

And not a moment too soon. The first of the rockets went up, and Leanora was caught in the magical spell of exploding lights and fire. She sipped from her glass as another rocket went heavenward and brilliant colors flashed against the dark sky.

She choked, for the punch tasted bitter. Could something have fallen into it, some ash from the rockets? She poured out the remaining liquid, sorry to have wasted such an excellent drink. A hush fell over the crowd, and she craned her neck to see a giant Catherine wheel begin its frenzied spinning.

Brilliant sparks shot away into the night as the wheel spun until it was nothing more than a blurred mass of colors. At last it slowed but continued spinning in hazy circles. Or was it the crowd that spun? Lights seemed to flash everywhere, and there was silence, though she could see the weaving head of the man before her, his mouth moving but no sound coming forth. And Deverell, above her, so far above her. . . .

Trees, stars, shooting flames, even people began floating about her in an unreal manner. Or was it she? She felt nothing, not the ground, not Deverell's hand that gripped her arm. Was he trying to say something? Her glass dropped from her nerveless fingers, her blurring gaze skimmed over the crowd and she felt herself falling, falling, without ever touching ground.

Chapter 14

Slowly, very slowly, Leanora became aware that her head ached abominably. How could it have gotten so bad without it awakening her earlier? She rolled over, burying her face in her pillow, wishing for some relief. If she opened her eyes, she had the distinct feeling that the top of her head might come off.

"She is waking up."

The voice, speaking such obvious words as if at a great distance, disturbed her, but it proved too great an effort to fathom its mysteries. There came a murmuring response, but that drifted off as sleep reclaimed her.

When her eyes at last fluttered open, sunlight streamed in through a crack at the curtained windows. It must have been well advanced into the morning. What was she doing still abed? The thought was incongruous, for she was always an early riser. A rustling of silken skirts penetrated to her still fogged mind, and she managed, with tremendous effort, to turn her head far enough to see that Mrs. Ashton sat in a chair beside her bed.

"Aunt Amabelle?" Her mouth felt strangely dry, and the words caught in her throat as if reluctant to be spoken. She moved her head again, and the room spun about her in a most unmannerly fashion.

"Leanora, my love!" her aunt exclaimed. Embroidery was flung aside as that lady almost sprang to her side. "Leanora, dearest, how do you feel?"

"Feel?" She tried to sit up, found her muscles strangely

reluctant to cooperate and sank back weakly against the pillows. "What—what . . . ?"

"Be still, my dear. Don't try to talk. You have been ill."

Ill? Her eyelids closed by themselves, shutting out the hurtful light. She remembered nothing, no illness, only a headache that had not completely departed.

When next her eyes opened, the room was lit by a pale, diffused light. A screen stood by her bed, shielding her from the direct glare of a branch of candles. Mrs. Ashton again sat nearby, and this time the contents of the room did not behave in a giddy manner when Leanora moved her head.

"Aunt?" she murmured, and was relieved that the simple syllable did not tear at her throat.

At once, Mrs. Ashton rose and poured water from a silver pitcher into a glass. "Here, my love, the doctor said you would be thirsty." She signaled to a maid that Leanora had not previously noticed, and the girl hurried forward. While Amabelle Ashton supported Leanora's limp form, the maid arranged several pillows behind her. This accomplished, Leanora was allowed to sink back into a semi-sitting position. Her aunt raised the cup to her lips, and she took a long, welcome swallow.

"I—I have been ill," she said slowly, still confused.

"Oh, my love, how you frightened us so! There you were, enjoying the fireworks, then you just collapsed. I vow, I do not know how we would have gone on, but Lord Deverell swept you up in his arms and carried you back to the box. If only you could have been aware of it all, for it was above anything romantic. That is, it would have been," Mrs. Ashton corrected herself conscientiously, "had you not been so terribly pale. Nothing we did would awaken you, and his lordship sent for a carriage and carried you back here. So attentive he was, and with his leg bad, but there! You would never have guessed it, so easily did he bear you, as if you were as light as a feather and not the least burden to him!"

Leanora shook her head, trying to remember. "Fireworks," she repeated to herself. Where—and why—had she been viewing fireworks? "Where . . ." she began, then: "Vauxhall?"

"But of course, my dear. We went to Vauxhall, with Lord Deverell and Reggie. Do you not remember?"

Leanora rested against the softness of the pillows. "No. It— it seems I must thank Deverell. And apologize."

But that last her aunt would not hear of. "For one cannot help falling ill, my love, as I am sure his lordship understands. A most superior gentleman, you must know, for he behaved exactly as one would wish and seemed to know just what was needed. Everyone has been so very good, my dear. You can have no idea."

"Everyone? How—how long have I been ill?"

"Why, this is the third day. Such an uproar as there has been, with both you and your dear father unconscious. I vow, I do not know how I would have gone on. But Gregory has been here, and Julia as well." Her aunt plucked at her skirts. "Julia has been particularly helpful, though little I would have expected it. You must know, my love, that she has taken to ordering everything in the household!"

"That must have made Mrs. Tremly happy," Leanora murmured. She felt a bit stronger and reached out for the water. Her aunt picked it up at once and held it to her lips again.

"Indeed, it did, though at first I was afraid she would not quite like it. But with the household at sixes and sevens, I was glad she took charge."

At the moment, it all seemed too much for Leanora. Julia, giving orders in her house. Gregory, making free of her papers, she had no doubt. What were they up to? She felt too weak, too dizzy to try and fathom the reasons. It was sufficient that the household continued to function. Everything else could wait until later.

She closed her eyes as a pleasant drowsiness overcame her. She dozed off and did not stir again until the morning light once more streamed through the window. This time when she tried to sit up, she found that her arms would cooperate. She pulled the pillows, which the maid must have removed, back behind her, then rested from the exertion. Shortly she was able to ring for her abigail and contemplate the prospect of tea and rolls with something approaching eagerness.

A short time later, as she nibbled at a freshly baked muffin, she found she was not as hungry as she expected. It was no wonder she was weak, if she ate so little! She picked up her tea, to which her maid had added liberal amounts of sugar and milk, and found it vastly satisfying.

She took another sip and tried to recall what her aunt had told her. She had taken ill at Vauxhall. . . . Vaguely, she remembered the party. She had walked with Deverell; he had been following someone. . . . It was all too hazy.

But what else had Mrs. Ashton said? Something that had disturbed her, about the house. . . . Gregory and Julia! She should be glad that they were taking charge, for her aunt had never been one to manage. But what . . . ? But Gregory . . . her earrings . . . papers. . . . Memory flooded back, and she sat up suddenly, splashing tea out of her cup and over the coverlet on the bed. Absently, she mopped at it with a napkin.

Solicitude was not noticeably one of Gregory's strong points. Nor, under normal circumstances, did he ever betray any desire to be of service to anyone but himself—not out of malice, of course, but out of a supreme and unshakable self-centeredness. Therefore, if he were in the house, he had reasons of his own. Was he looking for other things to steal and sell?

Or did he look for a certain paper, written in code, that he had no idea had already been found?

That thought could not be shaken off. She closed her eyes, sinking back against the pillows, hating her weakness. She had to get up, find out what was happening. Three whole days—or was it four?—had passed. What was Deverell doing? Had he discovered anything more of the Requiem Masque?

Her eyes flew open as the door creaked, then moved a few inches, and Mrs. Ashton peeped around the edge. Seeing her niece propped up and awake, she came into the room, beaming.

"How glad I am to see you better, my love. And you have eaten something! How often I have thought—"

"How is my father?" Leanora broke in quickly.

Mrs. Ashton's pale eyes misted over. "There has been no change in him, my dear, but the doctor keeps insisting that his pulse is stronger." She shook her head. "I am sure it must be so, but he does not *move*."

Leanora reached out a shaky hand, and her aunt took it in a warm clasp. "He—he will get better," Leanora insisted.

"Of course," Mrs. Ashton agreed, though somewhat doubtfully. "I have been telling everyone that when they call. Oh! Where have I put them?" She looked about, found her reticule dangling at her wrist and began searching through it. In a moment, she brought out a napkin in which she had wrapped a small handful of cards. These she handed to Leanora. "They have all been asking after you," she explained. "I promised I would give you their cards the moment you were awake."

Leanora accepted them and glanced through the names: Sir William and even Lord Petersham. The next bore Dalmouth's name, which surprised her until she recalled how unusually attentive and charming he had been on the last two occasions they had met. Deverell's card lay just beneath Dalmouth's, and in spite of the fact he could hardly have done less, it pleased her.

"And the roses, my love. Are they not pretty?"

Leanora looked up, and her aunt directed her gaze to a small table that stood near the window. A huge vase, filled to overflowing with fresh buds of yellow and white, had been placed upon it. Then she saw another, with large pink blossoms, on her dresser. A small bouquet of violets were arranged in a bowl.

"Who . . . ?" she asked, trying not to hope.

"Lord Deverell," her aunt told her, and there was more than a hint of smugness in her voice. "So kind of him. These are the third he has sent, you must know, for he wanted them fresh when you awakened. And Reggie, dear boy, brought the violets yesterday."

"It was very kind of both of them," Leanora asserted. "I must write and thank them."

"They are both sure to call this morning," Mrs. Ashton told her happily. "Oh, my dear, such flattering attention as Lord Deverell is showing! And he is so very much the gentleman! I cannot but be glad that Vincent had chosen such a man for his closest friend, for it shows that he, too, was a man of excellent character and must surely have thrown off the rackety ways

205

that I so deplored!"

For several more minutes, Leanora was obliged to listen to a mother's remembrances of a beloved son. She herself had shared those feelings, though had perhaps been more perceptive than her aunt of Vincent's shortcomings. There had been that devilry about him, that conviction in his own invulnerability, that sublime disregard for his safety. Nothing, she realized with sudden insight, could have prevented Vincent from entering full fling into his last mission. The love she could not give would have made no difference.

And Lord Deverell. . . . She was well aware of their likenesses, the barely leashed energy, the dashing air of romance and daring that hung about them. But she had recovered from the spell of Vincent's weaving. Would she do the same with Deverell's? She could only hope so.

"But I can see that you are tired, my love," Mrs. Ashton was saying. "I will come back later, when you have rested."

Leanora opened eyes she had not realized she had shut, and tears spilled down her cheeks. It must be the illness, laying her low to melancholy thoughts. It was time she gave her mind a new direction, left her bed, resumed her chores—and wove herself once more into the threads of her mystery. She sat up resolutely, then sank back as a wave of dizziness washed over her. Her determination out-stripped her strength, it seemed.

It was not until the following morning that she finally ventured out of bed. Over her aunt's protests, she requested her abigail to assist her in dressing. This accomplished, she was obliged to lie down upon a day bed until her weakness passed. Still, it required the assistance of both her maid and her aunt to support her down the stairs to the drawing room, where she was tenderly laid upon the couch with orders not to move. This was one time Leanora was willing to obey.

A breakfast tray was brought to her there, and Mrs. Ashton joined her, exclaiming that this was just like an *alfresco* meal, so quaint as it was to be eating from trays on such tiny tables. With the remnants of their meal carried away, both ladies sat sipping tea.

It was not long before a soft knock sounded on the door and

Tremly entered to announce the arrival of a visitor. Before he could ask whether or not they were receiving, Deverell stepped past the butler, his presence filling not only the doorway but the room as well. He came quickly forward and took Leanora's hand.

"Tell me at once if I intrude. I merely wished to assure myself that you were indeed better."

How could she possibly object to such a greeting? Warm color touched her pale cheeks as she told him he was most welcome and gestured for him to be seated. He turned to greet Mrs. Ashton, then drew the offered chair up beside the sofa. Her flush deepened as she remembered the services he was said to have performed for her when she fell ill, and she raised a shy face as he settled beside her. To her consternation, a warm glow lit the dark depths of his eyes. There were deep lines that she did not remember etched about their corners and also about his mouth. These seemed to lessen somewhat as he studied her countenance intently.

"So good of you to come, my lord," Mrs. Ashton declared in delight, momentarily drawing his attention. "You must know, your arrival is most perfectly timed. I did not want to leave you alone, my love," she added to Leanora, "but I wish to look in on your poor dear father. And now that Lord Deverell is here, I can leave you in safe hands for a little while. Pray, forgive me for running off like this." She rose, and Deverell followed suit at once, taking the hand she extended to him. She gave his a significant squeeze, threw a look pregnant with meaning at Leanora and left the room.

Her aunt lacked any semblance of subtlety! Leanora fumed. She could not possibly have made her meaning and hopes more obvious! To cover her embarrassment, Leanora rushed into speech. "I—I believe I must thank you."

Deverell's tantalizing smile played about his lips, further diminishing the lines. "For what?" A touch of humor lurked in his deep voice.

"The flowers. They are quite lovely. And according to my aunt, you had sent others, before, that I did not see."

"The merest trifles."

"But lovely, nonetheless." The next had to be said, and the

207

sooner she got it over with, the better. "I also must thank you for your assistance when I fell ill."

"Again, a trifling matter. I was glad to be of service."

"Trifling to you, perhaps, but not to me, or to my aunt. I do most sincerely thank you for taking charge of everything."

"It is not entirely an onerous occurrence when a lovely young lady faints in your arms." He managed to make light of the event, and the quizzing note in his voice effectively robbed her of embarrassment.

She was able to smile. "I cannot think how I came to do anything so silly."

"Can you not?" He drew an enameled snuff box from the depths of his coat pocket and took a meditative pinch. "Did you not feel unwell earlier?"

"Not in the least." Her brow furrowed as she considered the matter. "I have had some trouble remembering all that happened that evening," she said slowly, "but I am quite sure I was not experiencing dizzy spells or—or anything of that nature."

"I am quite sure you were not, either," he said and shut his box with a snap. "Tell me, what did you and Sir William talk about when you took that stroll?"

"Sir William?" she said slowly, considering for a moment. "I believe . . . yes, I am almost sure it was the papers. He teased me for having them the entire time. I don't think I remember anything else."

"So, you talked of the papers," Deverell murmured. His eyes were half hooded, his voice too smooth.

Leanora looked at him uneasily. "Is there any reason why we should not? Petersham told him, of course, as soon as he had them."

"And where did this discussion take place?"

Leanora did not like the almost purring note in his voice. "Why?" she asked. "Does it matter? We walked along one of the paths, I believe. I did not really notice. But we were not gone long, were we?"

"No, not long," he confirmed. "Just long enough."

"What do you mean?" Even as she asked the question, a cold touch of fear ran through her.

"You talked openly of finding the missing papers," he said, his voice biting with an unfamiliar edge of steel. "Anyone could have overheard you."

"I—I suppose so," she agreed, not liking this at all.

"And your . . . illness . . . came on quite abruptly. You were drinking a glass of punch, I believe?"

She shook her head. "I don't remember. There were fireworks. . . ." Her voice trailed off as she tried to recall.

"You were drinking punch," Deverell affirmed. "And a number of people came up and spoke to you and jostled your arm. Damn!" he swore suddenly, coming to his feet and taking several swift, halting strides about the room. "Any one of them could have done it!"

"Could have done what?" It was barely a whisper. Her eyes remained glued to his restless figure.

"Have you not guessed, my sweet innocent? Any one of them could have put something in that damned punch you were drinking."

"But—but *why?*" She shook her head slowly, trying to comprehend. "Do you mean . . . you *cannot* mean that someone tried to—to make me ill on purpose?"

"Possibly, but I doubt they hoped you would be merely ill."

The blood drained from her face, leaving her every bit as dizzy as she had been the last couple of days. "That—that is absurd!" she whispered.

"This whole business is absurd. But consider!" He sank back into his chair at her side and took her clenched hands between his own. "The death of your father's clerk and his own 'accident,' the very same night."

"No," she protested. "Holloway had nothing to do with this—did he? There have been funds missing at the Home Office. . . ."

"Possibly," Deverell said, but he sounded skeptical. "But the timing makes it too much of a coincidence. And do not forget the house breaking or the code. Then, as soon as it becomes common knowledge that you had that dangerous code, you are taken mysteriously ill."

"It—was it common knowledge?" She seemed to be floating in midair, surrounded by the oddest sense of unreality. The

209

pressure on her hands increased to a painful intensity, and vaguely, she realized that she was falling sideways from the pillows at her back. She straightened up, and his grip relaxed somewhat. With difficulty she concentrated on what he had just said. "You think someone overheard me talking to Sir William, was afraid I had seen their precious code and tried to—to silence me?"

"Silence," he repeated, an odd, unpleasant smile on his lips. "That is one way of putting it. How much of this does your father's secretary know?"

"Mr. Edmonton? Only about the papers. I did not tell him about the code."

"Good. Where is he?"

"At the Abbey. He received a letter from our bailiff and posted down. Last week, that must have been. It would have been the day after I found the papers."

Deverell nodded slowly. "Keep him down there."

Leanora stared at him through rounded eyes. "You are serious, aren't you? You really think someone tried to kill me."

"Whoever our man is, he does not take chances. He already made an attempt on your father, and Edmonton is the next likely target. Send him a message to stay where he is for now. As long as he is out of town, I don't think he will be considered a danger."

She hugged herself, feeling cold and empty and ill. None of this was real. It couldn't be! Deverell had to be wrong! But somewhere, deep within her, a little voice kept whispering *"what if he isn't?"*

Deverell dropped to one knee at her side. "I have distressed you. Forgive me, but you had to be warned, especially in your present state. You are too weak and vulnerable right now."

She looked up into his frowning eyes, meeting them squarely. "Do you think he—whoever he is—will make another attempt on me?"

"It is very possible," Deverell admitted.

She closed her eyes. What form would a new attack take? A runaway carriage? Another glass of punch? Both took planning. Her villain was a very careful, methodical person, it seemed. Suddenly her eyes flew open.

"Planning!" she exclaimed. "You cannot be right, my lord! If this—this man did not suspect until that night at Vauxhall that I had seen the code, then how could he have had something there to slip into my drink?"

Deverell rose and resumed his pacing. "It would not be impossible. In my—my travels, shall we say?—I have come across rings that have a cavity carved beneath the stone. A person may carry a powder or liquid safely within, ready in case of an emergency." He paused, regarding her narrowly. "I think," he said in a slow, lazy voice, "that it might be well if you retired to Sherborne Abbey for a spell."

Escape! It sounded tempting, to retreat to safety. If the doctor said a journey would not harm her father, they could leave any time.

"But there is so much unsettled," she said aloud, then realized the truth. "I am not so poor spirited, my lord." She gave a very shaky laugh. "I find I cannot leave town with everything up in the air like this. Not until we know what lies behind this Requiem Masque—and have captured the conspirators."

"It is hardly a safe occupation for you to engage in. You will be better off in the country."

"Perhaps, but I will not go." She met his determined eyes with defiance. "You wish me to go tamely into hiding. I cannot, my lord. It is not my way. I stumbled across this plot, it is true. But now that I am involved, I must see it through."

A warm, appreciative light danced in the depths of his eyes. "My lady, is there no making you see reason?"

"There is not."

"You are brave—or perhaps foolhardy." He resumed his seat, still smiling slightly.

"Just stubborn," she declared. "Do you have the copy of the message with you?"

He drew the much-folded sheet from his pocket and spread it out between them. "I have not been able to glean anything more from it," he admitted.

"*Grenville will attend Requiem Masque as planned,*" she read aloud. "It must be a masquerade at the Opera House. How can

211

we find out which one Lord Grenville plans to attend?"

"Petersham and Sir William might know," Deverell pointed out. "But I hardly think either of them would tell us, whether they are guilty or not. I think I shall ask at the Opera House when there are masquerades scheduled."

She gave this plan her approval, then returned her attention to the translated code. "*Assassination to take place at midnight.* Well, that seems fairly straight forward, does it not?"

"Quite uncompromising," he agreed.

"*Do not make contact. Watch D.*" She set the paper down. "Who is 'D', and why is he to be watched?"

"I seem to remember you asking that same question before," he murmured.

"It proves the question has validity and I have tenacity," she informed him flippantly. "Do you have any ideas?"

"The only 'D' I can think of is Lord Dalmouth, and that hardly seems likely, does it? He is not overly political."

"No," she agreed slowly.

"But?" he prompted her.

"But he has been acting differently of late. Quite friendly, where before he did not bother with me. Now I would almost say he is trying to ingratiate himself."

"Very suspicious," Deverell agreed, but she caught the humorous note that underlay his words. "You do not perhaps feel that his friendship is offered in all honesty?"

"It is possible," she admitted.

"Our friend 'D' could be almost anyone, someone we might never suspect. I think, on the whole, we will do best not to concentrate on our 'D.' There are by far too many possibilities."

She agreed, though reluctantly. It seemed the only real clue they had. She sighed deeply, aware suddenly of a vast tiredness.

"You are not to go about asking questions," he ordered her with a sternness that surprised her. "Is that understood? You are to let everyone know that you believe this to be an illness. And if anyone mentions those papers again, you are to pretend no interest in them whatsoever."

There was a strength of will in the man that could not but

thrill her. He was dynamic, his energy barely restrained, but for a reprehensible moment she longed to see his power unleashed. But right now she was so very weak, she could not withstand him. Deverell, she realized, was irritating, dominating and very much to her taste.

After further reassuring himself that she meant to conduct herself in a most circumspect manner in the near future, he took his leave. Leanora closed her eyes, sank back against the pillows and tried very hard not to think over all that Deverell had said. The visit had tired her more than she cared to admit, and it was not long before she drifted off to sleep.

When she awakened again, it was late afternoon. She felt refreshed but unbearably weak and was forced to ring for assistance to reach her father's chamber. Once there, she sank gratefully into her accustomed chair, glad to be off her feet and content for once to sit and do nothing except pet the pug puppy.

Her father would recover. One morning he would simply wake up. She had done so, and so would he. She repeated that thought, over and over, willing herself to believe it.

She remained by his side until exhaustion again overtook her. With considerable reluctance, she yielded to her aunt's entreaties and retired to her own chamber, leaving her father under the watchful eye of his valet.

In the morning, she returned to his room as soon as she had dressed. She had not been there long when Tremly entered, announcing that Sir William had called.

Supported by the butler, she made her way down to the Gold Saloon. There she found her sister-in-law entertaining her visitor. As she went in, Julia stood and went to her at once.

"Are you sure you should have come down, Leanora?" she asked as she helped her to a chair.

"My dear Leanora." Sir William came forward, took her hand and raised it to his lips. "How delightful to see you up, and in such looks." His eyes, filled with concern, searched hers. What he saw apparently satisfied him.

"As you see, I am recovering rapidly," she assured him.

"May mine be the honor of taking you for a gentle airing in the Park?" he asked.

213

"She is much too exhausted!" Julia protested.

Sir William acknowledged this. "I had hoped a gentle airing might be beneficial. If you think she is well enough?"

Leanora did some rapid thinking. The only way to stop suspecting everybody would be to eliminate people, one by one. And the best way to do that would be to ask subtle questions and see who had trouble answering. She would be glad to eliminate Sir William from the candidates for her villain. He was too old an acquaintance. To even for a moment think him capable of so dastardly a crime was despicable.

"I should be delighted," she declared, breaking in on Julia's polite refusal. She ignored the glare that her sister-in-law directed at her. "Though I fear I am not yet as strong as I could wish."

"Then I shall take the greatest care of you, upon my honor."

Apparently, Sir William meant what he said. He helped her from the house, handed her tenderly up into his curricle and himself arranged a lap robe about her in spite of the fact that it bade fare to be a warm day. She sank back on the seat and took a deep breath, glad to be in the fresh air.

"This should pluck you up a bit," he said. "Nothing is more depressing than to be forever sitting about indoors."

"I could not agree more." She fell silent, allowing the breeze to fan her pale cheeks, enjoying the feel of her ruffling curls. "How do things go on at the Home Office?" she asked, keeping her tone light and casual. "Has Petersham found great joy in his recovered papers?"

Sir William laughed. "He will never admit that they were worthless! Do you know, he has kept me there late for the past several nights, going over them repeatedly? And there is nothing there that deserves even half that much attention!"

She relaxed, glad that Sir William talked so freely and so much at his ease. He, at least, had nothing to hide—not even his contempt of his superior. Leanora could not help but smile at several of his barbed comments on inefficiency.

They lapsed into silence as he maneuvered the curricle through the London traffic near the Park. At last they turned in at the gate, and he was able to spare part of his attention from the horses. He cast a swift glance at her through narrowed eyes, and suddenly Leanora was tense, waiting.

"Have you noticed anything odd about Petersham of late?" he asked.

She looked up, startled, for she had not been prepared for that. "In what way?" she asked, and knew she was sparring for wind, as Gregory would say.

"I was not sure if it was all my imagination, but he has seemed nervous. And there is that peculiar taste he has developed for Lord Kennington's company when I would swear they despise each other. I have had the oddest notion that our dear Lord Kennington has some sort of hold over Petersham." He threw her a rueful glance. "I know, I should not be speaking to you of this. It might prove to be of a very sensitive nature. It is really Lord Sherborne I would like to talk to, but I know you are to be trusted. Can you not tell me I am wrong?"

She looked up and met his clear, piercing eyes. So he, too, suspected something was amiss. But how much did he know? She had best tread warily. "I wish I could tell you that," she admitted, reflecting that she only spoke the truth. "His—his behavior has seemed somewhat odd."

Chapter 15

Sir William did not keep Leanora out for long in the warm morning air. He turned the horses toward home as soon as she began to look tired, and in a very short while, they pulled up once more before the house in Berkeley Square.

A gig was there before them, a dilapidated affair, held by the youngest footman. Leanora stared blankly at it for a moment, then her eyes widened in sudden fear.

"James!" She hailed the liveried young man who stood at the horse's head. "Is the doctor here for my father?"

"Yes, my lady. He woke up a little while ago, Mr. Tremly says."

"He—" She broke off, her throat constricted so that she could not speak, her body trembling. She came unsteadily to her feet and clutched the front board of the curricle for support.

Without realizing she moved, she was scrambling down from the vehicle. Sir William came around, catching her as she stumbled in her haste. Supporting her still wobbly steps, he guided her into the house.

"He—he is awake!" she managed, her grasp tightening on his arm.

"So it would seem, my dear." He covered her hand with his own, pressing it gently. "It is wonderful news, indeed. But I would beg that you remember your own weakened condition. Lord Sherborne would hardly be pleased if his recovery signaled your collapse."

She gave a shaky, emotional laugh. "I—I am sorry. I have just been so worried! It is such a relief, you cannot know. . . ." Tears filled her eyes, and she blinked them back.

"May I assist you up the stairs?" They had reached the hall, where for once no servants stood at attention.

"Yes, please. I—I must go to him!"

Their arrival had been noted, for Tremly appeared on the landing. His face, heretofore always an imperturbable mask of propriety, crumbled at sight of his young mistress, and he gripped the banister railing.

"Miss Leanora! You have come back!" He hurried down.

"Is it true? Is he really awake?" she demanded. Leaving her companion's support, she took several wavering steps.

"He is." The butler reached her and in his agitation took the hands she held out to him. "He is not himself yet, but he has opened his eyes and is looking around."

"Does—has he recognized anyone?" The question came out in a whisper as a new, previously suppressed, fear forced its way to the forefront. What if he never did recognize anyone? What if his brain had suffered too extensive an injury? All she had longed for before was that he should one day open his eyes and move. Now she realized how shortsighted those prayers had been.

"Not yet, Miss Leanora." Tremly recollected himself and with an effort mastered his feelings. "The doctor was most displeased to find you from home, and not only for his lordship's sake. If you will come with me?"

Sir William bowed slightly to her. "You will be wishing me elsewhere, and one cannot blame you. I will take my leave now. May I have your permission to call later, to see how you and your father go on?"

"Yes, of course. And thank you, Sir William." She turned away, forgetting him at once, and started up the stairs. She took Tremly's arm and leaned on the banister, but by the time they reached the floor on which her father's bedchamber was situated, she was forced to pause and catch her breath. For several minutes she stood quietly, head lowered, waiting for her dizziness to pass before she could proceed down the hall.

Mrs. Ashton, with Artaxerxes dancing at her feet, met her

at the door of the antechamber. Tears streamed freely down her lined face. Silently she embraced her niece, then led her into the room. Leanora found she was trembling again and sank into the chair that was drawn up for her. Xerk, with tremendous effort, heaved himself at the great bed, dangled for a precarious moment with back legs desperately seeking a foothold, then scrambled up to the top. Heaving a sigh, he settled his ridiculous nose on his master's knee.

Pagget hovered anxiously at the foot of the bed while the doctor repacked his bag. The latter looked up and directed a quelling glare at Leanora.

"What were you doing out of your bed, miss?" he demanded.

Leanora ignored his words. "How is my father?"

His reply was a sardonic laugh. "Oh, he'll do. He's well on the mend now. A remarkably hard-headed lot, you Ashtons. Never take advice and survive accidents that would kill a normal man. Yes, you may stop looking so pale and frightened now. He'll be perfectly all right—in time."

She stood on shaky legs and crossed to the bed. "Thank you." She sank down on the edge by her father and took the hand that lay on the coverlet. His head moved on the pillow, turning so that his pale, tired eyes could rest on her. Something flickered in their depths, and his fingers twitched beneath hers. Tears filled her eyes and slipped unnoticed down her cheeks as she squeezed his hand.

She remained with him for the rest of the day, and to her relief she saw further signs of improvement. He drifted in and out of sleep, stirring slightly, but with each successive wakening, his eyes, which at first appeared watery and unfocused, took on a brighter appearance. His skin was still drawn tightly over his strong bones, but it now showed a warmer hue.

Artaxerxes remained with her, lying on the bed, his head between his paws, his unwavering regard focused on the earl. When Mrs. Ashton came to take him for a walk, he protested but at last allowed himself to be led away, his demeanor that of a martyr going to his fate with stoic resolve.

Leanora took her dinner on a tray, refusing to leave the

earl's side for a minute. It took the combined entreaties of her aunt and Pagget to convince her, for the sake of her own health, to leave the night watches to the devoted valet and Xerk. She could not argue the fact that she still felt far from well herself but took her departure with considerable reluctance.

The change in Lord Sherborne wrought wonders in her own recovery. She awoke in the morning with a fresh sense of energy and eagerness and, as soon as she was dressed, hurried down the hall to her father's chamber. Xerk greeted her arrival with a yelp of pleasure and attempted the daring leap from the bed to her lap as soon as she sank into a chair. Scooping up the portion of the little pug that did not make it, she gazed down uncertainly upon her father's sleeping countenance. Only Pagget's assurances that the earl had awakened three times during the night kept her from believing the day before had merely been a dream.

As if in response to her anxiety, her father's head turned restlessly on the pillow. His eyes opened, the bleary gaze sharpened and a flash of recognition registered in his blue-gray eyes. He opened his mouth, and she knew he tried to speak her name. Grasping the hand that lay nearest her, she squeezed it. To her infinite joy, his hand turned in hers to return the clasp.

Gregory arrived a little while later and slipped quietly into the room. Xerk stood in Leanora's lap and shivered all over in delighted greeting, and Gregory allowed his hand to be licked enthusiastically before pulling a chair up beside Leanora's. For some time he sat staring down at his sleeping sire, and there was an odd tightness in his voice when he finally spoke. "I can hardly believe he is getting better at last."

As if disturbed by the sound of voices, Lord Sherborne stirred and opened his eyes. They remained vague for a minute, then focused on his son and heir. Leanora could not be sure, but she thought his lips twitched into a slight smile. As the tired lids closed once more, she felt a touch at her sleeve.

Gregory gestured toward the antechamber with his head, and the two made their way out. "Plucky old gentleman, isn't he?" her brother remarked with a casual air that sought to hide his emotion.

"He is certainly that. Dr. Broughton ascribed his survival to his hard-headedness."

Gregory grinned, but it took him a moment to master a chin that seemed unaccountably to quaver. "Lord, Nora, if you knew how worried I have been!"

She laid a hand on his shoulder. "I have known. It—it has not been easy for any of us."

He gave a deep, ragged sigh. "When he is better, I think perhaps—" he broke off, as if unsure precisely what he wished to tell his sister.

"I have thought of taking him down to the Abbey," she said quickly. "But I shall have to provide him with entertainment if I mean to keep him there. Do you think you and Julia would care to come and stay for a few weeks? It would help me of all things."

He seemed on the point of demurring, then an arrested gleam entered his eyes. "You know, Nora, we might just do that! When were you thinking of going? In about a week?"

"If he is able to travel, yes. And that reminds me. I must go and send word of his recovery to the Abbey. Mr. Edmonton will be so relieved."

"I will stay with Father, then, if you want to do that now."

Leaving the earl under his son's temporary care, Leanora went down to her study and wrote a short note to her father's secretary. The composition of this took her no little time, for she wished him to remain where he was and not post instantly back to town. Nor did she dare mention the code or the potential danger to himself if he returned. In the end, she merely requested that he await their arrival, which now could not be far distant.

She had just finished dusting this with sand and affixing a wafer when Tremly announced the arrival of Lord Deverell. She rose at once, consigned the letter into the butler's care and went directly to the Gold Saloon.

Deverell stood by the mantelpiece, gazing thoughtfully down into the empty grate. As the door opened he looked up, then came forward quickly to take her hands. With touching solicitude, he led her to the sofa and obliged her to take a seat.

"I hardly hoped to see you so greatly improved," he

221

informed her. His critical eye ran over her, and a line formed between his brows. "You are doing too much," he announced.

"No. That is—but you cannot have heard! My father has awakened. It is only natural that we are all in an uproar."

He settled at her side and commanded her to tell him the whole. This she was quite glad to do, though it could not but be an emotional story for her, and she was forced to have recourse to her handkerchief. When she finished, he congratulated her warmly.

"And you?" she asked, remembering with difficulty that the last time she had seen him he was setting off to make inquiries. "How have you fared?"

"Alas, I wish I could bring you better news. I have been able to learn very little."

"But—surely you found out when the masquerade is to be held at the Opera House?"

"Yes, indeed. I have the dates of at least four masquerades. Unfortunately, not one of them has been titled as a Requiem Masque."

She leaned back against the sofa pillows, staring up at him in dismay. "Four masquerades?" she repeated helplessly.

He nodded. "One will take place tomorrow night. But have no fear, that is not the one. I visited an old friend who is now in the Horse Guards. I gave nothing away, you may be sure, but I gathered the prime minister is otherwise engaged that night."

Leanora bit at the tip of one delicate finger, digesting this piece of information. "How vexatious," she said at last, causing Deverell to chuckle softly at her understatement. She threw him a reproving look. "If there is no one we can trust," she said slowly, "perhaps the person we should approach is Lord Grenville himself."

Deverell rose and strode over to the mantelpiece. "And what can we tell him?" he asked. "Oh yes, I know, we can show him the code and the translation. But we have no proof it is not all a practical joke. We can hardly ask him to upset his plans on such flimsy evidence."

"But—my father's accident, the search for those papers, my own illness. . . ." she began, but broke off. "No, it is not proof, any of it," she admitted in dismay. "But we could at least make him aware of the potential danger!"

"A change in his plans would only serve to alert our conspirators that their plot has been bubbled," he said, rejecting her suggestion out of hand. "They would merely come up with a new one, and you and your father would become targets as well, being the only ones who could have exposed the original plan."

Leanora gave a shuddering sigh. "How very disagreeable of you to be right."

He smiled. "We shall step warily. But rest assured, the plot will be foiled and our conspirators captured. And as for now, just continue as you normally would, and that should prevent any suspicion of your knowledge of all this."

With that she had to be content. The next few days provided her little opportunity to think of the Requiem Masque, for with every passing hour she could detect new improvements in her father. By the afternoon of the second day, he was sitting up in his bed. He still showed little desire to talk but appeared to derive considerable pleasure from either his daughter or sister-in-law reading to him.

This continued until the morning of the fourth day when, much to Leanora's surprise, he greeted her with a request to have his secretary sent to him upon the instant.

Leanora crossed over to him and sat down on the edge of his bed. "Mr. Edmonton is down at the Abbey," she explained calmly. "Will I not do instead?"

"Some matters to discuss," he said thickly. "When—when will he be back?"

"He won't. We are going down to join him as soon as you can travel."

That only served to agitate the earl. Leanora did her best to assure him that all was well, but in the absence of his secretary he began to talk of seeing Sir William and Petersham. Nothing she could say would calm him, and at last she was forced to send an urgent message to the Home Office, begging that these two gentlemen come at once to set Lord Sherborne's mind at rest. Then, casting caution to the winds, she sent a message to Lord Deverell as well and sat anxiously awaiting the result.

In a surprisingly short time, Sir William and Lord

Petersham arrived. They greeted Leanora with assurances that they would do their best to calm her father, and she at once escorted them upstairs. She then went back to the main hall, where the newly returned footman awaited her with most unwelcome news. Lord Deverell was from home and was not expected back that day.

Robbed of his advice, she decided to take the matter into her own hands. Something distressed her father, and whatever it was had to do with his work and Lord Petersham. There were times when practicality must overcome the tenets of good breeding, and this was one of them. Creeping into the antechamber of the earl's apartment, she set her ear to the keyhole and tried to listen.

The result could not satisfy her. She could hear Petersham's ponderous tones, Sir William's more rapid speech patterns, even her father's slow, slurred words. An urgency underlay the manner of all three, though, and she longed to know the reason. What did they discuss? Did—*could*—her father's anxiety imply that he knew something of that code, or even of the Requiem Masque itself? If he sought to prevent the assassination, that would surely leave him distressed, knowing for how very long he had lain unconscious.

They must have rung for Tremly, for the butler entered the antechamber without warning. Not by so much as a raised eyebrow did he indicate any surprise at finding his mistress in that room. He bowed to her, then entered the bedroom and escorted the two gentlemen out.

She awaited them in the hall, trying not to look too curious. Petersham and Sir William both took her hand, but neither did more than murmur a polite leave-taking as they passed. That, alone, disturbed her. Why did they give her no reassurance? They knew she was concerned! In no little agitation of spirits, she hurried into her father's room.

The earl lay back against his pillows, his eyes closed, exhausted. One hand lay on the back of the pug, which nestled against him. Sherborne opened heavy lids to gaze at her, a puzzled frown on his beloved features. "Nora," he said softly and patted the place beside him.

She went to him at once, taking his free hand in both of hers.

"Are you easier now?" she asked. "What has been troubling you?"

He shook his head as if confused. "Don't really remember," he sighed. "Something bothering me, but they say nothing is amiss, everything is normal." He regarded his daughter, and suddenly his frowning expression gave way before a smiling light in his tired eyes. "Contradiction in terms, that," he told her with an attempt at his usual humor.

She bent over and kissed his forehead. "They probably mean that nothing out of the ordinary is amiss. Did they tell you they were practically living here for a time, studying your papers? I am sure you managed to solve problems for them, even when you were not there in person."

Her words seemed to reassure him, for presently he slept. When her aunt came to sit with him, Leanora went thoughtfully down to her sitting room. Her father's memory still had great gaps. What was he half-remembering? If only she could be sure of his safety—and of his ignorance of anything to do with that hateful code.

As she sat frowning down at her clasped hands, the door to the room was thrown wide, and Gregory stormed in. He slammed it shut behind him and glared at his sister.

"What the deuce do you mean by having Petersham here?" he demanded without preamble.

His entrance had startled her, but at his words her chin came up in defiance. "I would hardly have Petersham anywhere, brother," she said coolly. "My father sent for him, and it seemed best to let him have his way."

Gregory took a few agitated steps about the room. "What did that old fool want?"

"That is hardly a way to refer to my father," she told him.

Gregory spun about to face her. "You know very well I mean Petersham! What did he want?"

"Nothing. It was my father who summoned him."

Gregory was silent a moment, considering this. "You should not have allowed it," he said at last, and the heat of his anger had gone from his voice. "It could only do him harm."

"On the contrary. He was fretting so, I feared there was little choice. He is certainly tired, but I hope that Petersham and Sir

William were able to reassure him on whatever point was distressing him."

"You do not know?" Gregory demanded.

"How could I? I could hardly take part in their discussion. Nor did I wish to tax Pappa about it after they left."

Her brother ran a worried hand through his tousled blond curls. "Dash it, Nora, I—I wish he had not."

"So do I, but it appears to me that you are more upset over this than he was."

Gregory flushed, then tried an unconvincing laugh. "Lord, the things you say! I just don't want him to overtax himself." He hesitated, then managed a smile that was almost relaxed. "Came to ask you if you're going to the Strathmore's card party tonight."

"Tonight? No, I—I should stay with Pappa."

"Do you good to get out, you know. You stay here worrying too much."

That he wanted her to go, she could not doubt. But why? "I am only just recovering myself, you know," she pointed out. "I think an evening party would be rather strenuous activity for an invalid, do not you?"

"It's only cards!" he declared, exasperated. "You always used to enjoy a good game of piquet. Why don't you go? You'll enjoy being out. Leave my aunt and Xerk to sit with Father. You can come with Julia and me."

Was that it? Did he want her company for Julia? But which of them did he intend to be the chaperone for the other? If she could help with the trouble between her brother and his wife, then she really ought to go. He would never ask for her assistance directly; but she could tell that there was something on his mind, and it was most certainly not concern that she enjoy an evening.

"All right," she said slowly, though not without many misgivings.

"That's the girl. We'll call for you at nine and take you home the minute you get tired." Without giving her time to say anything more, he took himself off.

In spite of her good intentions to help Gregory, Leanora could not look forward to the evening. She was dressed and sitting in the earl's room, reading aloud from a lurid romance novel that had him smiling in amusement, when Tremly carried up the news that her brother and his wife were below. Dropping a kiss on her father's cheek, she promised to stop in to see him as soon as she returned home, then handed the book over to her aunt.

The party, as she would expect from the Strathmores, drew members of the political circles in which she was accustomed to move. News of her father's improvement had spread rapidly, and she found herself thanking an endless stream of well-wishers for their kind words.

In a very short while, Leanora took her place at one of the card tables, playing at silver loo with the wife of one of her father's associates, Lady Carmody and Julia. Under cover of playing the hand, she was able to keep a surreptitious eye on her sister-in-law.

Contrary to Gregory's fears, Julia displayed no pleasure in gaming. Even so harmless a pastime as silver loo did not interest her. If anything, Leanora thought as she watched the girl hesitating over her play, she did not enjoy cards in the least.

As soon as the three tricks were completed, Lady Carmody, who unlike Julia had enjoyed herself immensely, suggested that they play again. Leanora, herself no ardent lover of loo, looked quickly about the room, seeking some excuse to take her leave, to slip away to try her hand at piquet.

On the far side of the room stood Lord Kennington, observing a game of whist with that supercilious expression Leanora so detested. And Petersham, she noted with concern, was one of the players. She looked away, back down to her own table, and found to her further dismay that Lady Carmody had re-dealt the cards. She had no choice but to pick up her hand and give at least the semblance of her attention to the game. But try as she would, she could not prevent her eyes from straying back toward Kennington and Petersham.

As she watched, Gregory moved to join the whist game. He exchanged a light word with Petersham, then turned to Kennington and bowed slightly. The exchange that followed appeared amicable on the surface, but Leanora, who was well acquainted with her brother's every mood, sensed something amiss. She threw a measuring glance at Julia, and her suspicions were confirmed.

Her sister-in-law sat stiffly, her wide, beautiful eyes fixed on the two men. Leanora would have given a great deal to know what they said. Apparently, it was something that Julia would rather not have discussed—or did she just dislike any contact between her husband and the gentleman whose company she enjoyed too much?

Kennington let out a low, unpleasant laugh. Gregory straightened, and Leanora thought a dark flush colored his cheeks. Abruptly, he turned on his heel and walked away.

Leanora turned back to the card table, discovering that the game waited on her and that she had no idea what had been going on. She played a card at random and was instantly criticized by Lady Carmody.

Dalmouth strolled up and leaned negligently on the back of his sister's chair, watching with amused eyes while Julia hesitated. He leaned over, whispered something in her ear, and she hunched an angry shoulder. The game resumed, and Dalmouth raised his quizzing glass to better observe. As the last trick was taken, he shook his head.

"Lady Leanora, your heart is not in loo this evening. May I claim you for a hand or two of piquet?"

She stood at once, relieved to escape and grateful to Dalmouth for perhaps the first time since she had the dubious honor of making his acquaintance.

"Yes, I should like that. If you will excuse me? You will not miss my poor playing, I am sure. There is your daughter, Lady Carmody. I am sure she would be delighted to join you."

She hailed Eliza, and that young lady was indeed pleased to accept a place at the loo table. Leanora then turned to Dalmouth, who led her to a small table where fresh decks of cards already awaited them.

"I must thank you for my rescue," she said with a smile.

"No one, my dear Lady Leanora, can be expected to play at silver loo with Lady Carmody. She would appear to believe it the most important occupation that exists." He broke open a fresh deck and began to separate out the lower pips.

"Whereas we both know it to be piquet," she agreed promptly. "The stakes, sir?"

"My pockets are wholly to let. Shall we say shillings or pennies?"

She laughed. "Oh, pennies, by all means. It is the game I enjoy, not the stakes."

"How wise. More of us should follow your lead." He dealt the cards, then studied his hand.

Leonora discarded three and drew replacements from the stock. He shook his head, maintaining his own cards.

That drew a slight frown from her. "I make a point of seven," she declared.

He raised his eyebrows. "Yours, by all means, but it may hurt you elsewhere."

"That is still to be seen," she demurred with an enigmatic smile. "The run may be mine as well. Five?"

"Quite right. I cannot touch it." He lowered his eyes a moment. "Your father is a remarkable man," he added suddenly.

She looked up, surprised. "Why? Because he taught me to play piquet creditably? And will you allow three aces?"

"I will not. If you are missing the queen on your run, it is because I hold all four. So much for your hopes of a repiquet. But that was not what I meant about your father," he added as he watched her first play. "I find it remarkable that he concerns himself with his work when he is barely recovered. Most men would enjoy a much needed rest. One can only admire a man so ready to return to harness."

"It is hardly that." She took the first trick, then played a king. "But with the complexities of Lord Grenville taking office, and his establishment of All the Talents, it is only natural that my father is concerned that all goes well."

"All the Talents," he repeated musingly. "Do you really think Grenville's ministry is brilliant enough to deserve that name?"

"Fox certainly is. In time, I am sure they will work together most effectively," she responded with more loyalty than truth.

The game was quickly played out and the cards gathered up. Falmouth again shuffled the deck, and Leonora pretended interest in the loo table she had left. Why was Dalmouth going to such pains to make himself agreeable? He had been no more than cool to her for a very long time. Now, suddenly, he was charm personified.

Nor did she like his seemingly casual references to her father and his work. Was he merely being polite in his inquiries, or was there another reason? If that were so, then he might easily obtain his answers from Gregory. Her brother was possessed of very little subtlety, and a clever man could learn much from him.

As she picked up the cards that Dalmouth dealt, she looked up, met his lazy smile, and an uneasy chill ran through her. Gregory had never concerned himself overly much with his father's work. Dalmouth, who professed a close friendship with her brother, would have discovered that rapidly. Gregory's sudden interest in her father's papers rose once more to her mind. Were Gregory and Dalmouth involved in something together? Dalmouth, she feared, had the ruthlessness to make use of anything that Gregory might discover.

She selected her discards at random and placed them facedown. Were all these people trying to discover whether she and her father knew anything of the Requiem Masque? Or was she letting her worry turn polite inquiries into menacing probes?

Petersham rose from the whist table and strolled over to observe their play. Raising his quizzing glass, he examined Leanora's cards.

"Well, my dear! Good to see you enjoying yourself. Relieves me of my greatest fear, you know. You would never have come out if our little visit had tired your pappa. Tell me, did we answer his questions?"

She looked up into a face wreathed in smiles. Why must she sense danger everywhere? Surely Petersham, of all men, lacked the cunning necessary for a dangerous and treasonable plot. But there was something about his manner that did not seem right. Was he just a shade too jovial?

"He is still somewhat confused," she admitted, feeling her way with care. "I believe the less he thinks about his work for now, the better."

Petersham positively beamed on her. "Very wise, my dear, very wise. Well, you just—" He broke off in mid-sentence.

Leanora followed the direction of his gaze. Kennington stood in the doorway, an enigmatic smile on his face that made Leanora shiver. The look that passed between the two men was charged, practically shimmering in the air. Petersham dropped his gaze first, and Kennington's smile deepened.

"I—what was I saying?" Petersham stammered. "Oh, yes." Once again, he was in command of himself. "You just send me a message if I can be of assistance. Any time! Any time at all." Patting her on the shoulder, he strolled off with an assumed calm.

Leanora stared blindly at her cards. She was surrounded by mystery upon mystery! Or were they all interrelated in some strange, convoluted manner? Where was Deverell when she wanted him? How very like a man to be off when she needed him most! And why did he not tell her what he was about?

At some time in the foreseeable future, two or more men intended to assassinate the prime minister. And at the moment, she had no idea who they were or when it would happen! She was learning nothing! What if they were unable to discover enough to prevent the dreadful plot? Oh, where was that exasperating Lord Deverell?

Chapter 16

Leanora was to have her answer concerning Deverell's whereabouts the following afternoon. After spending a quiet day reading to her father, she ventured forth to the Park at the hour of the Promenade to exercise her mare for the first time since her illness. On her second round, as she approached the Riding House, she was privileged to observe that gentleman coming toward her astride his large, raw-boned roan.

He reined in at sight of her, and she brought her mare up to join him. Her groom fell back a discreet distance, allowing them to converse in something approaching privacy.

"I sent you a message yesterday," she informed him.

"And you see me presenting myself before you the moment I received it," he responded promptly, the twinkle in his dark eyes irritatingly pronounced. "You must forgive me for not returning home sooner."

She glared at him. "It is no easy thing for an unmarried female to be sending messages to gentlemen's lodgings, you must know."

"Then I am honored." His amusement, if anything, became more pronounced.

"Where were you?" She kept her eyes straight ahead, but her exasperation sounded clearly in her voice.

"Visiting friends" came the calm reply.

She turned her indignant gaze fully upon him. "Visiting friends? At a time like this?"

"Now, why should you assume that it has nothing to do with

our—our mystery?" he marveled.

"Did it?" she asked suspiciously. "I do not see where you have been exerting any real effort in uncovering our conspirators!"

"Unkind," he murmured.

She allowed herself a brief glance at his gently smiling face and instantly wished she had not. Merriment lurked in his eyes, but there were also lines of concern drawn deeply about his mouth. He intrigued her, and when she was caught in his spell she admitted to more interest in the mysteries he presented than in those provided by the code. And his enthralling web wove about her at that very moment.

"But you do not tell me," she protested quickly. "Whom did you see? And what did you learn?"

"Not as much as I had hoped," he responded, taking her second question first.

"And?" she prompted hopefully.

He laughed, a low sound that enveloped her. No other answer was forthcoming.

She straightened up in her saddle, turning to face him squarely. "Why will you not tell me?"

"Because the less you know, the safer you will be," he pointed out.

"What utter nonsense! If you are right, someone has already tried to kill me just on a suspicion of my knowing something! I can hardly be in more danger than that! Under the circumstances, I think I would be safer the *more* I know."

His lips tightened into a firm, determined line. "I prefer to be the judge of that."

"You intend to leave me out of this?" she demanded, anger causing her voice to rise slightly.

"You are looking marvelously improved," he told her affably. "One would never realize how ill you were, and so recently."

She counted to twenty very slowly. Her temper still seethed, but her voice remained under admirable control. "Has anyone ever informed you, my lord, that you are the most odious, irritating, exasperating man alive?"

He subjected this to a moment's consideration. "I cannot

remember if those were the exact words," he admitted at last. "But it does not sound wholly unfamiliar."

That brought a choke of outraged laughter from her. "You are totally beyond the pale!"

"Oh, completely, I should think. We have reached the gate, as you may have noticed. Do you mean to go back now, or would you care to abuse me further? I will gladly join you for another round of the Park."

"Shameless," she murmured, but her eyes could not help but twinkle in response. They rode in silence for a few minutes before she trusted herself to look at him once more. "I will not permit you to keep me in complete ignorance."

"I fear the choice will not be yours." His tone held only apology.

"But you cannot! It is *my* plot!" she informed him with considerable feeling. "I discovered it. It is not fair to keep me in the dark!"

He merely smiled with an amused understanding that did nothing to soothe her ruffled feelings—or lessen the effect on her of his overpoweringly masculine appeal. If he was going to be so disobliging, she fumed, the very least he could do would be to not stir her disobedient senses at the same time!

Furious, she urged the mare into a canter, wishing wholeheartedly it could be a gallop. The sedate pace irked her even more. When they once more returned to the gate, she took her leave of him with punctilious politeness, firmly declining his offer to escort her back to Berkeley Square.

At home, she hurried up to her room to change out of her riding habit and into a simple round gown. She went down the hall to her father's chamber, paused on the threshold to firmly oust any lingering thoughts of mysteries from her mind and went in. There she found her aunt, reading aloud from the morning's newspaper while Lord Sherborne listened with gratifying alertness. Xerk snored peacefully on the coverlet.

The earl looked up at her entry and held out a hand. She took it as she bent down to kiss his cheek. "Well, my dear?" he asked. "And how is the Park?"

"Quite beautiful. But you shall see for yourself in a day or two. Would you care to drive with me in my phaeton, or shall we parade you about like an invalid in the barouche?"

He chuckled, and her heart warmed at the sound. Slowly but steadily, he was becoming his old self again.

She settled down in the chair beside her aunt. "And what shall we do to entertain you this evening? I warn you, I have been practicing my piquet."

"What, no parties tonight?" he asked with mock concern.

"There is the Allinghams's ball, of course," Mrs. Ashton told him. "But we will not go."

"Why not?" Lord Sherborne raised an inquiring eyebrow. "Have you cried off?"

"No. To tell truth, I had forgotten it until a moment ago," Mrs. Ashton admitted.

"Do you tire of our company already, Pappa?" Leonora smiled at him.

"Impossible. But I am sleepy today and don't intend to sit up late. Go to your ball and enjoy yourselves."

Leonora demurred but at last allowed herself to be overruled. In truth, her aunt seemed wistful about the ball, and the earl did look as if he would enjoy an evening alone. He tried so very hard to be his normal, cheerful self when any of his family was about. It must have proven a terrible strain on him.

It should be safe to leave him, she decided. He no longer needed someone to sit with him every moment, and nothing could happen to him in his own room with the watchful Xerk at his side and Pagget either in the room or within easy call.

Mrs. Ashton immediately dispatched a message to Reggie, demanding the escort of her son to this affair. The footman returned shortly, though, bearing the news that Mr. Ashton had already departed to dine with friends before attending this event. His loving mamma bewailed this lack of foresightedness on the part of her son and kept up her lament throughout their early dinner. Nothing, she loudly declared, could be worse than being forced to attend a ball without a gentleman in attendance.

"Do not worry, dear Aunt," Leonora assured her as they rose from the table. "We will see him the moment he arrives and inform him of the rare treat in store for him for the rest of the evening."

"Really, Leanora, if anyone were to hear you! How improperly you speak!"

"Only to you, love, so you need have no fear. I conduct myself with the strictest propriety in company."

Her aunt threw her a reproachful glance and went away to change her dress.

As Leanora suspected they would, they arrived at the Allinghams's ball well in advance of her cousin. They were far from the first, though, for the hour was advanced and the rooms comfortably filled. Leanora had the satisfaction of seeing her aunt drawn off to the card room by Lady Carmody and knew she would be very happily entertained for some time to come.

She herself moved about the edge of the spacious dance floor, greeting acquaintances and watching the country dance that was in progress. Julia was going down a set near her, partnered by a young but solemn-faced lieutenant. At least it was not Kennington, Leanora reflected. She found an empty chair near an arrangement of potted plants and settled down to survey the crowd.

A swift glance around was enough to convince her that Lord Deverell was not present. Had he been, she would have sensed it without even seeing him. There was something about him, an aura of energy, a presence that made itself known. He was not a man who could be easily overlooked. And in spite of how very annoyed she was with him, she found she could still look forward to engaging in a lively repartee.

If he did not come, in fact, she would be heartily bored.

A moment later, that thought vanished. The dance ended, and Julia excused herself to her lieutenant and hurried away. At the door, she paused and cast a swift look about the room, then slipped out in a manner that smacked of intrigue.

Leanora hesitated only a moment. She was not about to let her sister-in-law, for whom she had always had a fondness, walk into trouble. If only Gregory. . . . But no, Deverell would be more to the point. He seemed infinitely capable of shouldering people's problems—and then refusing to allow that person to take any further part in what was after all their

237

own affairs! Well, Deverell was not the only person who could intervene and provide help in difficulties. On that thought, she followed Julia.

The girl flitted down the hall to an empty corridor, looked about, then entered a door that stood slightly ajar. To Leanora's relief, it did not close completely behind her. She followed, pushed it open a shade more and peered in.

Julia stood in the center of the room, staring about. From the low-cut bodice of her gown, she drew out a folded and sealed sheet of paper. This she shoved down between the cushions of a sofa. With a quick glance about the room, she started for the door.

Leanora had barely a moment to dart into an empty room across the hall. What was that paper? Another mysterious document? A code? Or, more like, an indiscreet letter to a paramour? And why must she be so suspicious of her own sister-in-law? Somehow, her entire world seemed to have been thrown into chaos of late.

She peeked out the door and almost gasped. Petersham emerged from the other room, and in his hands he held the paper. His color darkened to an alarming hue as he read the contents. He crumpled the paper, rammed it into his pocket and stalked off.

She waited several minutes, then slipped out of the saloon in which she had hidden and followed. What she could really use at this moment was a good dose of Deverell's irritatingly calm amusement to make her laugh at her uneasy fears.

As she turned toward the great ballroom at the back of the house, she glanced down the stairs toward the entry hall. Deverell stood there, slightly to one side, with a small, wiry man she recognized as his groom. The little man nodded to something his master said, then strode away toward the servant's hall. Deverell looked casually around, then strolled into one of the lower saloons where card tables had been set out.

What was he about now? Perhaps she could go in, claim that she was seeking her aunt. The door to the card room was thrown open, and Lord Petersham hurried out. He cast a furtive glance back over his shoulder, into the room, and almost bolted for the front door. A lackey, standing at attendance, opened this for him, and he departed without first claiming so much as his cloak. A moment later, Deverell also came out and went straight to the front door.

More curious goings on! Determined not to be excluded by Deverell again, Leonora hurried down the stairs after him. The lackey stared at her in surprise but opened the door for her as well.

Deverell was only about thirty yards ahead of her. He crossed the street to where a hackney was drawn up and exchanged a rapid colloquy with the driver. With a sense of shock, Leonora recognized this individual as Deverell's groom, who had been within the house only minutes before.

Under no circumstances was she allowing him to leave her out of this! As he started to mount into the hack, she ran across to join him.

"Deverell!" she called in an undervoice as she neared.

He stopped, spinning about to face her. His calm, somewhat amused mask settled over his features. "Good evening, my lady. But you must excuse me. I am in somewhat of a hurry."

"What is going on? I saw Petersham come out, and you follow." Her words came out as an accusation.

"Then you are aware of why I cannot delay. If you will kindly return to the ball?"

"I will not!" she exclaimed. "If you do not take me with you, I—I shall swing up behind this wretched vehicle as if I were a tiger!"

He laughed, a deep, vibrant sound of genuine amusement. "In a ball gown?" he demanded, still chuckling. His dark eyes glinted with merriment, shining in the light of the street lamps. "I believe you would! Come, get in, then. I'll not have you making a scandal of both our names." He took her arm and assisted her into the vehicle. "If we are seen, you know, your reputation will be ruined," he pointed out quite cheerfully as he swung himself up after her.

She settled onto the seat, moving over to make room for him. "Better that than I should die of curiosity."

That drew another chuckle from him. He leaned over, rummaged beneath the seat and drew out a dark cloak. "Here."

239

He handed it to her. "Your dress is rather noticeable. Next time you plan to chase after suspects, do not wear a yellow ball gown."

"You forgot to tell me what you had planned for the night," she shot back. She drew the cloak about herself, covering as much of her gown as she could.

"An oversight, I admit. I did not expect the honor of your company."

"No, you have done your best to exclude me, have you not?" She cast a darkling glance at him and did not know whether or not to be glad that he still seemed amused.

"My knowledge of you would appear to be insufficient," he responded on a note of apology. "I do not know why, but I had not credited you with so flagrant a disregard for the proprieties."

That stung, but she would not let him see. "Say rather you did not credit me with any determination or spirit," she corrected him. "I will not hide in some corner, cringing in fear, when there is something that must be done."

"No, that would not be like you," he agreed with disturbing readiness. "You are far more likely to charge in without considering the consequences."

He lapsed into silence, staring out the window. Leanora, momentarily robbed of speech, sat back against the squabs and subjected the situation to a moment's consideration. "Why are we following Petersham?" she demanded at last.

"*You* are following him because you must needs be involved in everything," he informed her with exasperating exactitude. "*I* am following him—because it is something that needs doing."

Not for the first time, she experienced an almost overpowering desire to strike him over the head with something. As nothing was at hand, she was forced to search for a stinging retort, which for the moment escaped her.

As if sensing her fury, he turned to face her, and for once his expression was serious. "I cannot like it when you follow people. It can be very dangerous, and you are not trained to this work."

"And you are?" She tried to keep her voice light, but the

240

solemnity that underlay his words took her aback.

"Yes, I am. You claim I led your cousin Vincent into this very sort of situation. But look at yourself. Am I not doing everything in my power to keep you safe?"

She looked down at her clasped hands, shaken by his concern. "I—I cannot just sit back," she repeated. "And sometimes I cannot help but overhear or see things, and—and know they may mean something."

"What did you hear—or see?"

She glanced up and found that he watched her closely, waiting. Quickly, she told him about Julia, the note and Petersham.

Deverell's eyes narrowed as he listened. As she finished, he nodded, as if he confirmed some suspicion of his own. "You do not know what it was about?" he asked.

"No. Unless it is the Requiem Masque, I have no idea."

He nodded again, but his dark eyes no longer saw her. "Petersham lacks finesse," he murmured, and she knew his words were not meant for her. He seemed oblivious to her presence.

The hackney drew to a halt, and Deverell glanced out quickly. Leanora, leaning across him, did not find the neighborhood familiar and said so.

"Pall Mall," he said shortly. "And that house, that one just there, would appear to be a very discrete gaming hell. Wait for me here. I am going in."

For once, she raised no argument. The dashing Lady Leanora Ashton might do a number of very odd things, but visiting a gaming hell was not one of them. She would have to let Deverell go on his own. The knowledge could not please her, but she settled back, determined to use the time in profitable thought.

She reviewed the situation, and a slight frown creased her brow. Petersham, to her, could not seem a likely suspect. As Deverell said, he lacked the finesse to be a conspirator in a plot as deadly as this. Yet he behaved very oddly, and Deverell evinced a considerable interest in him.

That line of speculation got her nowhere. Baffled on all points, she tried to be content with staring out the window and,

241

before much longer, acknowledged herself thoroughly bored. Time passed, and all she could do was sit and watch the various gentlemen as they arrived, knocked on the door, gave whatever magic password was required and were admitted to the house.

Suddenly she sat up, alert, for she recognized the gentleman just going up the steps. Lord Kennington knocked on the door and was admitted at once by the manservant. No password was required of him, she noted. She blinked, for a new thought occurred to her. How had Deverell gained admittance? Was he a *habitue* of this hell? And if not, how had he obtained the necessary password?

It seemed as if hours passed, but she suspected it was no more than twenty minutes before another familiar and most unwelcome sight met her eyes. Her brother Gregory, arm in arm with Dalmouth, strode up to the house. Dalmouth spoke whatever words were necessary, and the man within stood back, allowing them to pass.

She had barely enough time to wonder if any more of her jewelry would turn up missing when Deverell came out of the house. He looked casually about the street, then crossed over and climbed into the carriage. His features were set in grim lines.

"No sign of Petersham inside, anywhere," he told her.

"And what about the others?"

He looked at her in surprise. "What others?"

"But—Kennington, Dalmouth and my brother, of course."

He shook his head. "They were not there. What made you think they would be?"

"I saw them go in! Gregory and Dalmouth entered only a few minutes before you came out! No, do not look at me like that! I ought to know my own brother. I could not have been mistaken."

He looked over at the house, his gaze thoughtful. "There must be another room," he said slowly. "One to which I did not know the password, and one which I never saw. Interesting." He looked at her, and his eyes danced once more with eager lights. "I think this is one establishment that will bear watching."

"And what else does?" She leaned forward, partially across

242

him, following the direction of his gaze.

Before she realized what he was about, he threw one arm around her shoulders and dragged her ruthlessly against his massive chest. His lips descended onto hers, claiming them in a kiss that tore her breath away. To her shock, she found herself returning this unfamiliar caress, acting upon a previously unknown passion that flooded through her with alarming intensity. His manner might have been somewhat abrupt, but she could not find it within herself to object.

He released her slowly, and in the dim light of the interior of the hackney she could see his dark eyes glinting. "I was going to apologize, but I think maybe I won't, after all."

She stiffened, furious, pulling free of the arm that lingered about her. "I see. And to what do I owe the—the dubious honor of being mauled about by you?"

He laughed, low and soft, and her bosom heaved with indignation. "I cry pardon, my lady. But Kennington walked by. It was the—the impulse of the moment, I fear, an attempt to keep our identities hidden. This way, if he chanced to look within, all he saw was a gentleman sitting in a carriage with an agreeable companion. Nothing in the least to arouse suspicion."

A deep flush of mortification tinged her cheeks. His kiss had been nothing but a momentary convenience, and she had been fool enough to respond, snared in his mesmerizing spell! Gathering the remnants of her pride, she hunched an indifferent shoulder.

"You can have no notion how glad I am to have been of some use," she informed him with heavy sarcasm.

Deverell chuckled, a soft, deep sound that irritated her even more. He tapped on the roof, and the hackney set forward. Following Kennington, she supposed. As subtly as she could manage, she slid way from her imposing companion. She trembled with reaction to his kiss, but then she had never before been subjected to such a humiliating experience. Even the most ardent of her suitors had never dared to do more than kiss her hand. Perhaps that was why she had never been tempted to accept of their offers. But it was unforgivable that she should have been so carried away by Deverell that she

243

longed for him to repeat his offense!

She maintained a strict silence as the carriage wended its way through mostly unfamiliar streets. At last, they pulled up once more.

"Where are we?" she asked grudgingly.

"Bloomsbury," came the short reply. "Stay here. I am going to look into that house if I can." He slipped quickly out of the coach.

She watched him, her anger growing. She was not to be continually left behind, used as a convenience and then forgotten! He was not the only one possessed of intelligence and wits, and so he would learn! Disregarding his instructions, she followed him.

He had blended neatly into the darkness beside a house across the street, but as she watched closely, a slight movement in the shadows betrayed his presence. She crept up, peering over his shoulder. He glared at her and gestured back toward the hackney. She shook her head, then stood on tiptoe to peer into a lower window. He dragged her back and took her place. At last, he led her firmly away.

"Well, is this a gathering place for notorious spies?" she asked, her tone purely conversational.

"Notorious inamoratas, more like," he replied. "Now, how can our friend Kennington afford a high-flyer like that?"

Leanora felt a soft flush creeping to her cheeks. This was hardly the conversation for a gentleman to be holding with a lady—but then, their behavior had been somewhat odd this evening.

"Are you personally acquainted?" she asked before she could prevent herself from speaking the indelicate words.

"I fear the ladybird in question is quite above my touch," he assured her, smiling. "Shall we return to Pall Mall?"

Before Leanora had time to decide how Deverell was able to recognize a very expensive member of the muslin company when he had only recently returned from years upon the Continent, the carriage drew up once more before the gaming hell. Here they sat for some time in silence while other peculiar circumstances began to occur to her. Deverell had experienced no trouble entering this hell. He recognized Kennington's mistress—if indeed he had even seen her! Leanora could not remember a lady being in the room when she peeked in. What, exactly, did Deverell know or guess that he had not told her?

They remained watching at this post for some time, then at last gave up and returned to the Allinghams's ball. As the hackney slowed before the house, Deverell turned to Leanora with eyes that danced in amusement.

"Tell me, how do you plan to return?" he asked with all the air of one preparing to be entertained.

She stared at him, then one hand flew up to cover her pretty mouth as it dropped open. "I—I cannot just knock on the door, can I? The butler would be sure to make some comment to the Allinghams."

He grinned. "There is more to being a conspirator than at first meets the eye. I shall send my groom to order up your carriage. When you are safely within it, I shall go in search of your aunt and tell her that you developed the headache. We shall then collect your cloak, and I shall escort her out to join you. Will that be acceptable?"

"Odious man," she responded with feeling. "Why is it you must always know what to do?"

"Because I have been trained for this work," he informed her once again. "Secrecy and meddling in the concerns of others becomes somewhat of a habit."

In a very short while, Leanora shed the dark cloak and crossed the street to stand near the door of the Allinghams's own house with Deverell at her side. Barely a minute later, her barouche drew up, and Deverell, with a touching display of solicitude, saw her into it. Then, with an apparent unconcern, he mounted the steps, knocked on the door and was instantly admitted to the house. It did not surprise her in the least when, ten minutes later, he reappeared with Mrs. Ashton on his arm.

Her aunt noted nothing amiss. Her only concern seemed to be her niece's health, and she berated herself loudly for desiring amusement at Leanora's expense. By the time they reached Berkeley Square, Leanora felt extremely guilty for having sought refuge in that particular ploy.

The clock on the mantel in the Gold Saloon struck the quarter hour as they entered the house. It was after one o'clock! she realized in surprise. And she had spared barely a thought for her father! Leaving her aunt at the first landing, she hurried on ahead. She would just peep in to his bedchamber, and assure herself that he slept quietly.

As she paused before the door, she thought she heard movement inside. She knocked softly, then entered the antechamber. A harsh scraping sounded within the room beyond, and she hurried forward, raising her candle high to illuminate the darkened apartment. Beyond the bed, the window had been flung wide, and the heavy curtains billowed outward.

Surprised, she went to close it, then froze, gripped by terror as her gaze fell on the bed, and on the very large pillow that lay squarely over her father's face.

Chapter 17

A sob tore from Leanora's throat as she ran forward and grasped the smothering downy softness. She tossed it aside, then bent over the still figure of her father. His breath came in a ragged gasp, and her tears dropped unheeded upon his face.

She sank down onto the bed, taking his hand, gripping it tightly between her own. His breathing sounded steadier now. She reached out with a shaky hand and pulled the bell rope. How could they have ever left him alone? How . . . but how could she have guessed that he would be in danger here, that such a daring attempt would be made in his own home, in his own room?

While she awaited Pagget's arrival, she had ample time to think. How could she explain an attack, the purpose of which could only be a deliberate attempt to murder her father, without revealing her knowledge of that dreadful code? But to say nothing would leave the earl open to further attacks, for he could not, on her own, keep an around the clock watch on him.

By the time Pagget appeared, sketchily attired in a nightshirt shoved hastily into breeches, she had concocted a story of housebreakers. This, after assuring himself that his master was indeed all right, the valet listened to with a stony face.

"Yes, Miss Leanora," he said as she finished. "And if you will stay with him now, I will send for the doctor. Would you be wishful for the Runners to be summoned?" he added perfunctorily, though by no means with any enthusiasm.

247

She looked about the room, as if seeking inspiration. "I—I do not see what they could do. I doubt anything has been taken. My father must have awakened as soon as they entered. Let—let us see what he says, first."

But the earl, when they brought him around, was not able to tell them much. He remained hazy, unable to recall anything. He seemed confused to find his daughter and valet hovering about him in agitation. He had not the slightest idea who might have been in the room with him; he had been aware of nothing until suddenly something seemed to be pressed over his face.

Leanora sank into a chair, waiting while the valet went to rouse a footman for the doctor. If she had been even a few minutes later. . . . She forced back that thought. She had not been. She had arrived in time. And from now on, no one would get the opportunity to make such an attempt again. She would think of some excuse for the window to be bolted and to have the good Pagget spend every night where he could hear his master.

And Artaxerxes. . . . Where was he? Alarmed, Leanora looked about. Why had the little pug not raised an alarm and frightened off the intruder? He might be small, but his yips were piercing and his young teeth sharp and eager to bite, as her father's boots could attest.

The earl could shed no light on this mystery. When Pagget returned, though, the little dog came dancing at his heels. Thrusting past Leanora, he made a flying leap at the bed, not quite making it. His master provided a helping hand, and soon the pug curled up in his favorite place.

Leanora let out a deep sigh. "Where was he?" she demanded as she settled on the edge of the bed. Never would she have believed she could be so glad to see that ridiculous puppy.

"I am sorry, Miss Leanora. He made such a fuss earlier, I took him to the kitchens. A dreadful whining and running about. I thought he was taken ill. But he must have sensed someone prowling about. . . ." The valet broke off, aghast at the terrible results of his well-intentioned actions.

"It is all right," Leanora said quickly. "There was no way of knowing our Xerk was trying to be useful for once." She leaned over to stroke the puppy, which rolled to expose its stomach for a good rub.

The doctor arrived shortly, looked Lord Sherborne over and pronounced him to have suffered no real harm. If it seemed odd to him that a housebreaker should have attacked a sleeping man in his bed, he said nothing, merely recommending that the less fuss they made the better for the earl, and that they should all try to get some rest. Leanora saw him down stairs and thanked him, and was grateful that he did no more than stare at her fixedly from beneath bushy brows.

Her next step was to send an urgent message to Deverell. Even if she could not alert the Runners, he, at least, must be told the truth. She went back up to her father's room to await Deverell's response and found that the valet was already taking care of the window.

"I fear it was broken, Miss Leanora," Pagget informed her as she came to inspect his work. "We can get a carpenter to fix it properly in a few days time, but for now I have secured it closed—to keep the chill out."

"Thank you," she responded faintly. She touched the mullioned window and saw the narrow but solid boards that had been fastened immovably across it. No one would be able to enter by that way without alerting the entire house! She looked back at Pagget, who now busied himself with setting up a truckle bed in the antechamber. Anyone seeking to reach the earl from the door would fall over his devoted valet. Did the man guess the real danger? If he did, he did not speak of the matter but left her in no doubt that he intended to mount an efficient guard over his master.

The footman returned shortly with the news that Lord Deverell, upon returning to his lodgings after the ball, had startled his servant by packing a valise and departing on a journey in the middle of the night. Leanora could only stare at her messenger in stunned silence.

"In the middle of the night!" she repeated in dismay, finally mastering her voice.

"Yes, Miss Leanora. I left the message with his man, and he promised to give it to him as soon as possible."

Leanora voiced her thanks and dismissed him to return to his bed. It all seemed impossible! She had taken her leave of

Deverell a bare two hours before! How could he have disappeared so quickly, and what could have been so urgent as to call him away in so mysterious a manner? It was madness to travel in the darkness!

She went slowly back into her father's room, all desire for sleep flown. The earl lay very still on his great bed, drugged into rest by a sedative given by the doctor. In the room behind her, she could hear the sounds of Pagget settling down for the night.

She sank into the padded chair that the valet had set for her near the bed. She felt so very alone and vulnerable, bereft of Deverell's support. This was the second time he had not been available when she needed him!

She shivered, all too much on her own with her frightening thoughts. She could no longer deny the deadly seriousness of this maze they walked. Before, she had still harbored hopes that it was all coincidence, fabricated in her mind out of nerves. But now there could be no doubt. Someone wanted the earl of Sherborne dead. And it followed quite naturally that her own illness, as Deverell had suggested, was an attempt at murder, as well.

These were hardly cheerful reflections to comfort her during the long watches of the night. She huddled in the chair, drawing a shawl about her shoulders, her eyes fixed on her father's face. The attempt on his life had not succeeded. That had to make her feel better, even though only moments had made the difference. And still, the question haunted her of who, *who* wanted her father out of the way so desperately.

And poor Mr. Holloway. . . . She straightened up in her chair as a new thought struck her. If her father's clerk had been killed because someone thought he had seen that code, that meant the code had been among her father's papers before she left his office—and before she ran into Lord Kennington! Then either Petersham or Sir William must be responsible. . . .

She was getting ahead of herself. It was believed in the Home Office that Mr. Holloway had been involved in the missing funds. If that were the case, then his death had nothing to do with the Requiem Masque, and Kennington might well be behind the assassination plot, after all. Unless, somehow, those funds were tied in as well. . . .

She must have dozed off at last, for when she opened her eyes, thin rays of sun penetrated the heavy curtains at the nailed-up window. The pug stirred, yawned cavernously and regarded her through sleepy eyes. From behind her came sounds of movement in the antechamber, and Pagget tapped softly on the partially open door, then came into the room.

"You will be wanting to go to your room before his lordship awakens, Miss Leanora," he suggested. "Right angry he would be if he knew you had sat up all night."

She stood and stretched to ease her stiffened muscles. "Of course. Thank you. And Pagget. . . ." She hesitated, unsure how to phrase the request.

"If you do not mind, Miss Leanora, I mean to move back into the antechamber and spend more time in here. We don't want him fretting if he is left alone."

They exchanged a long look, and a wave of gratitude swept through her at the man's loyalty. Impulsively, she took his hand. "Thank you, Pagget" was all she could say, but she knew he understood.

In her own room, she rang for her abigail and began to remove her sadly crushed ball gown. What story could she possibly tell the staff? Very few had been awake last night, even her aunt had retired to bed without being aware of what went on. But with the morning, stories would spread rapidly below stairs. Her own maid must be beyond anything curious, for she had never been sent for to put her mistress to bed.

That question was answered very shortly. Ripton, her abigail, entered with a brisk, determined attitude. Not one question passed that privileged woman's lips. Instead, she saw Leanora fastened into a very pretty morning dress of peach crepe, combed out her long golden curls and arranged her hair in a simple but becoming fashion.

What went on in Ripton's efficient mind? At last, Leanora could stand the uncertainty no longer. Turning, she faced the woman. "About last night," she began.

"And what about last night, Miss Leanora?" Ripton asked. She compelled her mistress to turn away once more so that she could thread a riband through the curls at the top of her head. "Some time after you went to bed, his lordship had a turn. Pagget awakened Tremly, just as he ought, and they sent for the doctor. I am glad you awakened so early, for I am sure you will want to see for yourself that his lordship is quite recovered once more."

Leanora stared at her, then nodded. So the servants had settled it between themselves, and no hint of danger or murder would pass beyond these walls. Her composure threatened to desert her, but Ripton thrust her out of the room, informing her that she wished to attend to the straightening up before the housemaids arrived on the scene.

Leanora returned to her father's room where she sat beside the sleeping earl until the hour was considerably more advanced. Then she made her way down to the breakfast parlor, where she found her aunt, who had heard the fabricated version of the story from her own abigail upon rising. Leanora was able to assure her that the earl was already much improved.

As the morning wore on, Leanora found herself waiting for a message from Deverell. When Tremly announced that she had a visitor waiting below, desiring to speak with her, her disappointment bordered on the ludicrous when she learned that it was only Viscount Dalmouth. Stifling her emotions, she went down to the Gold Saloon.

As soon as she entered the room, she was aware that something was not quite right. His dress was impeccable, more so than usual, and his neckcloth was a wonder to behold. Even his dark locks were carefully combed and anointed with Russian oil. His bearing, though, seemed stiff, as if he were ill at ease.

He came to her at once and raised her fingers to his lips as he bowed low over her hand. To her surprise, he retained his hold as he lifted his eyes to her face. A slight frown crossed his brow. "You look troubled. Have I come at a bad time?"

"No, of course not. Will you be seated? What may I do for you?" She led the way to the sofa, then took a chair beside it.

He sat down opposite her. "I would hope my reason for coming might not be wholly unknown—or unguessed," he began. "You cannot be unaware of the regard in which I have come to hold you."

She blinked. At his first words, she had experienced a stab of fear, suspecting his visit had to do with the attack on her father. But now it appeared that he was bent on making her an offer!

"Lord Dalmouth," she began impulsively.

"No, please. Let me continue." He grasped her hands, but she pulled them free at once. "Can it be that you would not give me hope? I know our friendship is only of recent date, but the feelings that have long been buried within me can no longer be denied!"

She stood and took several agitated steps in an attempt to give herself time to recover from the shock of his words. "As— as you have pointed out, our friendship is new," she agreed, searching for words with which to express her utter amazement without embarrassing him.

"I have spoken too soon? Forgive me." He dropped to one knee, grasped the hem of her gown and kissed it.

"Oh, pray, do not!" she exclaimed, bewildered. From what she knew of Viscount Dalmouth, he was not a gentleman to indulge in so absurdly theatrical a display of romanticism. It only confused her more.

He came to his feet and possessed himself of one of her hands. Reluctantly, she allowed it to lie in his clasp. "Only give me leave to hope that we may come to know one another better!"

"There can be little doubt of that, because of the close tie that exists between our families. Believe me, Dalmouth, I am aware of the honor you do me, but we really should not suit."

He kissed her hand before releasing it. "I shall never give up hope, Leanora. I shall not stay and embarrass you now with further entreaties. And you may be assured that when we meet, it shall be as dear friends, which is what I hope we may always be." A wistful smile played about the corners of his mouth. "Perhaps the warmth of my affections may animate your regard for me."

He left her on that note, and she stared after him, at the door that closed behind him, bemused. What had ever induced him to offer for her? Certainly, they had enjoyed an agreeable evening of piquet, but there had been nothing in his manner then to suggest that he might propose to her in only two days time. Following so hard as it did upon the attack on her father, she could not but find the circumstance puzzling—and threatening, in some indefinable way.

She sought refuge from her thoughts in her father's apartment. As she entered the antechamber, Pagget bowed and indicated the room beyond where Mrs. Ashton sat at the earl's side. He was awake but somewhat vague, an after effect of the sedative. On the floor, Xerk growled threateningly at the tattered remains of a bedroom slipper, then pounced on it with glee. Leanora drew up a chair across from her aunt, picked up the novel that lay open on the bed and began to read aloud.

They continued in this way until late afternoon, when Tremly announced the arrival of young Mr. Reggie. He entered his uncle's room nervously and was relieved to find the earl asleep.

"Came to take my mamma for a drive in the Park," he explained.

"Oh, Reggie, that is the very thing!" his mamma cried. "An outing is just what we need, is it not, Leanora?"

It sounded tempting, but she did not want to be from home in case Deverell called. With no little regret, she shook her head. "You go, dear Aunt. I would rather remain here."

"But you must get out, my dear."

"Three in Reggie's curricle would be shockingly uncomfortable. No, you two go. I will walk in the garden later. Now hurry, Aunt Amabelle. You know how Reggie hates to keep his horses standing."

After their departure, Leanora sat in a silence broken only by Xerk's snores. This quickly grated on her already strained nerves, and she summoned Pagget. Leaving him once more on guard in the earl's chamber, she went out for a breath of air in the garden in the center of the Square.

It was a beautiful afternoon, warm with a slight breeze. Gladly would she relax and enjoy it if only dark and sinister mysteries did not lurk about her on every side. Finding no peace there, she started back to the house.

As she emerged onto the street, a dashing curricle turned the corner in style and proceeded toward her. Her heavy burden of worry lifted from her heart, and she remained where she was, aware only that Deverell was there, that he would take charge of everything.

He drew up the bays, climbed down and hurried over to her, a slight frown creasing his brow. He took her hand, and sudden memory of the warm firmness of his embrace the night before filled her. Soft color warmed her cheeks. He had kissed her, and it would have been a most thoroughly satisfying experience had his motives been for personal reasons rather than convenience.

"It is about time you showed up," she informed him tartly. It would make everything so much easier if the mere sight of him did not play havoc with her senses. "I have a few things to say to you."

"So I gathered from your note." He followed her up the steps, nodded affably to Tremly who opened the door to them, and handed over his hat and gloves.

Leanora strode into the Gold Saloon, her irritation with him vying with her anxiety to lay the whole at his feet. The latter won out. As soon as he pulled the door closed behind himself, she said: "Someone tried to murder my father last night."

Deverell checked, then came further into the room. "Dear me," he murmured with what to Leanora seemed hopeless inadequacy. With deliberate and irritating calm, he drew his snuff box from his pocket, opened it with a practiced flick of his thumb and helped himself to a pinch. He raised eyes that revealed a remarkable shrewdness. "It would seem that they did not succeed. Perhaps you had better tell me about it."

"I have been wanting to since last night," she snapped. She seated herself on the sofa, and he joined her. The happenings of the night before were quickly related to him, including the unexpected cooperation on the part of the servants. When she finished, he swore softly, drawing a startled but interested look from her.

"It would seem I have been less than efficient," he remarked with a return to his normal calm. "I must apologize. That was one move I had not anticipated, or I would have ensured against it."

"Could you have?" she asked, curious.

"Of a certainty." He stood, pacing slowly back and forth. "Your servants have performed admirably, but I think it would be unjust to expect much more of them."

"What do you mean? Surely they do not know the truth! Or do they?" Her anxious eyes met his sparkling ones, and something in his expression left her shaken. "But how . . . ?"

The door opened and Tremly came in, bearing a tray on which rested two decanters, glasses and a plate of assorted biscuits. He set this on the table and bowed himself out. Leanora watched his retreating figure with suspicion.

"Your butler, if you will remember, was also attacked upon one occasion," Deverell said smoothly as he poured Leanora a glass of lemonade. The other decanter contained Madeira, which he poured for himself.

"And?" she prompted as he fell silent and sipped the rich liquid.

"He and your father's valet—Pagget, I believe?—are quite excellent men. And under the circumstances, I felt it best they should be on their guard."

"You told them! But—how much?" Did this man stop at nothing? He certainly assumed complete command with an infuriating air—and without so much as asking her permission! She glared at him, indignation swelling in her breast.

"I told them the essentials, so that they would be aware of the danger. I did not mention the exact details. Enough only to assure your safety—or so I had hoped."

"You take a great deal upon yourself. Does it not occur to you that I might like to know if you talk to my servants?"

"I beg your pardon," he murmured, displaying an infuriating lack of sincerity. He returned to the sofa, having apparently come to a decision. "I believe it will be best if you and your father leave London as soon as possible."

She had come to much the same conclusion herself, but hearing the suggestion from him instantly set her against the scheme. He was behaving in too high-handed a manner, and he must learn that she, at least, did not dance to his piping.

"I am not so craven," she retorted scornfully. "I have no

256

intention of leaving until this business is settled, my lord. My father will be safe now. We are taking steps to assure that no one can again reach him."

"I would rather that you were both out of danger. I would suggest you set about packing at once. And you might convince your brother to go along with you. I will manage a great deal better without him, I believe."

"You may be able to order my servants about, but you will find you have met your match in me!" She came to her feet, her temper blazing. "I do nothing at your or anyone else's bidding!"

"Do you not?" He went to her and grasped her chin in his hand, forcing her face up so that he could gaze into it. His dark eyes glinted, sending a shiver of pure fear through her. "It is not wise to defy me, my dear," he said softly.

"Am—am I to take that as a threat?" She tried to turn her words into a joke, but she found she was honestly afraid.

"Do you doubt I could compel you to obey me?" His fingers caressed her jaw and closed gently about her throat.

She tried to look down, but the steady pressure of his hand kept her face raised to his. She trembled, but was it from fear or the sheer, overpowering will of the man? He was far too strong, too commanding. She felt herself drawn into the deep whirlpool of his eyes, sinking irrevocably, losing her will, wanting only to remain his captive.

"I—I must stay!" With almost superhuman effort, she tried to escape his spell.

"And what good do you think you could do?" Abruptly, he released her.

She fell back a pace, shivering. Had he created that aura of danger to make her yield—or had it been real? She took a deep breath and sought the fragments of her equilibrium. She had to trust Deverell! If she had been wrong, if he were a threat to her. . . . The thought was too horrible to contemplate.

"I—I would have no peace if I walked away from this—this plot." She held her head high, thrusting her panic and uncertainty behind her. Whether she had been right or wrong, she had committed herself to trusting him the moment she handed over that coded message. "Can—can you not understand? This is *my* responsibility. I involved *you* in this tangle, not the other way around! It would not be *right* for me to abandon it!"

An unexpected gleam of appreciation came into his eyes. "You would have made the devil of a good officer," he informed her as amusement replaced the menace in his manner.

She found it difficult to place. Unless. . . . But it was absurd! It was she who had involved him! He had known nothing of the code or plot until she had shown that paper to him. Yet the unnerving sensation remained that he knew far more of all this than did she.

She sank down onto the sofa again. "Will you tell me where you went last night?" she asked.

"Just asking a few questions" came his infuriating response.

"And did you get any answers?" Exasperation replaced the remaining shreds of her fear.

For a moment, he seemed wholly absorbed in the examination of his coat sleeve on which he had found a speck of dust. This attended to, he raised his bland gaze to meet her challenge. "A few," he admitted. "But not necessarily the ones I wanted."

And still he excluded her! Fury welled within her, overcoming judgment. "I assure you, my lord," she declared recklessly, "it would be much easier if you simply informed me of what you learn. I intend to find out anyway."

"Do you?" The considering look he directed at her held no little enjoyment. "Do you know, I think you may."

Chapter 18

Conversing with Deverell when he was in this secretive mood was less than useless, Leanora fumed as he took his leave of her. Why could he not tell her, unless. . . . She thrust her unwelcome fears away, refusing to face them. It was all nonsense! Deverell, of all people, could not be involved!

Restless and on edge, she went to her father's room and found him gratifyingly interested in a game of piquet. She spent the evening at play with him, and only his own weakened condition prevented him from being aware of her unusually erratic attention to the cards.

Her mind was far from piquet. Over and over, she reviewed her conversation with Deverell. In one respect, he had been right. No matter what lay behind the danger to her and her father, the only reasonable course would be to retire into the country. They should be safe at the Abbey, for there would be no reason for anyone to pursue them once they were out of town and posing no further threat to the Requiem plot.

But it wasn't only her lurking uneasiness that made her set her face against so tame a scheme. Nor was it due to resentment at Deverell's high-handedness. From the moment the first exciting events had invaded her humdrum routine, something inside her had come alive. An adventurous nature, previously unsuspected, lay buried within her, confined and restricted by society's dictums.

But all that had changed. Was it Deverell's reprehensible influence that made her restless, unsatisfied with the sedate lot of a lady of quality? She would not walk away from danger, though she suspected she was a fool. That knowledge, surprisingly, only made her want to laugh in a manner disturbingly reminiscent of Lord Deverell.

If he was going to be infuriatingly secretive, then she would find out a few things on her own. She would not—could not!—tamely submit to being excluded! Her options were limited, as was her experience in such a delicate matter, but she could ask questions. And ask them, she would.

A quick review of the people she suspected of being involved in some way led her to the conclusion that her brother Gregory would be the easiest—and probably the safest—person to approach first. Therefore, shortly after noon the following day, she took her courage firmly in hand and set forth on the short walk around the corner to Mount Street where she hoped to find him at home.

The afternoon was dark and overcast, with gray clouds hanging low in the sky. She glanced uneasily up at them, but rain did not seem imminent. Huddling more warmly into her pelisse, she quickened her pace.

She was too late. As she started down Mount Street, Gregory came out the front door of his house and down the steps. Without so much as a single glance in her direction, he set off along the street on foot.

Leanora hesitated only a second. Having steeled her nerves up to the point of a confrontation, she was not now about to be denied. She hurried in pursuit, almost running to bring herself within hailing distance of him.

He paused at the corner and looked impatiently about. Leanora, breathing hard from the unaccustomed exertion of trying to out-distance her long-legged brother, gasped in relief and slowed her own rapid pace. It would never do to be breathless when she caught up with him; it would put her at a disadvantage at the onset.

A number of carriages rattled past. Would he even hear her? She called, but to her frustration he did not turn around.

The next carriage slowed, came to a stop before Gregory, and the door was thrown wide from within. The interior remained shrouded in deep shadows, but as her brother climbed in, Leanora caught a glimpse of Lord Kennington. Gregory slid past him, took a seat, and Kennington pulled the door closed, sealing them into the privacy of the hackney.

Her brain whirled with conjecture, for the combination of Gregory and Lord Kennington seemed too ludicrous to be ignored. Here, at last, might be a real clue, and she would be a fool to let it slip away, all for the lack of a little resolution.

Without pausing for further reflection, she hailed the next hackney, and it stopped to take her up. The jarvey blinked at her rapid instructions to keep the other carriage in sight, but she seemed an affluent young lady. He was as well aware as any other member of his profession that the Quality were notoriously given to odd behavior and might be counted upon to slip a healthy *douceur* to anyone who aided them. As soon as she was safely within his vehicle, he put his horse into a rapid trot, bent on his errand.

Leanora perched on the edge of the seat, peering forward through the tangle of vehicles that made their way along the street. To her chagrin, the hackney turned down St. James Street and pulled up before White's. Somehow, it was the last thing she had expected, and the anti-climax of it left her momentarily bereft of coherent thought. She stared, perplexed, as the two gentlemen got out, paid off their jarvey and strolled into the club.

Well, she could hardly remain where she was. St. James was no place for a lady, especially one alone. Frustrated, she directed the driver to take her to the corner and set her down there, to give her a chance to consider. Her reticule, she was glad to perceive, contained a considerable number of coins. At least she would be able to get home again.

But what was she to do now? She could hardly stand there and wait! Already, several fashionable bucks were pausing in their perambulations, one going so far as to raise his quizzing glass, the better to observe her. She colored under the scrutiny and averted her face.

A drop of water fell on her cheek, then another as it began to sprinkle in a desultory manner. That was all she needed, she reflected wryly. A great investigator she turned out to be, standing in a place no well-bred lady should be, getting cold and wet. . . . The drops came faster and harder, and in a matter of minutes a heavy rain pelted down. All she had for protection was a merino pelisse, and it would not take long for this to soak through.

She hunched more deeply into it, seeking what protection she could while she called herself every derogatory name of which she could think. Why had she ever set forth on such a ridiculous expedition? Just what did she hope to accomplish, anyway? She had no business haring off after her brother in such a ridiculous manner! How shocked he would be to think that she would stoop to following him in a clandestine fashion. As if he were a common criminal and she a Bow Street Runner!

It was all Deverell's fault, of course. Had she never had the dubious honor of his acquaintance, she never would have behaved in this ridiculous fashion. And if he had not made her so angry by refusing to tell her anything, there would have been no need!

Only one course lay open to her. She would salvage what little dignity remained, summon another hackney and return home in defeat. She cast a dubious glance down the street. In fine weather, hackneys were to be found in quantity. But let the least bit of rain fall, and it was almost guaranteed that one would find oneself stranded.

The third vehicle to pass her stopped, and she climbed in before giving him her direction. They started forward, and she cast a last look of loathing at the front of White's.

"Wait!" she cried, and the carriage stopped on the instant.

"Yes, miss?" The driver looked down at her in reproach.

"Just—just wait a moment, please."

Gregory had come out, alone, and it was obvious at once that something was terribly amiss. He moved stiffly with his shoulders drooped, not freely with his usual arrogant stride. He hailed several hackneys until one at last stopped and he was able to climb in out of the rain.

"I want you to follow that hackney, please," she called to her jarvey. "Keep it in sight!"

The driver said something under his breath, but the steady beating of the drops upon the vehicle's roof drowned out his words. They started forward once more, and Leonora was forced to sit back in the seat to keep from getting even wetter. Not that it mattered much at this stage, she thought ruefully.

They turned east into Piccadilly, and with a sinking sensation she realized that Gregory was not returning home. She could change her mind, of course, at any time, but she was not one to give up easily. She settled down to watch the way, curious as to where her brother might be bound.

As they drove on and on, she began to grow somewhat uneasy. She no longer recognized any landmarks. They were off the main road now, driving through narrower streets lined with large, though not necessarily stately, houses. What district was this? At last, the hackney in front of her pulled up before an elaborate home, and its passenger alighted.

Her own jarvey drew up. "In there, miss," he called down to her.

She could see very well for herself. Gregory ran quickly up the steps to the house, knocked and was admitted almost at once. She stared hard at the place. There was something vaguely familiar about it. That porch, and that lower window. . . . She had it! It was the house she had visited the other night with Deverell. They were in Bloomsbury, and that home belonged to Kennington's mistress—or so Deverell had suggested.

She climbed slowly out into the pouring rain and paid off the jarvey. Kennington's mistress? What business had Gregory at this house? And he had been admitted without question, which implied he had been there before. She shook her head slowly, knowing she was out of her depth.

If she had any sense at all, she would summon that jarvey back and request to be taken at once to Berkeley Square. But it took no more than a second's reflection for her to realize that her mind must be wholly disordered, for she had no intention of doing the logical thing. She might be a fool, but she would see this through.

First of all, she wanted to discover what mysteries—if any—this house possessed. She crossed the street and walked slowly past, peering up at the window in what she hoped was a nonchalant manner. It was the same saloon into which she had looked the other night, elegant without being either pretty or welcoming. There was no one inside.

And what should she do now? Oh, if only Deverell were there and she were not so angry with him! He would undoubtedly know precisely what to do, irritating, exasperating man that he was.

One thing was certain, she could not linger there. In spite of the rain and the heavy clouds, it was not dark enough to provide her with any anonymity. Anyone who chanced to look out a window would be sure to see her trying to hide in a shadow.

Creeping about the front of the house was clearly ineligible. But what about the back? On inspiration, she turned and walked quickly down the street, counting the houses as she went. At the corner she turned, found the entrance to the mews and doubled back. It should be the fifth house . . . yes, that ought to be the one.

It was darker there, little more than an alleyway. The buildings behind her were partially converted, some still serving as stables, others adapted to rude dwelling places. She wrinkled her nose at the smell and turned her attention back to the house.

And what if Gregory was coming out the front while she was back there?

She wiped wet hair from her eyes and surveyed the building, feeling more a fool every minute. Having come this far, though, it would be a shocking waste to just walk tamely away without making the least push to discover what—if anything—went on there. Swallowing hard, and feeling distinctly ridiculous, she slipped silently up the back steps.

The door was bolted. She stared at it blankly for a moment, then suddenly grinned at her naivete. What had she planned to do? Walk right in and introduce herself to the servants? Ask if there might by any chance be anyone there who planned to assassinate the prime minister? How delightfully brilliant of her!

Hastily, she retreated back to the shadows to reconsider. She really had no notion of what she should do. Return home and summon Deverell, tell him of her suspicions? With her luck, he would be away from his lodgings, pursuing inquiries of

264

which he would tell her nothing! No, she would show him she was not entirely helpless, to be sent off to the country like a fox going to earth.

She regarded the back of the house with misgivings. She was a lady of quality, which was a severe handicap in her present endeavors. If only she had been raised in the fine art of breaking into houses, or of scrambling up iron gratings or drain pipes. She looked up toward the higher floors and could see lights in the windows above her.

It was quite a small house, really, and she reluctantly dismissed the suspicion that it might be a brothel. Such a simple answer would have explained a great deal—including Deverell's recognition of the mistress of the house! That thought disturbed her, so she returned to her contemplation of the building.

The back, she decided, was impregnable. The windows were above her reach, the door locked, and access to the first floor beyond her abilities. Discouraged—and secretly rather relieved—she retraced her steps to the front.

Here, in plain view of the entire street, she could hardly try a window. But there were two doors. The main entrance might be impossible, but there was still the servant's entrance in the basement. With a quick glance to assure herself no one was coming, she slipped down the iron area steps.

The door stood before her. With a trembling hand, she reached out for the knob, and to her consternation it turned. Silently, the door swung inward.

She swallowed hard. Her experience with the back door had led her to hope. . . . Well, in all honesty, she had expected to be thwarted upon every suit and to be able to retire from the field having been honorably defeated. Now it seemed she would either have to carry through with her investigation or admit herself a coward. She was frightened, but there was only herself to know that. Of course, if there were someone with her, like Deverell, he would probably have a fair idea of it from the way her shoulders were shaking.

The thought of Deverell buoyed her quavering nerve. He would not have the opportunity of laughing at her in his vastly superior way! He was not the only one who could face danger

265

bravely. But still she hesitated.

Just what did she intend to do? Try to get upstairs, to see if the house was a hotbed of conspiracy? Try to conceal herself somewhere and hope to overhear something useful? Behave, in general, as if she were a total fool? The latter was what she was doing! This was absolute insanity! She had best leave before she got herself into trouble.

A carriage rattled over the cobblestones and stopped frighteningly near. Leanora cringed against the block wall under the staircase as she heard a woman's far from refined voice. The newcomer ran through the rain, crossing the street, coming closer at every step. What if she was headed for the servant's entrance? Terrified of being caught, Leanora darted through the open door.

She found herself in a narrow hallway. Before her, the door to the kitchen premises stood ajar. The other way probably led to a pantry. She crept forward, peeked around the door and let out a sigh of relief. The kitchen was empty.

The iron stairs creaked with a heavy foot. The woman was coming down! Casting a terrified glance about, Leanora spotted a bulky cupboard standing out from the wall. In a moment she was behind it. She peeped back out, trying to see if she was hidden, and to her horror discovered a small puddle of water forming at her feet, dripping from her sodden pelisse.

An hysterical giggle rose within her, and firmly she bit it back. What on earth could she say if she was discovered? That she sought shelter from the storm? That she had mistaken the house? Or better, the street? That she was an escaped Bedlamite? If she were lucky, they might believe the latter. It came just a little too close to the truth.

"Rose?" a woman's deep voice called, clear and alarmingly near. "Where are you, girl?"

Light footsteps scurried from the pantry. "Here, Mrs. Applegate. I was just getting the vegetables, like you told me." Leanora heard something heavy being set down on the table, followed by a sigh of relief.

The first woman snorted. "Taking a nap, more like. I can't go out for more than a moment without you slipping off! Now, you cut those carrots on an angle, like I showed you, my girl.

266

I'll be wanting them in a moment. And the potatoes and onions, as well, mind! And you make sure they're attractive, like. Madam is having guests to dinner."

Leanora peeped around the corner of her cupboard. A scullery maid stood by a basin, scrubbing vegetables, and a woman dressed in the apron and cap of a cook stood behind her, her hands on her hips, watching. Merciful heavens, if they were about to prepare a meal, how long would she be trapped there? Long enough for her drenched garments to soak the entire floor? It could not yet be as much as four o'clock!

A bell rang, and the suddenness of it almost caused her heart to stop. The cook looked about.

"Where is that lout Albert?" she demanded.

"Dunno, Mrs. Applegate," Rose replied unnecessarily. "Want me to answer it?"

"You, girl? I should think not, indeed! I'll go." The cook pulled off her soiled apron and tossed it across a long wooden table. From a drawer she pulled a new one, tied it on and started up the stairs that led to the main floor. "You get some eggs from the pantry, Rose. And cheese. And I'll want it all ready when I get back!"

On that note, the cook made her exit. Rose dropped the carrots into the basin, hastily dried her hands on a cloth and hurried down the hall, away from the door that led to the street—and safety. It was enough for Leanora. In seconds she was out the door and darting up the steps to the street.

And she ducked down again. A carriage stood directly before the house, and above her someone was just coming out the front door. She peered up carefully and choked back a startled exclamation. Lord Petersham stood on the porch, adjusting a muffler so that it covered his ashen face. He stepped out into the rain and hurried across to the waiting barouche. A groom helped him into this, swung up onto the box, and the vehicle moved off.

Leanora stared after it in disbelief, for a moment forgetting her own precarious position. What was Petersham doing visiting this house? It seemed incomprehensible! Kennington, Gregory, Petersham. . . . And whose house was it? How did it all tie together?

267

She leaned back against the iron railing for support, trying to find some rational thread that might hold everything together. If there was one, she could detect no trace of it. None of this made any sense to her.

The next instant, all thought except her own safety fled from her mind as the front door opened again. Another gentleman came out. Gregory. And the bleakness of his expression left her shaken. What happened in this dreadful house to so upset people? And who else might be in there?

She remained where she was, just out of sight, watching as her brother came down the stairs. He appeared not to notice the rain. His posture was dejected, his head bent, and Leanora had to stifle an urge to go to him and offer comfort. She waited a discrete interval, then followed him once again. Under no circumstances did she wish to remain lurking about this house. She had had her fill of that!

He stopped at the corner and watched the carriages. It appeared to be a busy street, which was fortunate. After only a few minutes, he hailed a hackney. Leanora could only be glad, for she was absolutely drenched and uncomfortably aware of the stares she was receiving from the passengers in the various vehicles that passed.

Finding another hackney did not prove as easy as she had hoped. With a sense of growing frustration, she watched Gregory disappear up the street. Would she not be able to follow where he went next? She waved frantically at the next hackney. The jarvey slowed, took a good look at her bedraggled appearance and drove on.

Oh, the ultimate insult! Or at least she hoped it would prove the worst she would receive. But to be rejected by a hackney! She started to giggle, the absurdity of her situation finally getting the better of her. She had terrified herself, spoilt her clothing, wasted the afternoon—but it had not all been for nothing. She had something to tell Deverell about that house—though she might not tell him precisely how she had learned it.

The next hackney stopped, to her unending gratitude, and she climbed in. The jarvey was inclined to argue, though, when she tried to persuade him to catch up with another carriage that was no longer in sight. Furious, she clambered back out and waved him on, then set about hailing another.

It took her several minutes before the foolishness of that move penetrated her. If the last jarvey had no hope of catching Gregory, then how could another? She had lost her brother's trail, and she had only her temper to thank for the fact that she was not at this moment sitting in a dry carriage, being carried home.

At last another stopped, and she got in out of the rain before giving the jarvey her direction. He looked at her askance, seemed about to demur, then gave in. She cast a considering glance over herself and decided that perhaps he had cause to doubt her. She hardly looked as if she would be going to such an exalted address as Sherborne House.

She shivered as the wet and chill penetrated her garments. Even her feet inside the half-boots of kid leather were damp! If she had wanted to accomplish the complete ruination of her footwear—and bonnet, as well—she could hardly have set about it in a more efficient manner. Nor would her pelisse or walking dress ever be the same. Some spy she turned out to be! No wonder Deverell said to leave things up to him.

She hunched miserably back against the squabs, reflecting that she was undoubtedly ruining the hackney, as well. And what had she achieved? A vague suspicion? It was nothing more than that, really. She could not truly believe Gregory was involved in a treasonable plot. There must have been some perfectly reasonable explanation for his presence at that house. And Petersham's, as well.

She sniffed, depressingly close to tears. What a mull she had made of everything! And how Deverell would laugh if he ever guessed the truth. She shivered again, cold and wet and miserable. But even that might be bearable if she were not so utterly ashamed of her ridiculous behavior! What a delightful way to spend a day!

It was only when the carriage pulled up in Berkeley Square that she pulled herself together once more. She still had the servants to face! She straightened her appearance as best she could, smoothing back her dripping hair and ramming drenched curls under her bonnet at random. Holding herself at

269

her most regal, she paid the jarvey, added a generous *douceur* and sailed up the steps.

An astonished Tremly met her in the hall. She inclined her head to him in greeting and handed him her bonnet.

"You may dispose of that for me," she informed him, adding, by way of explanation: "It came on to rain."

He stared after her, open-mouthed, as she swept on past him and proceeded up the stairs. "Miss Leanora!" he exclaimed, recovering somewhat from the surprise of seeing his mistress in such a state.

She bit her lip, then turned to face him. "Yes?"

"Master Gregory has arrived, Miss Leanora. Only a few minutes ago."

She stared at the butler, then to his amazement she burst out laughing. "No, has—has he?" she managed. Her shoulders quaked with mirth at the sheer ridiculousness of the situation.

"In his lordship's study," Tremly informed her.

"Thank you. Please, tell him that I desire to have speech with him before he leaves. I—I will just go now to change my gown."

How many names had she called herself earlier? She could think of a few more now. She had worried about losing him, and he was bound for her home all the time! Oh, how glad she was that Deverell knew nothing about this! He would roast her unmercifully! It was almost—almost!—a shame to deny him the story.

She hesitated over summoning her abigail, then decided that good woman would discover the state of her garments sooner or later. She might as well be granted Ripton's assistance. She rang the bell, then set about removing her half-boots. She had been quite right. Unless Pagget could work the same miracles that he did on the earl's hunting boots, the soft leather was ruined.

Ripton, that most efficient of abigails, blinked upon being privileged to view her mistress. But rather than waste her time in useless exclamations and beratings, she went instantly to work stripping the young lady of her drenched garments. These she set into the basin where they could not damage the rugs. Towels were procured, and in a surprisingly short time

270

Leanora donned a clean round gown of figured muslin. Little could be done with her hair, but after drying it briskly on the soft towels, Ripton brushed it back and confined it with a riband at the nape of her charge's neck.

Once more relatively dry and comfortable, Leanora set forth to seek her brother. First, though, she would check on her father, who must be wondering by now where she had disappeared to. She opened his door and peeped in. Pagget, for once, was nowhere to be seen. In his place at the bedside, towering over the sleeping earl, stood Gregory. And in his hand he held a silver mounted pistol.

Chapter 19

Leanora gasped, and Gregory looked slowly around. His expression, his whole demeanor, was bemused, as if he were not quite sure where he was. His face was every bit as pale as when she had seen him in Bloomsbury, and his features were gaunt, haunted. He came slowly away from the bedside, toward her.

"Gregory!" It was little more than an anguished whisper. She shook her head, staring in horror at the pistol he clutched in his hand. "Gregory, you—you *cannot!*"

He was trembling, and not by so much as a glance did he acknowledge that he saw her. He walked past, out of the room, then turned to stare at her, his pale eyes filled with a boundless misery.

"I—I wouldn't have done it here," he told her. "Planned on using the study, but there wasn't a gun in there. Thought I'd check the old man's room, and I found it, just where I remembered, in the drawer of his bedside table." He gave a shaky laugh. "Here—here it is." He held up the pistol for her to see.

"What—what are you talking about?" One horror fled before the dawning of another. The face he raised to her was haggard in the extreme, his eyes huge and filled with pain, and for a moment it was as if she gazed into the torment of his soul.

"Put—put a period to my existence. Nothing left for me to do." He gave a hollow laugh at her dumbfounded expression. "Blow my brains out, you know," he went on to further elucidate his meaning. "Isn't that the accepted thing to do?"

She stared at him, for the moment bereft of speech, aware that things had gone hopelessly beyond her. What was Gregory talking about? That he had no intention of killing their father, she had grasped. But why should he kill himself? She took an unsteady step toward him, holding out her hands, and in a moment she clasped his shaking figure in her arms. He reeked of brandy.

"Oh, God, Leanora, I've got to!" he sobbed. His head came down to rest against hers, and she raised a hand to stroke his cheek.

"No!" She pulled away slightly. "Come—come down to the study. Tell me about it. We'll find a way out of this, be sure we will."

Somehow, she maneuvered him down the stairs, leading him to the back of the house to the earl's study where they would not be disturbed. Gregory seemed strangely biddable now, as if he had lost all will of his own. When she pressed him onto the sofa, he sat without protest. Next, she pried the gun from his now limp hand and stuffed it away in the back of a desk drawer.

She rang the bell, and when Tremly arrived she sent him for coffee. Gregory had imbibed more than enough brandy for one day. He sat bent over on the edge of the sofa, his head buried in his hands, his whole body trembling. Leanora perched beside him and slid a comforting arm about his shoulders. When the butler returned with the tray, she poured out a strong cup.

"Drink this," she commanded, holding it out to Gregory.

He raised his head, looked at the steaming cup, then took it with shaking hands. His sister was obliged to steady the cup so that he could sip the scalding liquid. He finished it, and she poured another. He waved this aside and dropped his face once more into his hands.

"Oh, God, Nora, what am I going to do?"

"To begin with, you are going to tell me everything." She kept her voice commanding, yet gentle. "And I do mean *everything!* If I am to help you, I must know the truth. What has brought you to such a pass?"

"Money." He spit out the dire word with loathing. "I'm in debt. Ruined, Nora. No hope of redeeming my vowels."

"Who holds them?"

"Kennington." He shook his head. "It's more money than I can even comprehend."

She let that pass for the moment. "How?" she prompted him.

"I don't really know. It—you can't understand it, Nora. You've *got* to game, or they shun you. And it seemed safe, going with Dalmouth. He's my brother-in-law! Knew he wouldn't steer me wrong. Or so I thought." He broke off and accepted the cup that she still held. He took a large gulp, seemed to feel better and went on. "He introduced me to a discrete little hell where I had the most wonderful run of luck. Said it was phenomenal, that I should back myself even higher when things went so well. So I did. He bet with me, and each time we raised the stakes. And I kept winning!"

"And then?" But she thought she already knew.

"The next time I went it was the same way—at first. I couldn't lose! Then, about halfway through the evening, I started to drop. But it didn't matter, because I'd won so much. But by then we were playing for such high stakes, only a couple of losses. . . ." The sentence trailed off, and he swallowed the rest of the coffee in one gulp.

"You found you'd lost more than you'd won?"

He nodded. "Wiped out my winnings of the night before, too. Scared me, I can tell you, but Kennington was there, watching. Said the only thing to do was to keep playing, that my luck would turn again." He gave a hollow laugh that sounded very like a death nell to Leanora.

"It didn't, did it?" She smoothed her hand over his tousled blond curls. "My poor Greg. What did you do then?"

"Not much I could do. I'd already lost more than I could afford, so I took Kennington's tip on a horse that couldn't lose. Damned screw didn't even place."

"How did you cover the bet?"

"Oh, no one could have been nicer than Kennington. Said he felt it to be all his fault for recommending the horse to me in the first place. So he offered to loan me the money to cover my reckoning at Tattersall's."

He lowered his head again in agonized memory, and Leanora

rose to pour more coffee. She could use a cup herself, very strong and very sweet. She had suspected Gregory of following a ruinous course, but nothing like this tale of reckless loss he was relating. She went back to him, handed over one of the cups and watched while he took a long drink.

"By that time, I was dipped so deeply there was no way of coming about," he went on. "My only hope was to win a fortune. So I kept playing. Didn't matter where, but usually at that hell in Pall Mall." He looked up at her, his eyes glittering with hatred. "Then I found out that fancy little establishment belongs to Kennington."

"*Belongs* to him!" Leonora exclaimed. "But . . . the scandal in government circles if that were to come out!"

Gregory gave a mirthless laugh. "Oh, there's no way to prove it, you may be sure. He's been most discrete—and most understanding. Never demanded a cent of the money I owed him. The only thing he wanted was that I be—complaisant, shall we say?—if he chose to flirt with my wife."

Leonora gasped. "Did—did he have the effrontery to actually suggest that to you?"

"Oh, not in so many words. But I knew what he meant. And then he suggested I bring a friend or two to his little hell."

"Like Dalmouth did to you. Is he in Kennington's debt, also?"

He nodded. "God, Leonora, if you knew how—how *trapped* I've felt!"

"Why didn't you just tell Pappa when you realized the trouble you were heading into?"

He stared at her as if she had just suggested he jump off the cliffs at Dover. "I couldn't!"

"How deeply are you scorched?" She had to know.

"About a hundred and fifty thousand pounds."

Her cup dropped from suddenly nerveless fingers. She stared at the puddle of coffee that seeped into the carpet, then reached for a napkin and began to mop at the mess. Sherborne could never pay such a sum! No one could! It was no wonder Gregory had thought to solve his problems with a pistol. She bit back hasty words of rebuke, knowing they would do no good. Instead, she asked: "What happened next?"

"Oh, he wanted me to pass on any bits of information my father happened to drop, anything that might be of use to the Opposition."

Leonora froze. "And—did you?" This shocked her more deeply than any of the rest.

"No! I couldn't! It would be betraying him! But Kennington kept on, dropping those subtle hints. I—I got the impression he would leave Julia alone if I got the information for him. And then—and then there was Father's accident. It seemed too good an opportunity to miss! Any information he had was bound to be out of date very fast. I could pass it on to Kennington without really hurting Father." He looked up at his sister, his eyes beseeching, seeking forgiveness.

She took his hand, giving it a tight squeeze. "Go on," she said softly.

"I think he knew what I was up to. I showed him a few papers, but he knew at a glance they were months old. So then he promised he would return all my vowels if I found him something really good."

"What?" Leonora demanded, holding her breath. What had Kennington wanted? The code mentioning the Requiem Masque?

"Anything. Just something he could use against All the Talents. He didn't care what."

Leonora's hopes fell. She had been so sure. . . . She took a deep breath and let it out slowly. "And what now, my brother?"

"I don't know. Oh, I can assure you, this business has cured me of gaming!" His shaky laugh sounded again. "Cured me of living, too! God, Leonora, to watch my wife encouraging the likes of Kennington . . . !"

"I meant what does Kennington demand of you now?"

"Money" came the hopeless response. "Can't pay, nowhere to turn. I saw him this afternoon. He's threatened to take the whole matter to Father. Says if he doesn't get the money at once, he'll create a scandal that will ruin Father politically. And he'd do it, Leonora. Nothing left to do but blow my brains out." He looked hazily around, as if seeking the pistol.

"Stop talking nonsense!" Leonora ordered. "You will not

277

have to pay any such sum, I am sure!"

He shook his head. "You don't understand. Matter of honor."

"Honor be damned!" she exclaimed roundly. "You may be very sure that gaming hell was not honest—and we'll prove it!"

Gregory straightened up, staring at her. A slight glimmer of hope shone in his eyes for the first time. "Do—do you think we can?"

She nodded firmly. "But it will take careful planning."

It was disconcerting that as soon as trouble struck, she forgot her uneasy suspicions of Deverell and instantly longed for his support. Not for a moment did she doubt his ability to do the trick! If they could destroy the hell, get Kennington arrested. . . . There must be a law against dishonest gaming!

"We must stall him," she said at last. "I will give you what money I can, enough to hold off his demands for the time being."

He clasped her hands, unable to find words with which to express his feelings. She returned the strong pressure of his grip.

"Don't worry, Greg. We'll get you out of this, and we'll make Kennington pay for what you've suffered. How much does Julia know?"

"Nothing. I—I've been too ashamed to tell her. And then she started flirting with Kennington! If you knew what that did to me, to see her turn away from me, and to him, *him*, of all men . . . !"

"It is only a flirtation," she told him sternly.

"I don't know. It could be more." His voice lacked any inflection whatsoever. "I—I haven't been able to interfere between them."

Leanora grasped his shoulder, pitying him deeply. At a time when his life fell apart about him, he was denied the support of the wife he loved. And Julia had undoubtedly been hurt by his apparent lack of caring. It was time these two were brought back together.

She crossed over to the desk and wrote two quick notes. She rang for Tremly, then carefully dusted and sealed the missives. When the butler entered the room, she handed them over with the request that they be delivered immediately. "And I hope there will be two more for dinner tonight," she finished.

"What are you doing?" Gregory asked as soon as Tremly had closed the door behind himself.

"I have just sent for Julia."

"What? No! Leanora, you can't!"

"On the contrary, I just have. No, sit down and be still. If we are going to extricate you from this mess, we are going to need a little help. I have also sent for Lord Deverell."

"Deverell? Why?" Gregory demanded, not pleased. "Lord, Nora, I don't want the whole world to know about this business!"

"It is not the whole world. Deverell has been helping me on—on another matter, and I can assure you he is discretion itself. There is a great deal more to him than appears at first glance. I would not choose to go against him."

Gregory looked dubious but was not yet up to argument. He sank back on the sofa and closed his eyes, in which position he remained for a very long while. He did not stir again until a soft rap on the door announced the return of Tremly, who ushered in Lady Julia Ashton.

"Leanora?" that lady asked, hesitating on the threshold. "What is this about? I—" She broke off, stiffening abruptly as she perceived her husband's sprawling figure. "Foxed, I suppose," she said in disgust.

Gregory raised his head at the sound of her voice. He looked her over slowly, from the top of her glossy dark curls to her walking dress of rose crepe and dainty slippers of matching satin. "Oh, God, you're beautiful!" he groaned, and allowed his head to fall back once again.

Julia stared at him, taken aback both by his words and manner. She turned to Leanora for guidance, and the emotionally charged atmosphere of the room at last penetrated her. Her lovely eyes widened, and she looked from one to the other. "What—what is going on?" she asked faintly.

"Sit down," Leanora told her. "We are waiting for someone else."

"Who?" Julia regarded her hostess in apprehension.

"Lord Deverell. I want him to hear Gregory's story as well."

279

Julia relaxed somewhat, as if she had been afraid that her sister-in-law would name someone else. Still, she regarded Leanora with no little curiosity though she held her tongue. Crossing the study, she took a seat well removed from the sofa.

To Leanora's immense relief, it was not long before the sounds of another arrival reached them, followed by the firm, uneven tread of Deverell's step. She stood, and as the door opened she went in relief to meet him, her hands extended.

He took them, raising first one and then the other to his lips. "I came at once," he said simply. "How may I serve you?"

His calm, soothing assurance filled the room, and her emotional turmoil began to subside. All at once she felt rather foolish, as if she had been making a great deal out of nothing. It was Deverell's capable presence, she knew, and could only be glad for it.

He led her back into the room, greeted Lady Julia and nodded to Gregory, who had straightened himself up. Leanora's grip tightened on his arm, and he covered her hand with his own. Looking at each of the drawn, worried faces in turn, he was forced to repress a slight smile. "It would seem that we are in for a dramatic evening," he murmured.

Leanora threw him a measuring glance. For once, his ever-present amusement seemed to be held decently in check. "We are," she confirmed.

"Then may I suggest that you send for some refreshment? Unless I am much mistaken, we may be here for some time, and all of us, especially your brother, will be the better for something solid to eat."

Leanora complied, ringing once more for Tremly while Deverell arranged chairs. Julia came closer with obvious reluctance, though she was unable to keep her worried gaze long from her husband's ravaged countenance. When Tremly returned with a loaded tray, Deverell took it from him and placed it on a nearby table.

Leanora filled a plate with a selection of biscuits and placed it beside her brother. "Go ahead, Greg," she urged him gently. "Tell them what you told me."

He cast her a wry glance, then stared down at the coffee cup he still held between his hands. His voice, when he started, was

280

raspy. He broke off, coughed, then resumed his tale in a tone that was barely audible. He took frequent sips of coffee, and Leonora took the cup from his shaking hands when he had drained it.

A ragged cry tore from Julia's throat when he reached the part of Kennington's demands. Tears slipped unheeded down her cheeks, and before Gregory had finished, she had dropped to her knees beside him and was convulsed in silent but wracking sobs. He reached out, tentatively touching her cheek, and she fell into his arms.

Deverell touched Leonora's shoulder, and when she looked up at him, he gestured toward the door with his head. She rose and accompanied him out of the room.

"Let's give them a few minutes," he suggested.

She nodded. "By all means. Poor Greg, he really fell into a trap, didn't he?"

Deverell's lips tightened. "He's been a fool, but I think he knows that. And he's not the first young pigeon to fall into the clutches of a Captain Sharp."

"What can be done about Kennington?" She looked up into Deverell's rugged face and knew complete confidence in his abilities to solve her difficulties.

A slow smile lit his eyes as they rested on her. "If Gregory is brave enough to play along with me, we'll see him brought to book," he promised.

"And that house in Bloomsbury? You will look into that?"

His eyes narrowed. "What do you mean?"

"I am not sure. But we must ask Gregory what goes on there!"

"I already have a fair idea," he informed her sternly. "What I want you to explain is what *you* know of the place."

Betraying color warmed her cheeks. "I—I followed Gregory today," she admitted. "He met Kennington, and I wanted to know why. And Gregory went out to that house in Bloomsbury, and—" She quailed under the anger in his expression.

"Good God!" The softness of his voice in no way detracted from his flaming temper. "Have you no sense at all, my girl? You know perfectly well what we are dealing with!"

281

"How *can* I know? You never see fit to tell me anything. If I want to find out what is going on, I have to investigate for myself!"

He grasped her shoulders and glared down at her, meeting a defiance that did not quite disguise the sudden alarm in her eyes. "Yes, I want you afraid," he breathed. "You're trembling." He took a deep, steadying breath and released her abruptly, muttering something that she could not quite hear.

She turned her back on him, pretending indifference to his wild, unsettling mood. She could not let him know how he affected her! She had trembled in fear at his touch, but there had been something exciting, as well. For a moment, she had experienced a tiny portion of that energetic power he normally kept so firmly under control.

"You will not do anything of that kind again," he commanded. "Someone tried to kill you once. Do you think they will hesitate to try another time if you are caught prying into matters that should not concern you?"

She hunched a shoulder and started back to the study. He was right, of course, a fact which left her terrified as well as rebellious. She threw open the door and stopped short.

Gregory still sat on the sofa, but he now held his wife comfortably upon his lap. Their arms were wrapped about each other, and her head rested on his shoulder. Julia raised a tear-stained face to her sister-in-law, but her expression was no longer one of misery. A shy, slightly embarrassed smile trembled on her lips. They appeared well on the way to reestablishing a very satisfactory understanding. Julia made a move as if seeking to rise, but Gregory held her firmly in place. She showed no desire to struggle.

Deverell came in behind Leanora and shut the study door. He crossed to the table and selected a tea cake, which he ate. Leanora poured him a cup of tea, and he resumed his chair. "I want you to tell me about that house in Bloomsbury," he directed Gregory.

The interlude with Julia had done wonders for her brother, Leanora noted with relief. The haggard lines had faded a bit, and there was a new energy about him. With his wife's support, they would see him through this.

"The place belongs to Kennington," Gregory said, holding Julia closer. "He has his mistress established there, but he also uses the house for his—his other arrangements. I'm not sure what all he's involved in, but it's undoubtedly nothing savory from what I've seen of him."

"What was Lord Petersham doing there?" Leanora asked, suddenly remembering the other visitor she had seen.

"Petersham?" Gregory repeated, perplexed. "Was he there?" He shook his head slowly. "I never saw him."

"He left only a couple of minutes before you did."

"Good God!" Gregory hugged Julia more tightly. "Do you suppose he is in debt to Kennington, too? I never heard he had a taste for gaming. I wonder what the connection between them could be?"

"Why, Petersham's collection, of course," Julia explained.

"What do you mean?" Deverell sat up, intent.

"That message you hid for Petersham at the ball?" Leanora asked.

"How did you know?" Julia stared at her sister-in-law. "But yes, I did take a note from Kennington to Petersham, and I thought he was being quite ridiculously dramatic about it all. You see, Petersham wanted some silly Roman vase, and Kennington came into possession of it. Only he didn't want anyone else to know, or he thought that business dealings between the Home secretary and a member of the Opposition wouldn't look good, or something. I don't really know, but he wanted it kept secret. So he asked me to carry the message."

Deverell ran a hand over his chin. "Sounds pretty simple, doesn't it? I don't see the need for such roundabout methods—unless there is more to it." He glanced at Leanora. "How would you describe Petersham's finances?"

She stared at him. "I have no idea. Comfortable, I should imagine."

He nodded. "Only comfortable. And how would you describe his collection of classical antiquities?"

"It's quite impressive—as anyone knows who has ever been so unfortunate as to ask him about it. It is his favorite and most boring topic."

"I wonder how he supports it?" he mused.

283

Leanora's eyes widened. "The Home Office funds?"

Deverell shrugged. "If Kennington has gotten his talons into him, who knows what he might have done? Petersham has a great deal to lose in a scandal."

Leanora let out a long breath. Just how many pies did Kennington have a finger in—and could the Requiem Masque be one of them? She could not like this new turn of events.

"Sir William might know about Petersham," she said softly, thinking aloud. "He always knows everything, even what he should not." She held Deverell's gaze. "If I know him at all, he probably has some suspicions of the Masque."

A bland expression settled over Deverell's face. "If you do not mind, I believe we will do best to keep our own council at the moment." The message in his eyes was unmistakable, and she realized she had almost given away too much before her brother.

Deverell need not have worried. Gregory paid them very little heed at the moment. Julia whispered something into his ear, and judging from his expression, nothing else mattered to him anymore.

Dinner was announced, and Deverell stood at once. "If you will excuse me, I cannot remain."

"But—" Leanora broke off, her expression comical in its dismay.

He took her hand, amused understanding filling his dark eyes. "You might find it somewhat difficult to explain my presence to your aunt," he murmured. "As it is, you will enjoy a quiet family party." He turned to address the young couple who rose reluctantly from the couch. "Can you do as you are told?" he demanded of Gregory.

"Yes, sir" came the instant response. "And so can Julia." He took his wife's hand, and she nodded.

So her brother called Deverell "sir." Did everyone respond to his air of command? In a way, she was glad that it was not only she who fell under his spell.

"Then I want you to continue exactly as you have been. Lady Julia, you must continue to encourage Kennington. You must," he pointed out as she protested, "or he will guess something has gone amiss with his plans. At the moment, our

284

first concern must be to protect your husband."

Julia raised frightened eyes to his and nodded mutely. Her other hand stole about Gregory's arm, hugging it close. Nothing, Leanora guessed with satisfaction, would make the girl hurt her husband.

"It—it will not be easy, but I'll do it. For Gregory." The look the couple exchanged spoke volumes.

"And you," Deverell turned his attention to Gregory. "You will have to give him some money to stall him. How much can you raise?"

"You can have my topazes," Leanora said at once. "The full set should bring you about two thousand pounds. Will that be enough for now?"

Gregory choked, having trouble finding words with which to express his feelings.

"If it isn't, I have some emeralds that were my mamma's," Julia said stoutly.

"Good God," Gregory exploded. "I can't take money from females! It ain't the thing!"

Leanora almost smiled. He must be feeling better, for he had made no objection when she offered earlier. And what about her diamond earrings and the housekeeping funds?

Deverell shook his head. "This whole situation is not 'the thing.' But it will only be for a very little while. If we handle this properly, we should be able to get the money back."

With that, the party broke up. Gregory and Julia went upstairs to the dining room, but Leanora accompanied Deverell to the door. In the hall she stopped him, suddenly remembering another point of interest.

"Yes?" he inquired as she drew him into the Gold Saloon.

"I just thought you ought to know. Dalmouth proposed to me yesterday."

"Boasting of your conquests?" A teasing light lurked in his eyes.

She flushed. "You can be very disagreeable when you want. I only told you because it might have some bearing on all this. You are somewhat acquainted with the gentleman. Do you really think offering for me is the sort of thing he would be likely to do?"

"No," he agreed with unflattering force after a moment's consideration. "It most certainly is not."

Leanora stiffened. "I am not quite such an antidote as all that!"

He had the audacity to chuckle. "I am quite sure you are not," he said with exaggerated kindness. "I merely intended you the compliment of not considering you to be Dalmouth's type."

She regarded him speculatively. "Dalmouth has somewhat of a reputation as a rake. I have it on good authority that he only pursues the most beautiful women."

Infuriatingly, Deverell laughed in that deep, whole-hearted manner that sent shivers through her. "My lady, I must not detain you from your dinner any longer. Rest assured, I shall call on you again very soon." He kissed her hand and, still smiling, took his leave.

Chapter 20

Leanora entered her father's chambers the following morning to find Pagget in the dressing room, hanging a coat away neatly in a cupboard. She looked beyond, and a short gasp escaped her at the sight that met her startled eyes. The earl, resplendent in a brocade dressing gown of deep mulberry, was seated in a chair beside the window with Xerk curled contentedly by his feet, snoring stertorously. She crossed the threshold, and her father rose and came toward her, leaning heavily on a cane.

"Pappa!" she cried and ran to him.

He clasped her against his chest, a soft chuckle shaking his lean frame. "Well, my girl, did you think to keep me abed forever?"

"No, but . . . is it wise? Are you well enough?" She raised anxious eyes to search his face.

"Of course I am. Would have risen long ago, but I can't seem to find a coat to fit me. Damme, if I don't get active again, I'll have to have a whole new wardrobe made!"

She laughed and knew it to be a release of tensions. She gave him a swift hug, then helped him back to the chair. "You look remarkably better," she assured him.

"Glad you think so." He eased himself back into the chair as if glad to get off his feet. The first time up was bound to be a strain. "Want you to do something for me," he added, eyeing her through half-lidded eyes.

"You reason with him, Miss Leanora," begged the

exasperated valet. "There's no getting him to see sense when he takes the bit between his teeth." He glared at his master with the license allowed such an old and loyal retainer, making his disapproval obvious.

A feeling of foreboding settled over her. "What do you want, dearest?" she asked.

"I want to see Petersham and Sir William," he told her, and there was a touch of defiance in his voice.

She looked over at the valet in alarm and met his pugnacious grimace. Apparently the request had already been put to him—and more than once.

"Now look here, my girl," her father started. "I will recover a great deal more quickly if I am not thwarted at every turn! I am not going out or exerting myself unduly. I merely wish to assure myself that all progresses smoothly at the Home Office. If you refuse to send for them, I can only suppose there is a great deal amiss and you hope to spare me."

She met the valet's dubious look and shrugged helplessly. "Very well," she sighed, and bent to kiss the earl's cheek. "You always did know how to get your own way."

It really was safest to give in, she reflected as she made her way downstairs to the breakfast parlor. He would be quite capable of ordering up a carriage and trying to go out if they refused him. The dear old gentleman, she thought fondly. He could be quite exasperating, but she would have him no other way.

But was it safe? Pagget could hardly be present at any meeting of the Home Office staff. Of course, it would only be Petersham and Sir William who came. Somehow, she could not see either of these gentlemen murdering her father in cold blood, and in the presence of the other. It should be safe enough. Oh, if only she knew who was responsible for all this! It was dreadful, having to doubt almost everyone she knew!

It had to be Kennington! She kept repeating that thought. If it were, then he would be put safely out of the way and Gregory would be free of his clutches. Deverell was keeping a close eye on him—she hoped! He would never give Kennington the chance to carry out his deadly plot at the so-called Requiem Masque.

But what if it wasn't Kennington who was responsible? This was something on which they could not afford to make a mistake! It would be comparatively easy to keep the prime minister away from that one event—providing they could discover when and where it actually was—but preventing this one attempt on his life would only make it necessary for the conspirators to try another, one of which they would know nothing until it was too late. No, they must find out for certain who had planned this monstrous scheme.

Following Lord Sherborne's instructions, she duly commissioned a groom to carry a message to Petersham and Sir William. A response arrived back within the hour, saying that both gentlemen would do themselves the honor of calling upon the earl at four-thirty. That left him with considerable time to rest—if he could only be prevailed upon to do so.

This did not prove as hard as she had feared. Tired from the exertion of dressing that morning, her father was surprisingly compliant when it was suggested that he retire to his bed and lie down for a while. He did issue strict orders that he was to be awakened in plenty of time to array himself in something other than his nightshirt for the meeting, but as this implied that he was willing to sleep for a time, Leanora assured Pagget that it would be all right to humor him.

She returned from a shopping expedition with her aunt a full half hour before her father was due to be roused. She peeked into his room at once and was pleased to discover that the earl still lay in the vast bed, his eyes closed and his breathing deep and regular. Providing he heard nothing from his associates to distress him, there should be no ill effects from this meeting.

Still, Leanora found reasons to remain in her study at the front of the house as the appointed hour approached. When the knock fell on the door, she was there to hear it, and she hurried out to the hall to personally welcome the two gentlemen.

Petersham bowed to her, and Sir William took her hand, raising it to his lips. "How is he?" the latter inquired.

"Overreaching himself, I fear," she said bluntly. "Nothing would do for him but to meet with you. I am sure there is no need to warn you that he is far from well. If you could reassure him on all points . . . ?"

"Of course, m'dear, of course," Petersham said jovially. "Good to see him taking an interest in our little affairs, good indeed. Now, don't you fret yourself, he'll come to no harm with us. Just have a couple of points I can't say I mind running by him. Good head, your father, always glad for his opinion."

"I will not let them get carried away," Sir William murmured as he released her hand. "Will you be within call if needed?"

She nodded. "There should be no problem, but—"

He winked at her. "I've had the dubious privilege of handling the pair of them for years," he assured her.

She could not but be glad. Although not going so far as to ascribe a kindly nature to Sir William, who was more inclined to seek his own comfort at the expense of others, he could be extremely adroit in his management of his associates. With only minor misgivings, she allowed Tremly to conduct them upstairs.

An hour passed, and the gentlemen did not come back down. Feeling that it was time to break up this meeting, Leanora made her way to her father's rooms. There she found Pagget waiting patiently in the antechamber, his arms folded and a look of resignation on his lined countenance. He sprang to his feet the moment he saw her.

"Is all well?" She gestured for him to resume his seat.

"Yes, Miss Leanora. All seems quiet. I cannot be sure what they are talking about, but then that would not be proper."

"No," she agreed, but somewhat wistfully. "Do you think he is strong enough to take much more of this?"

The valet permitted himself a prim smile. "There's no stopping him when he sets his mind to aught, Miss Leanora."

A slight scuffling as of chairs sounded within, and Sir William emerged into the antechamber. He stopped short at sight of Leanora, and he made her a mocking bow. "You do not trust me, my dear," he said, feigning hurt.

"It is my father I do not trust," she informed him, irritated at having been discovered hovering over them. "Are you finished?"

"I am the bearer of what to you will be bad tidings, I fear." He shook his head sadly, but there was a hint of a smile about his mouth, as if he looked forward to seeing how she would take his news.

"And that is . . . ?" she prompted, trying to conceal her sudden uneasiness.

"We have a great deal still to cover, and Sherborne requests that we remain and dine. He intends to come downstairs."

"Oh, no!" She could not prevent the exclamation, then blushed as she realized how this must sound. "And you need not look so offended, Sir William," she informed him tartly. "You know very well what I mean."

He laughed. "I do, and I am very sorry. But once your father has made a decision, I fear he will not be moved."

"Yes" came her bitter reply. "We were just remarking upon that."

He bowed to her. "And now that I have delivered my message, I had best return. There is no knowing onto what topic Petersham may have strayed."

Leanora was left to glare at the door as it closed behind him. "Now what are we to do?" she asked aloud.

Pagget gave a deprecating cough. "Send instructions to the kitchens, I fear, Miss Leanora."

She could hardly argue with such excellent good sense. She went in search of Tremly, whom she encountered in the lower hall, and relayed the information. Not by so much as a blink did that very proper butler reveal his amazement. He went at once to tell the cook that there were to be three more places laid and suitable dishes, appropriate to the occasion, prepared.

Next, Leanora went in search of her aunt, who had already retired to her room to dress for the meal. When informed of the turn of events, that lady stared at her open-mouthed, for once deprived of words. That happy state did not last for long.

"But—but my love, is it wise?" Mrs. Ashton asked as she recovered. "Think of the strain! Oh, we never should have permitted those men to come here in the first place! If only Mr. Edmonton were here! He could have handled all of this. Leanora, you must send for him first thing in the morning! To

291

think of it! Your father coming downstairs to dinner with us. Such an occasion! But truly, I do not think he should, for he has only arisen from his bed for the first time this morning. We must convince him not to make such an effort. Perhaps we could have a table carried up, and the gentleman could dine in his room?"

Leanora had already gone through this wave of tangled emotions herself. She was able to nod quietly, make gentle, soothing noises, then at last stem the flow of worried words.

"Yes, dear Aunt, but I think it will be best to let him have his way. You know how he can be when he is thwarted. Quite worse than any child, I am sure! If we try to change his plans, it will only upset him, and you know how exhausting that would be for all of us."

Mrs. Ashton agreed, though somewhat dubiously. "Very well, my love, if you think it wise. But you will send for Mr. Edmonton in the morning, will you not?"

Leanora hesitated. For her father's sake, it might be best, for his secretary would prevent him from doing anything too strenuous. But what of the dangers to Mr. Edmonton himself? He, no less than she and her father, would be a target for murderous attacks. If he came back, he would have to be told the truth about the attempt to smother the earl in his bed. At the moment only she, and probably Pagget and Tremly, knew it had nothing to do with mere housebreakers. For his own sake, Mr. Edmonton must remain safely at the Abbey until all this was over.

Leanora left her aunt and went to her own room to change her gown. How could she keep from sending for Mr. Edmonton without Aunt Amabelle demanding ticklish explanations? This troublesome question occupied her thoughts the whole time she was dressing.

Her abigail, putting the finishing touches on her hair, remarked that she was unusually silent that night. "And so happy as everyone is below stairs, Miss Leanora, to see his lordship up and about once more!"

At least someone was happy about it. If only she could be! But she did not want him to overtax himself. She gave a deep sigh. All she had to do was hint that he was too tired, and he would instantly turn stubborn and insist on doing more.

Of course! She had only to inform her father that she was sending for Mr. Edmonton to relieve him of worries at the Home Office, and the earl, ornery old dear that he was, would instantly forbid her to do any such thing! He would demand that Edmonton remain at the Abbey, awaiting their eventual coming. Pleased with herself, she made her way down to the drawing room to join her aunt.

Not wishing to put more strain on the earl than was strictly necessary, Leanora sent orders that he was to be assisted directly to the dining room. His arrival bore every resemblance to that of a monarch, for he came in state, preceded by Lord Petersham, supported by Pagget and the first footman, and followed by Sir William. The earl took his place at the head of the table and beamed at his daughter.

Talk throughout the meal naturally centered about Lord Grenville and his Ministry of All the Talents. Petersham, for once, did not hold forth as was his want, and Leanora found herself watching him closely. Did he disapprove of the government? Enough to wish to see the head of state assassinated? She would have expected him to be more forthcoming on the problems the new prime minister faced with the Opposition.

"Our dear Lord Kennington is certainly making his feelings known," Sir William commented when a momentary lull occurred in the conversation.

Petersham stiffened. "Damnable fellow" was all he said.

Lord Sherborne raised a questioning eyebrow. "Thought you were going to approach him on something," he said slowly, searching his mind for a hazy memory.

"No, no, nothing ever came of that," Petersham said hastily. "All nonsense. Curst rum touch, that fellow. Don't want to have anything to do with him." He looked up, caught Leanora watching him curiously and went off in a fit of coughing.

"No," Sir William agreed calmly. "He is too smooth a talker. One can fall under his spell if not careful, then awaken later to find oneself grossly misled." He directed a long, meaningful look at Leanora. "He is a good man to stay away from."

"French blood in him, that's the problem," said Sherborne. "No good ever comes of that."

Petersham laughed. "That's not always true, eh, William?"

Leanora, still smiling at her father's prejudice, turned to Sir William. "Have you French blood?"

He hung his head as if in shame. "I do. I admit it, though it is a fact I have always tried to keep secret. A flock of French cousins cannot add to my credit in this profession, you must know."

"Never held it against you, my boy," Petersham said heartily. "Lots of people have French relatives."

Leanora digested this. Could French family ties play any role in what amounted to a treasonable plot against England? It would not necessarily have to be the Opposition party that wanted the prime minister assassinated. Only think of the chaos such a crime would create! And with a leader like Pitt so recently dead, the war effort might very well fall apart!

What if they were totally wrong in thinking Kennington responsible? It could be French agents or sympathizers! It could be. . . . But here she came back to earth. The possibilities remained limited as they always had been. The code had turned up in that stack of papers. Someone who had access to them was still involved, for whatever reason.

"You are very quiet." Sir William leaned back in his chair and regarded her. "Has the shocking revelation of my tainted blood given you a distaste of me?"

"Not in the least. I was wondering if my father grows tired." She looked at her old acquaintance and experienced a sensation of guilt. She was considering him as a possible suspect! If he were behind the plot, because of his French connections, then he would hardly treat the matter as a joke! He made no effort to hide the fact or downplay it in the least. She was being ridiculous, seeing conspirators everywhere!

Tremly entered the dining room, cast a considering eye over the table and signaled for the footmen to begin clearing the covers. Lord Sherborne made no protest, and when, at Leanora's nudging, Sir William suggested that they dispense with any more talk for the night, he agreed. With relief, she saw her father escorted up the stairs, then turned to thank the guests for their consideration and to see them out.

She returned to discover that her aunt, who had retired to the drawing room following the meal, was comfortably ensconced in her favorite chair by the fire, absorbed in a novel. When Leanora called to her that she would go upstairs to make certain that her father had retired to his bed, Mrs. Ashton, who had just reached the point where the heroine was forced to flee for her very life from her dark and sinister guardian, merely nodded and wished her goodnight.

By the time she arrived at her father's room, Pagget had already assisted the earl to slide between sheets. The pug, which had been confined in the kitchens since the arrival of the visitors, danced about the room in delight at returning to his master, yipping steadily in its excitement. The exertions of the day showed clearly in the earl's face, but he seemed content nevertheless. Leanora could only be thankful and leave him to the tender guardianship of his devoted valet and dog.

Slowly, she made her way down the hall to her own room. Somewhere in the halls below a clock chimed nine. Well, it was time she had an early night for a change. She had not slept well for several weeks.

But sleep was long in coming. Gregory, who had never been far from her thoughts throughout the day, returned now to haunt her, the image of his distraught face intruding itself on her memory. What had he been doing? Should she have gone to see him? But she had not wanted to trespass on his reconciliation with his wife.

Also, she wished him to have the opportunity to dispose of the jewels and make his arrangements with Kennington on his own. He had gotten himself into a shocking mess, and it was very important for him to feel that he played a major role in disentangling himself. To have an older sister forever hanging about him would do little for his damaged self esteem. It had involved considerable restraint on her part, but she knew it

295

had been for the best. She would find some excuse to call upon him in the morning, though.

Thoughts of Gregory naturally led to Kennington, and she proceeded to review each one of her "suspects." When her tired brain was no longer able to make further sense, she drifted off into an uneasy sleep.

She awoke from this late the following morning with a violent headache throbbing behind her eyes. Only one thing would help it, she knew, and that would be to solve a few of the mysteries that had invaded her comfortable world. With the intention of relieving herself of one very major worry, she set off to visit Gregory as soon as she had breakfasted.

She found him in his morning parlor, attired in a dressing gown of vivid hue and fantastic pattern. He rose to greet her warmly, taking her hand and kissing her cheek. Julia sprang from her chair and subjected her to an enthusiastic embrace.

"Will you join us?" Julia asked, dragging her sister-in-law to the table.

"I have only come for a moment," she demurred, but a cup of tea was pressed into her hand. "I came to see how you go on."

Julia blushed adorably, casting a glance of such undisguised love at Gregory that Leanora experienced a pang of jealousy. The expression in her brother's eyes was no less intense, almost caressing his wife.

Oh, to love and be loved like that! A wave of longing and emptiness swept through her, unexpected and unwelcome. It had only been since meeting Deverell that she had become aware of the solitude of her single state. She had enjoyed its freedom before. But now . . . ?

Gregory resumed his seat and refreshed himself from a tankard of ale. "Kennington was somewhat displeased when I showed up with the money," he told her. Now that the worst of his immediate fears had been removed, he was regaining a measure of his usual good humor. "Says he wants more by next week." Here, he looked down at his hands, his expression suddenly grim. "Hope we have him laid by the heels by then," he added. "I'll never be able to lay my hands on the sum he wants now."

"We—we will manage!" Julia declared stoutly, laying a sustaining hand on his arm.

Leanora rose, satisfied. They had gained a week's respite, and anything could happen in that time—if they worked hard enough to bring it about. She would tell Deverell, find out if he had a plan. It was even possible, she realized suddenly, that the Requiem Masque might have taken place by then! And Kennington, if he were indeed involved in that plot, would have been dealt with most effectively indeed.

As she strolled thoughtfully back to Sherborne House, she saw a very familiar curricle and pair at the far end of the street, turning the corner. But the figure holding the reins was far too small to ever be confused with Deverell. If his groom walked the horses, that must mean that Deverell was within the house.

Trying to ignore the surge of elation that accompanied this knowledge, she hurried up the street. As soon as she entered the front door, she heard his deep, booming laugh, coming from the Gold Saloon. A murmur of voices followed, and she went at once to join the gathering.

As always, Deverell dominated his company. When he was present, she had barely a glance to spare for anyone else. Tearing her eyes from his elegant figure, she greeted her aunt and cousin, who sat together on the sofa. The greater part of her attention, though, remained fixed on the dark-haired giant who stood at his accustomed place, leaning negligently against the mantel.

He came forward, bowing over her hand, and if he noted the relief and pleasure in her eyes he did not betray it. He led her to a seat, but before she could think of a way to tell him about Gregory, Reggie spoke up.

"Dashed funny thing, Nora," he complained. "Went driving in the Park yesterday."

"Well, if you took your curricle, I doubt anyone else thought it was funny," she responded promptly.

"Dash it all, Nora! I ain't that bad a whip! Am I, Dev?" He appealed to his friend.

"Well," that gentleman said with great diplomacy, "I do not believe I would precisely label you a Nonesuch."

"But what happened in the Park, Reggie?" Leanora asked

quickly, cutting off Reggie's challenge to Deverell to see who could drive the most times through a narrow gateway unscathed.

"What?" He turned back to her. "Oh. Dashed peculiar." His face became grave all at once. "Saw Gregory with Kennington. *Kennington,* of all people!" He shook his head. "Fellow has a dashed casual way of tying his neckcloth. Tell you what, Nora, you keep an eye on Greg. If he sets up a friendship like that, you'll find him visiting the wrong snyders before long. What a figure he'd cut, in a coat like Kennington's!"

"Very true," Leanora agreed. "Perhaps you should warn him he stands in grave danger of shaming you."

"Well, I will," he said, totally missing her sarcasm. "And the sooner the better. Think he'll be at the Revesbys' ball?"

"Oh, my love," Mrs. Ashton exclaimed. "With your father so much improved, do you not think we might attend?"

Leanora blinked. "The Revesbys' ball. . . ." she murmured. "Oh, near Barnet, to be sure. I had forgotten it."

"Reggie has so kindly offered to escort us." She beamed upon her son. "So good of him, I am sure, for you must know that the very thought of crossing Finchley Common in the dark terrifies me." She gave an expressive shiver.

Leanora laughed. "You might have had cause, twenty years ago, but now it should be quite safe."

"What, does that infamous stretch hold no terrors for you?" Deverell asked.

"None, my lord," she informed him with an impish smile.

"Then if you will be there, may I claim your hand for the first waltz?"

"To sit it out with you?"

"As you say." His eyes twinkled. "To sit it out with me."

"How can I possibly refuse such a delightful offer? Of a certainty, my lord. The first waltz is yours."

Reggie rose to take his leave, and Leanora walked with their guests to the door. There was a great deal she wanted to tell Deverell about the talk at dinner last night and Gregory's activities. But how to speak to him without Reggie?

To her surprise, Deverell solved the problem for her. He

bowed low over her hand and retained it a moment longer than necessary. "Will you do me the honor of driving in the Park with me this afternoon?" he asked.

Did he guess? She looked up into his smiling eyes but could read no clue to his purpose. She started to speak but he shook his head. "Until later," he said softly, and took his leave.

It was not long before she discovered, to her intense dismay, that she looked forward just to being with Deverell every bit as much as she did to unburdening herself of her suspicions about French intrigue. It was not a situation she could like, for it threw her off balance and destroyed her normally good judgment. And in a maze this deadly, she needed all her wits about her.

Was his sole interest in her their mystery? That was one question she would dearly love to have answered. If they had never heard of the Requiem Masque, would he have sought her out for her own sake? She turned back into the hall, then stopped before the gilt-edged mirror that hung over a small table. She might be well past the first blush of youth, but she was still far from being an antidote! Her face stared back at her, a puzzled frown between her finely arched brows. She concentrated on smoothing this away. Was there anything there that Deverell might find attractive?

He had certainly enjoyed kissing her in that hackney when he hid them both from Kennington! And the sad truth was that she had enjoyed it, too. The masterful strength of his touch had sent shivers of pleasure through her. It was difficult for her to admit, but she would be very sorry if there was nothing more to bring him to Berkeley Square when this was all over.

She took even more than her usual care in dressing for her drive in the Park that afternoon. The first bonnet she selected did not seem quite right, the second was lined in a shade that did not become her as well as she had thought, but the third, decorated with a cluster of peach satin ribands that exactly matched her gown, at last satisfied her. She was just adding a final touch to the golden ringlets that clustered about her face when Tremly tapped on her door and announced that Deverell was below stairs. Giving the curls a final anxious pat, she hurried down to join him.

There was a disturbing light in his eyes as he took her hand and kissed it, and little thrills of excitement shot through her. There *must* be something more than the Requiem Masque that drew him to her! She hugged that thought to herself as he escorted her out to the waiting curricle and handed her in.

As soon as the horses were set safely in motion, he spared her a glance and asked: "What did you wish to tell me?"

She sighed. "Did I make it so obvious?" she asked dryly.

A slight smile curved his firm lips. "Your face, when I left you this morning, spoke volumes. I am sorry I could not delay my business then."

She flushed slightly. "I hope I do not inconvenience you."

A soft chuckle escaped him. "Not in the least. Let us say instead that you provide for my amusement."

She stiffened. "I realize, of course, that you enjoy the excitement and challenge of our puzzle. But must you make it so blatant that you do not take my role in all this seriously?"

"I believe we will for the moment ignore what I think of your role." A strange, almost angry note sharpened his voice. "What has occurred?"

She flushed, disconcerted and hurt by his tone. Fighting back her feelings, she told him of her father's meeting and the conversation over dinner. "Could not the assassination be a purely French plot, and have nothing to do with the Opposition?" she ended.

"Are you thinking of entering government service as an agent?" he inquired. To her further chagrin, he seemed to have considerable trouble controlling his amusement.

Her color deepened even more. "There is no need for you to be sarcastic. Do you expect me to show no interest when it is *I* who uncovered a plot of this nature? Would you rather I turned missish and had the vapors?"

"No, not you." An unexpected note of admiration warmed his voice. "But the situation is dangerous, more so than you perhaps realize. As laudable as your courage is, I do not think you are fully aware of what you are trying to get entangled with."

"That may be true," she admitted cautiously, "but I cannot sit idly by when my father—myself, even!—is so nearly

300

involved. Have your inquiries brought you any closer, yet?"

"I have a few ideas," he admitted, "though nothing definite." He looked at her and seemed to come to a conclusion. "Basically, that code could have come from one of three people: Kennington, Petersham, or your father."

"It is not my father!" she exclaimed hotly, forgetting to be impressed that for once he confided in her.

"No, I am inclined to agree with you," he went on smoothly. "And that leaves only the two, for no one else touched the papers."

Mollified, she subjected this last statement to consideration. "That is not strictly true," she said slowly. "Sir William was at that meeting with my father. And then both you and I touched them, when they fell on the floor."

A low laugh escaped him. "Thorough, my dear," he murmured. "I concede you the point. For the moment, though, shall we eliminate ourselves? Then let us first consider Petersham. His motives?"

"Kennington has a hold over him," she said quickly.

"Roman vases. That doesn't seem enough, does it? But there might well be more, such as gaming or borrowed funds. Definitely, he is a possibility. And what of Kennington himself? He has a flourishing fleecing operation going. Would he endanger that?"

"Well, he is already involved in at least one dishonest occupation." She glanced up at him. "Do you not think it possible he might have others? Gregory thinks so."

Deverell was silent for a moment. "He demanded papers from your brother. I suppose it is possible he could have drawn Petersham into the assassination plot."

"Then you really think Petersham is involved?" It did not seem possible—or did she just not want it to be true? She had known Petersham for so very long! She shivered, not liking the possibility at all.

"What of Sir William?" Deverell asked, ignoring her last question.

She shook her head. "All I know against him is that he has French blood, which seems pretty slim. I do not believe that he games, so there is no connection between him and

Lord Kennington."

Deverell slowed his team, and they entered the Park. They turned onto the carriageway, nodded to several acquaintances who were approaching on horseback and proceeded on their way.

"Sir William always seems to know everything that goes on," she added, having been given a moment to think.

"That is the sign of an inquisitive mind, not necessarily a criminal one," he said with a smile. "And then there is Lord Dalmouth and Gregory, if you will forgive me dragging your brother into it. The money he told us about may only be part of his problems. We have no proof he made a clean breast of it the other night."

"If we are to make such a complete list of possibilities, we really ought not to forget ourselves!" she responded at once with great cordiality to mask her anger at his suggestion. "And what of the clerks and assistants in the Home Office? Have you forgotten poor Mr. Holloway?"

Deverell shook his head. "There is no end to the number of people we might drag into this. All we want is a little ingenuity! For all I know, every one of them might be involved."

Leanora sighed. "What do we do next?"

"*I* will make more inquiries," Deverell informed her. "*You* will do nothing that might draw suspicion or interest to you."

She swallowed hard, averting her face so that he should not see her chagrin. "You have already made your feelings about my following Gregory quite clear," she said stiffly.

"Then I hope you have taken them to heart. Or have you already forgotten your illness?"

"But—but nothing has happened to me since. I am persuaded you must have been mistaken about that!"

Deverell appeared to take considerable interest in maneuvering his pair around another vehicle. "Possibly," he said at last, but did not sound convinced. "But since we cannot be certain, it will be best if you do not take any foolish chances."

A warm glow seeped through her. It was wonderful to experience the solicitude of a man like Deverell. She felt cared for and protected, as if he sought to put up a shield between her and the dangers that abounded. She *could* depend on him, in spite of her earlier qualms. He would discover and remove all threats to her.

But would he be able to do the same for the prime minister, as well? With regret, she relinquished her pleasant fantasy and returned to reality.

They were still no nearer than before to solving this terrible business, and time passed—rapidly!

Chapter 21

The feeling that they did not do enough to foil the assassination plot continued to haunt Leanora. As she descended the stairs for the Revesbys' ball the following night, fragments of half-remembered conversations still played through her mind. Had she remembered to tell Deverell everything that he might find useful? Or had she omitted some essential clue?

As she reached the hall, Tremly bowed to her, then sent a footman running to make sure that the carriage was on its way. He opened the door just as the vehicle pulled up before the house.

Mrs. Ashton, who had not had any momentous worries to delay her dressing, emerged from the Gold Saloon where she had been waiting. Seeing her niece, she subjected her to a critical scrutiny, but her unerring eye could detect not a single flaw in Leanora's appearance. She beamed on her in approval.

"My dear, how delightful you look!" she exclaimed, all admiration. "That is quite your most becoming gown, for I do feel a young lady is quite at her best in white crepe. And the blue trim! Exquisite, you know. I believe you should order another gown from Madame Celestine upon the instant, for I must say, she seems to know what becomes you better than any of the other *modistes*. Not, of course, that you do not look lovely in any gown, but Madame Celestine's creations always have such a distinctive flair, do they not? And those flowers!" She eyed the blue silk roses that were entwined in the thick blonde ringlets and sighed. "I vow, I have never seen you look so becomingly."

"Then we are a pair," she assured her aunt promptly. Indeed, Mrs. Ashton did appear to advantage in a figured robe of dull gold silk. A single plume, dyed to match, curled about her silvery locks and bobbed slightly as she moved.

The carriage ride to Reggie's lodgings was completed quickly, and within minutes of their arrival he joined them. He sank back against the squabs, complete to a shade in a coat of deep blue superfine and pantaloons of a delicate shade of yellow. A black silk cloak, lined in power blue silk, hung from one shoulder. He eyed his mother and cousin with a certain amount of trepidation. "Like it?" he asked, trying to sound casual.

"It is beautiful!" his mother responded, admiring the graceful folds that lay across the seat.

Leanora nodded. "This time, Reggie, I believe you have hit upon something that will make even Beau Brevin sit up and take notice. What a pity you must take it off before entering the ballroom!"

This threatened to throw a cloud over the evening for her cousin. He sat in his corner, frowning, until he hit upon the happy notion of remaining in the hall until as many of his acquaintances as possible should have been privileged to view his latest creation. His sunny disposition restored once more, he turned his attention to his companions.

"Well, you two look all the crack tonight," he announced appreciatively. "I say, Leanora, those roses ought to make someone sit up and take notice of you!"

Warm color crept into her cheeks, and she was glad that the interior of the carriage was dark. In spite of her preoccupation with codes and murderous plots, she had taken considerable pains over her appearance. The knowledge that Deverell would be there, and would seek her out for the first waltz, had taken firm possession of her mind. Would he admire her? But not for anything would she want Reggie to guess her secret hope.

They wended their way through London streets, then at last reached a district where long spaces stretched between the houses. In a very short time the dwellings ceased all together, and they entered the infamous Finchley Common.

Mrs. Ashton shivered. "I cannot like driving here!" she exclaimed, casting an uneasy glance out the window into the darkness.

"Shall I take out the pistol and hold it at the ready?" Reggie asked jokingly.

"Pistol?" her aunt cried, alarmed.

"Of course! Uncle Sherborne always keeps one in here. Loaded, too, I should think."

His mamma uttered a faint shriek, and Leanora turned a disapproving eye on him. "Then the only danger we are likely to encounter will be within this carriage, if you dare to draw it out!"

Despite his joking, Reggie, as well as Mrs. Ashton, peered out across the dimly lit heath. If he hoped to catch sight of any desperate highwaymen bearing down upon them and brandishing horse pistols, he was to be disappointed. The imaginary terrors of the Common were soon left behind, and they continued in peace through the countryside until they turned off the Great North Road just short of Barnet.

The house, a great sprawling building of Georgian design, lay in the midst of a secluded parkland. Numerous carriages filled the drive, dispersing elegantly clad ladies and gentlemen who mounted stairs lit with gaily colored lanterns to the front door that stood wide. Inside, the hall was crowded, filled with the elite of society.

Reggie breathed a sigh of pure contentment. Settling his cloak to display the lining, he followed his mother and cousin down the inner staircase and through the small knots of people in the hall. At the entrance of the Grand Ballroom, he turned back in a manner calculated to set the marvelous garment swirling gracefully about him. A quick check assured him that the glances he received were admiring and not contemptuous. His confidence swelling, he strolled back among the milling guests, pausing to exchange greetings and to give his fellow Pinks and Tulips a chance to gaze their envious full.

At last, he relinquished the cloak into the tender care of a footman and went to join the ladies, who awaited him by the ballroom. There, a lackey took their names and announced them in sonorous accents. Their host and hostess greeted them warmly, then moved on to welcome the next of their guests.

Leanora strolled to one side of the huge room, looking about. Almost the first person she saw was Gregory, who stood with a small circle of friends. Dalmouth, she noted, was with him. And Julia? She looked about, at last spotting her sister-in-law at the center of a small group of admirers. Gregory looked up, saw his sister and sauntered over to her side.

"We are following your instructions to the letter," he murmured for her ears alone.

Leanora looked searchingly up into his face. In spite of his scowl, he did not appear as haggard as he had of late. He winked at her, and she realized his sour expression was part of his act.

"Does it serve?" she asked softly. "Has anyone guessed that things are different between you and Julia?"

"Not even Dalmouth," he promised. "Mind you, we've nearly let it slip a couple of times. It's easiest if we attend different functions." He glanced over to where his wife was flirting with her fan in an outrageous manner. "I've a good mind to plant that lieutenant who's making eyes at her a facer!"

"Don't!" advised his sister. "At least not here. You might say something churlish to Dalmouth about it, though. And Kennington. Is he here? Don't forget to glower at him."

"Oh, that's easy enough," he responded. "Damnable fellow. I'll be glad to have a hand in laying him low."

He moved away, leaving Leanora prey to a new worry. Just how dependable was her brother? As long as he did not indulge in any heavy drinking, he could probably carry off this pose of desperate unhappiness. It was not that far from the truth, for while Kennington continued to hold his vowels he could not be easy.

She turned as the musicians struck up their first chords and found herself face to face with Dalmouth. His hazel eyes gleamed at her as if with too much wine, and the soft slur of his words as he addressed her confirmed her suspicions.

He bowed low. "My dear Lady Leanora, will you honor me with the first dance?"

She took his hand and allowed him to lead her to the floor

where they found a place in the lines that formed for the country dance. He smiled benignly upon her as he took his place opposite, then bowed in form as part of the opening movements. It seemed odd to go through the motions of the dance with him. The last time they had met he had proposed to her! But he made no mention of that occurrence, behaving, in fact, as if it had never taken place. His manner remained friendly, even flattering in a lighthearted way, and she soon relaxed.

But why was he not worried? If he, like Gregory, lay in Kennington's unprincipled clutches, should he not also feel desperation? None of the tell-tale traces of her brother's misery hung about him, and his manner, far from indicating overburdening concerns, seemed carefree. How involved was he with Kennington? Was he a victim—or a fellow villain?

When the dance drew to a close, Dalmouth escorted her back to where her aunt sat in conversation with her bosom friend Lady Carmody. Still smiling, he took his leave and went in search of his next partner. Leanora was claimed by a somewhat inarticulate friend of Reggie's, and once more took the floor.

Out of the corner of her eye, she saw Lord Petersham enter the ballroom. And there, in the next set, was Kennington. Apparently, her evening would not be dull.

As they moved through the stately steps, Leanora continued to look about. Gregory was nowhere to be seen; he had probably retired to the card room, where she could only hope he did not lose any more money. Julia danced nearby, partnered by Sir William. Both appeared to be enjoying themselves immensely. Deverell, she noted, had not yet put in an appearance.

She had just begun to despair of his arriving on time for their waltz when she heard his name announced and looked up to see his tall, imposing figure framed in the doorway. Suddenly, every other man in the great room seemed to fade into insignificance in comparison. He came forward, exchanged a word with his hostess and moved about the room, his eyes searching. Impulsively, she took a step in his direction, then stopped. It would hardly be the thing for her to go up to him as if she were anxious for his company!

She need not have worried. His gaze came to rest on her, and he began to stroll casually toward her, exchanging greetings with acquaintances, stopping to speak for a minute with friends. But always he moved closer to her, and that knowledge filled her with a fluttery, exciting sensation.

At last the musicians struck up a waltz, and he was before her, bowing over her hand. She looked up into his smiling face and found his eyes twinkling with a barely suppressed laughter.

"My lady, I beg you to sit this one out with me."

"A pleasure," she responded, and something of his inner merriment communicated itself to her. Had he learned something important? His energy enveloped her, leaving her nerves skipping and dancing with the pulsing power that emanated from him.

They went to the next room, procured glasses of punch, then found a quiet corner between potted palms where they could sit and talk undisturbed. As soon as he was seated, Leanora turned to him impulsively.

"What has happened?" she demanded.

"What makes you think that something has?" he countered, his eyes teasing. "If you can read me so easily, I shall have to control myself better."

Except for his energy and humor, she had the distinct feeling that every other part of his nature was held under the strictest governing. "Do not put me off," she begged. "Tell me!"

The laughing lights glinted in his dark eyes. "I fear I was a little late this evening. But you see, I have been trying to locate an old friend. He turned up tonight." His shoulders shook in remembered merriment.

"And?" she prompted. "Who is he?"

"I am not sure what name he chooses to be known under at the moment," he told her apologetically. "I met him when I first joined the army. He enjoyed what you might call a brief but highly diverting career there. He—er—was induced to resign. You see, he has an uncle who owns a gaming house in Florence, and I fear he not only picked up the tricks of the

310

trade, but can practice them in a manner that is positively awe-inspiring. He knows more ways to fuzz the cards than you would believe," he added reflectively. "And to look at him, he seems the veriest innocent! When you have the dubious privilege of meeting him, you will be led to believe—quite falsely, I assure you!—that he has never held a pack of cards above a half dozen times in his life. He is actually more accomplished than anyone else I have met at every method of dishonest gaming yet devised."

"And you think he can discover Kennington's secrets and discredit his hell?" she asked eagerly, her large, blue eyes opening wide in excitement.

"Not exactly." He held up a hand at her dismay. "I have something else in mind." A slow smile lit his eyes in a disquieting, almost unpleasant manner. "To borrow Reggie's term, Kennington is a curst rum touch. Now, consider a moment. A cornered cur is dangerous. If faced with Bow Street, do you think he would hesitate to create a nasty scandal?"

The eagerness faded from Leanora's eyes. "Then we cannot touch him! Oh, he is despicable!"

"*We* may not be able to touch him, but I assure you that my friend can! He will be thought a fine pigeon for the plucking by Kennington and his crowd, but he is more than adept at turning the tables on the wolf. I intend to see our dear Kennington ruined, and at his own game!"

"You mean. . . ." A delighted gasp escaped Leanora. "Oh, it is perfect! Deverell, it is far better than turning him over to the law! He will be utterly ruined! But can your friend do it?"

"He can!" Deverell replied with conviction. "All we need is for your brother to introduce an innocent young Italian nobleman to Kennington's hell. He'll manage the rest, and Kennington will never know what has happened until it is too late."

"What perfect vengeance," she murmured, her admiring gaze resting on his laughing face. "Gregory will be delighted to help, I am sure."

"Shall we let your brother pay off his debts with the money my friend fleeces from Kennington?" Deverell suggested.

She giggled, entranced with the scheme. "Can we tell Gregory tonight?"

He nodded, an odd smile in his eyes as they rested on her glowing countenance. "I will bring my friend to call on your brother tomorrow morning. With luck, they can begin their revenge by afternoon."

Leanora sighed and leaned back in her chair. "I cannot tell you how wonderful I feel! If you knew how desperately worried I have been. . . ." She let the sentence trail off, but her look spoke volumes. "I feel like dancing all night now!"

"I will be glad when I can oblige you. A celebratory waltz is certainly called for."

"Do you enjoy dancing?" She couldn't prevent herself from asking.

"Any man would be fortunate to claim you for his partner," he responded with prompt gallantry.

She was forced to laugh. "Very prettily said," she told him. "But you do not seem to me the sort of man who drops flowery compliments."

"I shall have to improve, then," he said softly.

Her gaze flew to his, and she felt warm color heating her cheeks. Confused, she dropped her gaze and brought her fan into play. Did he mean to pay her court? The idea was intriguing in the extreme! But there was still that note of teasing that underlay his manner. No, she dared not place too much reliance on his teasing words.

The dance ended, and Leanora's next partner claimed her, putting an end to their conversation. It was just as well, she reflected, though not without certain regrets. She was not at all sure of his intentions, nor of her own mind.

When the music ended, her partner escorted her back to her aunt. Julia flitted up, waving her fan, declaring the room to be dreadfully hot and begging her dear sister-in-law to accompany her out onto the terrace for a breath of fresh air. Instantly alert, Leanora acquiesced, and the two ladies slipped out of the ballroom.

"Gregory is being wonderful!" Julia informed her as they strolled along the paved stretch near the house. "He is in the card room but has not played a single hand. He is pretending to be odiously foxed, you see. And he is doing it marvelously well! No one is surprised that he does not game!"

"Tell him to seek out Deverell. He has devised the most wonderful plan for a certain gentleman's discomfiture," Leanora told her, but would not divulge the details, despite her sister-in-law's begging.

"Well," said that lady, giving up at last. "I shall be glad, whatever it is. Do you know, Dalmouth actually offered to take me to a public masked ball, just because Kennington will be there? As if that would be an inducement for me to do anything so improper!" She appeared the figure of outraged righteousness, as if barely three days ago she would not have accepted with alacrity.

"I should think not!" Leanora agreed, laughing at her private reflections. "A masquerade. . . ." She broke off, swallowed hard, then forced herself to continue in a light tone. "Do you know, perhaps you ought to go along with the idea? Just to keep your brother and Kennington from being suspicious? We want nothing to interfere with Deverell's plan. Where is the masquerade, by the way?"

"At the Opera House. In two days' time." She sighed. "I suppose I must go, then, unless Lord Deverell can be done with Kennington by then?" She ended on a hopeful note.

Leanora shook her head, her brain seething. A masquerade at the Opera House, in two days! And Kennington would be there. And Dalmouth! Could Dalmouth be the "D" of the code who was to be watched?

"Oh, I would dearly love to attend!" Leanora exclaimed with feeling. "I wonder—" She broke off, for footsteps sounded behind her. She spun about and found Sir William approaching.

"Fair enchantress." He kissed her hand, then turned to greet Julia in a similarly effusive manner. "Are you, too, escaping from the intolerable heat?"

"We are," Julia told him.

"And what is it you would love to attend?" he asked Leanora. Offering an arm to each lady, he led them back toward the ball room.

"A masquerade at the Opera House," Julia explained. "Is it

313

not nonsensical? But I have heard they can be the greatest fun!"

"This is a new come out for you! I would not have thought it at all your sort of entertainment," he told Leanora. "Quite vulgar, really. The company becomes quite free long before midnight."

"Very true," Leanora agreed with a feigned sigh. "It is just that I have never attended a masque before. I thought it would be fun to see for myself what it is like."

He laughed. "If you have your heart set upon it, I will escort you myself, though if your father ever comes to hear of it he will probably call me out!"

"I shall not put you in peril, then. I daresay I should hate it excessively."

They were once more inside the crowded room, and Sir William solicited Julia's hand for the next dance. They went off together, leaving Leanora very anxious to find Deverell. Did he know of this masque? If so, it was extremely disobliging of him not to tell her! But with so many people about, it would not be easy to relate this news to him without any number of people overhearing. In fact, anyone could already have heard her discussing the event with Julia and Sir William! That thought sent an uneasy shiver through her.

She spotted Deverell with a small group of gentlemen who were just making their entry from the card rooms. She hurried to meet him, just touching his arm.

"I have some information," she whispered.

He nodded that he had heard, but a laughing young buck turned back, slipped an arm through his, and led him inexorably off to where refreshments had been laid out.

Leanora turned away, trying very hard not to be vexed that he did not instantly spare her a minute. She could easily tell him later. She started back to where her aunt sat against the wall, conversing amicably with several other ladies of her generation.

Lord Dalmouth intercepted her with a low bow and a smiling word. "What, not dancing? For shame! Will you not honor me?"

It was another waltz, and to her surprise Dalmouth proved

accomplished at the art. As they moved easily among the other couples on the floor, he kept up an easy banter to which she could respond without having to tax her mental powers. He could be an enjoyable companion, she realized with surprise. Now, why had he always appeared stiff and affected, aping the manners of a set to which by natural inclination he did not now appear to belong?

They were intercepted by Deverell as they left the floor, and he requested the honor of taking her down for the first supper. Dalmouth did not appear pleased but bowed before the taller man's commanding presence. It would seem that few gentlemen cared to cross the dark-haired giant with the piercing eyes.

They joined the throng heading downstairs to the room that had been laid out with a lavish supper. Just being at Deverell's side lent a sparkling glow to her. Quite reprehensible of her, she knew, but she succumbed to the heady excitement of his companionship. He filled plates for them both and found places to sit at a tiny, intimate table.

"You are enjoying yourself," he commented.

"You have made certain of that, bringing me word of your delightful friend." She smiled at him, and their eyes met and held for a long moment. Nervous, she looked down at her plate, selected a lobster patty at random and found it delicious. Only one thing served to cloud her evening, for she dared not tell him of the masquerade in such crowded surroundings. But this night, even that did not weigh as heavily with her as it might have before. It was disconcertingly enjoyable just to sit near him.

She looked up again, encountered the warm, almost caressing glow that lurked in his mysterious eyes and in fluttery embarrassment glanced about the room. It *had* to be more than the dangerous mystery that brought him to her. She continued to scan the other diners, not daring to meet her companion's gaze for fear of revealing her chaotic emotions.

Lord Petersham sat in a corner, as far removed from the other guests as could be managed. His gaze darted from one table to another as if he sought to keep everyone under scrutiny. Leanora frowned. He had certainly been behaving

315

oddly of late, but never had she seen him so nervous! What could have occurred?

As she watched, Lord Kennington bore down on him. Petersham saw him coming and stood at once, moving away. For a few minutes, the Home secretary seemed to wander at random among the tables, but Leanora noted that he was actually edging toward the door. His next move brought him near her, he blinked rapidly and nodded an acknowledgment. His gaze came to rest on Deverell, and he looked away at once and almost ran from the room. Kennington made his slow but purposeful way after him, also stopping at their table to exchange an insincere greeting.

As Kennington crossed the threshold, he almost collided with Sir William, who made a belated entry. Kennington bowed stiffly and moved past, leaving Sir William to look after him through a raised quizzing glass. Allowing this to drop, Sir William strolled into the room, saw Leanora and came up to her.

"It's a wonder that fellow is received," Sir William declared. "Servant, Deverell," he added, nodding to that gentleman. "You have stolen a march on me by claiming Lady Leanora for your dinner partner!"

Deverell awarded this sally a polite smile. "Then the least I can do is ask you to join us."

This Sir William expressed himself quite willing to do, but in the press of finding a plate and filling it, he fell into conversation with someone else and failed to return. Leanora could only be glad, though she hoped this was not too obvious to Deverell. Carefully not looking at him, she concentrated her attention on the array of delicacies he had selected for her.

When they finished eating, they returned upstairs to find that the musicians had resumed their places and were striking up the opening chords of a quadrille. A young officer claimed Leanora's hand, and she was forced to part from Deverell. She took her place in the set, then began the intricate movements.

A sudden piercing stab struck her between the eyes. She faltered, then went on as the pain receded. She continued through the next group of moves, then the excruciating jab attacked her once again. She bit back a cry, but her partner stepped forward, grasped her elbow, slipped an arm about her waist for support and led her from the floor to the nearest chair.

Now the pain settled into a dull ache that grew steadily in intensity. Exhaustion, beyond belief, claimed her, and all she wanted was to sit there, not moving. But a ball was hardly the place for that. Was this the release of tension over her brother? Had she been so worried that she was making herself ill? Never could she remember being so tired!

A footman came up and held out a silver salver on which a note lay, inscribed with Leanora's name. She took it with a hand that shook alarmingly. The words blurred as she tried to focus on them, and the light from the hundreds of candles hurt her eyes. Still, she managed to decipher the cryptic message: "Send for your carriage and leave at once—alone. Deverell."

She closed her eyes. That was exactly what she wanted most to do, to slip quietly away from the ball. She had no desire for company, and there was no reason to spoil her aunt's evening. She could manage alone.

"Lady Leanora!" She heard her name called as if from a distance. She looked up into the worried face of her last partner, who hovered solicitously over her.

"Could—could you have someone send for my carriage?" she asked.

The young officer looked relieved. "At once." He gestured to the footman, who hurried off. "Should I find your chaperone?"

"No. Please, no." She closed her eyes, but the headache still increased. "Could you tell her? After I have left? She—she will be in the card room. I will send the carriage back for her."

Within a very short time, the officer handed her into the vehicle. The headache had settled down to a dull throbbing, much less intense, but she could barely keep her eyes open. A good night's sleep after so much excitement was all she needed, she was sure.

As they turned onto the Great North Road, she settled back in a corner. Closing her eyes, she swayed with the carriage, drowsiness overcoming her. Still, something tugged at the fringes of her mind. Deverell. . . . How had he known she should leave? But it didn't really matter. She could ask him tomorrow. . . . By the time they entered the dark expanse of Finchley Common, she was almost asleep.

A loud explosion sounded outside, but it did not seep into her hazy mind that it was gunfire until it was followed by a shout to stand and deliver. She came erect in a moment, fighting the fog that surrounded her brain. She was being held up!

The coach lurched to a stop, and she reached for the pistol that lay hidden in the pocket on the far side. She dragged it free, clasped it in both hands and pointed it at the door. Another shot sounded without, and the carriage door flew wide. A man rose up before her, his dark, menacing figure silhouetted against the sky. She pulled the trigger and recoiled from the explosion and kick of the weapon.

The man jerked back, then came forward into the carriage. Hazily, she knew she had missed. The heavily muffled figure loomed above her, raised one arm and brought it down upon her head. Blackness engulfed her.

318

Chapter 22

The first thing of which Leanora became aware was the dreadful aching of her head. The second was a scurrying, scratching sound that she identified, with something very akin to panic, as rats. Drawing in her breath sharply, she tasted, then smelled, the damp mustiness of mildew. She shivered, tried to sit up and discovered that she was firmly bound.

She struggled, twisting and turning against the ropes that confined her wrists behind her. Her ankles, also, were tightly secured. She sank back at last, exhausted, unable to free herself.

What happened? She had been at a ball. . . . She had become tired, her head ached, she had left, alone. . . . Something about Deverell, but she couldn't place what. Then vague memories of shots, a dark, dangerous figure . . . fear . . . an unfamiliar pistol, trying to shoot . . . a thunderous explosion from the gun . . . the highwayman looming over her with menacing intent. . . . He must have hit her over the head. That would account for the blinding pain.

Why wasn't she dead? Had she been robbed? She tried to see if she still wore her jewelry, but complete darkness enveloped her. Carefully she rubbed her chin along her collar bone and encountered the sharp metal and stone of her necklace. No, not robbery. If it had been that, she would have been left with the carriage.

Her heart sank. This must be due to her mystery. What a fool she must have been! A sick sensation of terror engulfed her, leaving her shaken and ill.

But she was not dead! She repeated that thought, over and over. She was not dead. That had to be a good sign! Apparently her attacker did not desire to kill her, merely keep her quiet. That must mean she was right about the masquerade! Someone realized she had guessed too much, and needed to keep her from issuing any warnings.

But it was still two days away! If she was to be kept wherever she was for all that time, surely someone would come to bring her food and water! Or was she to be left there to die, hidden away where no one would discover her until it was too late to prevent the prime minister's assassination?

"Fool" was too mild a word for her! How could she have been so stupid and clumsy as to have betrayed her knowledge? Deverell had been right when he said she was not fit for secret work. If only she had taken his advise and retired to the country where she would have been safe! She had no one to blame for her predicament but herself.

And Deverell! A fragment of her fighting spirit returned. If he had been less secretive about his investigations, she would never have been goaded into such unwise actions, not have felt it necessary to go asking questions and following people herself! And there was something she wanted to ask him. . . . No, it still escaped her. Perhaps she just wanted to tell him about the masquerade.

She lay there for a short while, brooding on Deverell's many faults. That she would have given a very great deal to see him at that moment she tried not to consider. If only he had told her more of what he was doing!

Presently, the throbbing in her head began to abate. She could think more clearly without the thudding crash between her eyes, and she turned her attention from Deverell's iniquities to her present situation. No good came from repining, and she had absolutely no desire to just lie there, waiting to see what would befall her next! If she was going to escape in time to save the prime minister, she had best get on with it.

With an effort that sent her head spinning off into space again, she dragged herself into a sitting position. Her hands remained firmly behind her, and she discovered that her knees as well as her ankles were bound. She was not going to be able to get around easily.

She closed her eyes tightly, creating a complete darkness, then opened them again. This time she was aware of a difference. A pale light seeped in from the ceiling, and she could make out several dim, dark shapes in the room. There, probably fifteen feet away from her, stood a table.

She tried to get to her knees, but with them firmly secured she was unable to crawl. She fell back to a lying position, aimed herself in the direction of the table and rolled over and over until she came to rest against one of the legs.

Again, she went through the painful process of pulling herself to a sitting position. Rising to her knees, she peered over the edge of the table and made out the shape of a plate with a loaf of bread. Somehow, that made her feel better. She and the rats had not been left to starve.

It was not the bread that interested her at the moment, but the plate on which it sat. Balancing as best she could, she threw herself against the roughly constructed table until it rocked. The plate slid several inches to one side, and she tried again. This time it clattered to the floor, and the bread went rolling. A scurrying sounded alarmingly close by, and Leonora closed her eyes again, glad it was the bread and not her ankles on which the rats feasted.

She inched her slow way around the table. The plate lay upside down on the far side. Maneuvering with care, she got her back to it, then picked up the coarse china in her bound hands. A table leg was within easy reach, and she brought the plate sideways against it with every ounce of strength she possessed.

It broke with a shattering smash into several large pieces which dropped on the floor behind her. One large shard remained clutched firmly in her hands, and she smiled in triumph. She now had a very serviceable tool. But how to brace it while she sawed through the ropes that held her? She felt the piece she held and found that it was curved with a wide lip. That solved the problem nicely. With a bit of further maneuvering, she managed to raise the heavy table by one leg, getting it almost half an inch from the floor. Bracing it against her back, she slid the smooth, curved rim into position beneath it. She lowered the table onto it.

The ragged edge stuck up in the air. Feeling insufferably pleased with her own ingenuity, she set to work sawing her bonds.

A sudden, insistent tapping reached her, and she jumped, then looked wildly about. It kept up, increasing to a rapid patter. From the roof, she realized, relaxing. It had started to rain. She resumed her steady work on the ropes that bound her wrists. Then the first drop landed on her face, followed by another, then several more. Her roof, it appeared, stood in desperate need of repair. She would really have to complain to her landlord—only think of the poor, wet rats who lived there on a regular basis!

She kept doggedly on, trying to ignore the increasing number of drips that landed on her head and slid down her face and neck. She had no idea whether or not she made any progress on her bonds, though she had a strong suspicion she was getting nowhere. It hardly mattered, she supposed. There was really very little else for her to do in the way of entertainment.

A rasping, grating noise sounded above her on the roof. It was repeated, as if there were somebody up there, scrambling along the uneven surface. She tensed, groping behind her for another of the plate shards. It was not much of a weapon, particularly since it was behind her, but at least it gave her some slight feeling of protection. The scraping along the shingles continued, then stopped abruptly. A resounding crash brought water and debris cascading down upon her, drenching her with rain and mud.

"Leanora!" Her name, called softly, reached her. Pale light flooded in through the newly created hole, and she could detect the outline of a man's head and shoulders lowered inside. "Leanora!" The call was repeated.

"Deverell!" Weak with relief, hoarse from she knew not what, she called out to him.

The silhouette shifted slightly. "Are you at home to visitors?" he asked, and a shaky laugh sounded in his voice.

"Really, you ought to leave your direction so people can find you. This is the third roof I have broken a hole into. Can you stand, by the way?"

"No. I—I am tied." She began to tremble. If it were not just like him, to treat this all as a joke!

He swung himself down into the room, hung suspended for a moment, then dropped to the floor with a thud. He straightened up with care.

"How—how kind of you to drop in!" she called, trying to match his bantering tone. "Such an unexpected surprise."

"A pleasant one, I hope." He reached her in three steps and sank down on his knees at her side. Taking her wet face between his cold, filthy hands, he kissed her with a thoroughness that made her forget everything except him.

He released her abruptly and began to search through his coat, then pulled something from an inner pocket. The streaky light glinted along the blade of a small knife. He set to work cutting her ropes, and she began to shiver with cold and reaction.

As soon as she was completely free, he dropped the knife and pulled her roughly against himself. Somehow her arms were about his neck, and she returned his kiss with a fierce emotion she only hazily realized was far more than gratitude. They remained like that for several long and contented minutes before the rain, which now pelted down with considerable force, recalled them to a sense of their dark and very dank surroundings—and the reason for it. Settled snugly against his broad chest, she told him of the masquerade at the Opera House in two days' time.

He swore softly, startling her with the range of his vocabulary. "Do you realize, if your captors had the least notion you had guessed so much, you would not be alive?" he demanded. He hugged her more tightly, and his lips brushed her hair, palliating the rebuke. "I want you to take your father into the country as soon as you get home."

She sat up and slightly away from him. "I most certainly will not! It takes more than this to frighten me off! I am not such a poor creature as that."

"I have a good mind to leave you right where you are, where

323

I know you aren't in any danger!" he retorted in exasperation.

"Very true. The rats and I are quite good friends by this time. But you might at least have the decency to fetch me a dry gown!"

He looked at her, an odd expression on his face, and suddenly he burst out laughing with the release of tension. "You look like a drowned rat!" he exclaimed when he could command his voice.

"Then that makes several of us," she replied shakily as his merriment infected her as well. "I—I am quite sure the occupants of this attic cannot be pleased with the—the alterations you have made. It was quite wet enough to begin with."

He frowned abruptly. "I am not worried about the four-footed variety of rat at the moment. But we had best leave before any of the two-footed ones arrive to see how you are doing."

He stood and helped her to her feet. She swayed alarmingly and was obliged to hold tightly onto his arm until the circulation returned to her legs and she could stand on her own. Leaving her leaning against the table for support, he made a quick survey of her prison.

"The door would appear to be locked," he remarked when he at last located it at the far end of the attic. He stepped back, squared his shoulder and threw himself against it. The word he muttered fortunately did not reach Leanora's ears, but she saw him rubbing his arm.

"Is that safe?" she asked. Moving slowly, surprised to find how stiff her muscles were, she joined him. "Will someone not hear you?"

"We are in an abandoned warehouse, and I did not see anyone during my—er—reconnoitering." He threw himself against the heavy wooden panel once more, then a third time. Steadfastly it refused to give way. He regarded it with baleful dislike before turning away in disgust. "Looks like we'll have to go out the way I came in," he announced.

Leanora looked up at the gaping hole in the roof. "Oh," she said, her voice strangely hollow.

A deep chuckle escaped him. "It won't be easy, but it should not prove impossible. I've been in worse situations."

"Have you?" She looked at him, marveling. "I—I must have led a sheltered existence indeed, for I fear I have never before had the pleasure of escaping through a hole in a roof. It must have been an oversight on the part of my governess," she explained. "Or perhaps my father, for not hiring a suitable teacher for me. It is quite a lowering reflection, you must know. This is not the first time I have noted a deplorable gap in my education."

He regarded her with considerable amusement. "Do you think your training will enable you to assist me in moving that table?"

They half-lifted, half-slid the coarsely constructed piece of furniture over to stand directly beneath the hole that Deverell had made. Climbing up onto it, he grabbed an exposed rafter beam, hooked an arm over it through the gap and slowly pulled himself up. A dangerous, creaking protest sounded, and more of the ceiling fell down upon Leanora's anxiously upturned face. She winced, brushed herself off and watched as he scrambled out onto the wet shingles. The maltreated roof groaned once more, but held secure.

Lying flat, he managed to turn about so that he could again lower his head and shoulders through the rough opening. "Now you," he directed.

She regarded her bedraggled ball gown, relieved that the skirt, which had been designed for dancing, was not as confining as the narrower ones of her day dresses. It still had not been intended for clambering onto table tops, however, and a little ingenuity was required to manage this. She succeeded by sitting upon the edge and swinging her legs up. Once there, she still had to stand, and without anything to grasp for balance, it was no easy task.

Nor was that the end of her problems. Standing erect with her arms stretched above her head, her fingertips could barely brush the rafter beam. Deverell reached down and grasped her upraised arms about the elbows, then inched himself away from the hole. She clutched at his coat sleeves and felt herself lifted upward until only her slippered toes touched the table. Deverell continued his careful maneuver, working his body

325

backward. Leanora kept her eyes closed firmly against the rain that beat down upon her as she rose slowly upward, inch by painful inch, dragged inexorably toward freedom. Her upper arms scraped against the rough, broken boards of the rafters, and she bit back a cry of pain. Even above the sounds of the storm, she could hear Deverell's strained breathing as he strove, confined by his awkward position, to haul her out of the attic.

Her necklace caught on a splintered board and jerked at her neck, almost tearing from her throat. Deverell's grip slipped, and she gasped as she dropped back. In a moment, his fingers dug cruelly into her flesh, catching and dragging her another few inches upward. This time the board missed her necklace, instead fastening in the fine white crepe of her low-cut bodice. The material, not as strong as the wrought gold chain, tore readily.

Her head cleared the hole, and an anguished gasp escaped her as her smooth, exposed skin grated against the splintered wood. She gripped his coat sleeve with numb but desperate fingers as the rain washed away the tears that sprang to her eyes.

"Grab—grab for the boards!" Deverell directed through gritted teeth.

Steeling her nerves, she released her hold on him and reached for solid wood. Her hands caught and held a broken beam, and she heard Deverell's exhaled breath as she relieved him of the greater portion of her weight. With more determination than grace, she dragged herself forward and up. Her skirt snagged on the same ragged rafter and ripped the entire length as she continued her progress.

Deverell released her arms, grasped her about the waist and dragged her toward him, free of the gaping hole. She collapsed at his side on the roof, and both gasped for breath. Rain streamed down upon them, not hard, but drenching and cleansing, rinsing much of the grime from their heads and arms.

When at last she raised her face to Deverell, he was staring at her in a frankly admiring way. She looked down, aghast to see that both her gown and chemise had been torn, exposing

326

her leg almost to the hip. Her bodice was nothing more than tattered shreds, and she flushed deeply as his gaze wandered across the mostly exposed fullness of her breasts. She escaped indecency by mere threads!

"A—a gentleman would avert his gaze and offer me his coat!" she declared coldly, embarrassed by his unwavering regard.

"Only a gentleman dead to all normal instincts," he responded with complete honesty. Nevertheless, he took off his ruined coat and helped her into it. It hung loosely about her, not quite reaching the areas that she most ardently desired covered.

She looked about, then clung to Deverell's arm for support. She had indeed been imprisoned in an attic, but she had not realized how terrifyingly far they were above the ground.

"Hold on to me," he directed, patting the hand that clutched his shirt sleeve. "The roof is slippery with leaves and debris."

He started off, crawling on his hands and knees, and she was forced to release his arm. Instead, she gripped one of his booted ankles and tried to keep near him. Slowly they worked their way along, running parallel to the peaked roof, until they neared the edge. Another building stood close by, the roofs only feet apart. Deverell stood and made the jump easily.

Leanora, shaking internally, came reluctantly to her feet. She must not look down! He reached back to her, taking both her hands in a reassuring hold.

"Jump," he ordered.

She jumped. Her foot barely touched the edge, she started to fall, then Deverell had her firmly in his arms as he dragged her away from the ledge.

"Only one more like that," he assured her.

Another one? For a moment she considered letting go of him and just dropping off the roof to get it over with. But Deverell helped her down to her hands and knees once more before he began crawling forward. As if robbed of all will of her own she followed, clutching his ankle tightly again.

They continued like that forever, until she doubted she could keep on. Her brain felt numb, and she wished she could say the same for her knees. They were raw and bleeding, but she kept on, step after painful step, yard after endless yard. She attempted to keep the tatters of her skirt between her savaged flesh and the sharp shingles of the roof, but it was to no avail. Abruptly she came up against Deverell and realized he had stopped at last.

He rose stiffly to his feet, wiped the rain from his eyes and leapt to the next roof. Leanora caught her breath, watching until he had steadied his balance and turned toward her, his hands held out. She closed her eyes for a moment, then grasped his offered arm and jumped.

The landing was easier this time, but she clung to Deverell's strong arms just the same. His lips brushed her hair, then her forehead.

"Just a little farther, now," he murmured encouragingly.

She nodded, and the rain slid unheeded down her face. It was agony to resume crawling, but somehow she did it, closed in a miniature world of torment.

"Stay here!" Deverell called back to her. He had stopped again, and to her horror he began to ease himself down the steep roof to the very edge. Lying flat, he peered over. He inched forward, leaning farther as he went, still looking. Raising an arm, he beckoned her to join him.

She could not do it. Just looking down that steep slope made her ill. But he waited. . . . She turned around and slowly—very slowly—crawled backward.

"Turn around," he called to her, enraging her with the chuckle in his voice. Had the man no nerves himself? He treated this as the merest nothing!

"But to be sure," she declared out loud. "I keep forgetting! You do this sort of thing every day, do you not?"

The deep, incongruous sound of his laughter surrounded her, momentarily easing her fear. "Not quite every day," he corrected. "Look over the edge."

"No." She stared at so absurd a suggestion.

"If you will, you will note that there is an open window just below us. It is the one I came through to reach the roofs."

"You came through a window and swung yourself up onto the roof?" she asked. She sat back on her heels, regarding him in fascinated horror. "You have confirmed my suspicions. You are obviously an escaped Bedlamite."

He laughed again, and it dawned on her that he actually enjoyed himself! It infuriated her, for she was little more than a quivering heap of nerves, but it also instilled her with a strange courage. She might be terrified, but at least he seemed confident. Cautiously she came closer and peeped over the edge, only to jerk back, trembling.

"Watch me carefully," he directed. "I won't be up here to help you get started." He slid a bit farther forward, sat on the edge and swung his legs over. Rolling onto his stomach, he grasped the guttering and lowered himself down.

A scream tore from her throat as he disappeared. All she could see were his hands, gripping the edge. Then suddenly they let go.

"I'm safe!" he called up to her, and she released her breath.

"If you think I am going over this edge . . . !" she began.

"I'm afraid you have your choice of that or spending the night on the roof," he called back.

She subjected it to serious consideration, casting a speculative glance at the sky. It was a mottled black, with not so much as a single star peeking out from behind the heavy clouds. The chances of the rain increasing seemed considerable. Even now, the drops were coming harder and faster. So it seemed she had her choice: to fall off the edge of the roof or die of an inflammation of the lungs.

"Are you coming?" he called.

"I'm thinking about it!" she yelled back.

His deep rich chuckle sounded from directly beneath her, giving her courage. Taking her lower lip firmly between her teeth, she rolled to her stomach as Deverell had done and began to let herself the rest of the way down the roof. Suddenly there was nothing but air beneath her feet, and she stopped, sick with a fear so intense it blotted out everything else.

"I can see you!" Deverell's commanding voice reached her. "Keep coming! Just a little farther now, take it slowly. I'm waiting to catch you." He kept talking, a calm, steady drone where the words were of less importance than the tone.

Obedient to his air of authority, she forced herself to descend a couple of inches farther.

329

"You think it will be quite difficult, but it won't," Deverell told her in a conversational manner. "There is almost no overhang at all on the roof. That means I am very close to you."

She kept going, encouraged by his quiet good sense. Her knees encountered the sharp edge, then they were over. Still he talked on, and he was right; it did not seem so very impossible. She concentrated hard on the feel of the rough shingles beneath her gripping fingers, not on the emptiness beneath her legs. Deverell called that it was not much farther, and she knew it was true, for already she felt her weight drawing her legs downward. She swallowed hard. Deverell was there; he would catch her. He had already made this same descent. It could be done. She repeated those words again, needing comfort. It could be done.

"When your hips reach the edge," Deverell called with a shocking lack of propriety, "your legs will swing in toward the building, and I can catch you!"

She could only hope that was true. But as her legs fell she panicked, screaming as she clutched the roof. A shingle broke loose in her fingers as Deverell's strong hands gripped her just below her knees.

"A bit farther!" came the order, and somehow she found another handhold and complied. Her fingers stung from their efforts. Determined hands worked their slow way up her legs, grasping her knees, then above, drawing her lower body inward—toward safety. But it was still so very far away. . . .

She was on the edge, with only her shoulders still on the roof. If she fell now. . . . Deverell could not yet have a firm enough hold on her. His hands crept higher, and shaking with fear as she risked everything, she lowered herself a fraction more. She balanced, but it would not be for long. . . . She was slipping . . . !

Horror-stricken, she grasped at the edge, dangling beneath it. Deverell's firm hold encircled her thighs.

"Let go!" he called.

Fear blocked her retort from her lips. She clung with every ounce of strength she possessed, too terrified to surrender this last hold, until matters were taken out of her hands—literally.

Her fingers slipped and she fell.

His grip held. Her back slammed against the window sill, knocking the breath out of her as he pulled her through. She was in his arms, gasping for breath, clinging to him as tightly as she had to the roof. She drew in air at last and began trembling as if she would never stop.

Deverell sank to the floor, breathing hard, drawing her with him and cradling her in his arms as if he still feared to drop her. They remained there for a very long while, until her shaking subsided somewhat. Now it was mostly the cold and wet that caused her shivering, though she was loathe to release Deverell.

"We had better get you home and warm you up." He spoke at last against her hair. "Do you think you can stand yet?"

He came to his feet and pulled her up to join him. The huge room in which they stood was in almost complete darkness, but he had no trouble leading her across the empty floor to a door that stood ajar. She followed slowly, clutching his hand as if her life still depended on it.

They felt their way across a hallway to the head of a staircase. The steps creaked alarmingly as Deverell placed a booted foot on them, and Leanora jumped, clinging even more tightly to him. He went down three more stairs, and she was forced to either follow or let go of his hand. She followed.

Step by step they descended into the inky blackness. She gained the impression of a huge empty space, but all that mattered to her was the solid footing beneath her and Deverell's capable presence just before her. It must be a very tall building, she had no idea how many stairs they came down, how many landings they reached. When she considered how high that roof must have been, how very far she could have fallen. . . . A wave of sickness engulfed her and she leaned against the wall until it passed.

Then suddenly they were at the bottom. In the distance a small rectangle of pale light could be seen: an open door. With Deverell's arm firmly about her for support, they headed toward it.

They were met just outside by his devoted groom, who ran to call the coachman. In a moment, a covered carriage pulled forward, stopping before them. Deverell helped her inside, and she sank back against the cushions, shivering, barely noticing when he wrapped a lap robe about her. He sat close, still cradling her tightly in his arms, and neither had the strength left to speak.

Her hopes that her ordeal was over were shattered as they pulled up in front of Sherborne House. The lower floor was ablaze with lights.

"What—what has happened?" she asked shakily, leaning forward to peer out the window.

"You, most likely," Deverell said, a soft laugh sending a mild tremor through his massive frame. He sat so near, she could feel it.

The groom jumped down, lowered the step, and Deverell climbed out. Turning, he lifted Leanora from the carriage and set her carefully on her feet. Huddling more deeply into his torn coat and trying to wrap the tattered remains of her skirt about her as she walked, she allowed Deverell to help her up the stairs.

The door was thrown open by Tremly, whose haggard face bore eloquent testimony to the worry he suffered. His jaw dropped at the sight that met his horrified gaze, and he so far forgot his dignity as to permit a gasp to escape him. He fell back several paces as Deverell almost carried Leanora through the doorway.

"Miss—Miss Leanora!" the butler exclaimed.

"I—I am all right, Tremly," she managed to say. Tears filled her eyes at her relief to be home.

"What is going on here?" Deverell asked, indicating the numerous candles that were lit.

"Sir." The butler turned a shaken face to Deverell. "The lights?" With a visible effort, he pulled himself together. "Mrs. Ashton, young Mr. Reggie and Sir William Holborne are in the Gold Saloon, my lord."

"What?" Leanora exclaimed, aghast.

Deverell's hand caressed her arm. "Go upstairs to bed. I will make the explanations," he said softly.

The plan was forestalled. The door to the saloon flew open, and Mrs. Ashton stopped just over the threshold, shrieking at sight of her niece. Reggie, just behind her, froze for a moment, then pushed past his mother and came to take Leanora's hands.

"Good God, Nora!" he exclaimed. "You'd better sit down!"

Between them, Deverell and Reggie led Leanora into the room. Too weak to resist, she sank into the chair that Sir William stepped forward to place for her near the fire.

"What in God's name happened to you?" her cousin demanded.

Her aunt, her face very white, knelt at her side and chaffed unnecessarily at her wrist. Deverell, more practical, returned to the hall and sent the wholly confounded butler for brandy.

"An accident, I believe?" Sir William asked gently. "My dear Leanora, how terrible for you!"

"Her coach was held up on the Common," Deverell explained curtly as he came back in.

Mrs. Ashton gasped, but no one paid her any heed. Both gentlemen's eyes were riveted on Deverell.

"The devil you say," Sir William breathed.

"No, dash it all, Dev! That's coming it too strong! Highwaymen?" Reggie exclaimed.

Deverell assented. "She was taken captive. Probably to be held for ransom."

Her aunt moaned and clutched at her niece's cold hands.

"I never heard such a thing!" Reggie exclaimed hotly. "That's—that's infamous!"

"It certainly is!" Sir William agreed shortly. "Common highwaymen to take a hostage?" He drew his snuff box from his pocket, opened it with a quick flick, then paused, his gaze coming to rest on Deverell. "And how did you come into this?"

"I left the ball shortly after Lady Leanora," he explained. "My carriage came upon hers just after the ruffians rode off. Naturally, I followed and had the good fortune to be able to free her."

Leanora glanced up at Sir William's frowning face. He took a pinch of snuff, snapped his box closed and restored it to his pocket.

"How . . . convenient . . . that you were at hand to perform the daring rescue," he said slowly, his eyes narrowing to watchful slits.

Leanora stiffened and a chill ran through her. What did Sir William imply? That Deverell's rescue of her might not be all that it seemed? She had not considered it before, having been only too relieved to see him, but now that she thought about it, it did seem strangely fortuitous.

But from Sir William's tone, he seemed to think it something more, something sinister! It was too much for her to take in at the moment. Too much had happened; she was too tired and still too frightened from her escapade on the roof tops. She sat shivering, then jumped as Deverell pressed a brandy glass into her hands. Trembling so much that she needed assistance in raising it to her lips, she took a tentative sip. A burning sensation shot down her throat and into her stomach, then slowly seeped through the rest of her, warming and strengthening.

"What did they do?" Reggie demanded, recovering from his stupefaction.

"Where did they take you, my love?" Mrs. Ashton chimed in. "Oh, my dear Leanora, how—how terrible this has been for you! And we owe her deliverance to you!" She threw herself upon Deverell's filthy chest. "Oh, how grateful I am to you!" she sobbed.

Reggie gave a shaky laugh. "Lord, Mamma, dashing about after highwaymen is much more to his taste than going to balls! I'm surprised he hasn't involved himself in something disreputable before now out of boredom!"

The odd circumstance of Deverell's having been on the scene to rescue her, his love of dangerous activity. . . . She forced the thoughts to the back of her mind. She was in no condition to try to sort things out right now! Instead, she turned to Sir William.

"How—how do you come to be here?" she asked unsteadily.

"Oh, my love, it was the most terrible thing!" Mrs. Ashton declared, releasing Deverell to return to her side. "When the carriage did not return, I was thrown into the most dreadful quake, for I made certain that some harm must have befallen you! And if only I had known how right I was! But I had no notion what to do, for the ball was coming to a close and still the carriage did not come back; and then I saw Sir William

334

and knew he would help us, for he is the greatest friend of your father's, and I knew he would not leave us in the lurch! And he so very kindly agreed to bring us home. Only imagine my distress when I discovered that you had not yet returned!"

"It was somewhat mystifying," Sir William agreed. "You see, your aunt was convinced that we should pass your carriage upon the road with a broken trace or a lame leader."

"But we did not, of course, so then I hoped that someone who left the ball after you would have stopped to give you aid! It was so very dreadful, not knowing what had become of you . . . !" Mrs. Ashton's easy tears slipped down her cheeks. "Oh, my love, whatever possessed you to leave alone? You should have come and told me you felt ill!"

"I—I didn't want to ruin your evening." But that wasn't it. There had been a reason . . . a note . . . from Deverell! That was what she couldn't remember! He sent her a message to leave at once, and alone! She spun about to demand an explanation, then realized that now, with so many people present, was not the time.

A new fear struck her, and she turned to her aunt. "Did—did anyone disturb my father?"

"Of course not!" Reggie declared, shocked. "As if we were not up to handling anything on our own!"

"I believe Lady Leanora has had a somewhat tiring night," Deverell suggested. "Do you not think she should go up to her bed?" He rang for the butler as he spoke, for all the world as if this were his own house. When Tremly arrived, he requested that a hot bath be carried to his mistress's room. "And now," he added as the butler disappeared to make the arrangements, "I will take you up."

Leanora stood and to her surprise discovered that her legs held her. She took an unsteady step forward, and her knees agreeably refrained from buckling. "I—I will be all right, thank you."

A soft tap sounded on the door, interrupting Deverell's reply. Ripton, Leanora's abigail, entered, took in the situation at a glance and went at once to the assistance of her mistress. With one arm firmly about her, she helped her from the room. At the door, Leanora paused, thanked Deverell again, managed a quavering goodnight and left with her maid.

As soon as they arrived in her room, Ripton began to remove the shredded remains of what had once been Leanora's favorite ball gown.

"Whatever has been happening, my lady?" she demanded as she dropped the sodden, ruined garment into the basin. Leanora repeated the story given by Deverell, and the maid dropped the brush with which she had been about to untangle her mistress's hair.

"Lawks!" the woman exclaimed. "Never have I heard of such goings on!" Unconsciously, she repeated Reggie's words. "How lucky you were that such a capable gentleman as Lord Deverell was on hand to rescue you. Why, it would have been quite the most romantic thing, if only you had not suffered so!" She sighed. "What a fortunate circumstance that brought his lordship on the scene!"

While Leanora sat wrapped in a dressing gown, two footmen carried in the large bathtub. The lower parlor maid followed bearing a can of hot water. The footmen hurried out, only to return shortly with more hot water.

At last, Leanora climbed into her bath, knowing as she did so that she would be stiff and bruised in the morning. Despite her headache, she refused the offer of burnt feathers, but accepted the hot brick in her bed to silence the anxious Ripton. The hot water stung the damaged skin of her knees and hands, but her tight muscles relaxed. She leaned back, sipping the hot chocolate that her maid produced.

Very soon she donned her nightdress and climbed into her comfortable bed. As Ripton pulled the curtains about this, Leanora glanced at the mantel clock and was surprised to see that it was only just after three. She closed her eyes, doing some mental arithmetic. She had left the ball quite early, probably at about eleven. That meant she had only been unconscious a bare hour, at the most. And Deverell must have located her within an hour of that, probably less!

Her earlier, nagging thoughts returned to haunt her. *Why* had Deverell sent her that message to leave—and alone? *How* had he arrived upon the scene in the nick of time to follow her abductors? Had he set her up for the abduction for some

336

unfathomable reason? And how had he known so precisely where she had been taken? He said he had checked into three attic rooms, but she might have been anywhere, even in a basement! Either Deverell knew more than he was telling her, or— A wave of sick fear swept over her.

Or Deverell was one of the conspirators.

Chapter 23

Leanora huddled in her bed. It didn't make sense! None of it did! But Sir William had thought something amiss, detected that something did not quite ring true in Deverell's story. . . .

If Deverell were one of the conspirators, why would he rescue her? Especially after making sure she could be captured so easily? Would he not want her to stay safely out of the way? Or did he feel that his confederates had committed a dangerous and unwise act? The abduction of the daughter of a peer of the realm would only heighten security about the prime minister, making the plot more difficult to carry off.

It *could* have been a ploy to direct any possible suspicion away from himself. But it was all too absurd! Why should he risk his life scrambling across the roof tops when his leg was bad? Unless it had been staged not only to clear him in everyone's eyes, but also to frighten her so severely that she would never again interfere? If so, it had gone a long way in accomplishing its purpose. A wave of nausea washed over her as she remembered hanging from that crumbling ledge of the roof.

Deverell. . . . She did not want to believe it! It could not be true! Every part of her cried out against casting Deverell in a villainous role. But Sir William had noted the improbableness of his story at once. And if she were thinking clearly, she must have done so, too. But her mind was clouded with fear—and with the heroic image she had created surrounding Captain Lord Deverell, daring British spy against Napoleon's troops.

There had to be another explanation! Deverell tried to prevent the assassination! He could not be guilty of treason. The very idea was repugnant to her. He might seem mysterious and even dangerous to her, but surely he could not be capable of such treachery! In her heart she believed in him, but her mind once again filled with numerous unanswered questions. It was a very, very long time before she fell asleep.

She was disturbed at last by noises in her room, and she dragged her tired eyes open when Ripton threw back the curtains from about her bed. It lacked only a quarter of an hour before noon, her abigail informed her in a relentlessly cheerful tone. And only think! Her carriage had turned up in the stable that morning with the coachman and footman tied up inside. They appeared to have suffered no ill effects from their adventure, a circumstance for which Leanora could only be heartily glad.

A tray with steaming chocolate and fresh rolls lay on the table nearby, and she eased herself up on one elbow, flexing her stiff muscles, grateful for not having to get up at once. It would take time to convince her body to cooperate that morning.

"How is my father?" she asked as Ripton moved about the room, straightening up a few details that had escaped her notice the night before.

"He doesn't know a thing about those nasty goings on last night, Miss Leanora," Ripton informed her proudly. "He was asking after you, but Pagget told him you came in quite late. We'll not let him be worried, and so you may be sure. And nor will Sir William."

"Sir William?" Leanora asked quickly. "Is he here?"

"Yes, Miss Leanora. Arrived about an hour ago. But don't you be worrying about him, neither. Pagget is sitting nearby, to make sure he doesn't tire his lordship."

Leanora sank back against her pillows, vaguely aware that she had never given full credit to the care the servants provided. "Where is my aunt?" she asked, suddenly curious. Knowing Mrs. Ashton as she did, she had suspected to find her hovering about her room or agitating the earl with her fluttery nervousness.

"Mrs. Ashton has gone for a drive to steady her nerves," Ripton informed her. "She was fearful of remaining in the house where her distress might betray to his lordship that something was amiss with you. I believe," she added primly, "that her destination was Bond Street."

A shaky smile tugged at Leanora's lips. Nothing would more surely soothe her aunt's nerves than a lengthy shopping expedition! When she at last returned, she would be quite her normal, comfortable self—and far too taken up with crepes and cambrics, laces and furbelows to notice her niece's unsettled frame of mind.

Leanora rose at last, wincing from the pain in her arms. There were large bruises about her elbows where Deverell had grasped her to drag her up through the hole. She shivered, looking at the bluish areas of skin. His injured leg had not hindered him in the least last night. It was a disturbing thought.

She selected a simple round gown made high at the neck and with long sleeves. Not fashionable, perhaps, but she desired to hide her deep scratches and bruises from her father's keen eye. As Ripton threw the dress over her head and twitched it into place with expert fingers, Leanora's mind continued to seethe with conjecture.

What did she really know of Deverell? Reggie accepted him unquestioningly as the best friend of the elder brother he had adored. His name had appeared often in Vincent's letters. And until she had allowed herself to fall under his charismatic spell, she had always blamed him for luring Vincent into the occupation that led to his death.

A new and horrible thought dawned on her. He had lured Vincent into becoming a spy. What if he, himself, had been a double agent, working for the French? What if Vincent's death were directly Deverell's fault? What if. . . .

She was being absurd, overreacting! She had to be objective! But when it came right down to it, she knew nothing about Deverell except that he was the most overpoweringly masculine man she had ever met. And that fact alone, unfortunately, did not mean she should trust him.

Rejecting her abigail's suggestion that she breakfast in her

341

room, Leonora made her way downstairs to the sunny parlor. There she found that all traces of the meal had been long since cleared away, but Tremly, who appeared almost at once, promised that a tray would be brought to her upon the instant.

It was in fact almost a half hour later that he reappeared, bearing a selection of dishes that contained a meal suitable in his eyes to sustain her after her ordeal of the night before. She stared at it in dismay, knowing she could never hope to eat even a small portion of the proffered delicacies. Assuring Tremly that she had all she required, she seated herself and made a few selections from the heaped plates.

She had just finished this light repast when Sir William's voice sounded in the hall as he descended the stairs. Setting down her tea cup, she rose as quickly as her aching muscles would allow and went out to the passage and called him.

"My dear Leonora!" He came back up the stairs to greet her. "I am glad to see you looking your usual lovely self. Have you quite recovered?"

"Indeed, I have, except for a few bruises. Come in for a cup of tea." She led the way into the parlor, found another cup and saucer on the sideboard and poured out. "Tell me, how is my father today?"

"Completely unaware of last night's stirring events," he assured her.

"How does he go on?" she asked, curious for the opinion of someone else. "You have known him both professionally and personally for a good number of years. Do you think he is recovering as he should?"

Sir William hesitated as if debating some point with himself, then raised troubled eyes to her. "I fear Sherborne is too anxious to return to public life," he said slowly, confirming Leonora's worries about her father. "It is my opinion that he needs more rest. But in London he is merely champing at the bit, eager to return to harness."

She nodded. "I—I feared that might be the case."

"Have you considered taking him down to the Abbey for a spell?" he asked. "The temptations would not be as great for him there, and perhaps you could induce him to relax. It would seem that you could do with a rest, as well."

342

A slight smile flickered in her eyes. "I will do my best to persuade him," she said. But as soon as the words were out, she knew she could not act upon them just yet. Her father would never go to the Abbey without her, and she had to stay in London—at least for two more days.

"May I ask you a question about last night?" he asked. "If the memory is not too painful for you?"

"I am not such a poor creature," she assured him. "Memories hold no terrors for me."

"Then were you able to see who attacked you? Could you give a description of the ruffians? I have been thinking about it, and I cannot believe them to be normal highwaymen! Do you have any idea who might want to hold you to ransom? What do the Runners say?"

She stared at him. "The Runners?" she blurted out. "I—I never even thought of them!" She looked down, willing her hands not to shake. "I—I must be more missish than I realized. I have been so shaken that even so obvious a course did not occur to me!" She hoped he accepted her bluff.

His eyes narrowed. "But did Deverell not suggest this?" He looked down, swirling the liquid in his cup. "Have you any notion of where you were taken? Ah, but then Deverell will know. I am sure he merely did not want to press you last night. It will all be taken care of today, I am sure." He rose and took his leave of her, and she began to tremble all over again.

Sir William suspected Deverell, but of what? It was obvious he sought to warn her! Did he know something of the Requiem Masque? If Petersham was involved, then it was very possible he had let something slip to his keen-witted assistant. Perhaps Sir William tried to prevent it and had no idea that she knew of it also. Did he believe Deverell to be one of the conspirators, but dared not tell her openly to avoid his company? Had she, in fact, turned to the wrong man for assistance?

If only she could think clearly! Did her heart betray her, making her long for a traitor's company? Or were her confused emotions correct all along, and Deverell *was* the man she could trust? And what would that make Sir William? A possible ally? A possible villain?

She retired to her sitting room, curled up on a sofa and tried

343

to sort through the tangled problem. None of the pieces fit properly! Deverell, Petersham, Sir William, Kennington, Dalmouth, even Gregory and Julia! They could not all be involved! Yet mysteries hung about every one of them!

She still sat there, lost in anguished thought, when the door opened and her aunt peeped about the corner.

"Leanora, my love!" she exclaimed and hurried into the room. Reggie followed in her wake with Xerk panting heavily behind.

Her cousin bent to kiss her cheek. "You don't look in the least like you went through an ordeal last night!" he told her handsomely.

"Such a ghastly experience." Mrs. Ashton shuddered. "If it were not for Lord Deverell, I dare not think what might have become of you! Why, I am certain it is only due to his quick thinking that you were saved from a Terrible Fate!" Her tone accented the words.

Reggie nodded. "Capital fellow, Dev."

Leanora agreed, though with a measure of reserve. These were exactly the sentiments she wanted desperately to hear. But were they the truth? She *had* to know! It tore her apart, wondering if a villainous nature underlay his laughing, captivating exterior! It was impossible! If he were evil, her heart could not have gone out to him so completely. . . . .

Reality dawned on her, momentarily eclipsing her aunt's recital of Deverell's manifest charms. She, a sensible spinster, had lost her heart for the first time. The realization shattered her, for never before had she been subjected to the heartaches and yearnings of love. But she could not give in to it! Not until she knew for certain the truth about Deverell. She could not permit her emotions to overcome her judgment.

"But you are looking fatigued, my love!" Mrs. Ashton exclaimed, breaking into her thoughts. "And it is no wonder, to be sure. You must retire to your chamber upon the instant and lie down."

Leanora managed a weak smile. "I am lying down, dear aunt. I shall be all right here, I promise you."

Her aunt blinked. "But to be sure, so you are. I declare, I do not know whether I am standing on my head or my heels, with

344

so many terrible things happening! I am certain we could not have managed without Lord Deverell of late. And only think, my love, if he had not left the ball early last night, he might never have been aware of your danger!"

Reggie shifted slightly in his chair. "Why did you leave early, Nora?"

"I—I had the most dreadful headache." Should she tell Reggie the truth? That she had felt so tired she acted upon Deverell's instructions without thinking? Should someone else know—just in case?

Reggie shook his head. "You should have taken my mamma with you, or called me."

"How very true!" his mother agreed at once. "Why, if we had all left together, and later of course, none of this would have happened. For with a number of carriages all crossing the Common at once, no one would have dared hold us up!"

"Come on, Mamma," Reggie intervened neatly, seeing the sudden strain in Leonora's face. "Nora needs to sleep." Taking his garrulous parent's arm, he shepherded her from the room.

Leanora sank back against the cushions and closed her eyes. They were absolutely right! If she had not developed that headache and become so tired, she would have gone straight to Deverell and demanded an explanation! Most likely, she would not have left the party until everyone else did as well. And with a steady parade of coaches crossing the Common, it would have been impossible for highwaymen—or anyone else—to hold up her coach and take her captive.

That could only mean that her indisposition was no mere chance. Someone must have given her something at the ball to make sure that she would leave early. A cold chill engulfed her. What would have happened to Reggie and her aunt if they had accompanied her? Would they, too, have been hit over the head? Would they have been taken captive or left with the carriage?

She swallowed hard, trying to calm her suddenly quavering nerves as she remembered her illness at Vauxhall. Poison. . . .

But *who?* Who had been near enough to her when she was either eating or drinking to have administered something?

Deverell had served her, both times! That thought refused to be banished. She closed her eyes again, trying to picture who else had been near her. Petersham, of course, and Sir William. Then Dalmouth, even Kennington. But Deverell had sent her that note. . . .

Tremly entered at that moment to announce that Lord Petersham had arrived and hoped to have a word with her. With an effort she set aside her terrifying thoughts and braced herself for what could only be an ordeal. But would it be one of boredom or something more sinister?

A few moments later, Petersham strode into the apartment, concern etched deeply in every line of his heavy face. He hurried to the sofa and took both her hands between his own damp ones. His relief at seeing her was almost comical.

"My dear Leanora!" he exclaimed. "William told me what happened! I came upon the instant to see for myself that you are all right!"

He released her hand, drew a handkerchief from his pocket and mopped at his brow, quite overcome. There was real anxiety in his manner, far in excess of what Leanora would have expected of one of his indolent nature.

"So glad I am that you have suffered no harm!" he added once more.

"As you see," she assured him. "I am merely tired."

"Ah! And one cannot blame you! Such a terrible experience! Such a shock to one's system! Has a doctor been to see you?"

At that, she smiled. "I have sustained no real injury, I promise you. I will be quite myself again by tomorrow."

He frowned. "But is it wise to resume your activities? I cannot think it a good idea. And your father has already suffered one relapse. . . . Have you considered taking him down to the Abbey?"

"I have," she said slowly. "We will certainly go there when he is well enough to travel."

Petersham heaved a deep sigh. "So fortunate he is to have a loving daughter to care for him. But you! With him ill, I am certain that no one concerns themselves with your health as they ought! Allow me, as one who has always stood in the position of an uncle to you, to guide your decision at such a time! Retire into the country! A gentle journey with frequent breaks will be quite enjoyable for Sherborne, and to be away from the bustle of London can only do you both good."

Leanora blinked. Petersham to have stood in the position of an uncle to her? The idea was laughable! Certainly she had known him for a goodly number of years, but he had never been more to her than one of her father's associates. Keeping that reflection to herself, she merely thanked him for his solicitude.

"Then you will go?" he pursued anxiously. "You look so pale, I am sure the air at the Abbey will be far more salubrious for you. And Sherborne need not concern himself with government matters! All will go well in his absence. He can return to take up the reins of office when you are both once more restored to health. Nothing, my dear, is as important as your safety—health, I should say! Such a wonderful climate, near Canterbury," he rushed on. "Makes me almost wish I could go with you. Haven't visited the Abbey in a dog's age! Beautiful place. Can't imagine anyone preferring to stay in London when they have a country seat like that!"

Leanora kept an artificial smile fixed firmly on her lips while her brain seethed. Never had she seen him so distraught! He knew something of the truth, of that she was certain. It was her safety—and that of her father—that concerned him, not all this nonsense about health. He knew something—but how much? Surely it was not he who wished them harm, he was too distressed for that! But was he one of the conspirators, or had he, like she, stumbled across the plot?

If only Deverell would come, she must tell him of her suspicions of Petersham. . . . But she could not! The cloud of suspicion must hang over Deverell, as well. She was truly on her own. When Petersham took his leave at long last, she retired to her bed with a severe headache.

It seemed like only minutes later when Ripton came to tell her that Lord Deverell was below, asking after her. Leanora hesitated, not knowing what to say to him. If she behaved any differently, he was intelligent enough to realize that she no longer trusted him. If he were innocent, he would think it funny. If he were not. . . . She felt chilled all over and longed to run to him for the comfort that this time he could not provide.

She found him leaning against the hearth in the Gold Saloon, staring thoughtfully down at the unlit grate. He turned as the door closed behind her, and came forward at once to take her hand and raise it to his lips. A warm glow lit his dark eyes, and she struggled against the answering response that leapt within her.

"I am glad to see you recovered," he murmured, retaining her fingers in a firm clasp.

"Oh, a trifle bruised and stiff, perhaps, but that is a small price to pay for the joy of scrambling over the roof tops," she responded lightly. She withdrew her hand from his and led the way to chairs.

"I have come to take you driving in the Park," he said, remaining where he was.

She stiffened, then forced herself to relax. He could not mean her harm, or he would never have rescued her the night before. She should be safe in his company. But would her heart? Just seeing him caused her pain, doubting him as she must. She longed to feel his strong arms about her once more, to know his strength and the security of his presence! But she dared not trust as she longed to.

"Is something amiss?" he asked gently, detecting the constraint in her manner.

"No!" she exclaimed at once. "Just—just let me fetch my bonnet."

In a very few minutes, she took her seat in his curricle, and they started for the Park. They drove in silence until they neared the Grosvenor Gate, then he turned to look at her, just touching one of her hands with a finger. "Did it upset you last night, more than you will admit?"

"Of course not!" she declared at once. "I am quite willing to admit I was terrified."

His lips twitched in a slight smile. "Why did you leave the ball so early, and alone? You never explained."

"But—you told me to!"

He stared at her. "What do you mean? When?"

"You had a note sent to me—" She broke off as she read the

darkening anger in his face. "Did—did you not?"

"Most assuredly, no! Do you tell me it was written in my hand?"

"I—I could barely make out the words. I had the most dreadful headache and everything blurred so. . . ."

"You were drugged again, then someone sent you a note you would not be up to questioning." He drew in a deep breath and let it out slowly. "Now will you go to the country?"

He hadn't sent that message? Her hopes surged. It was true; she could not be certain that message came from him! Oh, if only. . . . But it would be so easy for him to deny it all, now that his purpose, whatever it might have been, was accomplished.

"Why—why does everyone want me out of London?" she exclaimed, falling back on safer ground. "I will not go! I intend to stay right here and see it through!"

"That is hardly wise, under the circumstances," he pointed out.

"Are you threatening me?" she demanded, then realized that her words were incautious as she saw his dark brow snap down. He must not realize that she suspected him!

"Have I offended you?" he asked, his tone still gentle.

She looked down, shaking her head. "No," she managed in a very small voice. She felt the force of his gaze directed on her, and she looked about, anxious for a diversion. To her relief, she saw Gregory riding toward them, waving to attract their attention. He reined in at their side and turned his mount to accompany them.

"Glad to see you," he declared with a cheerfulness that had been noticeably lacking from his demeanor of late.

"How do things go with you?" Deverell asked, smiling.

Gregory grinned. "Couldn't be better. Lord, you should have seen Kennington's face when I appeared with the money! Thought he had me for sure! And then when I brought more just now!"

"More?" Leanora demanded. "Gregory, where did you get it?"

A soft laugh shook her brother's shoulders. "From Dev's friend! Honestly, Nora, that man is the most complete hand! I took him to Kennington's hell earlier today, and they took him for a complete flat and let him win. Only he broke the bank! I'll swear they still don't know how it happened. He'll go back tonight, and I'll bet he breaks it again!" For a moment, relieved laughter kept him from speaking. "To—to look at him, Nora," he finally managed, "you'd take him for a nobody, but Lord, when he plays cards, you can't even tell that he's fuzzing 'em. And he must be! But how he manages with the dice!" Gregory shook his head, baffled.

"He palms them and replaces them with his own which are not quite—balanced, shall we say?" Deverell explained, his tone one of apology.

That started Gregory laughing again. "Lord, Dev, when I think how frightened I've been. . . ." He shook his head, suddenly sober. "I'm paying off my debt with Kennington's own money. I'll have enough in a couple of days, but I won't give it to him all at once or he'll get suspicious. But I can tell you one thing, your friend will ruin our beloved Kennington!"

"He doesn't know you're not worried anymore, does he?" Leanora asked.

Gregory shook his head. "I maintain a properly cowed aspect, I promise you. And Julia is off with Dalmouth somewhere right now. That reminds me. Got something for you, Nora. Going to stop by on my way home and give it to you." He fished in his pocket and brought out a long, flat box which he tossed negligently to her. With another wave, he turned his horse about and rode off.

Leanora sat staring at the package, knowing without opening it that it contained her diamond earrings and the topaz set. Tears filled her eyes, and she looked hastily away.

"And so it seems that our friend Kennington is well on his way to being finished," Deverell mused.

Leanora nodded. "I am glad! I wonder how many other foolish boys he has entrapped! And to think I always thought he had no more than a moderate income, when all the time he was fleecing poor young fools like Gregory out of fortunes!"

"Not for much longer," he consoled. "When my friend is done, Kennington will be well and truly ruined. If he does not put a period to his own existence, I fear my friend may assist him. You need have no more worries about him. And as for Gregory, I think you will find he has learned a valuable lesson."

They completed another circuit of the Park, then Deverell headed for the street. As he pulled up at last before Sherborne House, he turned to smile down at her. "Will I see you at the Winnet's dinner party tomorrow night?"

"I believe so. For some reason, I have not been checking our engagements of late, but I am almost positive we are promised for that one."

"Then until tomorrow." He handed her down, then climbed back into the seat, waiting only until she entered the house before driving off.

She turned her pelisse over to the waiting Tremly, then sought out the solitude of her sitting room. If only she could have told Deverell about Petersham's distress! *Should* she have? How she wished she knew what to do! A vast sensation of emptiness seeped through her, leaving her very alone and frightened. She had no idea whom she could trust. She needed Deverell's comfort and encouragement. . . . No, if she were honest with herself, what she longed for was his love. Only that would satisfy her.

But was his attentiveness to her assumed for the sake of the deadly plot? Tears slipped unnoticed down her cheeks as she stared blindly out the window over the garden across the Square. Now that she had experienced the all-encompassing warmth and vitality of Deverell's companionship and affection, without it her life would become nothing more than an empty, meaningless shell.

Chapter 24

The night brought no council. Never before had Leanora felt so terribly and completely alone. Her first thought was to summon Mr. Edmonton back to her side, to tell him all that had happened and seek his advice. But he was not a young man, and his abilities lay in the organization of information and appointments, not in the capturing of traitorous conspirators. If she did send for him, all she would accomplish would be to provide the murderers with one more target, and one who would not have the least idea how to protect himself.

She awoke in the morning to the unwelcome realization that there would be a masquerade ball held at the Opera House on the very next night. And very possibly it would be the Requiem Masque. What, if anything, would Deverell do? Would Lord Grenville walk into a trap laid for him by people he erroneously trusted? Or would the conspirators be caught? Less than forty hours remained before the appointed time of midnight. *On which side was Deverell?*

She could not—or was it *would* not?—believe him capable of such treachery! Every questionable move he made would have a reasonable explanation. He was not guilty! But still . . . the life at stake was not hers, the potential chaos in the government disastrous. She had no right to take chances because she had been fool enough to fall in love!

It was time for her to stop depending on others and take definite action on her own. And first, she must visit Julia for the details of the masquerade, and as quickly as possible. If her sister-in-law carried out her instructions, she would be preparing to attend this event in the company of her brother Dalmouth. And Lord Kennington would be there, expecting to have her join him. Was she to be his excuse for being at the masque—and Dalmouth's, as well?

Shortly after ten o'clock, she collected her pelisse and bonnet for the short walk to Mount Street to see Julia. As she started down the stairs, she heard the sounds of an arrival in the hall below. Leaning over the banister, she saw Lord Dalmouth handing over his hat and cane.

She had always been one to accept the inevitable; her visit to her sister-in-law would have to be postponed. If only she dared ask her questions of Dalmouth! But the chance seemed stronger by the moment that he was the "D" of the coded message, the person to be watched. He would be at the Opera House that night, and in Kennington's company.

Forcing down her inward qualms, she went directly to the Gold Saloon, where her visitor had been escorted. He had just seated himself, but sprang at once to his feet and came forward wreathed in smiles to take her hand and kiss it. He released her as if that were the last thing in the world he wished to do, and with a certain amount of suspicion, Leanora took a chair.

"What may I do for you this morning?" she asked, though without much encouragement.

Possibly he caught the coolness in her voice. His confidence seemed to waver, but only for a moment. She still could not acquit him of being nervous, which was not at all like him.

"I hope you may do a very great deal for me," he averred. He hesitated, looking down at his clasped hands, then back up directly into her face. "I can only hope my coming here does not cause you any embarrassment, but I am being so bold as to renew my offer for your hand, now that you have had time to consider."

Surprise gave way to fear. Was this a threat? What was it she was supposed to consider? The attack on her? Did he mean that she could find safety only as his wife? But no, there was no trace of either danger or menace in his bearing. Rather, he seemed to be the one who was afraid—and most assuredly not of her. So it must be of Kennington. What would he do if he learned that his master was shortly to be laid by the heels? Renounce him in relief? Perhaps, even, betray the details of the Requiem Masque? She would have to move cautiously. . . .

"I—I have given your offer consideration," she said slowly, her eyes lowered as she felt her way with care. "But as I told you before, I am sensible of the honor you do me, but I do not believe we should suit." She cast a quick glance at him, and his demeanor gave her courage. Something was terribly amiss, and he obviously had no desire whatsoever to marry her. Daringly, determined to take charge, she rushed on. "Nothing, I assure you, will make me change my mind, so you may be quite easy. You may tell Lord Kennington that you tried your best."

Dalmouth started, his eyes wide as a rapid play of emotions flickered across his face. In a moment, he had himself mostly under control and gave a somewhat shaky laugh. "Really, my dear Leanora, I have not the slightest idea what you are talking about."

"Oh, do cut line!" she exclaimed shortly, borrowing an expression from her brother. "What hold does Kennington have over you?"

He blinked at the bluntness of her question, then hesitated, looking for all the world like a rabbit caught in a snare. He was very young, she realized suddenly, barely two years older than Gregory—and very vulnerable beneath his carefully polished exterior. And like Gregory, he was hopelessly trapped in an evil web beyond his understanding—and ability to control. For the first time, Leanora could feel sorry for him.

"Was it gaming, like Gregory?" she asked, her tone more gentle.

He paled. "What—what do you mean?"

"Gregory has told me everything." She went to the sidetable where a decanter of brandy stood, poured out a brimming glass and handed it over.

Dalmouth took a long, sustaining draught. "Did he?" he looked away, and his shoulders sagged as if he accepted defeat. "The—the whole?"

She nearly panicked. Just what was the whole? She could only guess at the extent of Kennington's activities! What if she were wrong, and Dalmouth wholeheartedly supported the

355

assassination plot? What if his dejection were all a ploy, to discover what she knew? She should never have tried to force his confidence! But now she had started, she had to say something!

"I—I know that it was you who introduced Gregory to the dishonest hells, and that it was at Kennington's orders." That much, at least, should be safe to admit. "And—and I am helping him to get free." She could only trust that *was* the whole, as far as her brother was concerned.

Dalmouth gave a hollow laugh, as if he dropped all pretences. "Then he can't have told you the total of his losses. God, no one could get free of that!"

"He will," she replied with a confidence that made Dalmouth sit up and stare at her fixedly.

"I thought he looked happier," he said. "And Julia, too. I'm glad of it!" he added savagely. "I tried to protect her from Kennington, but with Gregory appearing indifferent, it was not easy."

"Well, that is over now. And what about you? How deeply are you dipped?"

"I don't know!" The quaver in his voice sounded real. "He—he has had me in his clutches for over five years."

"Haven't you tried to do anything about him?"

"What? I've always suspected his places were dishonest, but try as I might, I have never been able to discover the methods or mechanisms of cheating. And don't think you can discredit him by bringing it out into the open that he owns gaming hells. He's covered his tracks too well."

"What has he demanded of you? Papers?"

Dalmouth gave a short laugh. "No, my father is not a political figure. My job has been to drag in useful and gullible young pigeons. They didn't have to be rich; all they needed was the right sort of connections."

Leanora let that pass, for it aptly described Gregory. "Why did he want you to propose to me?"

Dalmouth shrugged. "I have no idea. Probably he didn't trust Gregory. He was supposed to be bringing secrets from the Home Office, you know, but he never provided anything useful. I think he sought to get to your father through you."

Dalmouth raised tired eyes to hers. "He is not above creating a scandal and ruining people for his own ends, you know."

A chill hand seemed to clutch at her stomach. A scandal involving both her and Gregory would certainly ruin their father's political career. If she married Dalmouth, she would have been in Kennington's cruel hands every bit as much as any of his other victims. And it could be no mere coincidence, could it, that Dalmouth had not been ordered to pay her court until *after* she had come into possession of that hateful code?

It was on the tip of her tongue to demand if the name "Requiem" meant anything to him, but caution won out. Dalmouth's confession might be genuine, but it might also be purely for her benefit, to allay her suspicions—and make her even more vulnerable. For her own safety, she had best keep quiet and not admit any knowledge of the code.

"What else does he demand of you?" she asked, giving him the opportunity to mention it himself.

"Nothing, so far. I—I've been too damnably good at my job."

Nothing. But was that the truth? "Will—will he be angry when he learns I have turned you down?" she asked, trying to mask her whirling thoughts.

He made a fatalistic gesture. "I suppose I shall find out shortly. I have been ordered to present myself to him as soon as I leave here."

"You will not tell him about Gregory, will you?" She raised anxious eyes to his face. In her eagerness to have the truth out in the open, she had again behaved like a fool! Her indiscretion could jeopardize a great deal. Deverell was quite right; she was not at all suited to a life of secrets and intrigue.

Dalmouth smiled, though somewhat tightly. "Oh, have no fear. I look forward with great eagerness to seeing someone, just once, get the better of Kennington." He rose as he spoke and took her hand, pressing it. "Forgive me," he said simply.

"Of course." To her surprise, she meant it—as far as Gregory was concerned.

She remained sitting where she was for a long while after he took his leave. Had she said too much—or not enough? He had admitted his role in Kennington's fleecing scheme—but only

357

after she brought it up. And what of the Requiem Masque? Did his not mentioning it mean that he knew nothing of it—or that he was too deeply involved in the plot? He had volunteered nothing on his own, only playing to her lead. Was he, in fact, loyal to all of Kennington's plans? But it was too late for repining. She had done the damage, if damage it was.

So very few hours remained in which to thwart the plot at the Requiem Masque, and she no longer dared leave matters in Deverell's hands. He might have the situation well under control, or he might be deeply involved. After all, Dalmouth was not the only gentleman whose initial was "D." Deverell might just as easily be the person to whom it referred! On that unsettling thought, she prepared to set forth on her visit to Julia to learn the details of the upcoming masquerade.

She got no farther than the door. Pagget, his face a picture of concern, came hurrying down the stairs, stopping in relief as he saw her.

"Miss Leanora!" he called. "His lordship is very anxious to speak to you!"

"Is anything amiss?" She went to the valet at once.

"I cannot say, Miss Leanora. He was reading the paper, then started shaking all of a sudden and demanded that I fetch you."

"Oh, dear!" She almost ran up the stairs.

She found her father sitting up in bed with pages of the *London Times* scattered about. Xerk lay at his side, growling as he shredded a discarded sheet. The earl looked up as she entered and held a section out to her, jabbing a finger somewhere in the vicinity of the center of the page. She took it, frowning, and scanned the sheet until she spotted an article headed *Tragic Occurrence near St. James Street*.

It took a moment for the information to penetrate her already troubled mind, but then she sank slowly into a chair, re-reading the story with care. It concerned a certain Lord P——, a prominent member of His Majesty's government, who was set upon, robbed and brutally murdered by footpads while walking home from his club. A companion, Sir W—— H——, was also injured in the attack. After this brief description, it went on to comment on the upsurgence of crime and the inability of the Watch to protect honest and decent citizens.

The paper dropped from her nerveless fingers. Lord Petersham dead? And Sir William injured? Not for a moment did she believe the reference to footpads!

"Shocking thing to happen!" Lord Sherborne declared, shaking his head. "Tragic. I can scarcely believe it!"

Leanora raised horror-filled eyes to her father's lined face. He accepted the story, as it read! He had no idea that anything else might be involved! Relief flooded through her at this proof that her father was in no way tied into the deadly plot.

"Damme, I wish Edmonton were here!" he exclaimed. "With Petersham dead and William laid up. . . . Nora, you'll have to go to Whitehall for me! Find out what's going on!"

"But you cannot take over at the Home Office! You are much too ill, still!" She picked up the paper and once more read the first part of the article. "It does not say whether Sir William's injuries are bad. It is quite possible he can carry on. I will send a messenger to Whitehall at once to find out."

Her father leaned back against his pillows, his eyes closed. "Won't be the same there without old Petersham boring on," he mused.

"True, you may get home to dinner more often," she responded, then realized how callous that must sound. But she was badly shaken. She had never considered Petersham to be a possible target for murder. She had assumed him to be in the thick of the plot. But apparently someone had wanted him safely out of the way. Or had she been completely wrong? Perhaps Petersham had been trying to prevent the assassination!

"Are you all right, my dear?" he demanded suddenly, his piercing eyes narrowing as they rested on her face. "You are quite pale!"

"It—it is just the shock," she said. "I—I will go and send a message to the Home Office at once."

She hurried from the room. The impulse to keep going, to order the carriage and escape far away, all the way to the Abbey, was overwhelming. Petersham had not suffered an accident from which he would recover. He had not suffered illness or been imprisoned in a leaky, rat-infested attic. He had been murdered. And she, or her father, might be next—unless the prime minister beat them to this dubious honor.

With a sense of shock, she realized that her field of suspects had been decreased by one. That left only Kennington, Dalmouth, Sir William and . . . Deverell. Had one of them ordered Petersham's murder?

After dispatching a footman to Whitehall, she went to her study and locked the door so that she would not be disturbed. It was after noon. Less than thirty-six hours. How was she to prevent the assassination from taking place? Dear God, if only she could trust Deverell! She had to act, and fast, but what could she do alone?

She had to talk to someone! But there was no one left she could trust, no one except . . . Reggie. But what good could her cousin do? His intellect was far from superior. His only recommendation was that he had a good heart, and he was completely honest. If nothing else, at least he would know, in case something happened to her. . . .

She scribbled a rapid but urgent summons to her cousin, then sent for a groom to carry this to his lodgings. If only he were home and had not gone out to a club or to join a party of friends. . . .

She paced the floor, unable to sit still, trying to decide what to do. When Reggie strode quickly into the room barely twenty minutes later, she greeted him with such intense relief that he was taken aback.

"You all right, Nora?" he demanded. "Better sit down." He pressed her into a chair.

"Reggie, I need your help," she cried.

He blinked. "Glad to oblige, of course," he said with caution. "Uh, what did you have in mind?" He regarded her with no little trepidation.

"You must never repeat anything of what I am about to tell you!" she told him. "You must swear it!"

"Well, naturally. You know me, Nora. I know how to keep my tongue!"

"You most certainly do not, but this is serious, Reggie!" In as few words as possible, she told him of the code, the Requiem Masque and her suspicions of Petersham's death.

"But—but Nora! You're not bamming me?" he demanded as she finished. He subjected the matter to serious consideration. "Best leave the whole thing in Dev's hands, you know. Won't want us interfering."

"But I cannot! Oh, don't you see, *Deverell* might be involved! I have gone over and over it in my mind, and it is a chance we cannot take! Do you realize, he did not want me to warn the prime minister when we first discovered the plot? Surely that is the first thing that should have been done! And we must do it now!"

"You think he is behind it?"

"I—I don't know! It could be any—or even all!—of them!" She broke off suddenly, staring at Reggie. "Or only one," she repeated. "Reggie, Petersham might have been the only one from the Home Office involved in the conspiracy!"

"That don't explain why he's acted so strangely about Kennington," Reggie objected.

"Kennington. Oh, if only it is him!"

Reggie drew a snuff box from his pocket and helped himself to a pinch. "I always thought the fellow was an outsider," he announced at last. "Waistcoats are too showy."

"His—his collection might only have been a cover! They could have been joined together in the conspiracy!" That would explain Petersham's panic whenever Kennington approached him. A simple business arrangement over antiquities should not strike terror into his very soul. But a plot to assassinate the prime minister might very well. Leanora sprang to her feet, unable to sit still. Then Deverell had nothing to do with it. . . . Her heart soared.

Reggie replaced the little enameled box. "What does Dev say about Petersham?"

"I—I haven't talked with him since I read the news. Oh, Reggie, I have been so upset!"

"Send for him. He'd know if there was anything odd about the business with Kennington. Some sort of cousin of Petersham's, you know. By marriage. Second cousins, or something like that."

Leanora sank back into her chair as her happiness shattered about her. "No," she whispered, then mastered her voice. "I—

361

I did not know they were related."

Why had Deverell never mentioned it? That made a very strong tie between them, and one which they both kept secret. Where, she wondered uneasily, had Deverell been last night? She tried to shake the question off, but it refused to be banished.

What did she really know of the man? She had asked herself that same thing several times of late, and she had yet to find an answer that could satisfy her fears. What a fool she was, allowing herself to fall in love! Her suspicions tore her heart apart with a pain that left her screaming inside.

"We—we are going to have to act, and at once!" she announced.

"Think we ought to talk to Dev," Reggie cavilled.

"No! We must not let Deverell know!" she exclaimed as the door opened. She broke off, turning to stare at Tremly. And behind him, his massive frame looming tall and menacing, stood Deverell.

Chapter 25

Leanora stared at Deverell in horror, knowing he had heard her last words. He came into the room, an easy smile on his lips but an odd light in his eyes.

"What must I not know?" he asked, his tone quite affable.

"That I'm going to display a new buttonhole when I drive in the Park this afternoon," Reggie said, winning Leanora's admiration for this totally unprecedented display of quick-wittedness.

"Dear me. And am I not supposed to approve?" Deverell raised mildly surprised eyebrows.

"Nora thinks it ain't the thing, with Petersham just dead, and all," Reggie explained with unaccustomed aplomb. "Thought you might not approve, being related to him, but there it is."

"I see. But life must go on, after all. And I would hardly call my connection close."

Despite his voiced unconcern, his eyes narrowed, and he regarded Reggie with care. Leanora received the disconcerting impression that he was not at all deceived, but at least he asked no further questions. Instead, he turned to her.

"I called to see if you would care to go for a drive, but if you are busy I shall try another time."

Reggie stood at once. "Just about to pop off. Only came by to see how my uncle took the news."

"Ah, yes, Petersham. And how does Sherborne take it?"

Reggie blinked, threw a frantic glance at Leanora and, his

363

inspiration by this time exhausted, bolted for the door.

Deverell watched his departure with an air of amusement, then took his friend's vacated seat. "We can drive if you choose, but I really only wanted to talk with you."

She let out a sigh of relief, then caught herself up as she realized Deverell regarded her with a piercing alertness belied by his lazy manner. "Shall we stay here, then?" she asked with forced casualness. Here, in the house, she should be safe—though what she feared he might do, she had no idea.

"Of course," he said smoothly. He looked down at his immaculately manicured hands, then shot her a penetrating glance. "You have realized, have you not, that the Petersham affair is related to the Requiem plot? He has been too nervous of late."

"He certainly has behaved oddly. It—it must have been obvious to all." She swallowed hard. "Do you think he was a conspirator, or trying to prevent the assassination?"

"A conspirator, I fear," he responded with a cold certainty that left Leanora trembling, wondering how he could be so certain.

"And—and someone thought he could no longer be trusted?" she queried when she found her voice again.

Deverell nodded. "I am almost positive."

"And who else is involved?" His assistant? Or his business associate and political opponent who sent him into a nervous quake? Or his cousin by marriage? Desperately, she hoped it would prove to be Kennington.

"I have not been able to positively identify any of the other conspirators," Deverell told her on a note of apology. "But I am quite sure the motive is to throw the country into political chaos at this time. If you have been following the war, you must realize that we are at a very critical point. Napoleon achieved a tremendous victory at Austerlitz, and is marshaling his forces once more. If we are led properly, England will soon be sending many troops to the Continent. If we are not, Napoleon will be permitted to have his way until it is too late to stop him."

Leanora nodded. "If only we knew *who!*"

"I am fairly certain who the leader is, but I cannot prove it. And there will be at least two other co-conspirators, I should think. I have contacted several friends in the Horse Guard, and they will attend the masquerade tomorrow night and keep each of my suspects under close surveillance. At the first sign of trouble, they will act."

Was this true? Oh, why did she have to doubt? And why was he telling her things now, after being so secretive all this time? To keep her from taking any action on her own and discovering that he, in fact, did nothing? Her heart cried out against this idea, but she could not, for the sake of her country, take any chances! It was all his fault! If only he had told her everything from the beginning, she would never have doubted him for a moment.

Deverell rose. "You must excuse me. I still have a few loose ends to tie up." She also stood, and he took her hand, raising it to his lips.

"It—it was good of you to tell me your plans," she managed. To her dismay, she dared not look at him.

One strong finger touched beneath her chin, forcing her face upward until she looked fully into his dark, luminous eyes. A puzzled question lurked in their depths, and a slight frown creased his brows. His hand caressed her cheek, then smoothed back the soft golden curls. She swallowed, finding it strangely difficult to breathe.

"Trust me, my Leanora," he said softly. His hand slid around to the nape of her neck, and his lips, warm and demanding, found hers. Unable to stop herself, she let her hands creep to his shoulders, holding him, needing him desperately. Conscious thought ebbed away as she sank under the compelling spell of his embrace. Nothing mattered but that she should remain there, forever, safe in his strong arms.

He released her too soon. "It is almost over now. We shall win, never doubt it." His eyes glinted with anticipation and enjoyment.

Reluctantly, she came back to earth. Did he laugh at his power over her, at how ready she was to fall into his arms, to believe anything he told her? But with him so overpoweringly

365

near, it was hard to think rationally.

"Take care," she whispered, blinking back the tears that threatened.

He grinned suddenly in a manner that wreaked havoc on her already damaged heart. "You may be very sure I will."

He took his leave, and she sank back into her chair, staring at the fireplace with unseeing eyes. If only she could be sure! She wanted to trust; her every instinct told her she could, but she did not have the right to jeopardize the life of Lord Grenville because she was besotted. Deverell had behaved oddly about the business from the beginning, and there were questions to which she had not received satisfactory answers.

The door opened softly behind her, and she jumped, spinning about in alarm. Reggie entered the room, closed the door firmly behind him and came over to join her.

"Sorry, Nora. Didn't mean to startle you."

"Where did you come from?" she demanded. "Deverell has only just left."

"I know." He beamed at her with simple pride. "I went across the street to the garden and waited. Saw him drive off. Now, what do you propose to do?"

They retired to her father's study where she wrote a brief but urgent request for an interview with the prime minister. As she used her father's crested and engraved stationery, which bore his position in the Home Office emblazoned neatly in black letters, she had every hope of being attended to. A liveried footman was then dispatched, with orders that he was to find Lord Grenville and wait for an answer.

The minutes ticked slowly by. Leanora dared not go to see either her father or aunt, for her nervousness grew more obvious by the moment. Would the prime minister agree to see her? And would he take her warning seriously? She was not just anyone; she was Lord Sherborne's daughter. Surely that would weigh in her favor!

Reggie rang for refreshments and a deck of cards, but neither had much heart for piquet. They played hand after desultory hand, losing track of points without really caring. When the footman was ushered into the room at last, Leanora swept the half-played game aside without compunction.

"We are to go at once!" she exclaimed as she scanned the brief note the lackey handed her. Sending a message to the stables for the barouche, she hurried upstairs to fetch her bonnet.

Although Leanora had met Lord Grenville on several occasions in the past, she approached this interview with trepidation. As they were led into his office, she regarded his stern-featured face with misgivings. The whole situation suddenly seemed absurd to her. It was no wonder Deverell had counseled against this course of action!

They took seats opposite his great desk, and in a halting voice Leanora retold her story. From her reticule she drew out a copy of the code, complete with its decipherment, and handed them over.

He took them, scanned both sheets quickly, then laid them aside. "Thank you for bringing these to me," he said.

"You must stay away from the Opera House tomorrow night!" she urged him.

He smiled slightly. "My dear Lady Leanora. This can make no difference to my plans. I am grateful for the concern you are showing, but I promise you, I am well protected."

"You cannot realize how determined they are!" she persisted.

He picked up the uncoded paper and glanced at it again. "I shall do what it says and watch 'D,'" he said simply.

"Do you know who it is?" Suddenly, she could scarcely breathe.

"But of course," he said. "Do not you? I believe you are well acquainted with him."

"Who?" The syllable came out as little more than a whisper.

"Lord Deverell. Did you not realize? Who could be more likely, considering his connection with Petersham, and his— shall we say unusual?—background?" His mouth tightened in a thin-lipped smile. "I have been briefed on that gentleman quite fully. A truly remarkable man. He will definitely bear watching."

She shook her head, rejecting this confirmation of her worst fears. She could not focus her gaze through her blurring eyes, and a persistent ringing started in her ears. She half rose to her

367

feet to deny the accusation, then sank back, weak with shock.

Somehow, Reggie got them out of the room, out of the great man's presence and back to the carriage. He almost thrust her in, then climbed up after her.

"I don't believe it," he said dully, shaking his head. "Dev. *Dev,* of all people!" He took Leanora's cold, trembling hand. "Steady there, old girl. We did the right thing. We've warned him."

"He—he knew already!" Leanora exclaimed. "Did you not notice? He—he was not surprised or shocked at all. And someone had already checked on Deverell." Tears slipped down her cheeks, and a slight sob escaped her.

"There must be some mistake!" Her cousin slammed an agitated fist against his leg. "I just can't believe it, Nora!"

"We—we have to. What choice do we have?" She turned bleak, miserable eyes on him, then looked away hurriedly as they filled once more. "He fooled us completely. I—I only hope Lord Grenville will have enough men at the masquerade to protect himself."

"They will arrest Dev!" Reggie turned to stare at her as the horror dawned on him.

She nodded. They would arrest him, and he would be executed as a traitor. She couldn't bear the thought! If only she could prevent it! Should she tell him that the prime minister knew all? That he must abandon his deadly plan and escape now, before it was too late? But it had already gone too far for that. It was not only the attacks on her father and herself. Lord Petersham lay dead, and young Mr. Holloway, as well. That could not be ignored.

"Reggie? Will you take me to the masquerade?" she asked in a very small voice.

"What?" He stared at her, jolted out of his gloomy reverie. "Dash it, Nora, you don't want to go!"

"I—I have to."

"Lord, we've already done all that we can. From now on, we should leave it in the hands of experts! We've warned Grenville, it's up to him to take precautions if he won't do the sensible thing and stay home. You don't want to be there to—to watch," he ended lamely.

"If you will not take me, I will go on my own!" she threatened.

"Can't do that, Nora, be reasonable!"

"Reggie, there is nothing *reasonable* about any of this! I must be there! Can you not understand? I must see for myself what happens to—" She broke off, unable to complete her sentence, unable to admit how deeply she loved the treacherous, traitorous Deverell.

Her cousin cast an uneasy glance at her averted face, then reached across and patted her hand once more. "All right, Nora. I'll take you."

Chapter 26

Leanora pulled the folds of her black domino closer about herself as Reggie led her down a corridor at the Opera House. He had procured a box on the second tier, a circumstance that appeared to afford him considerable satisfaction. They would be close enough to the crowd of dancers on the stage to watch everything that took place, yet high enough to prevent Leanora from being accosted by ardent young bucks bent upon flirtation.

She slipped into the privacy of the box, glad to be away from the mingling and far from refined crowd in the hall. She went at once to the front and leaned over the edge to survey the merrymakers upon the stage below. Reggie set a chair and pressed her into it.

"You'll fall over the edge if you aren't careful!" he hissed at her.

"Can you see anyone yet?" she demanded, scanning the throng through the slits of her mask.

"I can see hundreds of people," he informed her, vexed. "Lord, Nora, how do you hope to recognize anyone when they're all in costume?"

"We shall know Deverell," she said, and could not prevent a note of bleakness creeping into her voice.

"Easy, Nora." He patted her hand ineffectually but with good intentions. "Everything will work out."

She continued to scan the people, hoping beyond hope that Deverell would not come. So far, though the company was far too free for her taste, nothing appeared to be out of the ordinary for a gathering such as this. The men danced and flirted outrageously, and the women seemed bent on encouraging them to take even greater liberties. Everyone who had warned her about public masked balls had been right. She would not have enjoyed such loose behavior under any circumstances.

On one side of the stage, a group of four men became conspicuous through their immobility. While the rest of the throng swirled about them, laughing and gesturing, this one group, garbed in black dominoes instead of outlandish costumes, stood aloof. There was something familiar about the man in the center who was flanked, as it were, by protectors.

"Reggie!" She tugged on his arm. "Is that not Lord Grenville? There?" She gestured with her fan, then continued to swing it in a sweeping gesture to disguise her purpose.

Reggie cast a considering glance at the four gentlemen in question. "Could be," he said slowly. "Looks about the same height and build. But only three guards? Doesn't look like he took us seriously, does it?"

"But only see how conspicuous they make him appear!" she sighed. "Oh, Reggie, it is almost as if he were *trying* to draw attention to himself!"

She cast a glance at the watch she carried in her reticule. The hour was rapidly approaching midnight. Tension gripped in the pit of her stomach, and she bit her lip. There was absolutely nothing she could do to prevent the tragedy that drew closer by every minute.

The wine flowed freely in the boxes and on the stage. The dancers were becoming more boisterous, behaving in a manner that would have shocked Leanora had she paid them much heed. Her gaze remained riveted upon the men in the black dominoes, who did not move. For what were they waiting?

The dancers were rapidly becoming unrestrained. The stage was alive with random movement as fewer and fewer people remained steady on their feet. Except one man. From the opposite corner, one figure clad in Elizabethan finery steered a straight course toward the gentleman in black. His mask effectively hid the upper portion of his face, and his ruff

372

higher than it should have been, disguised the lower portion. At his waist hung a scabbard from which he drew a very deadly looking sword.

Leanora sprang to her feet and started for the door.

"Nora! Wait!" She heard Reggie's frantic call but ignored him. Rushing from the box, she ran down the corridor until she reached the stairs to the lower level. She almost flew down these and came out in another hall below. Frantically pushing her way through the merrymakers lingering there, she emerged onto the stage.

She looked around, panicking when she could not see the men in black. But there, quite near her, came the man with the drawn sword. Light glinted off the sharpened steel, and the mouth that peeked out from behind the preposterous ruff was set in grim lines.

She shoved forward and threw herself against the man with considerable force. He staggered, and she thrust a foot in his way, neatly tripping him. He went down hard with a violent oath. She slipped quickly away as those of the crowd sober enough to notice turned to laugh.

All she had done was interfere, not stop anything! She looked about again, searching for the prime minister. Over there, not far away. . . . She started toward him.

Over the cacophony of music, shouting and revelry came the explosion of a gun. She jumped, spun about, but could see nothing. Another shot, as if in answer, fired from the opposite side of the stage, and if anything the crowd laughed more heartily. Amazingly, no one was disturbed, apparently taking the drama that unfolded about them as part of the evening's entertainment. Had those harmless shots been fired for just that purpose? To take away from the impact of the murder?

What a perfect place for an assassination! she realized with horror. If someone were killed, the crowd would believe it was an act, staged for their enjoyment, and applaud it!

Out of the corner of her eye she glimpsed a limping figure, swathed in the voluminous red folds of a domino, making his purposeful way toward the prime minister. Deverell! The Elizabethan gentleman loomed up at his side, and his sword flashed, slicing cleanly through Deverell's sleeve. Deverell

373

lurched sideways, but his crimson domino disguised the blood that flowed down his arm.

"Deverell!" The name tore from her throat. She rushed forward, aware only of a love she could not deny, desperate to reach him. Only yards away, she was thrown aside as a black-cloaked figure dashed for the prime minister.

Deverell, clutching his injured arm, shouted. Just beyond them, one man swung around, striking the Elizabethan gentleman a savage blow on the chin. He staggered backward, and his assailant followed, closing on him again.

Another man in a red domino stepped forward, raised a pistol and took careful aim at the prime minister. Deverell launched himself squarely against him, and they went sprawling, rolling together, locked in deadly combat. The revelers, hilarious in their enjoyment, stepped back to give them room, cheering them in unrestrained glee.

Deverell pinned the gunman's hand to the floor with his uninjured arm. The man gave a tremendous heave, loosening Deverell's grip and throwing him off. Grasping the gun that lay nearby, he brought it up and pointed it again at the prime minister.

Another cloaked figure rushed forward and brought the butt of his own pistol down sharply upon the man's head. He fell forward, unconscious. Deverell rose to his feet, wiping blood from a cut near his mouth. He took a shaky step to keep his balance and nodded at whatever his assistant said.

Three others, all in red dominoes, now came forward, two of them propelling bound men. The party about the prime minister went to assist, and two of them picked up the fallen gunman. All withdrew toward the hall.

Leanora, unable to break through the mirthful crowd to get closer, ran around them to join the group in the corridor. She burst through the opening and collided with a massive figure in a scarlet domino who swore roundly and swung about to face her. Recognizing her, he swept her against himself with his one good arm. Too shaken to demand answers, she threw her own arms about as much of him as she could reach and held on as if afraid to ever let go.

"Who . . . ?" she finally managed. Tears streamed down her

374

cheeks, unheeded, as she raised her bemused face to his.

"Did you not guess?" Deverell released her and strode forward to where the unconscious gunman slumped in a chair. Using only one hand, he untied the mask and let it drop. With a sense of numb shock, Leonora recognized Sir William Holborne.

She stared at Deverell, shaking her head in disbelief. "But—but he was injured. . . ."

"Carefully staged." He turned to a man who came up beside him, the one who had knocked Sir William unconscious. "Charley, get them outside." He gripped the man's hand, a sudden grin lightening his grim face. "It was a good run!"

The other man smiled broadly. "That it was, Dev. Thanks for bringing us in."

Leonora remained where she was, watching with wide, disbelieving eyes as the conspirators were taken out under guard. It didn't seem possible! It was over!

Deverell paused before her, his broad shoulders shaking slightly. "Did you expect something more?" he asked maddeningly, and she realized she had spoken aloud. "My dear Leonora, I told you I would handle it quite simply in the end."

She shook her head, still not able to comprehend. The prime minister was safe! She turned to him. "Lord Grenville. . . ." she began.

The man in the black domino held up a hand, smiling, stopping her. Wordlessly he reached up and untied his mask. It fell away to reveal a complete stranger.

Leonora stared at him in blank incomprehension, then turned bewildered eyes on Deverell. Her gaze fell on the arm that hung limply at his side.

"You—you are bleeding," she said unnecessarily.

Deverell glanced at the blood that dripped down his hand and fell to the floor. He drew up a corner of his domino and wrapped his arm loosely.

"We—we had better find you a doctor." She focused on the one detail she could assimilate and with which she could cope.

"Later," he said gently. "I'll just bind it up for now."

"We—we have a box." She looked at him, uncertainty in her blue eyes.

375

"Lead the way," he invited.

Still in a daze, she turned about, wondering which way to go. But there was Reggie, only a few feet away, watching events with apparent interest. She went unsteadily to him, and he shepherded them to the box.

Safe inside, Leanora almost fell into her chair. A bottle of wine and two glasses sat on the table, and when Reggie poured her one, she took it with gratitude. Deverell took the other and drank it off.

"Your arm!" she exclaimed suddenly. She unwound the domino carefully. The sleeve of his elegant coat of mulberry superfine was sliced cleanly, as was the fine lawn of his shirt. She was afraid to look further.

"It is not deep," Deverell informed her encouragingly as he tore back the ruined fabric and subjected his arm to a cursory examination. "I'll do fine for now if you'll just bind it up."

"With what?" she asked, still not thinking clearly.

"Well," he considered, his eyes twinkling. "According to the best novels, I thought heroines always used their petticoats."

That drew a shaky laugh from her. "Will a domino do instead?" Without waiting for his response, she tore at the hem of her black cloak. It refused to rend, but Deverell thoughtfully presented her with his pocket knife. Her hands shook too much to make the use of this dangerously sharp instrument advisable, so Reggie assisted. He handed her the first long strip, and she folded it into a soft, serviceable pad. This Deverell obligingly held to his arm while she tied another strip about it to keep it in place.

"It is over," Deverell said at last. He poured himself another glass of wine. Reggie, noting that his cousin had not finished hers, took the glass and tossed the contents off in one swallow.

Leanora let out a long, ragged sigh. "Explain!" she pleaded. "Who was that man? Where is Lord Grenville?"

"Beneath the stage," Deverell replied, answering her last question first.

"But how . . . ? Oh, I do wish you would tell me! How did they find someone so quickly who looks so much like him? And why is the prime minister here at all?"

Deverell hesitated, casting a measuring glance at Reggie. "He is meeting with a French agent who is selling out. This was the only place the man would consent to come, because he is being hunted by his own side. He hoped to lose himself in the crowd here." He took another drink of wine. "And as for the replacement prime minister, we had several weeks to find him, ever since I first told Grenville about the coded message."

"*You* told him!" she demanded, outraged. "Why did you not let me know? That is hateful of you, to make me worry, when I begged and begged you to go to him!"

He reached out, touching her cheek with one finger. "My dear Leanora, I have used you shamefully. You see, I have suspected Sir William for a very long time. And I did not underrate his intelligence. He knew you had seen the code, and he knew you were clever enough to discover what it meant. If he was to be fooled, that meant you had to remain worried. Otherwise he would guess you had taken steps to prevent the assassination. This way we have him safely captured."

"But why? *Why* did he do it? I still cannot believe it! I have known Sir William for ages."

"Consider what you know of him." Deverell eased himself in the chair, moving his bandaged arm carefully. Reggie refilled his glass for him, and he took a deep swallow. "You yourself told me that his greatest ambition had been thwarted, but it was not, as you suggested, sartorial. He desired political power, which had been denied him by his birth."

"There is nothing wrong with that!" Leanora exclaimed. "His baronetcy is very old, and—" Her eyes widened as his meaning became clear.

He noted her comprehension and nodded. "Socially, his position is excellent," he explained for Reggie's benefit. "Politically, he is not well enough connected. The higher offices that a gentleman of Sir William's abilities would covet would always be given to others, like Petersham, who have influential relatives. For years, Sir William has been forced to serve as the mere assistant of a man whose abilities were negligible at best. Did it never seem to you that he resented this?"

Leanora nodded slowly. "But to go to such an extreme! It—I

377

still cannot believe that he would."

"Perhaps he was promised a great position if the French conquered England." Deverell took another drink of wine, then held it out for Reggie to pour more. "I doubt we shall ever know his full motives, unless he chooses to disclose them himself."

"Who else is involved?" She asked the question that had been haunting her for weeks. "Kennington? I have not seen him tonight."

"Oh, he is here, but quite innocently. Or perhaps I should say he is not involved in this affair. I doubt if our dear friend Kennington could ever be considered completely innocent."

"But—"

"My poor Leanora," he said, and the teasing note was back in his voice. "Does it hurt to give up your favorite villain?"

She nodded dumbly.

"Well, I am sorry to have to disillusion you this once. Kennington is indeed one of life's less likeable characters. Dishonest in every way, I am certain, but not a part of this plot. Console yourself with the reflection that my friend will very soon bring about his ruin."

"But what of Petersham?" she managed to ask. "He—he was afraid of Kennington!"

"Ah, yes. Petersham." Deverell shifted slightly again to ease the throbbing of his arm. "Do you remember those missing funds from the Home Office? I greatly fear they went to finance some rather superb acquisitions to Petersham's collection of antiquities. Do not forget Kennington's unsavory connections. He came into possession of some very desirable pieces and dangled them before Petersham. When Petersham did not have the money to purchase them, he helped himself to those funds."

"Then. . . . Did Kennington kill him?"

"No, Sir William did that. I believe he found out about the missing funds and suggested to Petersham that in the chaos caused by the assassination, the thefts would never be discovered. So Petersham agreed to help." He swirled the dark wine about in his glass, watching it in meditative silence. "I do not believe Petersham proved an ideal conspirator," he went

378

on. "Sir William certainly realized this when the code went astray."

"Why did you never tell me you were related to Petersham?" she asked, her voice betraying her hurt at his not confiding in her.

He finished his wine but declined Reggie's offer to refill the glass once more. "It was only by marriage. I met him for the first time only two days before I met you. My friends in the Horse Guards had heard rumors of trouble, and I went to investigate. He is—was—no dissembler. I could tell at once that something was gravely amiss. For the sake of my cousin's memory, and the honor of her family, I stepped in to try and extricate him from a plot that was more serious than I think he realized at first."

"And what of my father's clerk?" Leanora was finding it difficult to take all this in.

"Poor Mr. Holloway." Deverell shook his head. "I believe he saw what to him appeared to be a page of idle scribblings and mentioned it to Sir William. Hence the swift attack on both him and your father, which fortunately, Sherborne survived. But by then, you had lost the papers, and Sir William was unable to recover the code."

"Then blaming Holloway for the theft of the funds was a—a ploy? To protect Petersham?"

Deverell nodded. "You see, he knew I was watching him rather closely, from the beginning."

"Then—then you were involved before I ever approached you," Leanora said slowly, chagrined. "You—it is a pity you were unable to accomplish your purpose of protecting him." She swallowed, wishing her voice did not sound so hollow and forlorn. He had made a mockery of her, from beginning to end, letting her play about the fringes and claim as hers the deadly game that was actually his own. His only use for her had been to satisfy Sir William's suspicions.

"No, Petersham did not make my task an easy one," he said. "He even warned his fellow conspirators about me."

Her head came up, her expression comical in its dismay. "'Watch D'?" she quoted. She turned to Reggie. "So that was what Grenville meant!"

379

"You believed *me* guilty," Deverell said, an odd note of pain in his voice.

"No! I—" She broke off, the misery and uncertainty of the last few days washing over her once more. "Oh, Dev, I have been so frightened, and it *was* a possibility with you behaving so oddly; and I had no right to endanger the prime minister just because I—I wanted to believe you. . . ." Just because she loved him, she meant, and tears of remembered heartache filled her eyes once more.

His expression softened. "I may have gotten involved for Petersham's sake, but I stayed with it for you. If you had not guessed, I have enjoyed myself immensely these past few weeks. Never before have I met a young lady with the courage to play at one of my games with me."

The warmth in his voice surprised her, and she looked up, meeting a smoldering glow in his expressive eyes. He reached across, and his one strong arm folded about her, drawing her tightly against his broad chest. His lips found hers with a force that left her breathless.

"I say!" Reggie expostulated. "Not here! Really, Dev, not the thing to be kissing Nora in public. Even if it is a masquerade. Devilish bad *ton!* Best continue that in a more private place."

"What a delightful idea!" Deverell said, a gleam of enthusiasm lighting his eyes. "I will be only too glad to continue—anywhere and everywhere the lady may care to name."

Hot color suffused her cheeks at his obvious intent. "I—I beg of you to consider the proprieties!" she ordered sternly as she tried to disengage herself.

"I am," he assured her at once. "I intend to marry you first." He released her with reluctance and drew a folded document from inside his coat pocket. He opened this and showed her the special license. "I obtained this two weeks ago," he said with a note of apology. He stowed the paper away again. "I suggest we find a clergyman at the earliest opportunity. There happen to be several matters I wish to—to discuss with you, and rather urgently. And to begin with, I would like to kiss you without being interrupted or without

380

you being dripping wet."

"I have not—" she began an indignant rejoinder, but he gave her no chance to finish her sentence. With his good arm, he gathered her once more against himself, and for a very long while she remained oblivious to everything except the joy that his touch sent flooding through her.